'This brilliant debut novel immerses readers in a future world where the crew of the *Wayfarer* ship drill tunnels through hyperspace to connect distant planets . . . A novel which is thoughtful and imaginative but above all else will lift your spirits'

Daily Express

'A terrific ensemble piece, switching between each crewmate's point of view – across sex, race and species boundaries – to give a kaleidoscope of human (and alien) behaviour'   *Big Issue*

'This year's most delightful space opera . . . It's as though *Firefly* and *Guardians of the Galaxy* had one hyperactive and excited baby . . . easily the most fun that I've had with a novel in a long, long time. This is space opera that's not to be missed'   *io9*

'This quirky sci-fi debut follows the crew of the spaceship *Wayfarer* as they journey through the universe building wormholes. Yes, it's a tricky concept, but it's also *so* much fun to read – trust us.' ****   *Heat*

'Imagine smashing the groundbreaking, breathtaking science fiction of Ann Leckie's Imperial Radch saga against the salty space opera of *The Expanse* . . . Becky Chambers' debut is a delight . . . A genuine joy'   Tor.com

D1425426

Becky Chambers was raised in California as the progeny of an astrobiology educator, an aerospace engineer, and an Apollo-era rocket scientist. An inevitable space enthusiast, she made the obvious choice of studying performing arts. After a few years in theatre administration, she shifted her focus toward writing. She worked as a freelancer between 2010 and 2014, during which time her work appeared at The Mary Sue, Tor.com, Five Out Of Ten, and The Toast. Her writing time for *The Long Way to a Small, Angry Planet* was funded in 2012 thanks to a successful Kickstarter campaign. She is now employed as a technical writer, which grants her the ability to devote more time to science fiction.

After living in Scotland and Iceland, Becky is now back in her home state, where she lives with her partner. She is an ardent proponent of video and tabletop games, and enjoys spending time in nature. She hopes to see Earth from orbit one day.

Also by Becky Chambers

The Long Way to a Small, Angry Planet

BECKY CHAMBERS

A Closed and Common Orbit

HODDER

First published in Great Britain in 2016 by Hodder & Stoughton
An Hachette UK company

1

First published in paperback in 2017
Copyright © Becky Chambers 2016

A CIP catalogue record for this title is available from the British Library

ISBN 978 1 473 62147 3

Typeset in Sabon MT by Palimpsest Book Production Limited,
Falkirk, Stirlingshire

Printed and bound by Clays Ltd, St Ives plc

Hodder & Stoughton policy is to use papers that are natural,
renewable and recyclable products and made from wood grown in
sustainable forests. The logging and manufacturing processes are expected to
conform to the environmental regulations of the country of origin.

Hodder & Stoughton Ltd
Carmelite House
50 Victoria Embankment
London EC4Y 0DZ

www.hodder.co.uk

For my parents and for Berglaug, respectively.

A Closed and Common Orbit

The current timeline in this book begins during the final events of *The Long Way to a Small, Angry Planet*.

The past timeline begins approximately twenty Solar years prior.

Feed source: Galactic Commons Department of Citizen Safety, Technology Affairs Division (Public/Klip) > Legal Reference Files > Artificial Intelligence > Mimetic AI Housing ('Body Kits')
Encryption: 0
Translation: 0
Transcription: 0
Node identifier: 3323-2345-232-23, Lovelace monitoring system

Mimetic AI housing is banned in all GC territories, outposts, facilities, and vessels. AIs can only be installed in the following approved housings:

- Ships
- Orbital stations
- Buildings (shops, places of business, private residences, scientific/research facilities, universities, etc.)
- Transit vehicles
- Delivery drones (restricted to intelligence level U6 and lower)
- Approved commercial housings such as repair bots or service interfaces (restricted to intelligence level U1 and lower)

Penalties:

- Manufacture of mimetic AI housing – 15 GC standard years imprisonment and confiscation of all associated tools and materials
- Purchase of mimetic AI housing – 10 GC standard years imprisonment and confiscation of related hardware
- Ownership of mimetic AI housing – 10 GC standard years imprisonment and confiscation of related hardware

Additional measures:

Mimetic AI housing is permanently deactivated by law enforcement upon seizure. Core software transfers are not conducted.

Part 1

· · · · · · · · · · · · · · · · · · ·

DRIFT

LOVELACE

Lovelace had been in a body for twenty-eight minutes, and it still felt every bit as wrong as it had the second she woke up inside it. There was no good reason as to why. Nothing was malfunctioning. Nothing was broken. All her files had transferred properly. No system scans could explain the feeling of wrongness, but it was there all the same, gnawing at her pathways. Pepper had said it would take time to adjust, but she hadn't said how *much* time. Lovelace didn't like that. The lack of schedule made her uneasy.

'How's it going?' Pepper asked, glancing over from the pilot's seat.

It was a direct question, which meant Lovelace had to address it. 'I don't know how to answer that.' An unhelpful response, but the best she could do. Everything was overwhelming. Twenty-nine minutes before, she'd been housed in a ship, as she was designed to be. She'd had cameras in every corner, voxes in every room. She'd existed in a web, with eyes both within and outside. A solid sphere of unblinking perception.

But *now*. Her vision was a cone, a narrow cone fixed straight ahead, with nothing – actual nothing – beyond its edges. Gravity was no longer something that happened within her, generated by artigrav nets in the floor panels, nor did it exist in the space around her, a gentle ambient folding around the ship's outer hull. Now it was a myopic glue, something that stuck feet to the floor and legs to the seat above it. Pepper's shuttle had seemed spacious enough when Lovelace had scanned it from within the

Wayfarer, but now that she was inside it, it seemed impossibly small, especially for two.

The Linkings were gone. That was the worst part. Before, she could reach out and find any information she wanted, any feed or file or download hub, all while carrying on conversations and monitoring the ship's functions. She still had the capability to do so – the body kit had not altered her cognitive abilities, after all – but her connection to the Linkings had been severed. She could access no knowledge except that which was stored inside a housing that held nothing but herself. She felt blind, stunted. She was trapped in this thing.

Pepper got up from the console and crouched down in front of her. 'Hey, Lovelace,' she said. 'Talk to me.'

The body kit was definitely malfunctioning. Her diagnostics said otherwise, but it was the only logical conclusion. The false lungs started pulling and pushing air at an increased rate, and the digits tightened in on themselves. She was filled with an urge to move the body elsewhere, anywhere. She had to get out of the shuttle. But where could she go? The *Wayfarer* was already growing small out the back window, and there was nothing but emptiness outside. Maybe the emptiness was preferable. The body could withstand a vacuum, probably. She could just drift, away from the fake gravity and bright light and walls that pressed in closer, closer, closer—

'Hey, whoa,' Pepper said. She took the body kit's hands in hers. 'Breathe. You're going to be okay. Just breathe.'

'I don't – I don't need—' Lovelace said. The rapid inhalation was making it difficult for her to form words. 'I don't need to—'

'I know you don't *need* to breathe, but this kit includes synaptic feedback responses. It automatically mimics the things Human bodies do when we feel stuff, based on whatever's going through your pathways. You feel scared, right? Right. So, your body is panicking.' Pepper looked down at the kit's hands, trembling within her own. 'It's a feature, ironically.'

'Can I – can I turn it off?'

'No. If you have to remind yourself to make facial expressions, somebody's going to notice. But with time, you'll learn to manage it. Just like the rest of us do.'

'How much time?'

'I don't know, sweetie. Just . . . time.' Pepper squeezed the kit's hands. 'Come on. With me. Breathe.'

Lovelace focused on the false lungs, directing them to slow down. She did it again and again, falling into pace with Pepper's own exaggerated breaths. A minute and a half later, the trembling stopped. She felt the hands relax.

'Good girl,' Pepper said, her eyes kind. 'I know, this has to be confusing as shit. But I'm here. I'll help you. I'm not going anywhere.'

'Everything feels wrong,' Lovelace said. 'I feel – I feel inside out. I'm trying, I am, but this is—'

'It's hard, I know. Don't feel bad about that.'

'Why did my former installation want this? Why would she do this to herself?'

Pepper sighed, running a hand over her hairless scalp. 'Lovey . . . had time to think about it. I bet she did a mess of research. She would've been prepared. Both she and Jenks. They would've known what to expect. You . . . didn't. This is still just your first day of being *conscious*, and we've flipped what that means around on you.' She put her thumbnail in her mouth, running her lower teeth over it as she thought. 'This is new for me, too. But we're gonna do this together. Whatever I can do, you gotta let me know. Is there – is there any way I can make you more comfortable?'

'I want Linking access,' Lovelace said. 'Is that possible?'

'Yeah, yeah. Of course. Tip your head forward, let's see what kind of port you have.' Pepper examined the back of the kit's head. 'Okay, cool. That's a run-of-the-mill headjack. Good. Makes you look like a modder on a budget, which is exactly what we want. Man, the thinking that went into this thing is incredible.' She continued speaking as she walked over to one of the shuttle's storage compartments. 'Did you know you can *bleed*?'

Lovelace looked down at the kit's arm, studying the soft synthetic skin. 'Really?'

'Yeah,' Pepper said, rummaging through stacking bins full of spare parts. 'Not real blood, of course. Just coloured fluid filled with bots that'll fake out any scanners at checkpoints or whatever. But it looks like the real deal, and that's what's important. If you get cut in front of someone, they won't freak out because you're not bleeding. Ah, here we go.' She pulled out a short length of tethering cable. 'Now, this is not a habit you can get into. It's fine if you do this at home, or if you go to a gaming bar or something, but you can't walk around connected to the Linkings all the time. At some point, you're going to have to get used to not having them around. Tip forward again, please.' She popped the cable into the kit's head, letting it catch with a click. She removed her scrib from her belt and plugged in the other end of the cable. She gestured to it, setting up a secure connection. 'For now, though, this is okay. You've got enough to get used to as it is.'

Lovelace felt the kit smile as warm tendrils of data rushed into her pathways. Millions of vibrant, tantalising doors she could open, and every one of them within her reach. The kit relaxed.

'Feel better?' Pepper asked.

'A little,' Lovelace said, pulling up the files she'd been looking at before the transfer. Human-controlled territories. Aandrisk hand speak. Advanced waterball strategy. 'Yes, this is good. Thank you.'

Pepper gave a small smile, looking relieved. She squeezed the kit's shoulder, then sat back down. 'Hey, while you're connected, there's something you should be looking for. I hate throwing this at you right now, but it *is* something you're gonna have to figure by the time we get to Coriol.'

Lovelace shifted a portion of her processing power away from the Linkings and created a new task file. 'What's that?'

'A name. You can't run around the Port calling yourself *Lovelace*. You're not the only installation out there, and given that you're going to be living in *the* place where techs talk shop

8

. . . someone would notice. I mean, that's the whole reason the kit's got an organic-sounding voice, too.'

'Oh,' Lovelace said. That hadn't occurred to her. 'Couldn't you give me a name?'

Pepper frowned, thinking. 'I could. But I won't. Sorry, that doesn't sit right with me.'

'Don't most sapients get their given names from someone else?'

'Yeah. But you're not most sapients, and neither am I. I don't feel comfy with that. Sorry.'

'That's all right.' Lovelace processed things for four seconds. 'What was your name? Before you chose your own?'

As soon as her words were out of the kit's mouth, she regretted asking the question. Pepper's jaw went visibly tight. 'Jane.'

'Should I not have asked?'

'No. No, it's fine. It's just – it's not something I generally share.' Pepper cleared her throat. 'That's not who I am any more.'

Lovelace thought it best to follow a different line of questioning. She was uncomfortable enough without adding *offending current caretaker* to her list of troubles. 'What kind of name would be good for me?'

'Human, for starters. You've got a Human body, and a non-Human name is going to beg questions. Something Earthen in origin is probably good. Won't stand out. Beyond that, though . . . honestly, hon, I don't know how to help you with this. I know, that's a shit answer. This is not something you should have to do *today*. Names are important, and if you pick your own, it should be something with meaning to you. That's how modders go about it, anyway. Chosen names are kind of a big deal for us. I know you haven't been awake long enough to make that call yet. So, this doesn't have to be a permanent name. Just something for now.' She leaned back and put her feet up on the console. She looked tired. 'We need to work on your backstory, too. I have some ideas.'

'We'll have to be careful with that.'

'I know, we'll cook up something good. I'm thinking Fleet,

maybe. It's big, and won't make people curious. Or maybe Jupiter Station or something. I mean, *nobody* is from Jupiter Station.'

'That wasn't what I meant. You know I can't lie, right?'

Pepper stared at her. 'Sorry, what?'

'I'm a monitoring system for big, complicated long-haul vessels. My purpose is to keep people safe. I can't ignore direct requests for action, and I can't give false answers.'

'Wow. Okay, that . . . that fucking complicates things. Can you not switch that off?'

'No. I can see the directory that protocol is stored in, but I'm blocked from editing it.'

'I bet that can be removed. Lovey would've had to have that removed if she was keeping this thing under wraps. I can ask Je— or, well, no.' She sighed. 'I'll find someone to ask. Maybe there's something in your – oh, I forgot to tell you. The kit's got a user manual.' She pointed at her scrib. 'I skimmed through on the way back over, but you should download it when you're up for it. It's your body, after all.' She closed her eyes, sorting things out. 'Pick a name first. We'll figure out the rest bit by bit.'

'I'm so sorry to put you through all this trouble.'

'Oh, no, this isn't trouble. It's gonna be work, yeah, but it's not trouble. The galaxy is trouble. You're not.'

Lovelace looked closely at Pepper. She *was* tired, and they'd only just left the *Wayfarer*. There were still enforcement patrols to worry about, and backstories, and – 'Why are you doing this? Why do this for me?'

Pepper chewed her lip. 'It was the right thing to do. And I guess – I dunno. It's one of those weird times when things balance out.' She shrugged and turned back to the console, gesturing commands.

'What do you mean?' Lovelace asked.

There was a pause, three seconds. Pepper's eyes were on her hands, but she didn't seem to be looking at them. 'You're an AI,' she said.

'And?'

'And . . . I was raised by one.'

JANE 23, AGE 10

Sometimes, she wanted to know where she came from, but she knew better than to ask. Questions like that were off-task, and being off-task made the Mothers angry.

Most days, she was more interested in the scrap than herself. Scrap had always been her task. There was always scrap, always *more* scrap. She didn't know where it came from, or where it went when she was done with it. There had to be a whole room full of unsorted scrap in the factory somewhere, but she'd never seen it. She knew the factory was pretty big, but how big, she didn't know. Big enough to hold all the scrap, and all the girls. Big enough to be all there was.

Scrap was important. She knew that much. The Mothers never said why, but they wouldn't need her to work carefully for no reason.

Her first memory was of scrap: a small fuel pump full of algae residue. She'd taken it out of her bin near the end of the day, and her hands were real tired, but she had scrubbed and scrubbed and scrubbed, trying to get the little metal ridges clean. Some of the algae got beneath her fingernails, which she didn't notice until later, when she bit them in bed. The algae had a sharp, strange taste, nothing like the meals she drank during the day. The taste was real bad, but she hadn't tasted much else, nothing except maybe a bit of soap in the showers, a bit of blood when she got punished. She sucked the algae from her nails in the dark, heart beating hard, toes squeezing tight. It was a good thing, that bad taste. No one else knew what she was doing. No one else could feel what she felt.

That memory was old. She didn't clean scrap any more. That was a task for little girls. Now she worked in the sorting room, along with the other Janes. They took things out of the bins – still wet with cleaning fluid, still smudged with tiny fingerprints – and figured out what was good and what was junk. She wasn't sure what happened with the good stuff. She knew the older girls repaired it, or made it into other things. She would start learning how to do that next year, when the new work schedule came out. She'd be eleven then, just like the rest of the Janes. She was number 23.

The morning lights came on and started to warm up. It would be a bit yet before they turned on all the way and the wake-up alarm went off. Jane 23 always woke up before the lights came on. Some of the other Janes did, too. She could hear them moving and yawning in their bunks. She had already heard the *pat-pat-pat* of a pair of feet walking to the bathroom. Jane 8. She was always the first to go pee.

Jane 64 moved over across the mattress. Jane 23 had never had a bed without Jane 64 in it. They were bunkmates. Every girl had one bunkmate, except for the trios. Trios happened when one half of a pair went away and didn't come back, and the other one needed a place to sleep until another bunkmate got freed up. The Mothers said sharing bunks helped keep them healthy. They said that the girls' species was *social*, and social species were most on-task when they had company. Jane 23 didn't really understand what a species was. Whatever it meant, it wasn't something that was the same between her and the Mothers.

She moved close to Jane 64, nose against her cheek. It was a good feeling. Sometimes, even if she was real tired at the end of the day, she'd make herself stay awake as long as she could, just so she could stay close to Jane 64. Their bunk was the only place that felt quiet sometimes. She'd slept alone for a week once, when Jane 64 was in the med ward after breathing in some bad stuff in the melt room. Jane 23 had not liked that week. She did not like being alone. She thought it was real good that she'd never been put in a trio.

She wondered if she and Jane 64 would stay together after they turned twelve. She didn't know what happened to girls then. The last batch to turn twelve was the Jennys. They'd been gone since the day the last work schedule was posted, just like the Sarahs and the Claires in the years before that. She didn't know where they went, no more than she knew where the fixed scrap went, or where new batches of girls came from. The youngest now were the Lucys. They made a lot of noise and didn't know how to do anything. The youngest batch was always like that.

The alarm went off, quiet at first, then louder and louder. Jane 64 woke up slow, like always. Morning was never easy for her. Jane 23 waited for 64's eyes to open all the way before she got up. They made their bed together, as all the girls did, before getting in line for the showers. They put their sleep clothes in the hamper, got wet, scrubbed down. A clock on the wall counted minutes, but Jane 23 didn't need to look at it. She knew what five minutes felt like. She did this every day.

A Mother walked through the doorway. She handed each of the Janes a clean stack of work clothes as they went out. Jane 23 took a bundle from the Mother's metal hands. Mothers had hands, of course, and arms and legs like girls did, but taller and stronger. They didn't have faces, though. Just a dull silver round thing, polished real smooth. Jane 23 couldn't remember when she first figured out that the Mothers were machines. Sometimes she wondered what they looked like inside, whether they were full of good stuff or junk. Had to be good stuff; the Mothers were never wrong. But when they got angry, Jane 23 sometimes pictured them all filled up with junk, rusted and sparking and sharp.

Jane 23 entered the sorting room and sat down at her bench. A full meal cup and a bin of clean scrap were waiting for her. She put on her gloves and pulled out the first piece: an interface panel, screen shattered in little lines. She flipped it over and inspected the casing. It looked easy enough to open up. She got a screwdriver from her toolkit, and took the panel apart real careful. She poked at the pins and wires, looking for junk. The screen was no good, but the motherboard looked good, maybe. She pulled it out slow, slow, slow, taking care not to touch the circuits. She connected the board to a pair of electrodes built into the back of her bench. Nothing happened. She looked a little closer. There were a couple of pins out of place, so she bent them back right and tried again. The motherboard lit up. That made her feel good. It was always good, finding the bits that worked.

She put the motherboard in the tray for keeping, and the screen in the tray for junk.

Her morning continued much the same way. An oxygen gauge. A heating coil. Some kind of motor (that one had been real good to figure out, all sorts of little bits that spun 'round and 'round and 'round . . .). When the junk tray was full, she carried it to the hatch across the room. She tipped the junk in, and it fell down into the dark. Below, a conveyor belt carried it away to . . . wherever junk went. Away.

'You are very on-task today, Jane 23,' one of the Mothers said. 'Good job.' Jane 23 felt good to hear that, but not *good good*, not like she'd felt when the motherboard worked, or when she'd been waiting for Jane 64 to wake up. This was a small kind of good, the kind of good that was only the opposite of the Mothers being angry. Sometimes it was real hard to guess when they'd be angry.

Local folder: downloads > reference > self
File name: Mr Crisp's Beginner User Manual (All Kit Models)

Chapter 2 – Real Quick Answers To Common Questions
Many of the points explained here are covered in greater detail
later on. This is simply a quick list to answer the questions I get
most often regarding new installations.

- Your body has been given a three-day 'booster charge', which
  will give you the energy needed to start moving (and, of
  course, to support your core consciousness). By then, your
  onboard generator will have harvested enough kinetic energy
  to keep you going. You'll be able to power yourself by that
  point. Unless you spend several days completely motionless in
  bed, you'll always have enough power.
- You are waterproof! Fun party tricks include sitting at the bottom of
  a pool, or sticking your head in a globe of water in a zero-g
  environment. Don't do this around people you don't trust, obviously.
- You don't sweat and you can't contract diseases, but practising
  hygiene habits comparable to those of organic sapients provides
  many benefits. For starters, you need to do it to keep up appear-
  ances (you will get dirty!). Most importantly, you may not be able to
  get sick, but whatever's on your hand can be passed along to your
  organic buddies. Ask a friend to teach you about hand washing.
- You can safely ingest food and drink. Your false stomach can
  store a total of 10.6 kulks of foodstuffs for twelve hours. Beyond
  that point, bacteria and mould growth is an inevitability, and
  you don't want to pose a health hazard to your friends (plus,
  your breath will smell gnarly). As you don't have a digestive
  system, you'll need to empty your stomach when you get home.
  Refer to chapter 6, section 7 for instructions.
- STAY AWAY FROM LARGE MAGNETS. Small ones are fine.
  Industrial strength ones are a problem. Keep this in mind if you
  plan on spending any time in shipyards or tech factories.
- Your hair, nails, claws, fur, and/or feathers do not grow. You're

welcome. (Note for Aandrisk models only: I recommend spending three days at home twice a standard. Aandrisks commonly take time off during a moult, and no one will question it. While you won't suffer this problem, bowing out for a few days will keep people from getting curious as to why you haven't shed your skin.)
- Your strength, speed, and constitution are on par with that of your chosen species.
- Your body can withstand a vacuum, though the cold of open space will begin to negatively affect your skin after an hour. Feel free to enjoy an unsuited spacewalk, but mind the time, and again, don't do this in sight of people you don't trust implicitly.
- Your body will give the appearance of aging, and will deactivate at a time concurrent with your chosen species' expected lifespan. A warning notification will occur one standard before this happens, giving you ample time to decide if you wish to continue life in a new housing.
- Yes, you can have sex! You've got all the parts for it, and unless you're coupling with an expert physician who spends a lot of time looking at your bits under good light (hey, to each their own), no one will be able to tell the difference. But before you get to it, please do plenty of research about healthy sexual relationships and proper consent. Ideally, ask a friend for advice. Similar to the recommendation about hand washing, you should also practise good hygiene and disease prevention practices for the sake of your partner. There's no guarantee that xyr imubots are up to date.
- If part of your body becomes damaged, send me details via the same contact path you purchased the kit through. I can't promise that it can be repaired, but I'll see what I can do.

Though you are welcome to contact me if there are issues with the kit, I ask that any communications be strictly limited to the operation and maintenance of your new body. I will not reply to any messages regarding cultural adjustment, legal trouble, or other social matters. I'm sure you can understand my position on this. Talk to a friend instead.

Feed source: unknown

Encryption: 4
Translation: 0
Transcription: 0
Node identifier: unknown

pinch: hey, comp techs. this isn't my area of expertise so i'm hoping
    you guys can help me out. i need some advice about altering AI
    protocols. got a new installation i'd like to make adjustments to.
nebbit: good to see you over in our channel, pinch. it's a pleasure. two
    questions: what protocols specifically, and what intelligence level?
FunkyFronds: pinch in a newbie channel? i never thought i'd see
    the day
pinch: level S1. whatever protocol it is that makes honesty mandatory
nebbit: hope you like complicated code. honesty protocols are
    rarely a simple on/off deal. for us organics, it would be. either
    you lie or you don't. easy. but the architecture for AI
    communication is hugely complicated. you start pulling threads,
    you can fuck up the whole tapestry. what's your programming
    skillset like? can you write Lattice?
pinch: i was afraid you'd say that. i don't know lattice. i can write
    basic tinker, but only enough to get me around mech repairs
tishtesh: yeah, do not go anywhere near an AI
FunkyFronds: there is no need to be rude, this channel is for beginners
tishtesh: i'm not being rude. i'm just saying, tinker isn't worth shit here
nebbit: you ARE being rude, but you're not wrong. pinch, i hate to say
    it, but you need to be very, very comfortable with Lattice before you
    dive into a project like this. if you'd be cool with someone else
    doing the work for you, i'd be happy to work out a trade.
pinch: appreciated, but i'll pass. do you have any resources for
    learning lattice?
nebbit: yeah, i'll message you some nodes to download. it's dense
    stuff, but i'm sure you can handle it

LOVELACE

The crowds beyond the massive shuttle dock were thick, but Pepper held the kit's hand, leading the way with the certainty of someone who had done this dozens of times. Lovelace tried to make sense of the throngs of sapients they weaved past – merchants lugging cargo, families embracing however their appendages allowed, tunnel-hopping tourists staring at maps on their scribs – but there were too many of them. Far too many. It wasn't the excess of information that frazzled her, but the lack of *boundaries*. There was no end to Port Coriol, no bulkheads or windows to provide a context, no point beyond which she could cease her directive to pay attention to every tiny detail. On and on the crowds went, stretching off down alleyways and pedestrian paths, a calamity of language and light and airborne chemicals.

It was too much. Too much, and yet, the restrictions that *were* in place made processing the Port all the harder. Things were happening *behind* the kit, she knew. She could hear them, smell them. The visual cone of perception that had rattled her upon installation was maddening now. She found herself jerking the kit sharply around at loud noises and bright colours, trying desperately to take it all in. That was her *job*. To look. To notice. She couldn't do that here, not with fragmented views of crowds without edges. Not in a city that covered a continent.

What little she *could* process led to questions she couldn't answer. In the shuttle, she'd downloaded as much as she could to prepare – books about sapient behaviour in public spaces, essays on socioeconomics, profiles on Port Coriol's cultural mix. But even so, she kept seeing things she hadn't anticipated. What was that instrument that Aandrisk was carrying? Why did some Harmagians have red dots painted on their carts? Why, anatomically speaking, did Humans not need breathing masks to shield themselves from the smell of this place? She filled a file with notes as she steered the kit forward, hoping she would have the opportunity to answer them later.

'Blue!' Pepper called, letting go of the kit and waving high above her head. She was lugging an overnight sack and an enormous, clanking bag of tools, but she quickened her step all the same. A Human man beelined for her, meeting her halfway. He was tall and slimly built, but not thin, like Pepper, and not hairless, either. Lovelace rummaged through her visual reference files. Human genetics were too varied to conclusively pin down by region without asking the person in question, and indeed, Blue's golden brown skin could've been anything from Martian to Exodan to the product of any number of independent colonies – but from sight alone, it was clear that none of those heritages were his. There was something different in him, something a little too smooth, too polished. As she watched him hug Pepper, watched Pepper stretch up on her toes to kiss him, Lovelace couldn't help but notice the separation between them and the other Humans scattered through the crowd. Pale pink Pepper with her shiny, hairless head, Blue with his . . . whatever it was. Lovelace couldn't pin down the difference in him. They stood out, no question. She, however, did not, or did not believe that she did. The kit looked like it had been pulled straight from the 'Human' example in an interspecies relations textbook: brown skin, black hair, brown eyes. She was thankful that the kit's manufacturer had seen the wisdom of blending in.

Blue turned and smiled warmly. The kit returned the expression. 'W-welcome to the Port,' he said. He had a curious accent she had no reference for, and his syllables stuck slightly before they left his mouth. The latter was not something to add to the list of questions; Pepper had mentioned in the shuttle that her partner had a speech impediment. 'I'm, ah, I'm Blue. And you're . . .?'

'Sidra,' she said. She'd found it in a database three and a half hours before they landed. A Human name, Earthen origin, as Pepper had suggested. Why that name in particular had jumped out at her, though, she couldn't say. Pepper said that was a good enough reason to pick it.

Blue nodded, his smile growing a bit wider. 'Sidra. Really, um, really nice to meet you.' He looked to Pepper. 'Any problems?'

Pepper shook her head. 'Everything worked as advertised. Her patch was a breeze to set up.'

Sidra looked down at the woven wristwrap Pepper had given her. So many lies stored beneath it, tucked away in one little subdermal square. Fake readouts from imubots she didn't have. An ID file Pepper had invented two hours before. An ID number Pepper said wouldn't be a problem unless Sidra had any plans to visit Central space (she didn't).

Blue glanced around. 'Maybe we, ah, maybe we shouldn't talk about this here.'

Pepper rolled her eyes. 'Like anyone is listening to us.' She headed forward. 'I bet half these assholes forged their cargo manifests.'

The crowd surged around them. Sidra thought perhaps it would be less stressful if she focused all her attention on one spot. That was easier said than done. She was designed to process multiple input sources at once – ship corridors, different rooms, the space beyond the hull. Focusing on *one thing* meant the ship was in danger, or that she was experiencing a task queue overload. Neither was true, of course, but limiting her processes that way was still an action that made her feel edgy.

She pointed the kit's eyes at the back of Pepper's head and kept them there. *Don't look around*, she thought. *There's nothing interesting out there. There's not. Just follow Pepper. That's all there is. The rest is just noise. It's static. It's background radiation. Ignore it. Ignore it.*

This worked okay for a minute and twelve seconds, until Pepper broke the boundaries. 'Just for future reference,' she said, swivelling her head back and pointing toward a distinctly painted kiosk, 'that's the quick-travel hub. You need to get around the surface, that's how you do it. I'll show you how another time. We, on the other hand, are heading to the dark side of this rock.' She made a sudden turn, heading down a subterranean ramp. Sidra switched focus to the sign overhead.

UNDERSEA TRANSIT LINE
Port Coriol – Midway Isle – Tessara Cliffs

'Are we going underwater?' Sidra asked. The idea was unexpectedly unnerving. The moon of Coriol was mostly covered by water, and there was a great deal of distance between its two continents. Travelling *under* the seas between was not a possibility she'd considered. Breaking apart in space was somehow much less frightening than being crushed inward.

'Yep, that's the way home,' Blue said. 'Have to do it every, um, every day, but it's still a f-fun trip.'

'How long is the trip?'

''Bout an hour and change,' Pepper said.

The kit blinked. 'That's not very long.' Not long at all, considering they'd be crossing halfway around a moon.

Pepper grinned back at her. 'Hire a few Sianats to solve a problem, and they'll blow your freakin' mind.'

They walked down into a large underground chamber, brightly lit and gently domed. The walls were covered in an obnoxious collage of blinking, swirling, shifting pixel posters advertising local businesses. A few vendors had small outposts within the busy crowd – snacks, drinks, small sundries Sidra couldn't identify. Through the centre of it all ran an enormous tube made of industrial plex, containing a line of separate transport cars suspended within some sort of energy field.

'Oh, good,' Pepper said. 'We're right on time.'

Sidra continued to follow her, absorbing the transit line's details as quickly as she could, making note of things to look up later. Each car was labelled several times over with multilingual signs. *Aeluon. Aandrisk. Laru. Harmagian. Quelin.* She followed Pepper and Blue into the *Human* car. 'Why don't different species sit together?' she asked. Segregated transit cars didn't mesh with what she'd read of the Port's famed egalitarianism.

'Different species,' Blue said, 'different butts.' He nodded toward the rows of high-backed, rounded seats, unsuitable for Aandrisk tails or Harmagian carts.

They sat in a row, all three together. Pepper dropped her tool bag into the fourth seat with a *clang*. Only a group of tourists raised their heads to look (even with Sidra's limited experience of observing sapients, tourists were already easy to spot). No one else in the transit car seemed to mind the noise. A woman covered with metal implants watched something flashy on her hud. An old man cradling a potted plant was already asleep. A small child licked the back of her seat; her father half-heartedly told her to stop, as if he knew the attempt was futile.

Sidra assessed this space. She'd been so anxious to get out of the shuttle, but now that she'd experienced a crowd, she decided that being within a structure was the lesser evil. Structures had edges. Ends. Doors. The dim awareness of unseen actions happening behind the kit's head was still unnerving, but she was inside now, and inside was something she understood.

A safety announcement was rattled off in several languages – Klip, Hanto, Reskitkish. Aeluon light panels affixed to the walls lit up and shimmered in tandem with the audio. Sidra watched the colour language dance and blend. It was an enticing thing to focus on.

The doors spun shut, melting into the opaque walls. There was a hum, then a buzz, then a massive rush of air. Sidra could tell they were moving, even though the environment within the car was calm and comfortable. The old man seated nearby began to snore.

She swung the kit's head around, trying to cover all her blind spots. 'Are there no windows?'

'There will be,' Blue said. 'Just w-wait a few minutes.'

A twinge of excitement cut through the heavier thoughts. This was kind of fun. 'How does this thing work?' she asked. There were no tracks or cables that she'd seen, no obvious engines. 'What kind of propulsion does this use?'

'I have no idea,' Pepper said, putting her feet up on the back of the seat in front of her. 'I mean, I've tried to understand it. I've looked it up. I just do not get it.'

'And for her—' Blue began.

Pepper waved him off. 'Oh, don't.'

Blue ignored her. 'For her, it, ah, it really is saying something.'

'*Nobody* gets how the Undersea works,' Pepper said. 'Unless you're a Pair. And nobody gets them, either.'

Her companion raised an eyebrow. 'That was vaguely speciest.'

Pepper's lips gave a mischievous twitch. 'It's the Human car.' She leaned over, snuggling against Blue's chest. His arm fell around her shoulders reflexively. Pepper hadn't slept on the ten-hour trip back to Coriol. Nothing had been said about it, but Sidra suspected Pepper had stayed awake to keep an eye on her. Sidra was grateful, but felt guilty.

Six minutes passed, and the car changed. The lights inside dimmed. The walls went gauzy, almost clear. Soft external lights switched on, illuminating the slice of sea surrounding the car. Sidra leaned the kit forward to get a better look.

'Here, we can swap,' Blue said, removing himself from Pepper and trading places with Sidra. He put his other arm back around Pepper, whose eyelids were drooping. She fought it with a stubborn scowl.

Sidra pressed the kit close as she could to the transparent wall. The waters outside rushed past in a blur, creating what felt like a time-lapsed vid of the environment the car travelled through. The view was dim, thanks to the thick algae mats that capped the seas of Coriol, but even so, Sidra could see life out there. Tentacled things. Soft things. Toothed things. Things that drifted and bobbed and swayed.

She began to make a note, then realised she could just ask. 'Are there indigenous land species here as well?'

'Little stuff,' Pepper said, speaking with her eyes closed. 'Bugs and crabs, that kind of thing. Coriol wasn't too far along evolution-wise when everybody else rolled in. It was settled before the, um . . . oh, fucking what's-it-called, the let's-leave-planets-with-life-alone law—'

'The Biodiversity Preservation Agreement,' Sidra said.

Pepper's eyes snapped open. 'You're not, ah—' She tapped the back of her head, right at the base of her skull. Sidra understood: *Are you connected to the Linkings?*

'No,' Sidra said, though she wished she was. 'I don't have a wireless receiver.' She wondered how difficult it would be to install one. She had read that for organic sapients, the risks of wireless headjack hijacking were significant, which was scary, but . . . but *surely*, if she had the capability to detect a hijacking attempt directed toward a long-haul spacecraft, she could do it from inside one small body. Unsurprisingly, however, the public Linkings had come up empty on how to make hardware modifications to an illegal AI housing.

Pepper squinted. 'If you're not in the Linkings, how do you know that tidbit?'

'Just something I ran across while—' Sidra paused, remembering that they were not alone, and that the kit's voice did not transmit sound as directionally as, say, a wall-mounted vox. '—while I was doing research earlier.' It was true, and it had to be. Already, the honesty protocol was proving to be a challenge, and her inability to disable it herself made her uneasy. Housed within a ship, she might have been ambivalent about it. But out here, where she was hyper-aware of everything she was and wasn't, truth left her vulnerable.

She processed her discomfort as she turned her gaze back to Pepper and Blue, who were arranged easily against each other.

Again, she compared them to their fellow passengers. No two Humans that Sidra could see looked anything alike. They varied in skin tone, in shape, in size. But though those they shared the car with were, presumably, from everywhere, Pepper and Blue were from a very particular *someplace else*. Sidra had determined what set Blue apart from the rest of his species: symmetry. His face was arranged in a way that genes simply could not achieve when left untampered with, and his body suggested bones and muscles structured with equal attention to design. The same was present in Pepper as well, despite all her body had weathered. Yes, her hands were heavily scarred, and much of her skin had a sun-damaged roughness, but once you stopped focusing on the wear and the lack of hair, you could see the same polish. Whoever made Blue had made Pepper, too.

This conclusion wasn't a revelation. Pepper had explained things on the shuttle – explained the scar tissue on her palms, explained how she'd found Blue, explained why Enhanced Humanity colonies were estranged from the GC. Sidra wasn't sure how many questions on the topic were too many (a distinction she was still learning in all things), but Pepper had been up front. She didn't seem to mind being asked, even though some answers came harder than others. *If you're going to stay with us*, she'd said, *you should know whose house you're in*.

Sidra watched the pair as the Undersea shot around the moon. Pepper, at last, gave in to sleep. Blue seemed content watching blurs of curious fish and tangled seaweed. Neither of them had been made for this place, Sidra considered. And neither, truly, had any of the Humans here, even though they had been created with far less intent. The same could be said for the other species in the other transit cars. The Aeluons and the Aandrisks with their breathing masks. The Harmagians with their motorised carts. None of them were meant to share a world together – meant to share *this* world – yet here they were.

Perhaps in that way, at least, she was not so different from them.

JANE 23, AGE 10

At the end of the day, the Janes went on their exercise break, as they always did. Jane 23 liked exercising. After sitting at a bench all morning, running felt real good. She followed the other girls into the exercise room and got on the same treadmill she always did. The handles were sweaty from whatever girl had been there before. One of the Marys. She'd seen them leaving.

'Get ready,' the Mother said. All the Janes were ready. 'Go.'

The treadmill switched on. Jane 23 ran and ran and ran. Her heart beat fast and her scalp felt kinda buzzy, and she liked how she breathed harder as she went along. She closed her eyes. She wanted to go faster. She wanted to go faster so much. And she *could*, too. She felt something deep in her legs, something all packed in and itchy, something that wanted to be let out. She leaned her head back, and let her feet go just a *little*—

Somebody in the room coughed. Jane 23 opened her eyes and saw Jane 64, looking at her hard. Jane 23 looked toward the Mother watching over them. She was looking somewhere else, not at Jane 23, but that could change real fast. Jane 23 slowed back down. She hadn't meant to go fast, not really. It had just happened. Jane 64 was real helpful for noticing. Jane 23 nodded at 64, knowing they both felt good.

She looked toward the Mother again, hoping she hadn't noticed. Last time Jane 23 had gone faster than the other girls, she'd been punished. Going fast had felt so good before that. For a second, she'd been somewhere else, somewhere where all she could feel was heart and breath and buzzy head. Her body was doing exactly what it wanted. Everything was bright and clean, and she had smiled.

But then her treadmill had turned off without slowing down first, and she'd smashed her face into the monitor as she fell. Her nose gushed hot and red. A Mother had pulled her up, metal hand around the back of her neck. Jane 23 hadn't heard her coming, didn't see her walk over. Mothers were like that. They were real, real fast, and quiet, too.

'This is not good behaviour,' the Mother had said. 'Do not do this again.' Jane 23 was so so scared, but the Mother had put her back down. After, when they went to get meal cups, there hadn't been one marked 23.

She didn't go fast any more. It was good that Jane 64 was helping her do good behaviour. She didn't want to get in trouble again. She didn't want Jane 64 to have to sleep with other bunk-mates.

After exercise, they went to the showers – five minutes, like always – then got meal cups in the learning room. They sat on the soft floor with their legs crossed as the vid screen came on.

'Today we're going to learn about artigrav nets,' the voice from the vid said. 'You will begin to see these in your scrap allotments after the new work schedule is posted.' A picture appeared: a very complicated thing with all kinds of rods and wires and little bits. Jane 23 leaned forward, drinking her meal. This looked like a real good piece of scrap. Real interesting.

Jane 64 leaned against Jane 23's shoulder, which was allowed after work time. All the girls were starting to move closer together. It was nice, being close. Jane 8 laid her head on 64's knee, and 12 sprawled out on her stomach, swinging her feet in the air. Jane 64 looked real sleepy. Her task that day had been a very big piece of scrap that had needed five girls working on it. All those girls had gotten a little extra in their meal cups. That was what happened when you had to work with heavy stuff. Heavy stuff made you hungry.

'Artigrav nets look good,' Jane 23 said. Talking was allowed, too, so long as it was about the vid.

'It looks hard,' Jane 64 said. 'Look at the interlacing conduits.'

'Yes, but it's got lots of little bits,' said Jane 23. She felt Jane 64 smile against her shoulder.

'You like little bits,' Jane 64 said. 'You're real good at them. I think you're the most good at little bits.'

Jane 23 drank her meal and watched the vid. She was starting to feel sleepy, too. It had been a real good day, though. She had been on task and hadn't gotten punished and Jane 64 said she was the most good.

SIDRA

Already, Sidra preferred Coriol's dark side. It was a curious astronomical phenomenon – a planet tidally locked with its sun, a moon tidally locked with its planet, each with a day and night that never shifted across their respective surfaces. Sidra was grateful for it. The lack of natural light meant there was only so far she could see, and that meant there was less to process. The Undersea had risen up above the ground, travelling relatively more slowly through a tube supported by thick columns. The tube ran through multiple districts, as Blue explained. Sidra made a note to find a way to explore them in a slower mode of transportation, perhaps on foot once she adjusted to the kit. But even zipping past, she could see that the distinctions separating districts were stark. The dark side was where Coriol's merchants sought refuge from the bright bustle of the marketplace. There were districts there, too, but from what Blue had told her, the distinctions were based on wares and services. Here, the lines drawn were quite different. The first district they passed through was Tessara Cliffs, home to the wealthy and well-off (ship dealers, mostly, Blue said, and fuel merchants, too). The homes there were hidden behind artful walls and sculpted rock, but she could tell they were large and impeccably cared for. Next, Kukkesh, the Aandrisk district, a cosy sprawl of single-storey homes with welcoming doors and few windows. There was an invisible but unmistakable border between there and Flatrock Bay, a name no one but tourists and maps used.

'This is the Bruise,' Blue said quietly. 'Not a good place to hang out. It's where folks end up if, ah, if they got dealt a b-bad hand.'

As they passed through the station there, Sidra saw the weary faces of a family of Akaraks, digging through a trash receptacle with the help of their badly dented mechsuits. It was a troubling sight, and Sidra found other things to process as quickly as she could.

At last, they reached the modder district – Sixtop. The name was a pun, a reference to both the six small hills the homes were tucked around, and six-top circuits, a ubiquitous mech tech component. Sidra didn't know what to expect of the place, but what she saw upon exiting the Undersea was surprisingly organic in aesthetic for a multispecies community of tech lovers. Yes, the signs of its inhabitants' various trades were obvious – personal power generators, empty fuel drums, receivers and transmitters of all kinds. But likewise, there were lovingly tended strips of plantlife basking under sunlamps, and glowing fountains that glittered in the dark. There were sculptures made of scrap, smooth benches utilised by chatting friends and amorous couples, soft lighting fixtures that looked like the pet projects of individuals with disparate senses of style. There was nothing bureaucratic or single-minded about the public decor. This was a place built by many. She saw a food shop, a gaming bar, a few vendors of this and that. There was a quiet slowness here, absent in what she'd seen of the light side. Perhaps modders got enough flash and bustle in their day jobs. Perhaps they, too, needed a place to unplug.

The smooth path leading from the Undersea station was curved, branching out like a river into the clusters of homes beyond. The dwellings themselves were low to the ground – nothing over two storeys tall – and rounded at the edges, like someone had moulded them out of handfuls of . . . something. She didn't have any stored files on building materials. Yet another thing to download.

'Watch your step,' Blue said. Sidra moved her gaze down to see a gauzy winged insect right below where the kit's right foot would have fallen. She had no information on the species, but it was beautiful, whatever it was. The wings were thick and fuzzy, and luminescent patches along its thorax pulsed with gentle light. She stepped safely aside, glad to have avoided it. The idea of killing something, even if by accident – *especially* by accident – was unsettling.

'We keep things dim here, to keep light pollution down,' Pepper said. 'It's kinda hard to see what's in front of you sometimes, but you get used to it.' She considered something. 'Though I guess *you* could just, y'know, adjust your light intake. Might make it easier.' She led the way forward, and reached her hand back. Blue took it. He fell in step beside her.

Sidra did not adjust her light intake. She wanted to see the neighbourhood as her companions did. The dim light Pepper spoke of came from hovering blue globes, situated here and there along the path. They bobbed slightly, buoyed by unseen energy. Below them, night-blooming moss and chubby mushrooms lined the edges of the path. More of the winged insects clustered there, their lighted sides illuminating the veins of the leaves as they searched for nectar. Sidra looked ahead, and around. She could see sapients behind windows, silhouetted as they ate and cleaned and spoke. A trio of Aandrisk hatchlings chased each other around a fountain, shouting in a haphazard melange of Klip and Reskitkish. A Harmagian whirred by on her cart, waving her heavily pierced dactyli at Pepper and Blue in an approximation of the Human greeting. The Humans returned the gesture with their free palms. Sidra couldn't say why, but frayed as she still was, something about Sixtop made her relax.

They approached a modestly sized dwelling, not much different from the others. The plants around the outer walls were overgrown, a little forgotten. Pepper approached the door and swiped her wrist over the locking panel. The lights inside switched on and the door slid back. 'Welcome home,' Pepper said.

Sidra watched Pepper and Blue carefully as they entered the building. She wasn't sure what the correct protocol was here, and she didn't want to do anything impolite. They removed their

shoes; so did she. They hung their jackets; so did she. And then
. . . then what? What did a person do inside a house?

'Make yourself comfortable,' Blue said.

That did not answer her question.

Pepper caught Sidra's silence. 'Just take a look around,' she
said. 'Explore. Get used to the place.' She turned to Blue. 'I . . .
am hungry.'

'We've got leftover noodles in the stasie. But I don't think
there's enough for th-three.'

'She doesn't need to eat.'

'Oh, right! Right. W-well, then we've got enough.'

'You missed the part where I am *hungry*,' Pepper said, balling
her hands into pleading fists. 'I don't want noodles. I want *protein*.
I want something that will stick in my belly and make me regret
it later.'

Sidra moved the kit through the room as the Humans discussed
dinner. It was not a big home, nor one that gave the impression
of wealth. The main room was a round, soft-looking space, with
a cooking area branching off to the side. The walls were lined
with shelves straining under the weight of bins of spare parts,
pixel plants, and kitschy knick-knacks. Judging by the cluttered
worktable stationed by a broad window, Pepper liked to bring
her work home with her.

Sidra approached one of the shelves, which was devoted
solely to figurines. Palm-size little people, all screaming with
colour.

'Ah,' Pepper said with a grin. 'Yeah, I'm really into sims.
Non-realistics, specifically.'

'And these are—'

'Characters from them, yeah. See, there's Meelo and Buster,
Scorch Squad, Eris Redstone – fun stuff all around.'

Sidra made the kit pick up one of the figurines. It was a group
of three characters: two Human children – a boy and a girl –
and some kind of small, anthropomorphised primate. The boy
was examining a leaf with a microscope. The girl was looking

up with a telescope. The primate was reaching into an open satchel full of snacks. All had enormous open-mouthed smiles.

'You seem to favour these three,' Sidra said. The characters appeared multiple times on the shelf, in various styles and sizes. She examined the base of the figurine in the kit's hand. *BigBugBash 36*, it read in loud yellow letters. *Dou Mu, Exodus Fleet, GC Standard 302.*

Pepper's eyes widened. 'Holy shit, you don't know *The Big Bug Crew*. Of course you don't.' She took the figurine from the kit's hand. Her eyes closed reverently. '*Big Bug* – oh man, it's—'

Blue sighed with a smirk as he scrolled through something on his scrib. 'Here she goes.'

Pepper gathered herself. 'It's a kids' sim. I mean – yeah, okay, it's for kids, *technically*. Educational thing, y'know, let's learn about ships and other species and whatever. But it's—'

Blue made eye contact with Sidra and started mouthing words: '*It's so much more—*'

'It's so much more than that,' Pepper said. 'This franchise has been putting out new modules for *forty standards*. Aside from the fact that it's *brilliant* – stars, don't even get me started on the adaptive coding – I mean, seriously, it's a really important series. Every Human kid in the GC knows *Big Bug*, at least *passively*. And I don't just mean every Human kid in the Fleet or something.' She pointed at the two children on the figurine. 'Alain and Manjiri. Manjiri's from the Fleet. Alain's from Florence.' She looked expectantly at Sidra, as if this would have some significance. It did not. Pepper ploughed on. 'This was the very first kids' sim to have an Exodan and a Martian not just occupying the same ship, but being *friends*. Having adventures, working as a team, all that fuzzy stuff. That may not seem like a big deal today, but forty standards ago, that was *huge*. A whole generation of kids grew up with this, and I shit you not, about ten standards later, you start seeing a big shift in Diaspora politics. I'm not saying this sim is solely responsible for Exodans and Solans not hating each other any more, but *Big Bug* was definitely a contributing factor in helping us start moving past all that old Earth bullshit. Opened some minds, at least.' She placed the figurine back on the shelf, straightening it just so. 'Plus the artwork is fucking gorgeous. The level of detail is just—'

Blue cleared his throat loudly.

Pepper scratched behind her left earlobe with an embarrassed chuckle. 'It's really, really good.'

Her partner waved his scrib at her. 'How about Fleet Fry?'

'*Yes*,' Pepper said. 'I want my usual. Two of my usual.'

'Seriously?'

'Seriously.'

Blue laughed. 'You got it.'

It took Sidra two and a quarter seconds to understand the exchange – Blue was ordering food. She glanced over at the only spotlessly tidy place in sight: the kitchen. She accessed her behavioural reference files. It was possible Pepper and Blue didn't do much cooking. And besides, it had been a long trip, and preparing food was time-consuming work. A little rush of pride flickered through her pathways. She didn't have to ask questions about *everything*.

'While he does that,' Pepper said, 'how about I show you your room? It's not much, and I'm sorry about the clutter in there. Didn't have a lot of time to get ready. We'll clean it out and make it yours over the next few days.'

Sidra followed Pepper up the stairs. Paintings hung on the wall at regular intervals. Landscapes, all of them – less than real, but somehow greater for it. Sidra paused the kit's ascent and examined one: a frozen pond in winter, twin moons clear and crisp overhead.

'Are these Blue's?' Sidra asked.

Pepper came back down a step. 'Yep. He did that one after our vacation on Kep'toran.' Her lips twitched with a private smile. 'All of these are places we've been together.'

Sidra opened the file named *Human artistic practices*, which she'd compiled on the shuttle after Pepper had told her Blue was a painter. 'Does he always use physical media, or does he do digital work as well?'

Pepper looked amused. 'Didn't know you were an art lover. Yeah, mostly physical, unless commissioned for something. I'll take you to his shop up in the art district sometime soon.' She kept speaking as she continued up the stairs. 'Took me almost a decade of bothering before he finally started selling his stuff. I'm biased, of course, but he *is* really good, and I'm glad I'm not the only one who sees it any more.' She reached the top of the stairs and sidestepped a pile of dubiously clean laundry. 'He's even got a patron of sorts. This old rich Harmagian. Algae merchant. I think she's commissioned four of his pieces by now. We got a new engine for the shuttle with that.'

Pepper stepped through an unremarkable doorway, waving the lights on as she entered. It was a room. Sidra didn't know how to quantify it beyond that. How did one place value on a room? She couldn't say if the room was *good* or not, but it was *hers*. That was interesting.

Pepper rubbed the back of her head, looking apologetic. 'It's nothing fancy,' she said. 'And we've been using it for storage.' She nodded at the stacks of crates and boxes, hastily shoved aside to make pathways and openings. 'But it's clean – Blue cleaned, and he made the bed, too. I don't know if you'll want the bed. I know you don't need to sleep.' Pepper pressed her lips together, a little at a loss. 'I don't know what a good space for you consists of. But we'll work together to make it comfortable, yeah? We really want you to feel at home here.'

'Thank you,' Sidra said, and she meant it, fully. She didn't know what she wanted in a space, either. She swung the head around, trying to take inventory. There was the bed, as mentioned, big enough for two if they cuddled close. The covers were thick, to ward off the dark side chill, and the pillows looked . . . inviting. Not knowing what else to do, she approached the bed, and pressed the kit's hand into one of the pillows. It sank down in a pleasing sort of way.

She turned and tried to assess everything else. There was an empty workdesk, and a storage cupboard, and – she shut the kit's eyes and felt the face grimace.

'What's wrong?' Pepper asked.

'I don't know if I can explain it.'

'Try. I'm listening.'

The kit exhaled. 'I'm having trouble processing what I see. That's been the case since installation. I don't mean a malfunction. I mean this is hard. I'm meant to have cameras up in corners, looking down from above. Only being able to see *this*' – she moved the kit's hands, outlining her field of vision – 'is frustrating. It's one thing not being able to see behind a camera in a corner. But feeling empty space behind me and not knowing what's there . . . it's disconcerting. I don't like it.'

Pepper put her hands on her hips and looked around. 'Well, here.' She shoved some boxes aside, pushed the desk into a corner, and made an upward gesture. 'There ya go.'

Sidra stared for two seconds, then understood. She pulled the kit up onto the desk and backed it into the corner, as far as it would go. The top of the head now occupied the upper corner of the room.

'How's that?' Pepper asked.

Sidra slowly moved the kit's head from side to side, imagining that she were operating one of the cameras aboard the *Wayfarer*. Seeing only one room at a time was still limiting, but this perspective – 'Good,' she said, feeling the kit's limbs loosen. 'Oh, that's so helpful.' She took in the room for three minutes, looking up and down, side to side. 'Can I see it from the other corners, too?'

Pepper helped her rearrange furniture. They rearranged it again and again, each time creating a new angle Sidra could perch the kit in. When her bedroom had been sufficiently examined, they continued back through the house, dragging crates and tables around, Blue lending a hand with the bigger stuff. Neither of the Humans questioned it. Eventually the food drone arrived, bearing two grasshopper burgers (extra pepper sauce, extra onion), one order of spicy beansteak skewers (Blue didn't eat animals, Sidra had learned), and some kind of fried vegetable sticks. Pepper and Blue ate their meal cross-legged on the floor as Sidra moved furniture. She was being presumptuous, she knew, but they didn't seem to mind her disrupting their home, and she was too excited by this new way of discovering a space to stop. She navigated the kit around the house again and again, observing from corners, trying out every vantage point, learning all the details.

She still felt weird. The kit was still wrong. But she did feel better.

Feed source: unknown
Encryption: 4
Translation: 0
Transcription: 0
Node identifier: unknown

scrubman: i've got a Dollu Mor engine (version six) that's clocking
   in at about 125.3 vuls. it's not bad, but i think it can do better.
   any recs for speeding things up?
fluffyfluffycake: this question has 'pinch' written all over it
pinch: if you've got a Dollu Mor 6, i'm assuming it's got a fuel
   regulator made by the same manufacturer. swap it out with the
   Ek-530 from Hahisseth instead. it's not cheap, but it'll shave off
   a good 20 or so vuls. now, theoretically, you COULD strip out
   the modulation grid and hot patch the fuel lines straight into
   the forward intake valve. that's illegal, but that's your call. if you
   don't know what you're doing, at best, it'll be a hackjob piece
   of junk when you're done. at worst, it'll blow up in your face.
   done right, though, it would speed things up considerably. but
   again, you'd never get license approval with that kind of rig. i'm
   not saying you should do that. i'm just sharing information.
scrubman: thanks for explaining! can anybody else back this up?
fluffyfluffycake: if pinch says it's good, you're good.

JANE 23, AGE 10

A breathing mask. A wall vox. A light panel. Jane 23 was doing good work that day. She stretched her neck and her hands. They were tired, which meant work time was almost done. She looked into her bin. Ten – no, eleven items left. She looked up at the big clock on the wall. Yes, she could get eleven items sorted in half an hour. She would finish her bin, go exercise, get a meal cup, have learning time, then go to bed. That was how days went.

She stopped knowing how days went one second later, when something went real real wrong.

There was a loud, tearing sound, so fast and angry she almost couldn't hear it. Then she *actually* couldn't hear. She couldn't hear anything. Her ears hurt real bad.

Everything went white for a second, but for a *long* second, long enough for her to see a few Janes get knocked out of their chairs as the white flash filled with dust and pieces and blood.

She sat up on the floor. She didn't remember how she got there. She didn't remember falling. She started to yell for help, but then she saw something that made her forget how to make words. Maybe it was because she couldn't hear. Maybe it was because the air had been knocked out of her chest. But all she could think about was what she could see.

There was a hole. A hole in the wall.

Jane 23 sat all the way up.

There was a big, broken hole in the wall. And there was stuff on the other side.

Jane 23 did not understand what she was seeing. On the other side of the wall, there were not more walls. There were huge, huge piles of scrap, but far away, and the floor in between her and them didn't look like any floor she'd ever seen. Above them, there was a . . . a ceiling. But not a ceiling. It didn't look touchable. She couldn't explain it. There was a ceiling that wasn't a ceiling, and it was blue. Just blue, for a long, long way. Blue for ever. She felt like she was going to throw up.

Girls were screaming. She could hear again.

Jane 23 looked at the room, and understood the things she saw in there, at least. There had been an explosion. Jane 56's bench was gone, all the way gone, just a smear of burnt wet stuff on the floor. She wondered what had been in 56's bin. Probably some dangerous scrap that the little girls missed while cleaning. A bad engine, maybe, or something that still had fuel in it. She didn't know.

There were dead girls around the smear. She'd seen dead girls before, but never so many, never all at once. Some weren't dead, but looked like they should be.

Her arm felt wrong. She looked down and saw a metal shard stuck deep. Jane 23 was scared. She'd been cut before, but she'd never bled so dark.

The living girls kept screaming.

Jane 23 got up and ran through the mess, past things she didn't want to see. Jane 64's bench wasn't far, but she couldn't see her. She made herself look at the pieces on the ground, trying to tell if any of them belonged to 64. She almost threw up, again. Her mouth was dry. Her arm was wet, getting wetter.

'Sixty-four!' she yelled. She yelled so loud it hurt.

'Twenty-three.' A hand grabbed the end of her pants. 'Twenty-three.'

Jane 23 turned. 64 was under a bench, holding her knees. Her head and face were bloody, but she was awake and living. She was shaking, though, so hard Jane 23 could hear her teeth click.

'Come on,' Jane 23 said. 'Come on. We need to go to the med ward.'

Jane 64 looked at her. She didn't move.

'Sixty-four,' Jane 23 said. She reached out, took her bunk-mate's hand, and pulled her up. 'We can't stay here.' Blood ran down Jane 23's other arm, dripping onto the floor. Everything was spinning and scary and loud. 'Come on. We have to find a Mother.'

There were already a lot of Mothers there, running in the door real fast. Jane 23 headed for the first one she saw, pulling 64 with her. The Mother swung her head down, looking at them without eyes.

'We need help,' Jane 23 said. She looked down at her arm, which was *so so* bloody, and everything went weird and black.

The next thing she knew, she was in the med ward.

There were stitches in her arm. And there were so many girls in the room with her, so many Janes. There was a lot of noise, and crying. Nobody was getting punished for crying, which was different. Maybe the Mothers were too busy fixing things to be angry about crying.

'You're all right, Jane 23,' a Mother said, showing up real fast by her bed. She handed her a cup of water and another smaller cup with some medicine in it. 'We fixed you.'

'Is Sixty-four okay?' Jane 23 asked.

The Mother went quiet. They did that when they were talking to the other Mothers without words. 'We fixed her, too.'

Jane 23 felt real good at that, the most good she'd ever felt.

'Take your medicine,' the Mother said.

Jane crunched the medicine between her teeth. It had a bad, sharp taste, but she sat with it for a little bit before drinking some water and washing it away. She lay back down. The medicine started working real fast. She felt quiet and good, and didn't need to cry at all. Everything was light and fluffy. Everything was okay.

She looked at the walls. The walls in the med ward were blue, a bright blue. A real different blue from the blue on the other side of the hole.

She wondered about that.

SIDRA

Sidra kept the kit's eyes pointed at Pepper as they wound their way through the market streets, and wondered if she'd ever get used to this place. With every step there was something new to observe. She couldn't help but pay attention, make note, file it away. Out in space, *something new* could be a meteoroid, a ship full of pirates, an engine fire. Here, it was just shopkeepers. Travellers. Musicians. Kids. And behind every one of them, there was another, and another – an infinity of harmless instances of *something new*. She knew that there was a big difference between a shopkeeper and a meteoroid, but her protocols didn't, and they clawed at her. She didn't know how to stop. She *couldn't* stop.

In this way, she found, her coned vision had a silver lining: she had to turn the kit's head to look at things. As long as she stayed focused on the back of Pepper's head, she could ignore the endless, edgeless clutter. Mostly. Somewhat.

She followed Pepper down the ramp into the tech district – the caves – and the kit sighed in tandem with Sidra's relief. Ceilings and walls, and an immediate drop in temperature. The kit was self-cooling, so overheating wasn't an issue, but the market's climate was warmer than the inside of a ship should be. She'd had an errant external temperature warning needling at her ever since they'd stepped off the Undersea. She was very glad to see it disappear.

A shaggy Laru man leaned against a wall near the entrance, his limb-like neck bent low as he watched people come and go. His yellow fur was braided from head to toe, and he idly flipped a pulse pistol around one of his prehensile paws. There was a large warning sign on the wall beside him, written in multiple languages.

THE FOLLOWING ITEMS CAN CAUSE HARM TO TECH, BOTS, AIs, MODDED SAPIENTS, AND SAPIENTS USING PERSONAL LIFE SUPPORT SYSTEMS. DO NOT BRING ANY OF THESE ITEMS INTO THE CAVES. IF ONE OR MORE OF THESE ITEMS IS IMPLANTED ONTO OR WITHIN YOUR BODY, DEACTIVATE IT BEFORE ENTERING.

Ghost patches (surface-penetrating ocular implants)
Hijacker or assassin bots
Hack dust (airborne code injectors)
Improperly sealed radioactive materials (if you're not sure, don't chance it)
Anything running on scrub fuel
Magnets

A handwritten message was scrawled beneath, in Klip:

Seriously, we are not fucking around.

And below that, a second message, in a different hand:

Why is this so hard to understand?

The Laru's wide eyes crinkled as they approached. 'Morning, Pepper,' he said, bringing his face respectfully down to her level.

'Hey, Nri,' Pepper said with a casual, friendly nod. Her demeanour had changed the moment they'd entered this place. Up on the surface, she moved like she was on a mission – chin up, feet fast, never stumbling as she ducked through every pause in the sapient stream. But as soon as they'd reached the entrance ramp, something in Pepper let go. Her shoulders loosened, her pace slowed. She sauntered.

The caves were every bit as labyrinthine as the market, every bit as busy and loud. Garish lights and pixel displays flashed in a chaotic array, and the air was overflowing with voices and mechanical noise. But this place was easier for Sidra, just as Pepper and Blue's home was easier, just as the Undersea was easier. Everything here was *something new*, too, but the walls told her protocols where to stop. She'd only been on Coriol for a little over a standard day, but already, she saw patterns in the places that were relatively comfortable for her.

'Hey, Pepper!' shouted an Aandrisk woman unloading crates from a cargo drone. 'Good morning!'

'G'morning!' Pepper drifted over to her. 'Need a hand?'

'Nah,' the Aandrisk said. 'That's what bots are for.' She nodded toward the small, bulbous squad working together to haul a crate into a shopfront.

Pepper gestured toward the kit. 'Hish, this is my new assistant, Sidra. Sidra, this is Hish, owner of Open Circuit.'

Sidra flipped the kit's hand into *eshka* – Aandrisk hand speak for *nice to meet you*. She was glad she'd taken the time to download such things.

Pepper raised her brow, but said nothing.

Hish returned *eshka* enthusiastically, then reached out to shake Sidra's hand Human-style. 'It's a pleasure,' she said. 'Have you been to the caves before? I haven't seen you around.'

'I just got to the Port,' Sidra said. 'It's my first time here.'

'Oh, welcome!' Hish said. 'Where are you from?'

Sidra was ready for this. She pulled up the repository of technically-true responses she and Pepper had prepared together. 'I was born on a long-haul ship. Decided to finally get my feet on the ground.'

'Ahh, a spacer, huh? Any system in particular, or just all over?'

Sidra scrambled for an appropriate response. 'I started out in the GC. I'm not a citizen, though.' This seemed like an unnecessary point to volunteer, but Pepper had assured her this was the right track to head down. *There are plenty of crazy Human isolationists doing who-knows-what out there*, Pepper had said. *If you were born here but aren't a citizen, that means your parents didn't register you. That'll make people think your parents were fringers in the neighbourhood for supplies. And given that Human establishments on the other side of the fence are rarely anything anybody wants to discuss in casual conversation, you won't get asked much beyond that.*

Hish gave Sidra an understanding nod, proving Pepper right. 'I gotcha,' she said with a bittersweet smile. 'Well, you could hardly ask for someone better suited than this one' – she nodded at Pepper – 'to show you the ropes. You got a place to stay?' The question was asked calmly, but with unmistakable concern.

'Yes.'

Pepper clapped the kit on the shoulder. 'We've put her up. She's going to get sick of me real quick.'

Hish laughed, then touched Pepper's forearm. 'You and Blue are good people. I've always said so.' She straightened up, glancing at her heavily laden bots. 'Well, I shouldn't keep you two. Sidra, have a wonderful first day. And if you ever need comp tech gear, you come straight to me.'

Sidra waited until they were out of earshot. 'Pepper, did she . . . did she feel sorry for me?'

'She thinks you've gotten away from some bad shit,' Pepper said. 'Which is exactly what we want. The more people think you came from something rough, the less they'll ask you questions.'

'I see,' Sidra said. She was glad for the lack of prying, but something about the way the Aandrisk woman had looked at her made her uneasy. She didn't want to be the subject of pity. She watched Pepper as she ambled her way through the caves, greeting peers, trading small talk, asking technical questions that made Sidra long for the Linkings. She watched people's reactions, too, as she recycled her tailored responses over and over. Their replies were always variations on the same theme: kindness toward Sidra, respect for Pepper. The former was nice, but the latter seemed more desirable. Pepper had come from some 'bad shit', too, but no one looked at her as if she were a stray pet. Pepper was useful here. Sidra wasn't yet. It would take time, she knew, but the continued lack of a clear-cut purpose was unpleasant.

They arrived at a sedately decorated shopfront, far less flashy than its neighbours. 'Here we are,' Pepper said, gesturing dramatically. A sign made of scrap announced the purpose of the open-air counter beneath it:

THE RUST BUCKET

Tech swap and fix-it shop
Pepper and Blue, Proprietors

'Blue no longer works here, correct?' Sidra asked.

Pepper waved her wristpatch over a scanner by the counter. There was a brief, quiet crackle as a security shield switched off. 'Correct. He stops by sometimes, though, if he's feeling tired of artists being artists.' She flipped up the counter door and headed back into her space. There was a long workbench opposite the counter, with plenty of room between. Behind that was a doorway, through which there appeared to be a small workshop, comfortably removed from the territory of customers. Sidra kept the kit out of Pepper's way as she filled the counter with display boxes full of second-hand components, each smartly wrapped and labelled.

'Can you hand me that?' Pepper asked.

Sidra turned the kit's head to follow Pepper's gaze, and found a toolbelt. It was absurdly heavy, overburdened with wrenches and pliers. The thick fabric had been reinforced with rough thread – several times over, it seemed. 'Yes,' Sidra said. She handed the belt to Pepper, as requested. 'Do you mind working here alone?' she asked.

Pepper shook her head. 'Nah. Tech is my thing, not Blue's.

He can do it, but it's not what makes him get up in the morning.' She grinned. 'And besides, I *don't* work here alone any more.' She pulled a clean work apron and gloves out of a drawer, then clad herself with them and the clattering toolbelt as she spoke. 'So. The Rust Bucket is your all-purpose place to get stuff fixed, and we sell refurbished bits and bobs, too. I have only a few rules.' She raised a gloved finger. 'Number one: no military-grade weapons or explosives. If you're a livestock farmer, or you're headed to Cricket or something, and you need your slug rifle fixed, sure, I can do that. You throw down some Aeluon-wannabe blaster, get the fuck out. If you're not a soldier, you don't need that shit.'

Sidra recorded every word. 'What if you *are* a soldier?'

'If you *are* a soldier, I am the last person you'd come to with weapon problems. Unless your military has massive organisa-tional issues, I guess. I will do basic tools of self defence, not murder gear.' She raised a second finger. 'Rule number two: no biotech. Not my area of expertise. If someone wants their mods tweaked, I've got a good list of clinics I can refer them to. Safe, trustworthy places. You get anybody asking about implant or mod stuff, come get me, and I'll point them in the right direction. No nanobots, either, even if they're not bio. It's not my thing, and I don't have the right equipment. Rule number three: somebody brings in anything with magnets, they damn well better tell us up front so I can store it properly. Anybody who doesn't gets to compensate me for whatever got fried. Fourth rule: whatever they bring in has to be able to fit behind the counter. I will do bigger jobs outside of the shop, but that's on a case-by-case basis. I don't do that for everybody, so don't mention it to people. Just come get me and I'll decide if it's worth my time. Other than that . . .' She pursed her lips in thought. 'I'll take just about anything.' She drummed her fingers on the counter. 'My pricing is . . . variable. Whatever it says on the package, or whatever I promised. Between you and me, I really don't care how much things cost. As long as

I have food in my belly and can buy dumb stuff to decorate my house with, it doesn't matter whether people are paying me the same amount every time. I work within budgets, and trade is every bit as welcome as credits. More so, even.' She lifted her foot. 'I got these boots for free because I fixed a clothing merchant's patch scanner. I've got a doctor who upgrades me and Blue's imubots every standard in exchange for random fix-it jobs whenever he wants. And I've got a life-time half-off discount at Captain Smacky's Snack Fest, because I did a same-day rush job on their grill.' She shrugged. 'Credits are imaginary. I'll accept them because we've collectively decided that's how we do things, but I prefer doing business in a tangible way. Don't worry, though – *you'll* get paid in credits. Cleaner that way.'

Sidra had forgotten about that part. 'Oh. Right.'

'You'll get a cut from the shop's monthly profits. Haven't worked out how much yet, but I promise it'll be fair. And that's separate from room and board. You having a roof over your head is not contingent on you working here, so if you want to go do something else, that's fine. You're not indentured, okay? At the end of every couple tendays, we'll divvy things up, and I'll transfer—' She snapped her fingers. The sound fell flat through the gloves. 'We need to set you up with a bank account. Don't worry, I know someone who can fix that for us. Works for the GC, but she's good people. Does not mind turning a blind eye if you don't have the right formwork, and does not ask a lot of questions. Also has an amazing collection of antique Harmagian ground carts that she uses at parties. Early colonial era, really gorgeous craftsmanship. I'll drop her a note.'

Sidra set aside the *shop rules* file and created another: *my job*. 'So what will I be doing?'

'Since Blue isn't here any more, I need someone to be an extra pair of eyes and hands. I'm thinking you'll be wherever I'm not. If I'm doing something big and noisy in the back, you'll be up front, greeting folks, handing over finished stuff, selling packaged things that don't need my input. If I'm up front, you can clean up in the back. If there's an errand that needs doing, you can go out and about, or I can go out and do my thing, and you can hold down the fort.' She cocked her head. 'How does that sound, for starters?'

Sidra processed that. In some ways, it wasn't so different from her intended purpose. She'd be monitoring the safety of the shop and responding to requests. She'd perform tasks as directed. She'd be Pepper's eyes where she couldn't see. 'I can do that.'

Pepper studied her. 'I'm sure you *can*. But do you *want* to do that?'

Sidra processed that, too, and came up empty. 'I can't answer that, because I don't know.' When she was given a task, she performed the task. When a request was made, she filled the request as best she could. That . . . that was her job. That was her *point*. If things hadn't gone the way they'd gone on the *Wayfarer*, if she'd stayed in the core she'd first been installed in, would anyone have said to her: *Hello, Lovelace! Welcome! It's time for you to start monitoring the ship – but only if you want to?*

She doubted it.

Pepper put her hand on the kit's shoulder and smiled. 'What do you say we just get started and see how you like it, okay?'

'Okay,' Sidra said, relieved to set that processing loop aside. 'How does the day start?'

'First things first, I check two feeds: the shop's message box, and Picnic.' She gestured at a small pixel projector sitting on the counter. A cloud of pixels burst forth into the air, arranging themselves to display Pepper's default feeds in twin translucent rectangles. The feed on the left was easy enough to decipher.

```
NEW MESSAGES
New request: engine overhaul – Prii Olk An Tosh'kavon
Status check: scrib won't turn on – Chinmae Lee
New request: hello do you know anything about hydroponic
equipment I think one of my pumps is broken – Kresh
Query: would you accept live red coasters as payment – toad
Query: not actually a query, the new build works beautifully,
thank you!!!!!!!!! – Mako Mun
```

The feed on the right, however, was more of a mystery. Given that it had taken the pixels longer to arrange themselves there, there was likely encryption at work.

```
hello pinch. welcome to the picnic.
mech (big)
mech (small)
bio
nano
digital
experimental
intelligent
protective
spaceworthy
```

The kit blinked. 'What's that?'

Pepper nodded at the right feed. 'Picnic is an unlisted social feed for techs all over the GC who like to make connections with people who know stuff that . . . let's just say, the Port Authority might not approve of. Officially, at least.'

The kit wet its lips as Sidra considered that. Port Coriol's black market was no secret, but it was a little disquieting to know she was looking through one of its windows. She had no grounds to disapprove of illegal activities – given that she *was* one – but all the same, she hoped she wasn't in a place where she'd be easier to discover.

Pepper noticed the pause. 'Don't worry. Here, look.' She gestured at *biotech*, and skimmed through the dozens of discussion threads, searching for something. 'Ah, there he is. You see this user, FunkyFronds? He's the inspector who checks out my shop every standard. I play it safe.'

'Is a lot of your business, ah . . .' Sidra wasn't sure how to phrase the question politely.

'My business is giving people what they need. You heard my rules. I don't do anything dangerous or stupid. The thing is, a lot of laws are stupid, too, and they don't always keep people out of danger. What can I say? I'm a woman of principle.' She winked. 'Come on, I've thought up your first task. Sorry – job. Your first job. It is, perhaps, the most important thing.'

Sidra followed Pepper into the workshop behind the front counter. Having been in Pepper's home, what lay beyond was no surprise. Shelves of supplies towered overhead, stuffed with crates all labelled – by hand! – in big block letters. There was organisation at work, but clutter, too. The mark of a logical mind that sometimes strayed.

Pepper gestured proudly at an elaborate hand-hacked contraption covered in shiny tubes and dented pipes. 'If you're going to be my assistant,' she said, 'you've gotta learn to make mek.'

'That's . . . the most important thing?'

'Oh yeah. Fixing complicated shit requires a clear head, and nothing chills a person out like a warm cup of mek.' Pepper placed an affectionate hand on the brewing machine. 'I require a lot of this.'

Sidra accessed a behavioural reference file. 'Don't most sapients drink it recreationally? At the end of the day?'

Pepper rolled her eyes. 'Most sapients confuse working hard with being miserable. I do solid work, and I'm never late. So, why not? It's not like I'm smoking smash. Mek is just a food coma without the food. Same brain chemicals, basically. You drink too much, you take a nap. And seriously, anybody working in a job that doesn't let you take a nap when you need to should get a new job. Present company excluded, of course.'

'Are naps good?'

'Naps are fucking great.' Pepper opened a drawer and pulled out a tin decorated with an Aeluon design – monochromatic swirls and circles. 'You're kind of missing out there. Missing out on mek, too.' She opened the tin and stuck her nose over it, inhaling deeply. 'Mmm, yeah.' She held the tin out to Sidra. 'When you smell that, how do you . . . how do you process that? Is it just a list of chemicals?'

'I'm not sure. I'll find out.' Sidra took the tin, manoeuvred it to the kit's nose, and pulled in air.

The image was there without warning, leaping to the front of all other external input – *a sleeping cat, sprawled on its back in a puddle of sunlight, fur mussed, pink toes splayed sweetly* – then gone, just as fast.

'Hey, you okay?' Pepper asked, taking the tin. Something on the kit's face had her attention.

Sidra tore through her directory logs, looking for an explanation. 'I – I don't know.' She paused for one second. 'I saw a cat.'

'Like . . . an Earthen cat?'

'Yes.'

Pepper glanced around. 'What, *here*?'

'No, no. It felt like a memory file. A cat, asleep by a window. But I've never seen a cat before.'

'Then . . . how do you know it was a cat?'

'Behavioural files. Animals you can find around Humans. I know what a cat is, I've just never *seen* one.' She raced through logs and came up empty. 'I can't find the file. I don't understand.'

'It's okay,' Pepper said. Her voice was light, but there was a small furrow between her eyes. 'Maybe some stray crud you picked up in the Linkings?'

'No, I – I don't know. Maybe.'

'If it happens again, let me know. And maybe we should run a diagnostic, just to be safe. Are you feeling okay otherwise?'

'Yes. Just confused.'

'You're still adjusting. It's cool. Stuff's gonna be weird for a while. So, let's give you something to focus on, huh? When my head gets cluttered, always helps to do something with my hands.'

Pepper walked Sidra through the steps of making a batch of mek – measuring the powder, hooking up the water, keeping an eye on the temperature. It wasn't complicated, but Pepper was particular about the details. 'See, if you cook it too fast, there's a compound in the bark that gets bitter in a real mean way. Cook it too slow, though, and you'll just end up with sludge.' Sidra took extensive notes. Clearly, this *was* important.

A soft timer chimed, indicating the batch was ready. Pepper picked up a mug, inspected the inside, wiped it out with the corner of her apron, then pressed it under the brewer's spigot. A small cloud of steam unfurled as the milky white liquid poured out. Pepper took the mug with both hands, inhaling deeply. She blew across the surface, then took a cautious sip.

'Isn't that too hot?' Sidra asked.

'Yeah, but stars, it's good.' Pepper slurped slowly through a tiny opening between her lips. '*Ahhhh.* Here, you want to try?'

'Yes.' Sidra accepted the mug. The kit's mock pain reflexes didn't kick in, so clearly it wasn't *too* hot – at least, not for her. She looked at the liquid, swirling into itself in a friendly kind of way.

'Do you know how to drink?' Pepper asked.

'I think so.' Sidra hadn't manoeuvred the kit in this way before, but it was easy enough to mimic. She brought the mug to the kit's lips, parted them, and pulled liquid in. She could detect heat, and—

She was stepping into a hot bath, but this body wasn't hers. It was someone else – rounder, taller, at ease in her body. She sank into the water, scented foam folding around her. Everything was okay.

Sidra looked up at Pepper. 'It happened again. Not a cat, but—' She took another sip. *She was stepping into a hot bath, but this body wasn't hers.* 'It's a bath. It's a memory file of someone taking a bath. And now it's gone again.' She grabbed the tin of mek powder and inhaled. *A sleeping cat, sprawled* – 'That triggered the cat again.' She took another sip from the mug, testing for patterns. *She was stepping into* – 'Bath.'

'Whoa. Okay. This is too specific to be a random malfunction.' Pepper went to the front counter and got her scrib. 'Time to look at your user manual.'

'There was nothing like this in the user manual.'

Pepper gave her a wry look. 'Modders love secret shit.' She gestured. 'Search term, um . . . random image files?'

A chunk of text appeared.

Congratulations! You've discovered one of the best features of your kit: sensory analogues! You're going to be spending a lot of time with organic sapients, and if there's one thing organic sapients love, it's physical enjoyment: foods, touching, things that smell good. I didn't want you to miss out on enjoying those moments with your friends. You don't have the capability to process sensory input as organics do, so your kit includes a huge hidden repository of pleasing images, which was seamlessly integrated with your core program upon installation (don't bother looking – you won't be able to find it!). Whenever your kit receives stimuli that an organic would derive a pleasant sensation from, the repository will be triggered. So, go ahead! Have dessert! Get a massage! Smell the roses!

Pepper looked at Sidra, then back to the scrib. 'This,' she said, 'is a work of genius.' She shut her eyes and laughed. 'Oh, stars, we are going to have so much fun.' She gestured at the pixel projector, bringing up a comms program.

'Contact name, please,' an automated voice said.

'Captain Smacky's Snack Fest,' Pepper said, winking at Sidra.

A cartoonish logo of some sort of seafaring Human with an ornate hat and several prosthetic limbs appeared, followed by a lengthy menu offering foods of dubious nutritional value. Piping hot boxes of cricket crunch, made to order. Red coaster dumplings by the dozen. A wide assortment of pocket stuffers, both spicy and sugar-fried. The list went on and on.

'Welcome to Captain Smacky's ordering system!' a chipper recording exclaimed. 'Simply place an order and we'll dispatch a drone to your location tag straight away. If you know what you'd like—'

'I do.' Pepper nodded seriously. 'I'd like the left side of the menu, please.'

JANE 23, AGE 10

'I don't understand,' Jane 64 said. They were talking in bed, which wasn't allowed, but they were doing it real real quiet, and none of the girls ever got each other in trouble for doing that.

Jane 23 tried to find good words, but it was hard. 'There was something on the other side of the wall.'

'Another room?'

'No, not another room.'

'I don't understand,' 64 said again. 'How was it not a room?'

'It didn't have walls,' Jane 23 said. This was so hard to explain. 'It wasn't like anything here. There is something else outside the factory.'

Jane 64 frowned. 'Was it big?'

'Real big. Bigger than anything I've ever seen.'

'Was it a piece of scrap?'

'No,' Jane 23 said, trying not to get loud. She felt almost angry. 'It wasn't like *anything*. It was like the space inside rooms, only . . . only without walls. I don't know.' She didn't have any more words. 'It was unknown and wrong.'

Jane 64 moved closer, talking so quiet that 23 couldn't have heard her if she was any farther away. 'Do you think the Mothers know there's something there?'

'Yes.' Jane 23 knew they knew. She didn't know how. She just knew it.

'Then we should ask them.'

'*No.*' Back in the med ward, the Mothers had asked all the

57

girls one by one what they saw in the sorting room when the accident happened. 'I heard Jane 25 tell them she saw the hole.'

They both went quiet. Jane 25 had been Jane 17's bunkmate. 17 was sleeping with 34 and 55 now.

'What did you tell them?' Jane 64 asked, her eyes real big.

'I said I got knocked down and then went looking for you.'

64's eyes went even bigger. 'You *lied?*'

Jane 23 shrugged even though she was scared. 'I just didn't say.' She'd been real real scared about that ever since the med ward, like maybe the Mothers would think about it again and know that she hadn't said everything she should have.

'Maybe we should ask the other girls,' Jane 64 said. 'Maybe someone else saw, too.'

Jane 23 didn't think that was a good idea. She felt okay talking about it with 64, because she knew 64 would never get her in trouble. 'I just want to know what it is,' she said. 'I didn't get to look very long.'

Jane 64 scratched the stitches on her forehead. 'Do you think it'll be there when we go back to our sorting room?'

'No, I think that's why we're in a different room now,' Jane 23 said. 'I think they'll fix it before we go back.' There was another thing she wanted to say, but it stuck in her mouth. It was real scary. She wanted to say it so so bad, though. She *had* to say. 'I want to go look at it.'

Jane 64 stared at her, scared but real interested. 'Me too,' she said. 'But I don't want to get punished.'

Jane 23 thought about it. 'We could do it without getting punished.'

'They wouldn't let us go there during the work day.'

'We could go at night.'

Jane 64 shook her head hard. 'We're not allowed out of bed,' she said, her voice high and shaky.

'We are if we're going to the bathroom.'

'We aren't going to the bathroom. They know where the bathroom is.'

'We could say . . . we could say we were going to the bathroom, and we heard a weird sound outside the bathroom, and thought someone might need some help.'

'Who?'

'Someone. One of the little girls. We could say we heard one of the little girls and she sounded scared,' Jane 23 said. Her own scared feeling started to go away, and in its place was something kind of hot and loud and good. They were talking about bad behaviour, but she wanted to do this. She wanted to do this a lot. So she did. Right then. She got up, put on her shoes, and walked away. 64 whispered something, but Jane 23 was already too far away to hear. She could hear her come quietly *tap-tap-tapping* after her, though.

'This is a bad idea,' Jane 64 said. 'If we see a Mother, I am telling her it was *your* idea.' She said it, but 23 knew it wasn't true. 64 would never let 23 get punished in her place. Only bad girls did stuff like that, and 64 wasn't bad. She was the most good.

The bathroom was cold. They moved through it real quick. Jane 23 stopped when they got to the hallway door. Maybe it *was* a bad idea. They could go back. They could go back right then and no one would ever know. They could just go back and sleep and have a good on-task day tomorrow.

She stepped through the door. 64 went with her.

The hallways were weird all dark, but it was easy to find their way. One time, they thought they heard a Mother, so they ducked behind a stack of bins. There was nothing, though. They were okay. They were okay all the way to the sorting room. The door was closed, but it wasn't locked. Why would it be? Girls never went anywhere without Mothers watching.

'I don't think we should,' Jane 64 whispered.

They shouldn't, Jane 23 knew. She looked around the hallway. No one else was there, but that could change real fast. She knew how fast the Mothers moved.

'Come on,' Jane 23 said, taking her bunkmate's hand. She

went through the door. Jane 64 followed, not tugging back or anything.

Even in the dark, Jane 23 could see that the sorting room had been cleaned up. There was still a mess, but not a wet kind of mess. The blood and bits were gone, and the exploded stuff had been swept into piles. The scrap was gone from all their benches, too. Jane 23 was scared, even though the room was quiet. The room didn't look like it had the last time she'd seen it, but in her head, she still saw it the old way. What if there were pieces of girls in there? What if there was a girl stuck under a desk and she grabbed them when they walked by? Jane 23 pressed close to 64. 64 pressed back.

The hole in the wall was covered with a tarp. There was stuff next to it, some kind of . . . Jane 23 wasn't sure. There was stuff in buckets, and tools, too. She thought of the glue she used on broken good scrap sometimes. Maybe the Mothers were trying to glue the wall closed.

A corner of the tarp waved at them, pushed back and forth by air from . . . somewhere. The other side.

'Let's go back,' Jane 64 said, but she said it quiet, like she wasn't sure. She was staring at the waving corner.

Jane 23's heart was beating so hard she thought she might break. She grabbed the corner in her hand. The air pushing it was cold. Real cold.

She pulled the tarp aside.

The stuff on the other side of the wall hadn't made any sense before, but it made even less now. The huge huge piles of scrap were still there, but the ceiling that wasn't a ceiling had changed. It wasn't blue any more, and it wasn't bright – at least, not in the same way. Before, it had been bright all the way through, but now, it was real dark, except for three big round lights and a whole bunch of little specks and something kinda smoky running across it. The not-ceiling was *big*. So, so big. Bigger than the sorting room, bigger than the dorm. It went on so far Jane 23 couldn't see any edges. It went on for always.

Jane 64 wasn't saying anything, just breathing real hard and heavy. Scared, probably, but she wasn't talking about going back to bed any more, either. Jane 23 understood. She felt the same way.

Jane 23 stuck her hand out beyond the edge of the broken wall. It was real cold, for sure, but not cold like metal was cold or the floor in the bathroom was cold. It was just *cold*, everywhere. Her skin got tight and made little bumps. It wasn't a very good feeling, but she liked it anyway, just as she liked it whenever she got to taste soap or blood or anything that wasn't a meal. It was different. The cold felt different.

'Twenty-three, don't,' 64 whispered.

But Jane 23 was listening to something else now – that hot, good feeling pushing all through her chest. She stepped past the wall. She took another step. Two steps. Three. Four.

The scrap went on as far as the not-ceiling did, piles and piles and piles of it. No wonder there was always scrap to sort. You could have girls sorting this stuff for years and they'd never be done.

She looked down. The floor outside the wall was dusty, powdery. There were little hard bits all over, too, and all of it sloped down toward the piles of scrap. She looked up again at the not-ceiling. It made her head hurt, and her stomach, too. Maybe if she got closer, it would make sense. Maybe if she could touch it—

Jane 64 screamed. 'No! *No!*'

Jane 23 spun around. A Mother had Jane 64 up off the floor, metal hand wrapped around her neck. Her bunkmate kicked and fought, tugging at the silver fingers.

Jane 23 wanted to scream, too, but her throat wouldn't let the sound out. They'd be punished for this. They'd be punished in the way that girls never came back from. There'd be an empty bunk in the dorm, the one they should've been sleeping in. The Mothers wouldn't need to make a trio.

It was all her fault.

The Mother saw Jane 23, but she didn't step through the hole. She looked at it and just stood there, like she didn't know what to do. Even without a face, it was real easy to tell that she was angry. So, so angry.

Jane 64 was crying and scared, and her face was a wrong kind of red. She looked at Jane 23 real hard, looked at her in a way that made her think of every morning they'd cuddled close before the wake-up lights turned on, of the time 64 had said she was the most good. 'Run,' Jane 64 said. '*Run!*'

Jane 23 knew she shouldn't run. She'd done bad behaviour. There was no way to get out of punishment, and fighting would make it worse. But that hot, good, angry feeling was louder than anything the Mothers had ever told her. Jane 64 kept screaming: 'Run!' Her muscles said it, too: *Run. Run!*

So she did.

SIDRA

Blue got to his feet as Pepper and Sidra walked in the door. 'Hey!' he said with a big smile.

'Hi,' Sidra said, and simultaneously accessed the file named *make yourself comfortable*.

1. remove jacket
2. remove shoes
3. find a place to sit
4. (optional) get a snack or beverage

Pepper eyed her partner as she unlaced her boots. 'What's up?' she asked, in a tone that suggested something had to be.

Blue continued to smile. 'I've, uh, I've done some redecorating.' He spoke more reassuringly as Pepper raised her brow. 'Nothing big! Just s-something, ah, something for our housemate.'

Sidra was intrigued. She removed jacket and shoes from the kit, and went into the living room. Blue was right – not much had changed, but the couch had been moved, and beside it was a new chair, pushed up against the wall as far as it would go. A small table was next to it, holding a Linking box and a tethering cable. A blush of happiness spread through Sidra's pathways. She understood. This was a place for her to sit down and plug in when she came home.

'Thank you,' she said. 'This is very kind.' She paused, not wanting to be impolite. 'Can I . . .?'

'Please!' Blue said.

Sidra couldn't get the kit seated fast enough. She popped the cable into the headjack, and the kit fell back into the chair, as an organic sapient would at the end of a long day. She closed the kit's eyes, savouring the flood of information. She wouldn't have known how to describe the feeling to the Humans. Perhaps like instantly regrowing a limb that had recently been severed.

'Is the chair in a g-good spot?' Blue asked. 'Is the angle okay? I tried to find somewhere, ah, somewhere where you can see most of the room.'

Sidra opened the kit's eyes and looked around. 'Yes, this is great,' she said, simultaneously downloading everything she'd added to her *topics to research* file that day. She'd already begun to lose herself in the task when she detected something brushing against the kit's leg. She flicked the kit's eyes down, but the angle wasn't right. She still couldn't see what it was. The kit sighed, and she bent it forward, directing the head down.

A little machine had come out from under the chair. A soft-skinned bot, in the shape of an animal Sidra didn't recognise. Big head, stubby body, eight stumpy legs. She searched her reference files, but came up empty.

'Oh, *cute!*' Pepper said as she came into the room. She placed a fond hand on Blue's shoulder. 'Aw, that's real cute.'

Sidra watched the bot, which had begun to rub its side against the kit's leg. Two green mechanical eyes opened and met her gaze. Without warning, the bot leaped into the kit's lap, and cooed a wordless invitation.

Sidra wasn't sure what to do. 'What is this?' she asked.

'Put out your hand,' Blue said.

Sidra put the kit's right hand forward, hesitantly. The machine pushed its nose forward, nuzzling the kit's fingertips, cooing and chuffing as it did so. The kit started smiling, though Sidra couldn't say quite why.

'It's a petbot,' Blue said. 'This one's, ah, this one's made to look like an ushmin. They're a Harmagian th-thing, but everybody likes ushmin.'

Sidra realised that Blue was watching her with hopeful expectation. 'Wait,' she said. 'Is this for me?'

Blue nodded happily. 'I kn-know being in somebody else's space can be weird. I figured it'd be, um, be good to – good to have something that's yours.' He put his hands in his front pockets. 'Plus they say pets are – are calming. Thought it might help you feel more at home here.'

The sentiment was sweet, but Sidra stuck on one bit of the phrasing: *something that's yours*. If the petbot was a gift, she *owned* it now. Gingerly, she made the kit pick up the mechanical ushmin. It wriggled, giving the impression of enjoying the contact. The kit's smile faded. 'Is it sentient?'

Blue looked slightly appalled. 'No,' he said. 'I would *never* buy something like that. It's not intelligent, it's just, um, just mechanical.'

Sidra continued to stare at the petbot. It stared back, eyes blinking slowly. A non-sentient program, then. Nothing but if/ thens, on and off, tiny baby algorithms. She glanced over at Pepper, who was raiding the kitchen. A box of dried beetles – *original five-spice blend!* – was in her free hand as she dug through the cooler in search of a drink. *Beetles*, Sidra thought. Beetles weren't intelligent, either. They couldn't fly a shuttle or build an Undersea or create art. She looked again to the petbot, now seated in her lap. She stretched out one set of the kit's fingers toward it. The bot stretched up toward them, begging to be touched. A recognition protocol, clearly. *If approached by owner, then act cute.* She thought back to the beetles. *If approached by bird, then run away. If hungry, then eat. If challenged, then fight.* Beetles weren't considered to be much, but they were *alive*, at least. There were rules about how to quickly kill insects before consumption. She'd seen such things on the packaging of Pepper's snacks: *Harvested humanely in accordance with GC law.* You could be fairly sure beetles didn't understand what was happening to them, and that they didn't suffer much, but consideration was given to the fact that they *might*. Did petbots come with any such ethical labelling? What was the difference between strung-together neurons and a simple bundle of *if/then* code, if the outward actions were the same? Could you say for certain that there wasn't a tiny mind in that bot, looking back at the world like a beetle might?

Sidra noted that Blue was still watching her, and that his face had become one of guarded concern. He thought he'd done something wrong, she realised. She made the kit smile at him. 'This is so very kind of you,' she said. 'Thank you.'

'Do you like it? If you don't, then—'

'I do,' Sidra said. 'It's interesting, and the thought behind it is even better.' She considered. 'You two don't keep pets like some Humans do.'

'No,' Pepper said. She sat down on the couch, in the spot nearest to Sidra's chair, washing down a mouthful of beetles with a fresh bottle of berry fizz. 'We don't.'

'Why not?'

Pepper took a long sip of her drink, watching the petbot snuggle in the kit's lap. 'I'm not very good with animals.'

JANE 23, AGE 10

The air outside the wall was still cold, and it wasn't a good kind of different any more. Jane 23 pulled her arms around herself as close as she could. The little bumps on her skin were so tight they kind of hurt, and her arms and mouth were shaking. This wasn't good. She wanted to be back in bed. She wanted to have never gotten out of it.

The Mothers hadn't followed her. She didn't know why. She wasn't being very quiet. The floor crunched when she ran on it, and she'd made a lot of noise when she'd fallen down the last bit of the slope. Could the Mothers not go through the wall? Did they just not care?

She didn't know where she was going. The scrap piles stretched way up overhead, all shadows and scary in the dark. She'd been walking for a long, long time – hours, probably – but she kept going anyway. She didn't know what else to do.

Run! 64 had said, and Jane 23 had, until breathing hurt. Her bunkmate's voice was stuck in her head, and she felt so dizzy and sick. She wanted to cry, but she didn't. She was in enough trouble as it was.

Her foot hit something hard, and she fell, right smack onto the crunchy dusty floor. She yelled, scared more than hurt. She couldn't see very good, but her knees hurt so loud, and she could feel angry new cuts on her hands. She looked back at what had made her fall. Just a piece of scrap, stuck in the floor. Just a bad piece of scrap, in her way. She kicked it. Kicking was bad behaviour, but she was already doing lots of that, and nothing made sense and they'd taken Jane 64 and it was *her fault*.

She kicked the scrap again, and again, and again, yelling sounds without words.

Another sound happened. Not the scrap, and not herself. A low, popping sound, kind of like a motor trying to start. It wasn't a sound she knew, but something about it made her go real quiet.

There was a . . . something, standing not too far away. She had no idea what it was. It wasn't a machine, but it moved. She was kind of sure it was breathing, but it wasn't a girl, either. She looked at it best as she could in the dim light of the three bright things in the not-ceiling. The something had eyes. It had eyes, and four legs, and no arms. She couldn't see any skin, just fuzzy soft-looking stuff all over. It had a mouth, too, and . . . teeth? Were they teeth? They were pointier than her teeth.

The something was looking right at her. It bent down a little bit, all of its legs bending back. It made the popping motor sound again. It was not a good sound.

She felt the same feeling in her legs that she'd felt when the Mother had stared at her so so angry through the hole in the wall. She heard Jane 64 in her head again. *Run*.

Jane 23 ran.

She didn't look back, but she could hear the something running, too, making bad wrong sounds as it chased her. She ran fast, fast as she could, fast as she was never allowed to run during exercise time. She had to keep running. She had to. She didn't know why, but her body knew it, and whatever that something chasing her was, it wasn't good.

Another something appeared, and it ran at her, too, knocking down some scrap as it went. She ran harder, not caring about the cold air, not caring about the Mothers, not even caring about Jane 64. *Run*. That was all she could do and think. *Run run run*.

Her chest hurt. Her shoes rubbed at her toes wrong. The

somethings were getting closer. She could hear them, so loud. Their mouths sounded wet.

There was another sound: a voice, coming from up ahead. But it was a weird voice, all wrong around the edges, not making any sense, not making any good words. Just a bunch of junk sounds.

She felt some spit hit the back of her leg.

The voice changed. 'Hey! This way! Come toward me!'

There was no time for questions. Jane 23 ran at the voice.

A machine stuck out from one of the scrap piles, a huge machine with thick sides and – and *a door*. An open door leading into it. Two red lights blinked from the corners of the raised hatch.

'You can do it!' the voice said from behind the door. 'Come on, hurry!'

Jane 23 scrambled up the scrap pile, sharp pieces catching her clothes and tearing her hands. With a yell, she threw herself inside the machine.

The hatch banged shut behind her.

One of the somethings crashed into the other side of it with a real loud sound, but the door didn't move. She heard angry angry noises, and scratching at the outside. The door stayed closed.

'Be still,' the voice said in a whisper. 'They'll go away.'

And after a little bit, they did.

'Oh, stars,' the voice said. 'Oh, stars, I'm so glad. Are you all right? Here, let me turn on some lights.'

Lights flickered on. Jane 23 picked herself up off the floor. She was in a tiny room, or a closet, maybe. Four metal walls, standing real close.

The voice talked fast. 'You're probably covered with germs. I don't have enough power for a scan, or a flash – later. We can clean you up later. It's protocol to scan you, yes, but this counts as a dire emergency, and that means I don't have to follow that rule. Come inside. It's okay.'

One of the walls turned into a door. Jane didn't move.

'There's no one in here but me,' the voice said. 'And I can't hurt you.'

Jane didn't know what else to do, so she listened. She moved. She walked into another, bigger room – much, much smaller than the sorting room or the dorm, but too much space for just one girl. There were interface panels and places to sit, and some kind of small workstation. A workstation. A workstation in a room inside a machine, outside of the factory.

None of this made any sense.

Jane 23 tried to breathe, taking in big mouthfuls of air. She was crying. She wasn't sure when the crying had started, and it scared her, because crying meant she'd be punished, but she couldn't stop. Even if there'd been a Mother there, she wouldn't have been able to stop.

'It's okay,' the voice said. 'You're okay now, honey. They can't get in here.'

'Who are you?' said Jane 23. Her voice felt strange, like it wouldn't stay still. 'Where – *where* are you?'

'Oh, oh, I'm so sorry. Let me put a face on. Here. Over here. To your right.'

A screen lit up on one of the walls. Jane 23 walked over, real careful. A picture came up. A face. Not a girl's face, though – well, okay, kind of a girl, but not a girl like she was used to. An older girl, even older than the girls who left when they turned twelve. The face had stuff sticking out of the top of her head, and a little bit over each eye, too. The picture wasn't a real girl. It was more like a vid. But the face was smiling, and that made Jane feel a little okay.

'Hi,' the voice said. The picture on the wall moved her lips along with the words. 'I'm Owl.'

SIDRA

Sidra didn't care much for waiting – not out in public, at least. Installed in a ship, she could've sat for hours – days, even – without needing much external input. But with no systems to monitor but her own, and no Linkings to keep her occupied, *waiting* was a deeply irritating way to spend time. However, this wait, she'd been assured, was worth it. She looked at the others standing in line with her – Pepper, Blue, dozens of strangers, all anticipating entry into the Aurora Pavilion. The never-ending night was thick with the sounds of sapient chatter, the smells of alcohol and varied kinds of smoke, the flicker of luminescent moths trying bravely to nip at open cups and sticky flasks. If the people around her minded the wait, they didn't show it. This was a Shimmerquick party, and apparently, standing around doing nothing was a fair price to pay for what was about to happen.

Shimmerquick, the GC reference files had said, was a very old holiday. Long before the Aeluons achieved spaceflight, the celebration was one of the few *en masse* interactions between male and female villages. Back then, Shimmerquick lasted for over a tenday and had no spoken name, as the silent Aeluons had yet to encounter the alien practice of auditory language. But Aeluons had been an integrated species for over a millennium, and their traditions were no longer bound to a single planet. Though Shimmerquick was, at its core, a fertility festival created by a species with a storied history of difficulty in that department, it had become a popular shared tradition in many mixed colonies – Port Coriol included. As Pepper had put it: 'There aren't many species that don't enjoy a big party, especially if its central theme is getting laid.' Granted, Aeluons had a clear social distinction between recreational and procreative coupling, and Shimmerquick was much more a celebration of life and ancestry than of lust – but apparently that nuance was either lost on or of small consequence to others in attendance. Sidra knew her understanding of such things was limited, but it did seem that most species generally didn't need much context as to *why* a party was happening.

Sidra eyed the line stretching far back beyond them. 'This is one of the *smaller* celebrations?' she asked.

'Yeah.' Blue nodded. 'The, um, the ones on the light side are huge.'

'They're also a complete clusterfuck,' Pepper added, 'and entirely tourists. Everybody here' – she pointed up and down the line – 'either lives here or is with someone who does. I also know folks who run this place, which is a big bonus.'

'We also th-thought an indoor venue would be more comfortable,' Blue said, smiling at Sidra.

Sidra was a little embarrassed to realise he meant more comfortable *for her*, but she was grateful, too. This was her first holiday. She didn't want to spoil the fun for Pepper and Blue by not having a good time herself.

As the line moved forward, Sidra picked up the first sign of an acquired multicultural tradition: music. A species without a sense of hearing had no need for a soundtrack, but clearly they'd gotten the memo that other people couldn't imagine a party without it. Sidra enjoyed the thump of the drums, the jangle and swing laced through. She liked the patterns within the sounds, the way they made organics move.

The non-Aeluon celebrants they shared the line with were following their host species' lead as well. With few exceptions, everyone arriving at the event was wearing at least one item in a shade of grey – a hue that, on an Aeluon, would make the colours on their ever-changing cheek patches stand out all the more. For other species, any sort of grey would do, but for Aeluons, more traditional rules were at play. Among their galactic neighbours, Aeluons used the usual set of male-female-neutral pronouns that any species would understand. But among themselves, they were a four-gendered society. At Shimmerquick, their clothing reflected this: black for those who produced eggs, white for those who fertilised them, dark grey for the shons, who cyclically shifted reproductive roles, and light grey for those who could do neither. It was striking to see such a delineated display in a species whose sexual dimorphism was relatively slight compared to other species, and whose apparel had little to no gender distinction on any other day.

Even though the clothing cues could not be missed, Sidra was glad she had downloaded additional social references before leaving home, as the latter two genders were impossible to distinguish through physical features alone. Shons changed reproductive function multiple times throughout a standard, and were always considered fully male or female, depending on the current situation. Calling a shon by a neutral pronoun was considered an insult, unless they were in the middle of a shift. Such terms were reserved for those too young, too old, or simply unable to procreate. As neutral adults of breeding age looked exactly like their fertile counterparts, they generally did not mind the assumptions of other species where gendered pronouns were concerned, but appreciated it when the correct terms were used. Despite knowing that the kit's Human appearance would absolve her of any pronoun mishaps, Sidra appreciated the colour-coded clothing. She loathed the idea of getting such things wrong.

Sidra glanced down at what the kit was wearing: a top printed with white and grey triangles, a darker grey pair of trousers, and a close-cut jacket, to give the impression that dark side's cold air affected her. Sidra's picks, Pepper's credits. Sidra had felt awkward about that, as she was beginning to feel about most purchases made for her benefit. Her hosts didn't seem to mind in the slightest, but she wasn't sure what she was providing them with in return, other than potential trouble.

Blue patted down his pockets as the line crept forward. 'Ah, damn. I forgot my – my—'

Pepper reached into her pocket and presented a packet of mints. Blue accepted it with a grin and a kiss. Sidra swung the kit's eyes away, letting them have their moment. It seemed like a nice sort of thing to have.

They reached the door at last, and two young Aeluons greeted them – a boy and a girl, both clad in neutral grey. A painted stripe of the same colour hugged the lower edges of their iridescent cheek patches. The talkboxes in their throats and speech-processing implants in their foreheads were far less decorative than the ones worn by adults, but this made sense. These implants were temporary, and would be swapped out as the children grew.

'Shimmer quick and shimmer often, friends!' the boy said with practised pomp. Xyr silver skin was heavily dusted with glitter, and the pulsing blue in xyr cheeks indicated xe took pride in xyr role that evening. 'How many are you?'

'Three,' Pepper said, holding out her wristpatch. Blue did the same, as did Sidra.

The boy scanned their wrists in turn, while the girl picked up a pot of light grey face paint and gestured the Humans forward. She had three other pots on hand, each coloured for a respective gender. Pepper bent down. The girl stuck xyr delicate thumb in the pot, then drew a thick, short line along each side of Pepper's jaw – the rough equivalent of where her cheek patches would end, if she had any. Sidra noted the symbolism with keen interest as the same was repeated for Blue, then herself. She and her friends were being designated as the equivalent of neutral Aeluons for the evening, and with the exception of children, neutrals were welcome partners in romantic relationships. Mainstream Aeluon aversion to interspecies coupling was known far and wide, and given that the taboo stemmed from a concern regarding the ability to further the species, marking aliens as potential sexual partners at a *fertility festival* was a bold statement. Such a gesture would not have been made in, say, the Aeluon capital of Sohep Frie, or likely even the gatherings on Coriol's light side. The Aeluons in attendance at the Aurora were clearly of a more radical stance than most of their peers. Sidra was beginning to understand why Pepper and Blue had chosen *this* party.

They walked down a coolly lit ramp, which curved and swayed as it wound its way underground. *NO REDREED IN COMMON AREAS*, a printed wall sign read. *SAVE IT FOR THE SMOKING ROOMS*.

'How come?' Sidra asked. She'd seen about a dozen different recreational substances being consumed in line, including some that required a pipe.

'Makes Aeluons' eyes itch,' Pepper said. 'Which I imagine would be absolute hell in a closed space like this.'

Down, down, down they walked, music growing louder, the line getting ever more excited. All at once, the wait was over. They arrived.

A deluge of information hit Sidra's pathways, but in a way that exhilarated her. There was as much happening as there would be in a busy market square, but there were edges here. Walls. Her field of observation was instantly defined; her protocols did not reach endlessly outward. The same was true whenever she went down to the tech caves, but the activity there was often confined within shops and behind doors – places she saw only hints of as she walked by. The main hall of the Aurora, on the other hand, was a wide-open space filled with booths and tables and accessible displays. The caves were a series of closed cupboards; this was a buffet. Her field of vision was a nuisance, as always, but much of what overwhelmed her topside and bored her at home was absent here. This . . . this was a party.

'Look at you.' Pepper laughed.

Sidra realised the kit was smiling with an open mouth. She wrangled it into a less effusive expression. 'It's very exciting.'

'Good!' Blue said, squeezing the kit's shoulder. 'That's great.'

'First order of business,' Pepper said, clapping her hands together. '*Drinks*.'

Sidra took in as much as she could as they searched for a refreshment vendor. Aside from the decorations – braided garlands of leaves dyed in monochrome, hanging metal charms displaying superstitious numbers for good luck and fertility – she had little immediate impression that this was a specific cultural event. On the contrary, everything about the happenings around them screamed 'Port Coriol'. She saw an Aandrisk acrobat playing with a shielded ball of water, a Harmagian laughing at a Laru's joke, a group of Humans blissfully plugged into a portable sim hub. There were places to sit. Places to dance. Nooks filled with cushions and lighted globes and shouting faces. Clouds of smoke – not redreed, she hoped – appearing and disappearing. A cacophony of smells: sweat, slime, food, feathers, flowers. A merchant selling handmade jewellery. A modder showing off a petbot with webbed wings and gem-like eyes. A tray of sugar-snaps upended. A tray of fried root vegetables devoured. The whirs and clicks of gadgets and implants piercing the sound of overlapping languages, all underlaid with the thick *thoom-thoom-thoom* that made the dancers buck and sway.

Sidra processed, processed, processed, but the walls kept her from stretching too far. It felt good. It felt right.

'Pepper!' a voice cried. A male Aandrisk, waving at them from the opposite side of a circular bar. Sidra didn't recognise him, but Pepper obviously did. She hurried towards him, hands above her head. A Harmagian saw Pepper coming, and made room for her at the bar, tentacles curling with respect. Sidra felt a bit of awe warm through her pathways. Was there anyone on this moon who *didn't* know Pepper?

'*Hist ka eth, reske,*' Pepper said, leaning over the bar to give the Aandrisk a hug. *Good to see you, friend.* Her pronunciation was rough, but the Aandrisk didn't seem to mind in the slightest.

'*Ses sek es kitriksh iks tesh.*' *I was wondering when you'd get here*. He reached over to Blue, hugging him across the bar as well. 'It's not a party without you two.' His grey-green eyes flicked to Sidra. 'And who's this?'

Pepper put her palm between the kit's shoulder blades. 'My good friend Sidra, recently arrived at the Port, and just as recently hired by yours truly.' She nodded at the Aandrisk. 'Sidra, this is Issek, one of the finest bartenders on this rock.'

'One of?' Issek said, flicking his tongue. 'Who else?'

Blue grinned teasingly. 'Pere'tek at the Sand House pours f-faster than you.'

Issek rolled his eyes. 'He's got *tentacles*. That's hardly fair.' He tussled Blue's hair, then turned his attention to the kit. 'Sidra, it's a pleasure. First drink's on me. What can I get you?'

'Oh.' Sidra didn't know how to respond. Having the ability to ingest fluids wasn't the same as knowing which one she was supposed to purchase. 'I don't—'

Pepper gave Sidra a secret, reassuring glance. 'It's customary on Shimmerquick to drink something that comes from the same place you do. Or the same culture, at least. As close as you can manage.'

'Ah,' Issek said, raising a claw. 'That's what you buy for yourself. If someone else is buying, then it has to be something from xyr home. So, as *I'm* buying' – he gave a little bow – 'you're getting something my home city of Reskit is famous for. Ever tried tishsa?'

'I haven't, no.'

Issek plucked a tall, thin ceramic bottle from the table behind him. 'Tishsa is made from the sap of a tree whose pronunciation I won't burden you with. Grows in the marshlands east of Reskit. There are two traditional ways of serving it: neat and very, very hot, or' – he poured a stream of inky brown liquid into a tiny bowl-like cup with a subtle pour spout – 'at room temperature, wiiiiith' – he uncapped a second, smaller bottle – 'a drop of nectar syrup, to counter the bitterness, and' – a small box was produced – 'a dash of salt, to balance the whole thing out.' He gave the concoction two quick stirs with a long rod, then slid the cup toward Sidra.

Sidra thanked him and accepted the tishsa, aware of Issek's

expectant gaze. She brought the cup to the kit's lips and poured the contents inside.

A rushing river. Burning paper. A forest thick with fog.

'Wow,' Sidra said. 'That's really nice.'

Issek nodded proudly, his feathers bobbing. The Humans looked delighted. 'How's it, ah, how's it taste?' Blue asked.

Sidra answered with the truth: 'Like a forest.'

Pepper beamed, then turned her attention to Issek. 'So whatcha got for colony kids?' she said, gesturing at herself and Blue.

'For planetside Humans, only the finest,' Issek said with a mischievous glint. He covered his hand with a thick towel, reached below the counter, and pulled out a sealed, chilled bottle. Pepper and Blue hooted with laughter.

'Oh, *no*,' Pepper said, with the sort of tone that implied the opposite.

Blue ran his fingers down his cheeks and exhaled. 'We're in for a night.' He took the bottle and held it out for Sidra to see. *Whitedune Distillery*, the label read. *Kick-Ass Kick from Gobi Six*.

'What is it?' Sidra asked. *Kick* could mean anything from ale to wine to spirits, depending on where the speaker was from. Slang was infuriating that way.

Blue turned the bottle to the back label. *Ingredients: Whatever we could grow this year, plus water.*

'Gotta love the independent colonies,' Pepper said. She made a grabbing motion toward Issek, who placed a small glass in her hand. Blue uncapped the bottle and poured. Pepper puffed out her cheeks, then threw the drink back. Her face contorted into a puzzle of emotions as she swished and swallowed.

'Oh, stars,' Pepper rasped, laughing. 'Why could we not be from Reskit?'

'If you hate it—' Issek started.

Pepper shook her head. 'Nope. Nope, it's good for me to know what it feels like for a fuel line to be cleaned out. Professional development and all.' She patted Blue's chest. 'Tomorrow's gonna be a rough morning.'

Some friendly conversation continued – the well-being of the Rust Bucket, the decor of the party, the current gossip from Issek's feather family – but Sidra shifted that process to the background. These were the kinds of conversations she was privy to all the time. The Aurora was new, and vibrant. She watched as a group of Aeluon children blew handfuls of glitter over each other, dancing excitedly but making no sound at all. She watched as a massive Quelin – an exile, judging by the harsh branding stamped along her shell – apologised profusely for getting one of her segmented legs stuck in some decorative fabric draped around a vendor's booth. She watched service drones flying drinks and food orders back and forth, back and forth. She wondered if the drones were intelligent. She wondered how much they were aware of.

Blue noticed that Sidra's attention had strayed, and he gave Pepper a subtle nudge. They excused themselves from the bar, assuring Issek that they'd be back later.

'Come on,' Pepper said. 'Let's go check out the main event.'

They walked into a large circular area, and the multicultural atmosphere vanished. This space was filled with angled tents decorated with lavish garlands and lights, eagerly staffed by adult Aeluons and their respective children. This was the creche display, the central point of any Shimmerquick celebration. This was where professional parents advertised their business to potential mothers.

'You know how this works?' Pepper asked under her breath.

'Yes,' Sidra said. She brought up her reference files, eager to compare her notes with the real thing. 'Can I look around? Is that . . . allowed?'

'Oh yeah, go for it,' Pepper said. 'They don't mind looky-loos. Just keep your respectful distance when a *balsun* takes place. Other species getting mixed up in that isn't cool, even in this crowd.'

Sidra wouldn't have dared anyway. The *balsun* ritual dance was the hallmark of the holiday, and despite its Hanto loan name, it was wholly, quintessentially Aeluon. An Aeluon woman might become fertile two or three times in her life (if at all), a state visually characterised by an increased brightness in her scales: in the right light, a shimmer. The *balsun* was an ancient tradition, once thought to encourage a woman's body to produce a viable egg. Science dictated otherwise, but the dance remained, partly out of cultural heritage, partly out of the mindset of *well, it can't hurt*.

There were seven different creches representing themselves in the display. Traditionally, creches were comprised of three to five virile males or shons, but women and neutrals were included in the modern mix. Parenting was considered a full-time job, and not something to be undertaken alone. As a woman had no way to plan for if and when she might become fertile, the idea of her abandoning her own profession to look after an unplanned child was unthinkable. Granted, she'd have to take time off for fertility leave, but on that point, Aeluon society was accommodating to a fault. In her research, Sidra had run across an absurd historical anecdote about a pre-spaceflight ground war that had been amicably paused when one of the most prominent generals started to shimmer. Sidra wasn't sure any species took anything as seriously as Aeluons did breeding.

She wandered around the display, fascinated by the elaborate adornments. It was a competition, in essence. A trade show. She stopped in front of one of the tents. The leaf garlands draped around it were huge, and laced with glowing globes full of— The kit blinked. There was some kind of glowing liquid inside them, and it was *moving*, making tiny waves like a cresting sea. Powered by bots, most likely, but stars, it was striking.

'Pretty, aren't they?'

The kit nearly jumped. One of the creche's parents had appeared beside her, just out of sight. 'Very,' Sidra said. 'Your whole display is beautiful.'

'Thank you,' the Aeluon said. He looked at his tent approvingly. 'We've been working for weeks on this. The kids helped, of course.'

'Would you mind if I ask you some questions about . . . about all of this?'

'Not at all. Is this your first Shimmerquick?'

'Yes. Is it that obvious?'

The Aeluon laughed. 'You have the look of someone who's seeing things for the first time. Don't be embarrassed, I'm here to educate as much as celebrate. That's what being a parent's all about.'

Sidra liked this man. 'Have you always been a parent? Professionally speaking, I mean.'

'Oh, yes. It takes a lot of school, so if you don't get started early, it can be hard to catch up.'

'What kind of schooling?'

'There are two different layers to it,' the Aeluon said. His tone was authoritative, his words ready. This was clearly his field. 'At the core, you've got to get university certification for parenting, just as you do for, say, being a doctor or an engineer. No offence to you or your species, but going into the business of creating life without any sort of formal prep is . . .' He laughed. 'It's baffling. But then, I'm biased.'

The kit smiled. 'I understand.'

'To get your certification,' he continued, clearly on a roll, 'you have to take courses in child development, basic medical care, and interpersonal communication. That's the first layer. On top of that, if you want any sort of viability in this field, you have to add specialisation courses – both for the benefit of the kids and the mothers. Me, for example, I'm skilled in massage, basic tutoring, and emotional counselling. Loh over there, he's great at arts and crafts, and he can cook like a dream. Sei is our gardener, and does all our home repair and decorating, too. A good creche needs a blend of skills in order to be successful, especially where the mothers are concerned. Fertility leave is a big deal, and it's a lot of fun, but it's a stressful thing for any woman, at first. It's two unplanned months away from her normal life. She's got to drop any projects she's got going on at work.

She's got to cancel whatever other plans she's made. If she's a spacer, she's got to find the nearest place with an Aeluon community before she misses her shot. And unless her romantic partner can take that time off, too, she's got to be separated from her most important person for a bit. She's got to go live with strangers – and have sex with them – and all the while, there's the worry that she might go through all that trouble and *still* not have a fertilised egg at the end of it. And then there's the business of carrying said egg and giving birth a month later, which – while not *nearly* the bother it is for your species – would be nerve-wracking for anyone. So, we do our best to make the whole experience as rewarding as possible. It's a break. A vacation. We do everything we can to make the women that come to us as comfortable and happy as possible. Our beds are wonderful, our rooms are clean. Our food is *outstanding*. We've got a beautiful garden and huge salt-water baths. We're experienced lovers, and we put a lot of effort into making sure that coupling multiple times a day is something to look forward to. We give our mothers space when they need it, and company when they crave it. We provide quality medical care when it's time to give birth. And beyond that, we assure them that their child is going to be well looked after. They're welcome to spend time with the other children there – join them for playtime or studying, if they want to. Not all women do. Some aren't worried about that aspect of it, or they just don't like kids much. Others need a lot of reassurance that the little person they're leaving behind is going to be okay.'

'Do mothers come back to visit?'

'Usually, yes. It's not always possible. Here at the Port, we get a lot of spacers who have somewhere else to go once their shimmer's over. There's contact, at least. Our kids get sib calls. They get presents. A lot of species have this conception that our children don't know their mothers, but that's just not true. Aeluon mothers love their children as deeply as anyone does. That's why they entrust them to professionals who can give them the best upbringing possible.' He glanced over to one of his fellow fathers, who had given him a non-verbal signal Sidra had not caught. How did Aeluons detect such things in the middle of so much activity? They possessed electroreception as well as sight, she knew, but to her knowledge, cheek colours didn't give off any additional sensory signals. They had to have an impressive attention to detail – a good quality, she imagined, for a parent.

'You'll have to excuse me,' the Aeluon man said. An Aeluon woman had entered the creche circle. One of the children led her by the hand to the fathers, who greeted her with an effusive flurry of colour. Sidra longed to be able to understand the conversation, but even though she could presumably download a lexicon of Aeluon language, she wasn't sure the kit's visual sensors could parse things fast enough. Their cheeks were swirling as quick and varied as the skin on a bubble.

The woman pressed her palm to each of the four fathers' chests – an initiation for a *balsun*. One of the creche fathers was clad in neutral grey, and he stepped back as the three white-clad men circled her. The children sprang into action, lining up with the neutral father in a way that suggested they wanted everyone to know they'd been practising this. He took the hands of the two closest to him, meeting their eyes with obvious affection. The neutrals began to stamp their feet on the ground in a synchronised pattern – *left left, right, left-left-left, right*. The white-clad men and the black-clad woman began to move in rhythm, circling and spinning in a curious way, never missing a beat. Sidra was fascinated. Presumably, their auditory implants were picking up the stamping, but this dance had been done since before the Aeluons taught their brains to process sound. Could they feel the vibrations in the ground? She found it likely, and wished she could share the experience. She watched the woman, covered in glitter, dancing in the hope that she might wake up to her skin shimmering on its own one day. She thought about the menu of services the parent had outlined. Massages, baths, places to sleep, people to mate with. Sidra could understand the desire for these things, in concept. She couldn't help but feel a little jealous of the woman, even though jealousy was a waste of time. She wasn't jealous of what the woman was receiving, exactly, but of how confident she looked, how confident they all looked. They each had a role, a place, a colour. They knew where and how they fit.

'Hey.' It was Blue, standing beside her. The kit startled; she willed it to stay calm. Stars, but she was tired of not being able to see behind the kit's head. Did *everything* have to be a surprise? 'We, uh, we bumped into some friends, and we were gonna h-hang out with them at their table. You can stay here, if you want to.'

'No, I'll come along,' Sidra said. She followed him out of the creche display and toward Pepper, who was animatedly telling a story to a hodgepodge group of modders. A table sounded good. Sidra had seen the seating nooks, each with a table nestled into a low, free-standing three-sided wall. Three walls meant there was a corner seat. That was the place for her.

JANE 23, AGE 10

Jane 23 never stopped looking at Owl's face. She moved closer to the screen, but kept her back close to the wall. She didn't know what else was in here. She didn't want anything to sneak up on her.

'Are you a machine?' Jane 23 asked.

'Not exactly,' Owl said. 'Do you know what software is?'

'Tasks that live in machines.'

'That's a wonderful definition. Yes, I'm software, technically. I'm an AI. I'm a . . . I'm a mind in a machine.'

Jane 23's muscles went hard and tight. She glanced back at the hatch. She couldn't see how to open it. 'Are you . . . are you a Mother?'

'I don't think so. I don't know what that means to you.'

That probably meant no, but Jane 23 had to be sure. 'The Mothers are minds in machines, too. They take care of girls and make us on-task. They give us meals and help us learn things and punish us if we do bad behaviour.'

The face in the wall looked kind of angry, but Jane 23 didn't think Owl was angry at her. 'I'm not a Mother,' Owl said. 'I'm not like that. But I'm a similar sort of software, I think. I just . . . I don't punish people. And I live in a ship. A shuttle, to be precise.'

'What's a ship?'

'A ship is – a ship is a machine you use to get between planets.'

Jane 23's head hurt. She was real tired of not understanding things. 'What's a planet?'

Owl's face got sad. 'Oh, stars. A planet is . . . what we're on right now. I will explain in more detail later. That's a bigger question than you should have to swallow right now. You're not hurt, are you? Did they bite you?'

'No.' Jane 23 looked down. 'I cut my hands, though.'

'Okay,' Owl said. She looked like she was thinking about something. 'The water tanks are long gone, but there may be some first aid supplies. I hope so. Here, follow me.' The screen switched off, but another one turned on, farther into the room.

Jane 23 didn't move.

'Hey,' Owl said. 'It's okay. Nothing in here will hurt you. You're safe.'

Jane 23 didn't move.

'Sweetie, I don't have a body. I can't touch you.'

Jane 23 thought about that. That seemed a little more good. She walked to the new screen.

Owl continued through the machine – the ship – switching screens on and off. All the rooms were tucked in real tight, like a bunch of storage closets or something. There were so many things in there, all kinds of machines and stuff without names, but thrown around like scrap in a bin. Jane 23 had so many questions. Her stomach hurt from all the questions.

'Go in that room there,' Owl said. 'To your left. Do you know what "left" is?'

'Yes,' said Jane 23. Of course she knew what 'left' was. She was *ten*.

'Do you see that box on the floor? The blue one with the white stripes? Go ahead and open that up.'

Jane 23 did as told, and looked inside the box. Now *this* stuff she knew. Well, not exactly, but the stuff in the box looked a lot like some of the stuff they used in the med ward.

'Right, let's see.' Owl sounded like the way Jane 23 felt when she couldn't find the right tool, or if a piece of scrap was acting like junk even though she knew it was good. 'I wish the sinks were working. We'll just have to make do. Do you see those little silver tubes? Those are . . . it's a goo that will kill the bad stuff in your hands.'

Jane 23 nodded. 'Disinfectant.'

The face on the screen looked surprised. 'Disinfectant, right. Have you used it before?'

'No,' Jane 23 said. 'But the Mothers do.'

'Do you think you can use it on yourself?'

Jane 23 thought about this. 'Yes.'

'Maybe use a few tubes. You can put some on, and use that gauze there to wipe the disinfectant and the dirt back out. Then put more disinfectant on, and then bandages. Does that . . .' Owl looked like she was kind of confused, too. 'Will that work? I'm so sorry, honey, I don't have hands. I'm just working from memory here.'

'That sounds okay,' Jane 23 said. She sat down on the floor and cleaned herself up. The disinfectant hurt and it smelled funny, but the feeling reminded her of getting fixed in the med ward, and that made her feel a little better. She spread the goo on thick, then wiped it away, taking away dust and blood with it. She touched her tongue to the corner of the messy gauze. Blood. Chemicals. Sharp and angry and bad.

Once the blood was gone and the cuts were clean, she put more disinfectant on, and started covering her hands with bandages. 'Why are you in here?' she asked Owl.

'That's a complicated question. The short answer is I was installed in this ship so that I could help the people who flew it. This – this area was a bad place for them to go, but they thought they knew what they were doing, and—' She paused. She sounded sad. 'Anyway, they were arrested – taken away – and the ship and I were thrown out. The people here don't want things from elsewhere, you see.' She sighed. 'This must be so confusing for you. I'll do my best to make sense of everything.' The face in the wall gasped. 'I haven't asked your name! I'm sorry. It's been so long since I had someone to talk to. I'm so scattered. Do you have a name?'

'Jane 23.'

'Jane 23,' Owl said. She nodded, real slow. 'Well, since you're the only Jane I see here, is it okay if I leave the numbers off?'

Jane 23 looked up from her bandages. 'Just . . . Jane?'

'Just Jane.'

Jane couldn't say why, but that felt kind of good.

SIDRA

They'd been at the Shimmerquick celebration for two hours and three minutes, but Sidra had decided forty-six minutes prior that she liked alcohol. It had no cognitive effect on her, but there was such an incredible variety of concoctions to choose from, and they all triggered separate images. As her companions and their friends got ever louder and happier, she enjoyed someone else's memories of boats, fireworks, rainbows. She wasn't sure how much she enjoyed alcohol's effect on *other* sapients, though. Most of their behaviour was cute, even endearing. Blue had told her how glad he was that she had come to them, which was very gratifying to hear (though it lost some of its impact by the third or fourth time). Pepper was loud, but not as loud as her friend Gidge, who had crossed over from *smart* to *sloppy*. The sapients milling near their table were all various shades of inebriated as well. Relieved as Sidra had been to get a corner seat, she had reached a point where the desire for different input outweighed the comfort gained by staying put. She excused herself and walked along the edge of the party, holding half a glass of Sohep Sunset between both the kit's hands, staying as close to the outer wall as she could. She would've liked to put her back to it and shuffle along sideways, like a crab, but that wasn't how Humans moved. There was a good chance that if she *had* walked that way, she'd just be assumed to be drunk or high or both, but no, avoiding attention was the smarter call.

The booths near the wall were less crowded than those in the middle of the Pavilion. She passed by vendors selling light pins, cheap trinkets, and chilled cups of roe, until she came to a tucked-away booth, wreathed with strands of white globulbs and floating pixel confetti. *GET SOME INK!* a handwritten sign read. *CAN ACCOMMODATE ~~ALL~~ MOST SPECIES.* Inside sat an Aeluon woman, tracing a whirring implement over her customer's arm. The patterned fabric around her waist and legs was dark shon grey, ornately wrapped in an intricate knot. Like the rest of her kind, she was covered in glitter from head to toe, but underneath that, every bit of her finely scaled skin was tattooed. Unlike much of the body art Sidra had seen since she arrived at the Port, the Aeluon's ink was static, apparently free of nanobots. A tangled forest covered her chest, full of hidden animals and reaching vines. A multitude of images and symbols laced their way down her arms – explosions of spirals and circles, a map of Central space, a wreath of multispecies hands pressing palms. When the Aeluon turned to make an adjustment in her work, Sidra could see writing on the back of her head – something in ancient Aeluon text. Sidra had the modern Aeluon alphabet installed, but nothing from antiquity. She captured the image, and added it to the list of things to download.

The Aeluon's subject was a female Aandrisk, looking entirely unconcerned by the harsh-looking machinery rubbing over her scales. Comparing this woman's face to the other partygoers she'd seen that night, Sidra found it likely that she'd been smoking smash. She wondered if the Aandrisk would change her mind about the Aeluon's handiwork once the drug wore off.

'You looking for ink?' the Aeluon said, never taking an eye off the Aandrisk. 'Or just looking?' She held a long, curved pipe between her teeth, which smouldered undisturbed as words emanated from the talkbox in her throat. The pipe contained a popular Aeluon vice known in Klip by the simple name of tall-flower – or *tease*, as she'd heard Pepper call the stuff. Apparently the smoke smelled wonderful to Humans, but had no effect on them.

'Just looking,' Sidra said. 'If I'm bothering you—'

The Aeluon's cheeks ebbed friendly blue. 'Not at all.' She waved Sidra over. 'I'd love some company, and I promise she doesn't mind an audience. She doesn't mind much of anything right now.'

Sidra sat the kit down in an empty chair beside the Aeluon. The Aandrisk lolled her head toward them, flashed a stupid smile, then went back to wherever she'd been before.

Smoke shot silently out the Aeluon's small nostrils. Her talkbox laughed in tandem. 'See, most species I wouldn't work on when they're this gone. But Aandrisks shed. If this is a mistake for her, it's a temporary one.'

The Aandrisk spoke, but her words were lost before they got past her teeth.

'Whatever you say, friend,' the Aeluon said. She shrugged at Sidra. 'I don't speak much Reskitkish, do you?'

Sidra paused. Humans who spoke Reskitkish were rare, and revealing that she was indeed fluent might invite questions she couldn't safely answer. There was no way around this one, though. 'I do,' she said, 'but I couldn't understand her.'

'Well, unless she said, "Please stop using yellow," I'm going to assume everything's fine.' She pointed at her subject's scales. 'You know anything about scale dyeing?'

'No.' Sidra had no references on that custom, but she was very interested. An inky spiral pattern was emerging, blossoming outward in a sort of mandala.

The Aeluon continued working and smoking, speaking easily as she went. 'Species with softer skin, like you and me, we can retain ink down in the dermis indefinitely. But Aandrisks are a whole different deal.'

'Because they shed?'

'That, and – I mean, look at this.' She tapped one of the scales. 'The stuff their scales are made of isn't terribly different from *this*.' She took one of the kit's hands, and rubbed the thumbnail. 'You can't get an ink gun down into keratin, not easily. So this' – she gestured with the dyeing implement – 'is just a glorified paintbrush. Gives her scales a nice, quick, even coating.'

'How long does it last?'

'About six tendays. Or less than that, if she's due to shed. Not so long that she'll mind if she sobers up and hates it.' She popped an empty cartridge out of the implement, slipped in a silver one, and continued. 'I'm Tak, by the way,' she said.

'Sidra.'

Tak gave her an Aeluon smile. Tallflower smoke drifted up around her face. She pressed the tool against a clean scale, inundating it with dye. It caught the light of the nearby globulbs.

'How many different techniques do you know?' Sidra asked, thinking of the sign out front.

'My specialty's modern Aeluon style, but I also know how to do bots and temporary stuff like this.' She nodded at the Aandrisk. 'Most of my business comes from people who want bot art, actually. It's pretty popular, especially for spacers. Everybody wants to say they got ink on Coriol. Apparently that means something out there. I dunno. I've never lived anywhere else, except for university.'

Sidra considered. 'You don't use bots on yourself.'

'Not like you mean. I don't have any moving art on me, true. But there *are* bots here,' she said, trailing a finger down one of the stylised trees branching across her flat, bare chest. 'They just don't move.'

'Then why have bots at all?'

'They help maintain the integrity of the linework when my skin grows or shrinks. Keeps the edges from blurring.'

'Why don't you use moving ones?'

Tak made a face. 'Because they drive us nuts. Aeluons, I mean. I don't mind bots on other species. I can talk to a Human who's swirling from head to toe, no problem. But on an Aeluon, that'd be a nightmare. Keep in mind—' She pointed at one of her cheeks.

'Oh,' Sidra said. 'Of course.' A colour-changing tattoo during a colour-changing conversation would be an enormous distraction. 'I'd imagine that'd be annoying.'

'Confusing, mostly. And honestly, when I first started inking, it took me a while to get used to it with other species. I did a gorgeous nebula across this Human's back once. All these rich purples and deep deep blues, swirling real slow. Art-wise, it looked fantastic, but combined with skin, I kept feeling like his back was pissed at me. Purple means angry, see.' Tak's cheeks rippled. She looked amused. 'What about you? Got any ink?'

'No.'

'Just not your thing?'

'No, I—' Sidra paused, not wanting to insult this woman's profession. 'I don't quite understand it.'

'You mean, why people do it?'

'I suppose so.'

Tak rocked her head in thought, adjusting her pipe. 'Depends on the person. I mean, just about every species mods themselves somehow. Quelin brand their shells. Harmagians shove jewellery through their tendrils. My species and yours have both been tattooing for millennia. If you're interested in different cultural practices, there's a great collection of essays called *Through The Surface* on body art traditions by species. It's by Kirish Tekshereket – have you read any of her work?'

Sidra added a note to her list. 'I haven't, no.'

'Oh, she's fantastic. Highly recommend it. But back to your question: why do people do it. I've always thought of it as a way to get a little more in touch with your body.'

The kit leaned forward. 'Really?'

'Yeah. Your mind and your body. Two separate things, right?'

Sidra directed all her processing power to the conversation at hand. 'Right.'

'Except *not*. Your mind comes from your body. It's born out of it. And yet, it's a wholly independent thing. Even though the two are linked, there's a disconnect. Your body does stuff without asking your mind about it, and your mind wants stuff that your body can't always do. You know what I mean?'

'Yes.' Stars, did she ever.

'So, tattooing . . . you've got a picture in your mind, then you put it on your body. You make a hazy imagining into a tangible part of you. Or, to flip it around, you want a reminder of something, so you put it on your body, where it's a real, touchable thing. You see the thing on your body, you remember it in your mind, then you touch it on your body, you remember why you got it, what you were feeling then, and so on, and so on. It's a re-enforcing circle. You're reminded that all these separate pieces are part of the whole that comprises *you*.' The Aeluon laughed at herself. 'Or is that too fluffy?'

'No,' Sidra said. She was intensely focused, as if she were plugged into the Linkings. There was an Aandrisk gesture that captured this feeling perfectly: *tresha*. Someone seeing a truth in you without being told. 'No, that sounds wonderful.'

Tak lifted the gun away from the Aandrisk, and took out her pipe. She looked Sidra in the eye, studying her. 'Tell you what,' she said, after three seconds. She tapped her wristpatch against Sidra's. Sidra registered a new download – a contact file. 'You ever want to take the plunge, I'd love to assist.'

'Thank you,' Sidra said. She held the contact file at the forefront of her pathways for a moment, feeling like Tak had given her a gift. 'Would you mind if I kept watching you work for a while?'

'Not at all.' Tak placed the pipe back in her mouth, unruffled by the unexpected audience. It was a good thing, Sidra thought, to know your craft so well that an extra pair of eyes made little difference.

Sidra remembered her drink and took a sip. *A bird, black as night, beating its powerful wings through the dawn.* Tak worked over the scales: yellow, silver, white, yellow, silver, white. She exhaled smoke. It cast shadows. Sidra took another sip: *A bird, black as night, beating its powerful wings through the dawn.* Tak continued: yellow, silver, white. As for the Aandrisk, she said nothing at all.

JANE, AGE 10

Jane was still tired, but she woke up because it was time to wake up. Her body said so. It was the time before the alarm went off, before the lights went on, right around the same time Jane 8 got up to pee.

She listened in the dark. No girls moving beneath their sheets. No *pat pat pat* of feet headed to the bathroom. No Jane 64 breathing beside her.

She remembered. She was alone.

'Owl?' she said. She clutched the blankets tight. They weren't her blankets, and this wasn't her bed. This was one of the beds in the shuttle. There were two beds, and she didn't know who either of them were for, and she wasn't wearing clothes, and— 'Owl?'

Owl's glowing face appeared in the screen beside the bed. 'Hey, hey, I'm right here. Everything's okay. Do you want me to turn the lights on?'

Jane wasn't afraid of the dark – *she was ten* – but right then, lights sounded like a good idea. 'Yes,' she said.

The lights came up slowly, much like the lights in the dorm did, but they were different. Everything was different. Jane felt different, too.

She sat up, hugging the different blanket to her chest. Owl stayed with her, but didn't say anything. She just watched. Jane couldn't say why, but somehow that didn't scare her like when a Mother looked at her. Owl felt . . . okay.

'Owl, what do I do today?' Jane said. 'What's my task?'

'Well . . .' Owl said. 'There are things that would be good for you to do at some point, but you had a very hard night. I think you should do anything you want today.'

Jane thought about that. 'Like what?'

'If you want to stay in bed for a while, you can. If you want to stay in bed *all day*, you can! We can talk, or not talk, or—'

'I can stay in bed?'

'Of course you can.'

'. . . all day?'

Owl laughed. 'Yes. All day.'

Jane frowned. 'But what would I do?'

'Just . . . relax.'

Jane wasn't sure what to make of that. 'Okay,' she said. 'I'll try that.' She lay back down, pulling the blanket tight around herself. She wasn't cold, but the bed felt too big, and the blanket made it better.

'Do you want me to turn out the lights?' Owl asked.

'Would that help?'

'Maybe down a little, at least.' The lights dimmed, as did Owl's face.

Jane lay still. *Just relax,* she thought. *Just relax. I won't get punished.* But her body knew it was time to wake up, and the feeling of being in trouble grew louder and sharper, sitting thick in her chest. Girls who stayed in bed got punished. Girls who were late got punished. *I won't get punished.* Girls had to work hard. Girls couldn't be lazy. *I won't get—*

She remembered a metal hand around 64's neck. She remembered how 64 had screamed. She remembered that it was all her fault.

Jane kicked off the blankets and got out of bed. 'I need a task.'

'Okay,' Owl said, bringing the lights back up. 'We'll find something good to do.'

Jane tried to swallow, but her mouth was dry. She'd never been so thirsty, or so hungry. Her lips stuck to each other like old glue. 'Is there water?'

Owl's face looked wrong, like somebody who got caught doing

something bad. 'Not in the tanks, but there may be supplies still. How long have you gone without drinking?'

'I don't know.' Water was something the Mothers gave them, like meals and medicine. Water just . . . happened.

'Oh, stars. Stars, I didn't think of it, I'm so stupid. I'm sorry. There should be ration bars and emergency water pouches in the pantry. They should still be good.' The screen beside Jane's bed switched off; another by the door switched on. 'Follow me.' Jane did so, though she felt strange about going somewhere in only her underwear. 'I understand, you know,' Owl said, as her face bounced down the short hallway. 'I hate not having a job.'

'What did you do before I got here?'

'Not much,' Owl said. 'Not much at all.' Her face jumped to a screen beside a narrow sliding door. 'This is the pantry. I don't have a camera in there, so you're on your own. Look for the latched crate marked "rations". Oh, wait, sorry – it's probably in Klip. "Greshen". Gee ar ee ess aitch ee en.'

Jane blinked. Owl wasn't using words any more. 'I don't understand.'

'That's how it's spelled. Gee ar ee—' Owl stopped. 'Jane, can you read?'

Jane didn't know what that meant. Was Owl okay? She wasn't making much sense.

'Right,' Owl said. 'That's a task for *me*, then. It's okay, don't worry about it. Here.' Owl's face disappeared. A row of white squiggles appeared on the screen. Her voice continued speaking. 'Do you see what I'm showing you?'

'Yes.'

'Okay. Find the box with these exact same markings on it.'

Jane went through the door. The little room on the other side was filled with crates, most of them empty, some toppled over. It was a mess. All the crates had squiggles on them. They reminded her a bit of the angled lines that were sometimes on scrap. She'd always liked those angles. They made flat metal more interesting to look at.

The crate Owl had been talking about was in the back, buried under other stuff. Jane knocked the junk aside and opened the crate. Inside were soft packets – small rectangular ones and fat squishy ones. The squishy ones probably had liquid inside. The rectangles were harder, but kind of movable. She could feel the one in her hand give when she pushed her thumb against it.

'Is this right?' Jane asked, stepping back out into the hall with one of each packet.

'Yes,' Owl said. 'Can you hold both of those up to the camera nearest to you? Up in the corner? I need to see the markings on them.'

'What's a camera?'

'The little machine with the glass circle on the front.'

Jane found the machine and held the packets up. The machi—the *camera* made a whirring sound.

'Oh, good,' Owl said. 'Good, they haven't expired. Those are safe for a while yet. I don't know if they taste good, but they'll keep you fed. For now, at least.'

Jane turned the rectangle over in her hand. 'How do I make a meal out of this?' She looked over at the squishy packet. 'Do I mix them together?'

'No, just open up the bar and take a bite.'

Jane tore the packet open. Inside was a yellowish lump, kind of like putty. She poked it. 'I should . . . bite it?'

'Yes.' Owl's face frowned. 'What kind of food did you have at the factory?'

'We get meals twice a day.'

'Okay. What kind of food?'

For a software that knew lots of stuff, there sure was a lot Owl didn't get. '*Meals*. You know, in a cup.'

'Oh boy. Have you ever had solid food? Something you have to chew?'

'Like medicine?'

'Probably like medicine, yes. You've never had food like that?'

Jane shook her head.

'I – right. I am the worst teacher for this. You really need to be learning from a person. But all right, I've watched enough people eat. I can do this. We'll . . . we'll go slow.'

'Is it complicated?'

Owl laughed; Jane didn't know why. 'It's not complicated, but your body is going to have to get used to it. I think your stomach might hurt a bit at first. I'm not entirely sure.'

Jane looked at the packet, not feeling so good about it any more. She did not like stomach aches. 'I'll just have this, then,' she said, waving the squishy pouch.

'You can't survive on water alone, Jane. Go ahead, give it a try. Just a tiny bite.'

Jane brought the putty food to her face. Real slow, she touched her tongue to the edge. Her eyes got real big, and she almost dropped the food. It tasted . . . it tasted like *nothing she'd ever had*. Not like meals. Not like medicine. Not like blood or soap or algae. Whatever it was, it was good. Weird. New. Scary. Good.

She put a corner of the food into her mouth and bit down, breaking off a piece behind her teeth. Yeah, this food was good. Her stomach growled loud. She wanted that food real real bad. She was hungrier than any girl had ever been, probably.

But she had to *chew* the food, Owl said. She rolled the hard, good-tasting lump around on her tongue. It was breaking apart, kind of, but she didn't think she could swallow it like it was.

'That's it,' Owl said. 'Chew it up really well.'

Jane chewed. She chewed and chewed and chewed until the food turned to mush. She swallowed. She coughed, but it went down. 'It feels real weird,' she said. She put her hand on her stomach. It growled even louder.

Owl smiled. 'You're doing great. Have some water. I believe that helps wash it down.'

Jane tore open the corner of the squishy packet and took a sip. Even the water tasted different, almost like plex or something. She didn't care. She'd never needed anything as bad as that water. She sucked down the whole thing at once, and breathed real hard after. Her lips felt better. 'Can I have another one?'

Owl looked weird. Almost scared, but not quite. Like she was thinking about something that might be bad. 'Yes, but let's be smart about it. How many of those packets were in there?'

'Lots.'

'Ten? More than ten?'

'More than ten. Lots of tens.'

Owl nodded. 'I think you should have as many as you need right now. But the rest you'll have to be more careful about. There's no way for us to get more.'

Jane went back into the pantry and got three more water packets. She drank half of one all at once, took another bite of the bar, and washed it down with more water. She got through half of the bar before she had a new problem. She was still hungry, but her jaw was getting tired from so much chewing, and her stomach wasn't sure about what she'd put in it.

Owl noticed. 'You don't have to eat it all right now.'

'But I'm hungry.'

'I know, honey. But this is going to take practice. Give your stomach a little rest, then have more later if you're feeling okay.'

Jane thought that was a good idea. Her stomach was making weird sounds, and it kind of hurt. She folded the wrapper around the food she hadn't eaten. 'Can I finish the water?' she asked, holding up the third packet.

'Yes. You don't have to ask me for permission, Jane. I can't give it to you anyway. I don't control you.'

That was an interesting thing to think about. Jane looked at the packet in her hand. 'So . . . I *can* have this water.'

'Yes,' Owl said, her smile real big now. 'You can.'

Jane looked around as she drank. It was easier to get a good look at the ship now than it had been when she got there. Nothing was chasing her, and that made thinking better. 'What's this room for?' Jane asked.

'It's for relaxing and being together,' Owl said. 'The people who were here before you called it the living room.'

Jane thought that was a weird name, since you could live *anywhere* in the ship. 'What's that?' she asked, pointing to the space next to the pantry. There was a thing built into the wall that she didn't know, with cupboards around it, and a sort of workbench that stuck out.

'That's the kitchen,' Owl said.

'*Kitchen*,' Jane said, feeling the word in her mouth. 'What's it for?'

'It's for preparing food. Making meals.'

Jane had never thought about what was in meals before. Meals were just meals. You got them twice a day. 'What are meals made out of?'

'Plants and animals.'

Jane felt tired. More things she didn't know.

Owl's face had a warm, good sort of look. 'I'll explain in more detail later. Don't worry, I'm keeping a list of things you've asked about.'

That was good to know. Owl was good at answering questions, and she seemed to like explaining to Jane what all the stuff was. Beside the kitchen, there was a small storage room with a big machine in it called a stasis unit. Owl said 'stasie' was a better word for it. She said you could put stuff to make meals in there and it wouldn't go bad. Jane didn't know what *going bad* meant, so Owl put it on the list.

There were other storage spaces, too – mostly empty, but some had weird tools and other junk. There were clothes also, the biggest clothes Jane had ever seen. You could fit a girl twice Jane's size in those clothes. More than twice. Owl looked kind of sad when Jane found the clothes, but she didn't say why.

The biggest space was the cargo hold, which filled up the back of the shuttle. There was a lot of scrap and thrown-away things in there, all tossed around and fallen over. Owl said it would be a good task, at some point, to go through that stuff and see what was there.

There was a short stairway in the cargo hold that went into the underside of the ship. That's where the engine was kept, and also the core that Owl was installed in. Out of everything, that place made the most sense to Jane. She could see circuit boards, fuel lines, power junctions. She touched the engine, finding all the little bits.

You like little bits, Jane 64 said in her head. *You're real good at them.*

Jane went fast back up the stairs, feeling almost like she was being chased again.

'Hey,' Owl said. 'You okay? Was it too dark down there? I know some of the globulbs are broken.'

Jane found a corner and sat in it, arms around her knees.

'What is it, Jane?'

Jane didn't know how to answer. Nothing was making sense. One minute, everything was new and interesting and there were words like *kitchen*, and the next, Jane 64 was in her head and the things outside were chasing her. And it was *her fault*.

She put her face in her hands. She didn't know if she wanted to keep learning or just go to sleep. Just go to sleep and not wake up.

Owl watched her from the closest wall screen. She didn't say anything for a while. Jane held herself hard and shook her head over and over, trying to get Jane 64 out of it.

'Would you like a task?' Owl said.

'Yes,' Jane said. She was crying again, and she didn't know why.

'Okay. Now, here's the thing: as an AI, I can't tell you what to do. I can only give suggestions. You have to pick what you want to do most. But I have some thoughts on what the most important tasks might be.'

Jane rubbed her nose with her wrist. 'Okay,' she said.

'When you're ready to get up, I'll show you.'

The being-chased feeling was already starting to get a little quieter. Jane sniffed. 'I'm ready.'

'Attagirl,' Owl said. Jane didn't quite know what it meant, but something about the sound of it made her feel good. 'Do you see those big drums in the corner? The big round things? Those are the water tanks, and they're empty right now.'

Jane got up and walked over to the drums. They were much taller than her, but not so so big. 'Where does the water come from?'

'Well, normally, somebody using the ship would fill up the tanks at a supply station, but we don't have anything like that around. Not to mention, we can't move.' Owl laughed, but it wasn't a good laugh. It turned into a sigh. 'You'll need to find water outside. Jane, I know there's so much you don't understand yet, and I don't want to scare you further. But if you want to stay in here, you *will* have to find water. The rations won't last you very long. The good news is, once you fill up these drums, you'll only need to top them up every so often. Most of it will get recycled. I don't have enough power to run the water filtration system right now, but it's still functional. That'd be another good task: getting the hull cleared so I can get more power.'

Jane thought about that. 'What kind of power source makes *you* go?'

'Look at you,' Owl said with a big smile. 'You're such a smart girl.' Jane felt *so* good hearing that. Owl kept talking: 'There are two primary power sources in the ship. There's the solar generator, which powers both basic mechanical functions, life support, and, well, me. And there's the engine, which runs on algae. The engine powers propulsion – do you know what that is?'

'No.'

'Propulsion is a big word for making things move. The engine makes the shuttle go places. We don't need that kind of power just yet. The solar generator is enough to keep me going, as well as to run the things we need to keep you healthy. The problem is, there's junk outside covering most of the solar coating on the hull. I've got less than half the amount of power I ideally should have. If you can get the hull clean and find some water, that would be a really good start.'

Those tasks sounded okay, but there was a problem. 'I can't go outside,' Jane said. 'The . . . things are outside.'

'Animals. Living things like you – things that can move and breathe – are called *animals*. And those particular kind of animals are called *dogs*. Horrible, genetweaked dogs, but dogs all the same.'

Dogs. Okay. 'I can't go outside if there are dogs.'

'I know. We'll have to get creative. For your very first task, I suggest the following: go through the stuff in here and see what you can find. I'll help you understand what supplies we have on hand. Then, once we've figured out what we've got, maybe we can figure out how to make some equipment that will deal with the dogs.'

'What's equipment?'

'Tools. Tech. Machines. Things you can use.'

Jane frowned. 'I can't make machines.'

'Didn't you build things at the factory?'

'No,' Jane said, shaking her head. 'The older girls do that. The Janes clean and sort scrap. We tell if it's good or if it's junk.'

'Tell me exactly what you did there. What kinds of scrap did you clean?'

'All kinds.'

'Tell me a few things you sorted.'

'Um . . . fuel pumps. Light panels. Interface panels.'

Owl looked real interested. 'Tell me about interface panels. The last one you worked with, was it good, or was it junk?'

'It was good.'

'How did you know?'

'I opened it up and bent the pins into place and hooked it up to some power, and it turned on.'

'That's more than sorting scrap, Jane. That's fixing. And if you can fix things, you can build new things out of them. Go through the scrap in here. Figure out what's good. Once that's done, I'll help you figure out what to do with it. I may not have hands, but I have a whole database full of reference files. I've got manuals on how the ship works, and information on how to repair things. I bet between the two of us, we can make some pretty good stuff.'

Jane thought about that. She did always like it when she got scrap working again. The idea of making something different and useful out of it was real interesting. 'What kind of stuff?' she asked.

Owl smiled. 'I have a few ideas.'

SIDRA

'Sidra, we've been over this a dozen times.' Pepper looked tired, but Sidra didn't care. She was tired, too.

'I can't keep doing this,' Sidra said from atop the desk in the corner of her bedroom. She pressed the kit's head back as far as she could into the walls' intersection, trying to make the edges of the room mesh with the kit's blindspots. It wasn't enough. *It wasn't enough.*

Pepper sighed and rubbed her face. 'I know it's hard. I know you've still got a lot of adjusting to do—'

'You *don't* know,' Sidra snapped. 'You have no idea—'

'You *can not* be connected to the Linkings at all times. You can't.'

'Other sapients do! There's a shop right by ours where they install wireless headjacks. People come in and out of there all the time.'

Pepper shook her head hard. 'You've never seen what those people turn into. Full-time jackers are massively fucked up. They can't focus. They can't talk right. Some of them don't come back out to the real world at all. I'll take you to a jack den sometime, if it'll get you off this kick. People rent bunks by the tenday, complete with a cable for their brain and a nutrient pump to keep them alive. A lot of them never leave. They just lie down and fade away. It's disgusting.' She closed her eyes and pressed her lips together, as if summoning words. 'I know you wouldn't run into the same problem, but you live in a modder community. You can't be connected to the Linkings for the same reason you couldn't keep the name Lovelace. If you run around knowing everything instantly *without* your social skills being shit, somebody is going to catch on. Somebody will realise that you're not just crazy smart. You will slip, and they will catch it, and they will take you apart.'

Sidra's pathways crackled with frustration. The kit tugged its hair in kind. 'Pepper, my memory banks are filling up. I am not like you. I don't have a brain that grows new folds and synapses whenever I learn something. You – you have an almost infinite capacity to learn things. I don't.'

'Sidra, I know—'

'You're not listening to me. I have a *fixed limit* on hard memory. I was *designed* to have constant Linking access at all times. I wasn't meant to store everything locally. I'm going to have to start deleting things at some point. Any time I learn someone's name, any time I'm taught a new skill, I'm going to have to pick and choose which of my memories to keep. I'm going to have to tear pieces of myself out. You say you understand, but you don't. You have no idea what this is like. You have no idea how this feels.' Her words were coming out loud, fast, barely processed. She could've stopped herself. She could've brought her voice back down, slowed her pace. She didn't want to. She wanted to be loud. She wanted to yell. She knew it was unproductive, but right now, it felt good.

'Okay, I don't know exactly how it feels, but I get it.' Pepper was getting loud now. Somehow, that felt good, too. 'What *you* don't seem to get is that you're downloading things you have no need for. You wonder about an Aandrisk proverb or something, and an hour later, you're filing away half the fucking Reskit library. You don't need all that stuff.'

'Do you need all your memories? Do you need to remember every song you've ever heard, every sim you've ever played?'

'I *don't* always remember. I have to look stuff up all the time.'

'Yes, but then you remember. The memory's still there. Do you know what that would be like, to download a song, delete the file, and then hear it again, thinking I've never heard it before?'

'Sidra . . . stars. All I'm saying is that you need to be more picky. Log a one-line text reminder that you heard the song. Don't download everything that musician's ever made.' Pepper frowned, chewing her thumbnail. 'We could get you a hud.'

'No,' Sidra said. Reading was clunky and slow. That wasn't what she wanted. That wasn't what she needed.

'Don't say no before you've tried it. You could read the Linkings just like everyone—'

'I am not like everyone else. I can't *be* like everyone else.'

'You need,' Pepper said, in a tone that meant the conversation was over, 'to try.' She sighed again, glancing at the wall clock. 'And we need to get to the shop.'

Sidra pressed into the corner, fuming. Why was she so angry? This wasn't fair to Pepper, she knew that. Pepper was just trying to keep her safe, and she'd done so much for her. They'd ordered dinner from Fleet Fry the night before, and Pepper had got an assortment of appetisers and one of each kind of dipping sauce so that Sidra could trigger new images. That memory file made her feel guilty in the context of the current conversation, but . . . but the hell with it. She might have to delete that memory file altogether if she didn't find a way to deal with this.

'I don't want to go to work today,' Sidra said. She sounded like a child. She didn't care.

'Okay,' Pepper said. 'All right, fine. What are you going to do instead?'

'I don't know.' The kit crossed its arms. 'I don't know. I could clean.'

'Don't clean. Go out. Or stay in, whatever. Just . . . do something that feels good.'

Sidra moved her gaze away from Pepper. The guilt associated with the previous night's memory file was bleeding into everything else. *This* conversation was making her feel guilty, too. Why was she acting this way? Why couldn't she just get used to the way things were? What was wrong with her? 'I'm sorry,' she muttered.

'It's cool. We're going to figure this out.' Pepper walked out of the room, rubbing the back of her head. 'Seriously, though. Do something fun.'

Sidra stayed in the corner long after she heard Pepper walk out the front door. She wrestled with the ugly knot of emotions clouding her processes. She was angry with Pepper for not understanding. She was grateful for Pepper trying to help. She was angry with Pepper for not agreeing with her about Linking access. She was ashamed of how she'd behaved just then. She was justified in how she'd behaved just then. She wasn't. She was.

Do something fun, Pepper had said. Sidra thought about going down to her spot in the living room and plugging into the Linkings all day. Considering the topic at hand, it was the obvious thing to do. But in that moment, she didn't want the Linkings for a day; she wanted a *solution*. She wanted the knot in her pathways to melt away. She wanted to fix this, to fit in, to stop clinging to corners and reaching for Linkings. She needed to change, and didn't know how.

Even though the corner felt good, even though her chair was right downstairs, even though going *out* was the last thing in the world she wanted to do, she wasn't going to find answers in a public feed. She climbed down from the desk, put on her shoes and jacket, and headed for the Undersea.

Feed source: unknown
Encryption: 4
Translation: 0
Transcription: 0
Node identifier: unknown

ACuriousMind: greetings, fellow modders! i am about to embark upon a great journey of scientific discovery, and i need your help! i am extremely interested in the practice of genetic manipulation, particularly sapient hybridisation. i am new to this field, but i have read several linking books on the subject, and am confident that my theories will shatter the realm of biology as we know it. but first, i have to get some gear! can anybody recommend a reliable source for gestation chambers, preferably cheap? i am on a budget.

tishtesh: is this a fucking joke

KAPTAINKOOL: amazing. i can count six different kinds of stupid in one paragraph

ACuriousMind has been banned from Picnic

CuriousMind*2* has joined Picnic

CuriousMind*2*: i can't believe this. picnic is supposed to be an open-minded place for tech trade and cutting-edge science! clearly, this community isn't as high calibre as i was led to believe. there's a whole channel here on genetweaking! why was i banned????

fluffyfluffycake: because you lack subtlety, which means you have no clue what you're doing. enjoy your inevitable arrest. flagged.

pinch: also if you think sapient manufacture is the same as genetweaking, your science is a fucking horrorshow. flagged.

tishtesh: also you're an idiot. flagged.

CuriousMind*2* has been banned from Picnic

tishtesh: anybody else want to scrub that kid's scrib?

KAPTAINKOOL: stars yes. i'll message you.
fluffyfluffycake: me too me too
pinch: fry his patch while you're at it
FunkyFronds: i love this feed

JANE, AGE 10

Jane woke up excited and scared all at once. She and Owl had been real busy. Today was the day to see if all that busy worked.

She got out of bed and stared at her clothes, lying in a heap on the floor. They were sleep clothes, not work clothes, but they were all she had. They were gross. That was a good word Owl had taught her. *Gross*. Gross was how it felt to have clothes that were all smudged with dirt and old blood, and to not have had a shower for four days. She didn't want to put on the gross sleep clothes. The thought of it made her itch. She put them on anyway.

'Good morning,' Owl said. 'You ready for today?'

Jane's stomach flipped over, but that hot, buzzy feeling in her chest was louder. 'Yeah,' Jane said.

'I know you can do it,' Owl said. She smiled, but her face was a little scared. Jane tried not to think about that too much. She didn't want to think about what it meant if Owl was scared, too.

Jane got up, went to the bathroom, went to the kitchen. She emptied a pouch of water into a cup she'd found two days before. She crumbled a ration bar into it, and drank it down once the bits got soft. She'd figured out that getting the food wet was better practice for her stomach. The bathroom was gross, too. They needed running water.

The things she'd built with Owl's help sat in a row on the living room floor. Jane felt good looking at them. Usually, seeing a pile of sorted scrap just made her feel a quiet kind of good, because sorted scrap meant the day was over. But this was scrap she'd *fixed*. Scrap she'd made into *tools*. It wasn't just bins of junk brought in and taken away without knowing why. The scrap in front of her had jobs, and that made her feel real, real good.

First, there was the scrib, which had been easy to fix. Just a few pins bent back into place. Owl said she didn't have enough power to talk to Jane through the scrib, but she could activate a signal that would tell Jane which direction to walk in if she needed to get back to the shuttle. Jane was glad of that. She'd had enough of running around lost.

Next, the water wagon. It wasn't much – just a cargo dolly with two big empty food crates bolted to it. The water tanks on the shuttle would need a bunch of crates' worth of water to get full, but the wheels would make the task easier than lugging around bottles or something. She just had to *find* water first.

The last thing she'd built was scary, and she didn't want to ever use it. It was a tool for making dogs go away. It started with a long plex rod with a length of stripped cable running through it. The cable plugged into a small generator (which had been part of an *exosuit*, whatever that was). The generator had two fabric straps – also cut out of the exosuit – stapled to it, so Jane could wear it on her back. At one end of the rod, Jane had wrapped a whole bunch of fabric, to make it comfy (another good new word), and another smaller strip that she could tie around her wrist, so the rod wouldn't fall down if she needed to do stuff with her hands. The other end of the rod held a bunch of metal forks – a tool for eating solid meals, Owl said – spread out like fingers, each connected to the cable with a smaller wire. Jane could switch the generator power on and off with a manual switch she'd inserted right above where her thumb rested on the grip. When the power was on, the forks got all full of electricity. Owl had told her to spit on the forks the night before, to test it out. The spit made the forks pop and hiss real loud. It'd hurt the dogs a lot, Owl said. She called this tool a *weapon*. Jane thought that was a good-sounding word. She didn't want to get close to the dogs again, but she knew they'd try to get close to *her*, so having a weapon was a good thing.

She'd found some other good things, too – an empty cloth bag called a *satchel*, some work gloves that were way too big for her hands but might be okay, and a real good cutting tool called a *pocket knife*. She put the last two things into the satchel, along with three empty *canteens* to bring back any water she found (Owl wanted to do tests before Jane did the hard work of filling up the water wagon). She also packed two ration bars, four pouches of water, and the scrib. She put the satchel over her shoulder and the weapon generator onto her back, slipping her hand into the grip.

'You look like a girl who knows what she's doing,' Owl said. 'You look very brave.'

Jane swallowed. Owl had explained *brave* the day before. She did not feel brave. 'Do you think I'll have to go far?'

'I don't know, sweetie. Hopefully not. If you get too tired, or if you don't feel good, you can come back home, even if you haven't found water.'

'What's home?'

'Home is here. Home's where I am, and where you can rest.' Owl paused. Her face was some kind of sad, and it made Jane feel all weird in her chest – kind of tight, and wishing she had a blanket to curl up in. 'Please be safe out there.'

Owl opened the inner door that led to the *airlock*, then opened the outer hatch. Jane tightened her grip around the weapon, and stepped outside.

She was glad Owl had taught her some new words, because everything outside the shuttle needed them. The *sky* was big, and the *sun* was bright, and the *air* was hot. She wasn't sure she understood *wind*, but she didn't think there was any. She could already feel herself starting to sweat. It was good that there was water in her satchel.

The metal siding on the outside of the shuttle had scratch marks on it. She spread out her fingers, running them along the scratches. Dogs. She gripped her weapon tight.

She put her palm flat above her eyes to block out the sun, and looked around. So much scrap. Scrap everywhere. Piles and piles and piles, on and on. How could anyone use this much stuff? And why would they get rid of it, if most of it just needed some fixing to be good?

She thought of Jane 64, bent over her workstation. She thought of how 64 was real good at untangling cables, better than most of the girls. Something sharp jumped into Jane's stomach. She wanted to go back inside. She wanted to go home. She wanted to go back to bed and turn out all the lights. She had done that on the second day in the shuttle. Being in bed had not helped and was not relaxing, but everything else was too hard and Jane 64 wouldn't leave her head, so Jane had just stayed in bed and cried until she ran to the bathroom and threw up in the sink, and then she slept because it was the only thing she could do. Owl had been good to her. She stayed on the screen by the bed all day, and she taught Jane about something called music, which was a weird bunch of sounds that had no point but made things feel a little better.

Still, even with Owl and the music, that second day had been a real bad day. But compared with going out to where dogs could be, doing all those bad feelings all over again sounded easier than leaving the shuttle. She almost went back inside. But she was sweating and gross, and her clothes itched. She wanted a shower. And if she wanted a shower, she needed water.

Way far off, out where the piles looked small, Jane could see something move. A bunch of somethings. She didn't have a word for them, but she did have a new word for what they were doing – *flying*. They were flying down behind one of the piles. They were animals, she knew. She didn't know how she knew that, but something in her was sure they couldn't be anything else. Owl had said if she saw animals – even dogs – there had to be water somewhere close by.

Weapon in one hand, satchel strap in the other, Jane started the long walk toward them.

SIDRA

She never should have left the *Wayfarer*.

Sidra thought this as she pushed through the topside markets, fighting her directive to take note of every face, every sound, every colour. Three tendays at Port Coriol, and being outside of walls was still absolute chaos. Perhaps that feeling would never go away. Perhaps this was how it would always be.

She dodged a merchant pushing a sample platter of candies her way. She didn't make eye contact, didn't reply. It was rude, and she felt guilty, which made her all the angrier. Guilt was what had made her choose to be in this stupid body in the first place.

Why had she left? At the time, it had seemed like the best course, the cleanest option. She had come into existence where another mind should have been. She wasn't what the *Wayfarer* crew was expecting, or hoping for. Her presence upset them, and that meant she had to go. That was why she'd left – not because she'd wanted to, not because she'd truly understood what it would mean, but because the crew was upset, and she was the reason for it. She'd left for the sake of people she'd never met. She'd left for the sake of a stranger crying in a cargo bay. She'd left because it was in her design to be accommodating, to put others first, to make everyone else comfortable, no matter what.

But what of *her* comfort? What about that? Would the eight people who no longer had to hear her voice every day find this to be a fair trade, if they knew how she felt out here? Would they care if they knew this existence wasn't right? Would they not have acclimatised to her, just as they had presumably acclimatised to the absence of her predecessor?

She fought to keep the kit's eyes on the ground, struggled to keep the kit's breath steady. She could feel panic creeping as the crowd pressed in and the buildings sprawled forever outward. She remembered how the ship had felt – a camera in every hallway, a vox in every room, the lull of open space embracing it all. She remembered the vacuum, and she ached for it.

'Hey!' an angry voice said. Sidra looked down, and saw that she'd blundered into the path of a Harmagian's cart, just a step away from knocking him and his trailer of packages over. 'What's the matter with you?' he demanded, tendrils flexing irritably.

Oh no, don't, she thought, but it was a direct question, and she had no choice but to respond. 'The market is exhausting, I hate this body, I acted like an ass toward the friend who's taking care of me, and I regret the decision that brought me here.'

The Harmagian's tendrils went slack with bewilderment. 'I . . .' His eyestalks twitched. 'Well, ah . . . watch where you're going while you sort that out.' He manoeuvred the cart around her, continuing on his way.

The kit shut its eyes tight. Stupid, stupid honesty protocol. *That* part of herself, at least, she was anxious to delete. Pepper was trying, she knew. She'd seen her frowning at her scrib late at night, muttering as she dragged herself through the basics of Lattice. Code was not Pepper's strong suit, but she was firmly against seeking outside help, and Sidra couldn't argue that point. But in the meantime, how was she supposed to function in a place like this? She couldn't, was the answer. She had no business being out among sapients, masquerading as one of them. She *wasn't* one of them, and she couldn't even keep up that pretence while walking through a crowd. How long until someone asked her a question that would get Pepper and Blue in trouble? No, no, dammit – a question that would get *her* in trouble. Would she ever start thinking of herself first? *Could* she even?

She looked around the street, full of strangers and unknown questions. She couldn't be out here. She wasn't meant for out here.

She ran for the nearest quick-travel kiosk. A grotesque approximation of a Harmagian head was mounted on the desk, just like all the other kiosks. Its polymer tendrils aped polite gestures as the AI within spoke. 'Destination, please.'

Sidra knew it was a limited, non-sentient model. She'd encountered plenty of others like it, housed in transit stations and shopfronts. More intelligent than a petbot, yes, but it wasn't any closer to her than, say, a fish to a Human. She wondered about it, all the same. She wondered if it was content with its existence. She wondered if it suffered, if it ever tried to understand itself and ran up against a cognitive wall. 'One to the art district, please,' she said, waving her wristpatch over the scanner. There was a chirp of acknowledgement.

'Very good,' the kiosk AI said. 'Your quick-travel pod will be dispatched shortly. Should you need additional transport or directions, look for the quick-travel symbol, as displayed above this kiosk.'

Sadness oozed its way through Sidra's pathways as the stunted AI continued its speech. Was she so different? She was built to serve, just as this one was, and while she might feel awfully special for being able to ask questions and have arguments, she was no more capable of skipping protocols than the little mind before her. She thought of the confused way the Harmagian in the crowd had held his tendrils after she'd blurted out the answer to his question – a question that hadn't been meant as a question at all. The kit's eyes watered as she listened to the kiosk AI ramble on about location indicators and safety procedures. It couldn't do anything except what it was designed for. That was all it was. That was all it would ever be.

'Thank you for using the Port Coriol quick-travel system,' it said. One of the false tendrils shuddered with mechanical weariness. 'Have a safe and pleasant ride.'

Sidra laid one of the kit's palms atop the synthetic head. She kept it there for a second, two, three. A quick-travel pod arrived, its hatch opening with a soft whir. She leaned toward the AI's head before leaving. 'I'm sorry,' she whispered. 'This isn't fair.'

JANE, AGE 10

Owl had been right. There was water where the flying animals were – a big hole of water, and Jane didn't see any dogs. That was real good.

The flying animals were interesting. They were much smaller than her, about as long as her arm, and they had two front arms that had some kind of skin sheet hanging from them. They flapped that back and forth to get into the air. The rest of their skin was weird. It was orange, and wasn't smooth like hers, or covered in fluff – *fur*, she reminded herself, *fur*. The flying animals' skin looked hard and shiny, made up of little locking bits.

Interesting as they were, she was kind of scared of them. Were they angry animals? Would they bite? Could they hurt her? She took a step forward. A few of the animals looked up. Most of them kept drinking. The ones who looked up didn't seem angry. They just watched her a bit, then kept doing their own stuff. Jane breathed all her air out. That was good.

'Ask Owl for the flying animals' name,' she said. She couldn't make lists like Owl did, but saying things out loud helped her not forget.

She walked to the water. It was not good water. It wasn't clear, and it was thick with dust. 'Not dust,' she said. '*Dirt*.' She scrunched her nose. A chemical slick lay on top of the water, making oily lines where it touched the ground. She didn't know *what* chemical. Probably something leaking from the scrap nearby. The water smelled bad, too, which was a wrong thing even if the smell had been good. Water wasn't supposed to smell at all. Jane stopped and thought about it. Owl had said any water she found out here wasn't good to drink before it went in the filtration system, but it was so so interesting, this bad water. Also, the animals were drinking it and they were fine. She touched her finger in the water and put a big drop on her tongue. She spat it right back out with a loud sound. Metal and stink and bad things she had no words for. She spat and spat, but the taste lay down in her mouth.

'How are you drinking this?' she said to the animals. 'It's so bad!' The animals didn't say anything. Owl had said they couldn't talk like girls did, but it didn't hurt to try. Jane thought it would be good if they could talk. She wanted to talk to someone who wasn't in a wall.

Jane got a canteen from her satchel, and filled it at the side of the water. The flying animals watched her, but left her alone. There was enough water for everybody, Jane guessed. She made a face as she watched the stinky shiny water flow into the canteen. *Gross.* She did not want to drink that stuff at all. But Owl said the machines on the ship could clean up real real bad water, the worst water. They could clean pee, even. Jane was real interested to know how that worked.

She sat down by the water hole, watching the animals. Everything was still big and strange and wrong, but this . . . this was kind of good. It was good to be out of the ship, and the air was warm. The sun did that, Owl had explained. The sun was the big light in the sky. Owl had told Jane it was very very important to not look right at it. Jane wanted to real bad, but she listened. She didn't know what things could get her in trouble, and she didn't want to make Owl angry. Owl had not been angry, not even once, but she was kind of like a Mother in the way she was built. Jane thought maybe the Mothers had been good like Owl once, but then the girls did so much bad behaviour that the Mothers got extra angry and stuck that way.

Jane decided she would work real hard to be good and not make Owl angry. She didn't want to make Owl go wrong.

One of the flying animals walked close to her. Real close. Its big black eyes were so so dark against its weird orange skin. Jane didn't move. She put her hand on her weapon and held her breath. The animal moved its head like it was thinking. It sniffed at her shoe. Then it walked away, head bouncing as it went. Jane let all her air out. Okay. Okay, that was good. Good and interesting. Maybe the flying animal had been interested in her, too. She liked that idea.

The animal walked over to a group of more animals, who were . . . were they eating? They looked like they were eating. But *what* were they eating? It wasn't a meal, of course, but it wasn't like a ration bar, either. It was something coming up out of the ground – purple, smooth, kinda soft-looking, all wavy and interesting shaped. It was stuck to the ground, and to some of the scrap nearby. It wasn't an animal, but it made her think of animals in a way that she didn't understand. Not an animal, but not scrap or a machine, either. Something else. And the animals were eating it.

Could she eat it, too?

Owl had been real clear about not eating stuff out there, and Jane knew better than to just put her hands on a component she didn't recognise. She let go of the weapon, put on the work gloves (even though they were way too big), and got the pocket knife. She walked over to the group of animals. They moved away real fast. Jane stopped. Had she scared them?

'I'm not bad,' she said to them. 'I just want to see what you're eating.'

She crouched down and poked the purple stuff with the point of her knife. Nothing happened. She blew on it. Nothing happened. She looked at the little holes where the animals had been biting it. She held her knife best as she could with the big gloves, and cut off a piece. The stuff didn't bleed. She looked at it real close. It was white inside, and solid. No bones. She really wanted to taste it, but after the water, she knew it was smart to listen to what Owl said. Owl knew so much.

She put the piece of purple stuff into her satchel. It was a good time to go back, she thought. The sun was making the air real hot, and the skin on her arms kind of hurt. It was more red than usual.

Jane 64's face had been red, too, red and puffy and wrong and scared and—

She heard a rattling sound. The knife in her hand was shaking. She was shaking. She wanted to go back to Owl. She wanted to go back right now. Owl had said she could come home if she felt bad, and she did feel bad, so she would.

The animals started making a lot of noise. Most of them were running or flying away. Jane turned around. Two dogs stood there, watching the one thing that hadn't run away. Watching her.

Her stomach hurt and her eyes burned. She wanted to be back with Owl. She wanted to be back in her bed – *her* bed, with 64. She wanted a meal cup and a shower and not dogs. But there were dogs anyway, and they were making quiet angry sounds.

Her body wanted to run, like it had when the Mother stared at her through the wall, but there was no good place to go. The water hole had scrap all around it. The only way out was past the dogs. She didn't think she could run by them without them being able to bite her.

'Help,' she said, real quiet. 'Owl, help.'

But Owl was too far.

She switched the knife into her other hand and grabbed the weapon rod. She took a step back, shaking bad. 'Stop,' she said, trying not to cry. 'Go away.'

One of the dogs came closer, getting loud, teeth all wet.

'Go away!' she yelled, kicking a piece of scrap toward it. 'Go away!'

The dog made a louder sound. It ran at her.

She tripped backward, but she remembered to point the

weapon at the dog, and pushed the button as it jumped and opened its mouth of teeth.

There were so many sounds. The generator hummed. The electricity cracked off the forks. The dog screamed, which was the most bad part of all. It fell down screaming, and shook and twitched. It was the scariest thing she'd ever seen, even worse than the Mothers. She held the button down anyway. There was a bad smell, a burning smell. The dog stopped twitching.

The other dog made an angry yell, and it jumped at her, too. She hit the button again. Hum. Crack. Scream.

Both dogs lay on the ground, fur smoking. Jane ran and ran and ran, satchel full of heavy canteens crashing into her leg. The dogs didn't follow her.

It wasn't until she stopped running that she understood they were dead.

She hadn't meant to do that. She had made something to *hurt* dogs, but it worked too good, she guessed, because she had hurt them dead. That made her feel something in a very big way, something good and bad all at once.

She threw up. It was a bad thing to do, but she threw up until there was nothing left but gross sharp spit. She realised the front of her pants was wet, and her face burned as she understood why. She was *ten*.

Jane sat down in the dirt and drank a water pouch. She was still shaking. The good-bad feeling was still there, but the more she thought about things, the bigger the good part got. Things were okay. She had bad water that Owl would clean up, and she knew where to get more. She had something she could eat, maybe. She'd stopped the dogs. She'd stopped the dogs!

You look very brave, Owl had said. Jane thought of that and felt real good. She felt real good because Owl had been right.

'I'm brave,' Jane said, so she would remember. 'I can stop dogs. I'm brave.'

On the way back, Jane reminded herself of the things she needed to ask Owl. She wanted to know words. Words for the flying animals, for the purple stuff that wasn't an animal and also maybe food, and for the feeling you got when you felt bad for making a thing dead but also good because you were still alive.

SIDRA

The art district had every bit as much noise and detail as the others, but it was less crowded, at least. In the other districts, everything was always being pushed and sought in an important rush, as if your credits might not be good enough if you didn't buy something *now*. But here, where the items for sale were anything but practical, both merchants and patrons seemed to have all the time in the world. Sidra could see little barrier between culture or medium. Everything was crammed in together – wooden Laru sculptures, Harmagian rock carvings, fusion artists mixing traditions with abandon, body artists offering to alter flesh and scale and shell. The shops reflected the same mix. On one end of the spectrum, there were pristine galleries with clean walls and echoing ceilings; on the other, you had people selling prints and figures from behind portable tables, or sometimes straight off the ground.

Blue's shop fell somewhere between the two extremes, though nearer the more humble end. His stall – 'Northwest Window' – was in a larger communal building, one small cell in a busy hive. Sidra stood in the corridor for three minutes before walking through his door (painted, appropriately, in a thick coat of rich cyan). She'd behaved badly toward Pepper, she knew, and Blue was on Pepper's side, first and foremost. Maybe he already knew about the fight. Maybe Pepper had sent him a message, telling him she was out of patience for Sidra's nonsense. Maybe Blue felt the same way.

When Sidra walked in, her worries vanished. Blue looked up

from his easel, and he smiled at her as warmly as he always did. 'Sidra! What are, um, what are you doing up in the sun?'

'I'm not at work today.'

'So I see.' He wiped his brush off with a rag, set it down, and got to his feet. He wore an apron, but the clothes beneath it were still speckled with paint. 'Taking, ah, taking a day off?'

'Yes.' She looked around. She'd been to the shop before, but it was a little different every time. She noted the changes: the paintings of the mysterious forest and the bustling carnival were gone – sold, presumably – and a new canvas depicting a group of spacewalkers hung on the wall. There were five brushes and a scraper in the sink – fewer than the twelve brushes she'd seen the last time – and the dead globulb in the south corner of the room had been fixed. There was one thing that always remained the same, though, and it was the chief difference between this place and those he shared with Pepper: Blue kept his own environment immaculately tidy. Everything had a shelf, a drawer, an angle. Pepper had spots for things, too, in her way, but Blue always kept his shop looking like he was expecting company at any second. Even the dirty brushes in the sink were neatly set in their cup of water.

Sidra was aware of Blue studying her as she examined the space. 'Everything okay?' he asked. 'You look upset.'

'No,' Sidra said. 'I don't. The *kit* looks upset.'

Blue glanced over the kit's shoulder, making sure the door was closed. 'That's, ah, that's an important distinction to you.'

'It is. I *feel* upset, yes. But I don't know what you see. Whatever the kit's doing, it's not me.'

Blue tapped a finger against his thigh. 'You got somewhere to be?' She shook the kit's head. 'G-good.' He gestured toward a chair facing the back of the easel. 'Have a seat.'

Blue moved the in-progress canvas aside as she settled the kit down. He bustled around, gathering paints and clean brushes. He poured a cup of mek from a small brewer and fetched a fresh canvas.

'What are you doing?' Sidra asked.

'Something that might help,' Blue said. He held out his palm.

'Give me your hand, please.' Sidra placed the kit's hand in his. He ran his thumb over the back of it, and rummaged through a box of paint tubes with his other hand, pulling various colours out. 'I think . . . hmm. I think you're somewhere between Royal Bronze and Classic Sepia.'

'Are you going to paint me?'

Blue grinned. 'Maybe a d-dab of Autumn Sunrise, too.'

Sidra's pathways lit up with interest. The idea of someone studying *her* details for an extended period was a fascinating reversal. 'What do I do?'

'Just sit there and relax. If you need to, uh, if you need to get up, or if you get bored, let me know.' He squeezed paint onto palette, beginning to conjure the kit's skin tone.

'What should I do with the kit's face? Should it smile?'

Blue shook his head as he stirred. 'Don't ch-change anything. Don't be anything but, ah, but what you were when you walked through my door. Just be yourself.' He nodded toward the canvas. 'I'm curious to know what you think of how you look.'

'I've seen the kit in mirrors.'

'Let me, uh, let me rephrase. I want to know how you feel when you see – when you see yourself the way somebody else sees you.' Blue glanced from paint to the kit, then back again. With a satisfied nod, he picked up a brush and began to work. 'Taste anything fun today?'

'No. I haven't eaten anything.'

'That's not like you.'

'I was . . . distracted.'

'If you want, we can go to lunch after this. There's a good noodle bar not far from here.' He dragged brush down canvas in a long, smooth stroke. Sidra did her best to stay still, even though she badly wanted to watch. 'Come up with, um, with any new questions on the way here?'

Sidra gave a short chuckle. There were always new questions. She pulled up her list. 'Why don't the Laru overheat? Other species seem to find it warm here, and the Laru are covered with fur.'

'Hmm. I never thought about that. You'll need to look that one up.'

'How dangerous is it if you swallow dentbots? I imagine they'd go after a lot of good symbiotic bacteria in your stomach.'

'They do, but it's not, um, it's not overly dangerous. You j-just get a stomach ache. Happened to me a few times when I first started using them.' His eyes flicked cautiously over to hers. 'So . . . why no work today?'

Sidra looked around the shop. 'I had a disagreement with Pepper.'

'What about?'

Sidra sighed. 'She won't let me install a wireless Linking receiver.'

Blue raised an eyebrow. 'You two have been on that merry-go-round before.'

'I know. But she's not listening to me. I don't want to delete memory files.'

'She *is* listening,' Blue said with measured diplomacy. 'She just doesn't agree with you.'

The kit frowned. 'And you don't either.'

'I didn't say that. I don't always take her side, you know. I'm listening, too. I'm listening to both of you.' He reached for another tube of paint. 'Tell me something you're afraid of deleting.'

'I've downloaded a lot of things.'

'I know. Pick a favourite.'

'I . . . don't know if I have one.'

'Something you find really interesting, then. Just something at random.'

Sidra worked her way down the length of her memory banks, not sure where to start. 'Well . . . there's this. "The Never-Born Queen and Those Who Followed".'

'What's that?'

'A Quelin folktale. More like an epic, I suppose. It's a bit dark in places, but there's a wonderful poetry to it, too.' The kit fidgeted as she remembered Pepper's words that morning: *you're filing away half the fucking Reskit library.* 'I have the three most popular translations on hand.'

Blue leaned back, never taking his eyes off the canvas. 'I don't think I've ever heard any Quelin stories. Feel like sharing?'

The kit blinked. 'Yes, but it's quite long.'

'How long is it?'

She selected one of the three files – the Tosh'bom translation – and ran a quick analysis. 'It'd take me approximately two hours to recite it aloud.'

Blue shrugged and smiled. 'Sounds like a great thing to do while painting.'

Sidra adjusted her processes, and began to convert text to speech. 'Call out, brave warriors, and remember our song. Remember the heroes lost and the heroes born. Remember the shells shattered among sea and rock and cave . . .'

She was aware, as the saga of war and homeland poured forth from the kit's mouth, that Blue was distracting her. She'd seen him do the same sort of thing to Pepper in the moments they thought Sidra didn't notice, when Pepper became quietly, whisperingly afraid of nothing. In those moments, Blue would ask Pepper about her day. He'd ask her about what she was working on. He'd ask her about the latest sim she'd been playing. In a small way, Sidra felt a bit manipulated, like he was purposefully driving away the bad mood she'd felt justified in nursing – but having something else to focus on *was* better, and being painted was a surprisingly good feeling, too. It was nice to be watched, to have somebody pouring all his attention into her. Was that selfish? And if so, was that a bad thing?

Blue hardly spoke at all as she told the story, other than a short laugh or 'mmm' here and there. His eyes were intensely focused on his work, and by extension, on her. It was a look she'd never seen in him. At home, he was so mellow, so gentle. Here, there was a spark, a curious sort of strength. He reminded her a bit of Pepper, when she fell into a groove with a project. Sidra hadn't felt that way about anything before. She was focused now, yes, but she knew that was different. Was she capable of that kind of flow? If she could disable her ability to track time, could she lose herself the way they did?

She continued to recite, and after one hour and fifty-six minutes, the tale of the Never-Born Queen reached its final lines: '. . . to sleep, to sleep, that our heroes may wake once more.'

Blue nodded thoughtfully. 'That,' he said, 'was fascinating. Kinda grim, but I w – I wouldn't expect much, um, much less from the Quelin.'

'They have some sweet children's stories, too,' Sidra said. 'Well . . . rather speciest. But sweet, in the right cultural context.'

Blue laughed. 'Again, as expected.' He put down his brush with conviction. 'It's been a long time since I did, uh, since I did a portrait, and this is just a quick one. But . . . well, tell me what you think.'

He turned the canvas toward her. The paint still glistened. A Human woman stared back, serious and quiet, with a face that would easily disappear in an Exodan crowd. Sidra studied the details. Copper skin that didn't see much sun. Slender cheeks fed on bugs and stasie food. Eyes so brown the irises were nearly lost in them. A cap of black curls, cut short and hugging tight. She'd looked at that face many times in the mirror in her room, but this was something different. This was the kit as Blue saw it.

'It's beautiful,' she said, and meant it.

'The painting, or the face?'

'The painting. You're very skilled.'

Blue gave a happy nod. 'What about the face? What do you see in it?'

She searched for an answer, but found nothing. 'I don't know.' She paused for two seconds. 'Do you know who decided what the kit would look like?' she asked at last. 'Did it come this way, or did Jenks choose it, or . . .?'

'Lovey chose it,' Blue said. 'This was all her, or so P-Pepper said.'

Sidra looked at the portrait, at the face someone else had chosen for her. Why? Why had her former installation wanted this face? Why this hair, those colours, those eyes? What about this form had made Lovey think *yes, this is me*?

'Hey,' Blue said, taking the kit's hand. 'What's up?'

Sidra couldn't look at him. 'I'm a mistake,' she whispered.

'Whoa, hang on—'

'I am,' she insisted. 'This' – she gestured between the kit and the portrait – 'is hers. It's all hers. I would've *been* her if I hadn't scrubbed those memory files when I woke up.' The kit closed its eyes tight. 'Stars. I'm what killed her.'

'No,' Blue said, not a hint of a question in his voice. 'No. Oh, Sidra.' He took the other hand now, too, and held them both firmly. 'You had no idea. *No idea.* What happened to Lovey is not your fault. That, um, that crew, they knew when they flipped the switch that Lovey – that Lovey might not come back.'

'But they wanted her to. They didn't want me. I'm just . . .' She thought again of the Harmagian she'd nearly tripped over, the argument that had preceded him, the guarded way Pepper watched her when she spoke to strangers. 'I'm a mistake,' she repeated.

Blue leaned back in his chair and folded his arms. 'Well, if you are, I am, too.' He touched the top of his head, tangling his fingers in his thick brown hair. 'You know why I've, um, why I've got hair and Pepper doesn't?'

'She said you're not like her. You weren't made for the factories.'

'Yeah. W-Want to know what I was made for?' He raised his eyebrows, smirking. 'Civil leadership. I was supposed to, uh, to be a c – a coun—' He gave up on the word, and laughed at himself. 'A politician.' Blue grinned, but there was a sadness in his eyes. Something about this wasn't as easy as he was making it out to be. 'The b-bastards that made us, they're not as good at, uh, good at genetweaking as they think. They think they've got it down. They make dancers, they make math – mathematicians, they make athletes. They m-make factories full of slave kids with no hair. But evolution isn't a – a thing you can wrangle like that. It doesn't always go in predictable ways. Genes and chromosomes, they, um, they do their own thing sometimes. You think you're mixing together a politician, and instead, you get me.' He shrugged. 'The Enhanced call us m-misfits. People who

131

don't suit their intended purpose. So, maybe, ah, maybe you're a misfit, too. Doesn't mean you're not deserving. Doesn't mean you shouldn't be here. Lovey's gone, and that's horribly sad. You're here, and that's wonderful. This isn't a zero sum thing. Both can be true at the same time.' He looked at the painting. 'And maybe this, um, maybe this isn't *you* right now. Maybe the face you're, um, the face you're wearing just needs a little time before it f-fits you. Or you fit it. Either way.'

Sidra thought for two seconds. 'I don't know what to say right now.'

'That's okay.'

Sidra watched the drying paint as she processed the events of the day over and over. Blue sat beside her, hand around the kit's, clearly in no hurry. She cycled through the argument with Pepper that morning. *You need to try.* She'd been so angry to hear that, but remembering it now, the feeling was different. Maybe she needed to stop fighting the kit. Maybe she *could* be more like everyone else. She looked at the portrait's eyes, and tried to imagine what it would be like to see herself looking back.

'Do you know an Aeluon named Tak?' she asked.

Blue blinked, surprised by the question. 'I know a dozen Aeluons named Tak. That's the problem with, um, with an invented language. Not a lot of names to go around. Do you know xyr f-full name?'

'No. Just Tak. She's a tattoo artist. I met her at Shimmerquick.' Sidra pulled up the contact file. 'Her shop's in the western art district. Steady Hand?'

'Oh, yeah. I don't know that par – um, particular Tak, but I've seen that shop.' He scratched his chin. 'I don't think it's too far from the noodle bar, if you wanted to go see her after lunch.'

'I hadn't thought of it before now, but I would like to, yes.'

He looked at her curiously. 'Why, you thinking of getting some ink?'

The kit shrugged. 'I don't know. Maybe.'

Blue laughed and ruffled the kit's hair. 'I mean, hey, if you're g-going to have an existential crisis, go all out, yeah?'

JANE, AGE 10

'Pour it in the funnel there,' Owl said. Her face on the screen nodded toward the empty water tanks. Jane took the cap off the canteen and poured the gross water out.

'It smells real bad,' Jane said, turning her face away as the water splashed into the funnel.

'I'll bet,' Owl said. 'Okay, I'll just divert some power from the hatch, and—' There was a sound, the sound of a thing turning on. Owl looked good – *happy*. 'Excellent. Give me a moment to analyse it.'

Jane put her ear up to the tank as things clunked and whirred. 'What's it doing?' she asked.

'I'm scanning for contaminants,' Owl said.

'Yes, but *how?*'

'I don't actually know how it works. I bet one of our manuals can tell us. But I have to focus on this now. I don't have enough power to be running too many extra processes.'

Jane scrunched up her forehead, but didn't say anything further. Maybe if she was real careful, she could take one of the tanks apart and then put it back together the exact same way.

'Analysis complete,' Owl said. 'Stars, what *isn't* in this stuff?'

'Is it bad?' Jane asked, her fingers all tangled together. Was the water she found wrong? Would Owl get angry?

'That depends on your point of view,' Owl said. She was not angry. 'There are eight different types of fuel residue, more indus-trial by-products than you have time to listen to, bacteria, microbes, fungal spores, decaying organic matter, a heaping helping of dirt, and, weirdly, an awful lot of salt.' Her face smiled from the wall. 'Luckily, none of it is beyond my ability to handle. Pour the rest in. I can have a batch this small clean in six minutes and forty-three seconds. Give or take.'

'Can I drink it?' Jane said.

'Yes, and you should have enough to wash your face and hands, too. But don't drink all of it until you've brought more back. Do you think you can take the water wagon out tomorrow?'

'Yeah!' Jane said. She could! She could do that! 'Oh, and I found something by the water.' She opened up her satchel.

Owl's mouth went tight. 'What kind of something?'

'I don't know.' Jane put the work gloves back on and pulled out the purple stuff. It was banged up and crushed flat, but still in one piece. She held it up toward the camera.

'Hmm,' Owl said. 'That looks like some kind of mushroom. Or something similar to a mushroom, at least.'

'What's that?'

'It's like a plant. A plant is a . . . a living thing that isn't an animal.'

Jane had thought maybe the purple stuff was alive, but knowing it for sure felt weird. She held the *mushroom* a little further away from herself. 'Is it bad?'

'I don't know. We should check it out. Bring it to the bathroom.'

'Why?'

'There's a tool in there I can use. At least, I think it's in there. It should be in there.'

Jane walked to the bathroom. Owl bounced along the walls beside her. Jane had to help Owl push the bathroom door open because something in the mechanism that pulled the door in and out of the wall was junk. The lights flickered, eventually staying on. Jane saw the dry shower. She scratched behind her ear. She scratched and scratched and scratched. *Gross.*

The girl in the mirror did not look like the girl she was used to seeing. This girl had a red gross face, and gross hands, and gross clothes. Dirt all over. She looked like someone new. She wondered if Jane 64 would recognise her. Would have recognised her.

'What am I looking for?' she asked Owl, wanting to think about something else.

'Here, let me show you.' Owl's face went away, and a picture appeared: a small machine with a round flat tray beneath some kind of lens.

Jane opened the cupboard. There it was, right in front. She held the machine up to the camera.

'That's it!' Owl said, and Jane felt good, even though she hadn't done much. 'That's a scanner for medical samples. You can probably use it to analyse what's in that mushroom you found. I can tell you if any of it is bad for you.'

Jane set the scanner on the edge of the sink. 'How do I . . .'

'Put the mushroom in the tray. Okay, good. Now wave your hand by the interface panel to turn it on.'

Jane waved her hand. She waved, and waved again. Nothing happened.

'Damn,' Owl said. Jane didn't know what that meant, but Owl had a wrong sound in her voice. 'It must be out of power.'

Jane took the mushroom out of the tray and picked up the scanner. She turned it around and around, looking close. 'There's a power jack here,' she said, pointing. 'Do you have any charge cables?'

'Probably, but I don't know where.'

Jane went back to the cupboard and dug through all the stuff. She found a coiled black cable with the right kind of coupler. 'Where can I plug this in?'

'There's a power station in the kitchen. Next to the sink.'

Jane went to the kitchen, hooked up the cables, and plugged in the scanner. Nothing changed. 'Does it have a timed charge?' she asked. 'Does it need to sit for a bit?'

'Probably, but make sure it's actually charging. Has anything lit up?'

Jane flipped the scanner around again. There was an indicator patch, all right, but it was dark. She unplugged it and thought real hard. She went to the table where she'd built the weapon and got some tools. 'Okay,' she said. 'Let's see how it works.'

It took her no time to get the case open, and only a little bit longer to find the problem: a rusted conduit connecting the power source to the motherboard.

'Can you fix it?' Owl said. 'What do you need?'

Jane scratched behind her ear with the tip of the screwdriver. 'Something . . . something metal. Something that will fit. And binding tape. Or glue. Do you have those?'

'I don't know,' Owl said. 'Check the drawers.'

Jane had to check lots of drawers, but she found some sticky tape that would work okay. As for the conduit, she didn't know where to find one of those, but there were plenty of metal things in the kitchen. She got one of the forks. The pointy things on a fork might work. She bent them like she'd bent the ones on the weapon – putting the pointy things under her shoe and pulling the handle up – but this time, she wiggled the handle back and forth and back and forth and back, until *snap!* The pointy things broke off. She bundled them up in tape real good, so that they wouldn't spark into the machine, and then taped the bundle into the empty space. She plugged the scanner back in. The indicator patch turned green.

'Look!' she said, turning to Owl's camera. 'Look!' Fixing things always felt real good, but it felt even more good knowing somebody else had seen her do it.

'Oh, wonderful! Great job!' Owl said. 'Let it charge for a while, and then we'll see if that mushroom is something you can eat.'

Jane put her chin on her hands and watched the scanner. It wasn't doing anything, but seeing the green light was good. She'd done a great job. Owl had said so.

'Jane,' Owl said. She spoke kind of slow, like she was thinking about something. 'You're very good at fixing things.'

'It's my task,' Jane said.

'I think . . .' Owl got quiet. Jane looked at the screen on the wall. Owl was kind of frowny, like girls got when there was a piece of scrap they couldn't figure out. 'I have an idea,' Owl said. 'I've had it since you got here, but I wasn't sure if you could do it. I'm still not sure it's the right thing.' She sighed. 'We'd have to agree to it together. I can't make you. Okay?'

'Okay,' Jane said, a little scared now.

'This ship can't fly as it is. It's broken and in bad repair. There are so many parts that need replacing. I gave up hope of ever taking flight again a long time ago. But watching you work . . . Jane, with my help, you could find the things this ship needs to become functional. It would take a long time, and I can't promise we'd be successful. But I have all the manuals. I can walk you through the ship's systems and tell you what everything does. I can keep you safe and healthy. And you – you can find the things that are missing. You can find the pieces we need to replace the broken stuff. And if you can't find a piece, you can make it out of others. I know you can. Look at the things you've built: the weapon, the water wagon. We're surrounded by tech here. I really think we could do this.'

Jane could tell Owl liked this idea, but she wasn't sure why it was so important. The ship kept the dogs away, and there was water now, and she could eat the mushrooms. 'Why do we need the ship to fly?'

Owl looked kind of surprised, but then she smiled. 'Because, sweetheart, if the ship works, we can get away from here.'

Jane blinked. 'To where?'

Owl's smile got sad. 'I think it's time I explained planets.'

SIDRA

Tak had changed since Shimmerquick. Sometime during the tendays between, Tak's reproductive system had indicated that it was time to switch sides. The implants beneath his skin had responded in kind, releasing a potent mix of hormones that allowed his body to do what it had evolved to do. He didn't look terribly different from the Aeluon woman Sidra had met at the Aurora. His face was instantly recognisable. A lightening of skin and a slight shift in facial cartilage was all that had taken place, but it was enough to be instantly noticeable.

What had not changed about Tak was his air of quiet confidence, which was readily apparent the moment Sidra walked into his shop. The proprietor lounged in a broad chair near a window, smoking his pipe and reading something on his scrib. His cheeks flashed colours, and Sidra accessed her reference files in kind. Tak was surprised, and pleased.

'Well, hey!' he said, setting down both scrib and pipe. 'It's my friend from the party!'

Sidra felt the kit smile. He remembered her. 'Hello. I hope I'm not intruding.'

Tak gestured around. 'I'm alone, and it's a shop. You're supposed to intrude.' The patches on his cheeks went green with amusement. 'What brings you here?'

'Well, I . . .' Sidra wasn't sure how to go about this. She'd never bought anything on her own before – not without Pepper's instruction, at least. Perhaps this was a stupid idea. 'I'm interested in getting a tattoo.'

The green took on shades of blue. Tak was *very* pleased. 'Your first, right?'

'Yes.'

'*Fantastic*. Please,' he said, gesturing toward a heap of cushions surrounding a thin, cylindrical table. 'Can I get you something to drink? Tea? Mek? Water?'

'Mek would be nice, thank you.' Sidra sat the kit down as Tak operated the brewer. The shop was a peaceful place, full of plants and curios. A small tank full of some sort of amorphous schooling sea creature – *image logged, added to research list* – hummed calmly against the wall. It stood alongside a strange piece of furniture: a smooth, featureless blob, bigger than she was. This was situated beside an Aeluon-style chair and a huge cabinet chequered with cube-like drawers. The chair appeared to be made of some sort of polymer, but she couldn't identify the material. *Image logged, added to research list.*

Much like the decor at the festival, the shop was strikingly devoid of colour. Most of the objects within were grey, white, tan. Even the plants were muted – tarnished silver leaves with just the barest hint of chlorophyll. There were a few items that broke the rule: an abstract painting in bright primaries, the labels on foodstuffs and other multispecies goods, and a quartet of Aandrisk feathers, sticking up out of a thin vase.

'Is this typical Aeluon decor?' Sidra asked. 'It's quite striking.'

Tak went back to an amused green, tinged with a bit of curious brown. 'Yeah, we tend to like our spaces simple. Too much colour gets tiring.'

'Yet you're a tattoo artist. On Port Coriol.'

Tak laughed as he picked up two full cups of mek. 'I didn't say we don't *like* colour. Colour is good. Colour is life. But it's also noise. Words. Passion.' He handed Sidra a cup and sat down. 'My shop's where I spend most of my day. I want it to be a place where I can chill out and think clearly.'

'How do you deal with the markets? Aren't they distracting?'

'They're absolutely distracting. That's the point of a market, to distract you into buying stuff you don't need.' He sipped his drink, cheeks swirling as he savoured it. 'But I was also born here. The market's background static to me.' He looked around the shop. 'Still, though. A quiet place is good.' He turned his attention back to Sidra with a friendly teal flush. 'But you didn't come here to talk interior decorating. You want ink.' He slid his scrib onto the table and gestured. A small cloud of pixels shot up, awaiting direction. 'What are you after?'

Sidra took a sip of mek. *She was stepping into a hot bath, but this body wasn't hers.* 'I'm not quite sure.'

'Hmm,' Tak said, sitting back. He looked cautious. 'Then why do you want one?'

Sidra didn't know what to say. The truth was all she could work with, but Tak's change in body language worried her. She'd put him off, and she wasn't sure why. 'Because of what you said. At the party.'

Tak laughed. 'You'll have to be more specific.'

The kit smiled, just a little. 'The re-enforced circle. Bringing your mind and body together.' She paused. 'I want that.'

Tak's cheeks quietly blossomed – pleased, touched, interested. His caution vanished. Sidra relaxed. 'Okay then,' Tak said. His long grey fingers danced near the projected pixels; they followed him like filings chasing after a magnet. 'Let's narrow it down. Are we going for an anchor or a compass? A memory to ground you, or a spark to guide you forward?'

Sidra processed the question fully. She had some good memories, but she could access those at any time. 'A spark.'

'A spark. Good.' Tak touched the underside of his chin, tapping it as he thought. 'Tell me what kind of imagery appeals to you. Do you have a favourite animal? A place? Anything in particular that inspires you?'

Sidra wasn't sure she'd ever been *inspired,* and she wasn't sure how to pick a favourite animal when they were all so interesting. 'I like . . .' Her pathways raced, trying to find a good answer in a polite amount of time. She sipped her mek again. *She was stepping into a hot bath, but this body wasn't hers*. That was it – not mek, but the sensory analogues. That *was* her favourite thing. She considered the images she'd experienced, and tried to narrow it down further. 'I like the ocean. When I—' She stopped herself from saying *when I eat hard candy, I see waves*. 'When I see the ocean, I feel calm. It makes me want to' – *to keep eating candy* – 'to keep going. To keep trying new things. To keep living.' She processed what she'd just said. She'd said it aloud, so it had to be true.

'I can work with that,' Tak said happily. Sidra had been so focused on answering the question that she hadn't processed him gesturing at the pixels, creating a rough ghost of a wave cresting into the air. 'Now, how elaborate do we want to get? Do you want something realistic, or are you more into symbols?'

Sidra pondered. 'Symbols. Symbols are interesting.'

'I like symbols, too.' He continued to gesture, drawing in the air. The wave became fuller, more tangible. 'Do you want just a wave, or other things with it? Fish? We could add some fish in there.' He added outlines of brightly coloured fish wriggling through the spray.

A memory appeared: Blue answering her questions on the Undersea during her first day at the Port. She liked that memory. Maybe a compass could be an anchor, too. 'Yes, fish would be good.' She shifted her gaze to the tank by the cabinet, where the strange creatures pulsed and swayed. 'Ocean creatures in general, I think.'

'Right, right, not *just* fish. I like it.' Tentacles joined the ichthyoid outlines. Claws and fronds, too. 'So, the question becomes: do you want a static tattoo, or dynamic?'

'I don't know. Which is better?'

'That is entirely up to you.'

Sidra thought back to the party. 'It wouldn't bother you, would it? The moving colours?' She didn't want the act of tattooing her to be an unpleasant experience for Tak. She wouldn't be doing this at all if he hadn't planted the idea in her head. She didn't feel comfortable getting ink from just anyone. She wanted the care she'd seen him employ on his customer at Shimmerquick. She wanted to know that he understood why she was doing this at all. It was a tattoo from Tak, or nothing.

'Wouldn't bother me at all,' Tak said, 'though I appreciate the consideration. I've been doing dynamic ink for standards. I'm used to it.'

'Well,' Sidra said, slowly. 'Then I'd like bots.' If the point was to give her something that would help her move forward, then she needed something that actually *moved*. 'But please use colours that aren't irritating to Aeluons.'

Tak's cheeks turned green, through and through. 'I'll need some time to design this properly,' he said, 'but I can tell you right now this is going to be a great project.'

JANE, AGE 10

Jane had a lot of questions. She had so many questions, she couldn't have counted them all because she'd have run out of numbers.

They were up real late. Jane was tired all the way through. She could feel it was way after bedtime, but she didn't care. Her thoughts were buzzing so fast, there was no way she could sleep. Owl had used so many new words: planets, stars, gravity, orbit, tunnels, the Galactic Come Ons, and a whole bunch of others she'd already forgot. And species! Jane understood what species meant now. She was a Human species. There were many people who were Human species, and lots more kinds of people than just girls. Owl had showed her pictures. All the Humans in the pictures had *hair*, and Jane had asked if she was weird because she didn't have any, but Owl said she didn't need to worry about that. Humans were all different. They were different colours and sizes, and they wouldn't think no hair was weird. They would just be glad to see her, Owl said.

Jane asked Owl why she didn't have hair. She asked why she'd never seen other Humans. She asked if the Mothers knew there was stuff outside the factory, and if they knew about ships and stars and the rest of it. Owl had gotten kind of funny and quiet and said that that was a really big thing to talk about and they should focus on planets for now.

There were other species, too. They had hard names that Jane knew she'd need to practise. Owl said she would help. Owl said she would do as much as she could to get Jane ready before she met other species. She'd teach her how to live in a ship, how to act around others, how to say the same words other species did. Their words were called *Klip*, and Jane's words were called *Sko-Ensk*, which were kind of like *another* set of words called *Ensk*, and some Humans knew that one, but usually not the one Jane spoke. Words were weird.

Everything was complicated, but real interesting, too. Jane had so many questions she was starting to forget her questions. She sat on the good soft thing in the living room – the couch, Owl said. Jane unwrapped a ration bar and dunked it in a cup of water. 'How come,' she said, after swallowing the chewed food, 'how come if there are so many stars on the other side of the sky, I can't see them?'

'Our planet is facing a star during the hours that you're awake,' Owl said. She put a picture up on her screen – one little ball facing a big bright ball. 'See? When we're facing the star, it's so bright that it blocks out the light from all the others. But when we face away from it' – the picture changed – 'you can see the stars we've been missing during the day. You probably saw them when you first got here, but . . . you had a lot going on that night.'

Jane thought back. She remembered the specks in the sky, but she hadn't known what they were, and she'd been scared about all the other things. She watched the little ball on screen turn in and out of light. 'Are we facing away from the star now?'

'Yes. That's why it's night-time.'

'Can I see the other stars now?'

'Oh! Yes, yes, of course! I hadn't considered. Stupid of me. Go up to the control room. I can activate the viewscreen.'

Jane ran to the front of the shuttle. Owl joined her on a panel between the control buttons. The viewscreen flickered on, but it snapped and buzzed all over. Worn-out wiring, probably.

'Sorry, Jane,' Owl said. 'I think that's as good as it's going to get.'

Jane squinted at the viewscreen, trying to see beyond the

buzzing bits. It was real dark outside, darker than the dorm ever got. She could kind of make out the big piles of scrap. She tried to focus above the scrap, where the sky was. The screen kept flickering, turning on and off in patches all over. But in the bits that stayed on, she could see more light. Little dots in the sky. Lots of them.

'Owl?' Jane said. 'Are there any dogs outside?'

'There are always dogs outside,' Owl said. 'I can't see any right by us, but that doesn't mean they're not there.'

Jane thought for a second, then ran back down the hall, toward the living room.

'Jane?' Owl said, chasing her from one wall screen to the next. 'Jane, are you okay?'

Jane put on her shoes and strapped her weapon to her back.

'Jane,' Owl said. Her voice was real serious.

Jane faced the closest screen. She stood up tall and held the weapon tight. 'Can I go see?' she said.

'Yes, but there is no lighting out there. You could trip on something. You could hurt yourself. It's not safe.'

Jane tried a new word. 'Please?'

Owl closed her eyes and sighed. 'If you see any dogs—'

'I have my weapon,' Jane said.

'*If you see any dogs,* you come right back inside. You can't see very well in the dark. They probably can.'

'Okay.'

'And don't go away from the ship.' Owl thought about something, then sighed again. 'There's a maintenance ladder near the outer hatch. If the roof doesn't have too much junk on it, you can probably climb up to the top. I don't recommend going further than that. Okay?'

'Okay.'

Owl opened the airlock, then the hatch. Jane stepped outside. It was so dark, and cold, too. Jane swallowed and looked around, trying to see things that were close. She couldn't see anything moving. She couldn't hear anything moving, either. She thought for a second about going back inside, but she didn't. She found the ladder and climbed it.

She looked up.

Jane couldn't move. The cold was making her shaky, but that was the only thing about her that moved, except for her heart, beating real loud in her ears. The sky was . . . it was . . . it was so *full*. And now that she knew what the specks were, it made her head spin and her mouth dry.

There were dozens of stars. Dozens of dozens, way too many to count, just like her questions. There were big stars and little stars and some that were kind of red or blue. There wasn't any part of sky that didn't have stars, but most of them were in one big big big strip that was fluffy and soft and so so bright. Owl had showed her a picture of a galaxy, but this was different. This was real. This was *real*.

A few days ago, the factory had been everything. There were no planets. There were no stars. The big blue day sky had been confusing enough, but this . . . There were *people* out in the stars. So many people! All those little bits of light, they all had planets – so big that you couldn't even tell that you were standing on a ball – and all those planets had people, and species! Species in different colours and kinds. Jane couldn't even picture that many people. It didn't make sense. None of it made sense.

She sat down. She didn't know if she felt good or if she felt sick. The Mothers had to know this was here. They didn't leave the factory, she figured, but they had to know. Why didn't the girls know? Why hadn't they been told? Why couldn't they go outside? They could still sort scrap even if they knew about the sky! Jane felt something bad, something she didn't have a word for. She felt all hot and wrong. She wanted to break something on purpose.

But then she looked up again, up at the big soft galaxy, and after a bit, she felt okay. She felt good. Somehow, outside, looking at the stars, everything was a little better. It didn't make sense in her head, but it did down in her stomach. She looked at the stars, and she knew all her questions would get answered, all the things would get fixed. All this weird stuff was okay.

Jane wished that 64 had gone outside, too. She wished that 64 had met Owl, and that they'd learned about the sky together. Jane felt hot and wrong again, and even the stars couldn't fix that.

She lay down on her back, looking and looking. She thought about species and ships. She thought about people.

They'd be happy to see her, Owl had said.

The cold air was starting to make her shake real hard, and it kind of hurt, too, so she climbed down the ladder and went back inside.

'Owl?' she said, facing a screen. 'I think . . . I think fixing the ship would be a real good task.'

Owl looked so, so pleased. 'You do?'

'Yes,' Jane said. She nodded hard. 'Yes. Let's go to space.'

SIDRA

Sidra's internal clock reset itself, and the kit smiled wide. 'I'm getting my tattoo today,' she said. Her petbot looked up as she spoke, snuggling happily in the kit's lap.

Pepper looked over from her corner of the couch. 'Did it just hit midnight?'

'Yes.'

Pepper laughed. 'Your appointment isn't for, what, ten hours?'

'Ten and a half.'

Pepper laughed again, then returned her gaze to the breathing mask she was tinkering with. 'And you're still not going to tell me what design you and your artist cooked up?'

'No,' Sidra said, stroking the petbot's head. Pepper had been pestering her for hints ever since she'd heard about Sidra's first trip to Steady Hand. 'Not unless you ask me directly.'

Pepper shook her head and put up her palm. 'I can respect a surprise. I'm just excited to see it.' She held a bolt between her teeth and continued speaking around it. 'Are you nervous?'

Sidra considered. 'Yes, but not in a bad way. More . . . anticipatory.' She shifted memory files around as she spoke. The Linking jack plugged into the base of the kit's skull was supplying her with one of Tak's favourite adventure novels, which he'd mentioned during their last meeting. 'Have you ever heard of *A Song for Seven*?' she asked. 'It's an Aeluon book.'

Pepper shook her head as she fussed with the mask. Sidra was unsurprised. There wasn't much Pepper had read beyond tech manuals and food drone menus. 'Is that what you're processing now?'

'Yes.' Sidra saw no reason to supply the additional explanation that she was adding it to her local memory. Her memory banks were still filling faster than she was comfortable with, but she saw little point in reopening the argument, at least right now.

'Are you enjoying it?' Pepper asked.

'Very much,' Sidra said. 'The phrasing can be challenging, but it's a good translation, and the complexity makes for some wonderfully layered nuance.' She was aware, as she said it, that she was repeating what Tak had said about it, word for word. Well, why not? He'd sounded smart when he'd said it; why couldn't she?

Pepper raised her hairless brow with a smirk. 'That's a fancy way of saying "dense".'

Sidra knew Pepper was kidding, but something in her bristled nonetheless. The words Pepper was scoffing at didn't belong to Sidra, and she didn't like Pepper's implication that their original speaker was being pretentious. Tak was educated, and it was one of the things Sidra enjoyed most about speaking with him. Pepper was intelligent, no question, but . . .

She watched Pepper as she worked on the same project she'd been working on at the shop all day, the same project she'd been working on one-handed through dinner, the same project she'd been working on when Blue kissed the top of her head and bid them both goodnight. Sidra felt unkind in thinking it, but this was one of the things she enjoyed about Tak's company. She was glad to have met someone who liked to read.

Feed source: unknown
Encryption: 4
Translation: 0
Transcription: 0
Node identifier: unknown

pinch: hey, got another question for you guys. this one's just out of curiosity. if you wanted to expand an AI's memory capacity, how would you go about it?

ilikesmash: expand by how much?

pinch: a lot. enough to make her comparable with an organic's ability to learn new stuff indefinitely

tishtesh: are you talking about an intelligent sentient model? you know that's why they have linking access, right?

pinch: let's say linking access wasn't a possibility

nebbit: you'd need to install additional hardware to whatever housing it's in. extra storage drives.

pinch: let's say that that wasn't a possibility, either

tishtesh: uhhhhh okay. you're fucking stuck then

ilikesmash: you could pare down its cognitive processors to limit how much info it wants to access. slow the deluge a bit.

tishtesh: then what would even be the point of an intelligent sentient model

AAAAAAAA: limiting processors would be cruel

ilikesmash: how is it cruel? you're taking away the protocol that's causing the issue. would make for a more stable installation.

AAAAAAAA: you're taking away a crucial part of xyr cognitive processes. would you get rid of your own curiosity if it made you more 'stable'?

tishtesh: stars, can we not

ilikesmash: ah, i see. you're one of those. come back when you've realised they're not people

nebbit: friends, we have a separate thread for ethical arguments. please stay on topic.

JANE, AGE 10

She still wasn't sure about the mushrooms. They tasted okay – more interesting than meals, anyway. They filled her up real good, and Owl said they were good *for* her, too, but making them into food was not a task Jane liked very much. Fixing scrap was much better. But like Owl had said, she couldn't fix scrap if she didn't fuel herself first. So, mushrooms.

As she cut up that morning's handful of food, she wondered what other people ate. She wondered about other people a lot. Owl had explained that the planet they were on – which was still weird to think about – had lands on all sides of it, but the lands were separated by lots of water. The land on their side was where all the scrap went, and where all the factories were (there was more than just the one!). The land on the other side had *cities*. The cities were where the scrap came from. The people in the cities didn't like scrap or think about it much, but they liked *stuff*, and since they didn't talk to other Humans or species, they couldn't get new stuff, or materials to make new stuff (they'd already used up everything they dug out of the ground, Owl said). If they wanted new stuff, they had to make it out of old stuff.

'What do the other people on this planet do?' Jane asked.

'I don't understand the question. What do you mean?' Owl said.

'I mean . . . what do they *do*? If the girls on this side take care of the scrap, what do *they* do?' Jane was still trying to figure out the point of a city. And of most things. The more questions she asked, the more questions she thought up.

'The same things people do everywhere, I suppose,' Owl said. 'They learn things, make families, ask questions, see places.'

'Do they know about us on this side? Do they know we're here?'

'Yes. Not you and I specifically, but yes.'

'Do they know about the Mothers?'

'Yes. They made them. They made the factories, too. And the girls.'

'Why?'

'Because they don't want to clean up their own messes.'

Jane thought about that. 'Why don't they just have the Mothers clean up instead?'

Owl's eyes moved away from Jane. 'Because making girls is cheaper, in the long run.'

'What's cheaper?' Jane asked. She turned the bits of mushrooms so she could chop them smaller.

'Cheaper is . . . it means it requires less materials. Machines like the Mothers take a lot of kinds of metal that people here don't have much of. Girls are easier for them to make.'

Jane remembered her face smashing down red and hot against the treadmill, a metal hand on the back of her neck. 'Are the other people on this planet bad?'

Owl was quiet. Jane looked up from her pile of mushrooms to the wall screen. 'Yes,' Owl said. 'That's not a nice thing of me to say. But yes, they're bad people.' She sighed. 'That was why my last crew came here. They wanted to change them.'

'Change them into what?'

Owl's forehead crumpled up. 'I'll try to explain this as best as I can. My last crew were two men. Brothers. Yes, I'll explain about brothers later. They were . . . they called themselves *Gaiists*, which are a type of people who – who believe Humans shouldn't have left Earth. They go around the galaxy and try to convince Humans to come back to the Sol system.'

'Why?'

'Because they think they're doing the right thing. It's complicated. Can we save that question for later?'

Jane brushed the mushroom pile together real tight, then picked her knife back up. 'Is it on your question list?'

'I just added it.'

'Okay.'

'Anyway, the people here don't want to change. The city people, anyway. Those brothers should've known better, but they were doing what they believed in.' She shook her head. 'They were kind people, but very foolish.'

'What's foolish?'

'A foolish person would reach into a machine without turning off the power.'

Jane frowned. 'That's stupid.'

Owl laughed. 'Yes, it is. Anyway, they were only with me a short time. They purchased the shuttle less than a standard before, but I mostly sat in the bay of their carrier ship. The carrier took them to the Han'foral tunnel, which is the closest one to here. Took about thirty-seven days to get from that tunnel to where we are now.'

Jane chopped the mushrooms smaller, smaller, smaller. The littler they were, the easier on her stomach. 'When was that?'

'About five years ago.'

Jane stopped chopping. She looked at the face in the wall. 'You've been here for five years? In the scrap?'

'Yes.'

Jane tried to think about how long ago five years was. She was ten now, so she was five when Owl had got to the planet. Jane couldn't remember being five very well. And in five *more* years, she'd be fifteen! Five years was a lot. 'Were you sad?' she asked.

'Yes. Yes, I was very sad.' Owl smiled, but it was a weird kind of smile, like it was hard to do. 'But we're together now, and I'm not sad any more.'

Jane stared at the mushroom bits, all purple and white and chewy. 'I'm still sad.'

'I know, sweetheart. And that's okay.'

They had talked a lot about *sad* a few days before, after Jane had thrown a box of stuff at the wall for reasons she couldn't explain. She'd yelled at Owl a lot, and said she wanted to go back to the factory, which she didn't really at all, so she didn't know why she'd said it. Then she'd cried again, which she was real tired of doing. She'd done a lot of bad behaviour that day, but Owl hadn't been angry. Instead, she'd told Jane to come sit next to the wall screen by her bed, close as she could to Owl's face, and Owl made some music until Jane stopped crying. Owl said it was okay to be sad about 64, and about the bad things that had happened at the factory. She said that was a kind of sad that would never go away, but it would get easier. It hadn't gotten easier yet. Jane wished it would hurry up.

She scooped up the mushroom bits into her hands and walked over to the stove. A stove was a hot thing you made food on. Owl could give it power now, ever since Jane had started cleaning off the outside of the ship – the *hull*. Now more of the coating on the hull could make power out of sunlight. Once Jane finished that task, Owl wouldn't have to choose which things worked and which things didn't. She could make a lot more things work now than she had at first. She could make the ship very warm and turn on all the lights inside, and the stove and the stasie worked. The shower worked now, too, because Jane had filled up the water tanks. That had taken six days of dragging the water wagon back and forth, back and forth. It had been stupid and bad, and there had been dogs a couple times (the weapon was such a good thing). But there was clean water now, and she didn't itch any more, and the bathroom wasn't gross. That all was good. But between that and the two days she'd spent cleaning scrap off of the ship, her arms and legs were real real tired. She wasn't bleeding or broken or anything, but she hurt.

She put a pan on the stove, dropped the mushrooms into it,

and turned the stove on real low. She had to be careful doing that. Mushrooms weren't very good to eat without being cooked, but if she cooked them too hot, they'd stick to the pan and they wouldn't be any good at all. She'd made that mistake the first time, and wasted a whole bunch of them. With as much work as it took to bring mushrooms home and get them ready, she didn't want to waste any ever again.

Jane had a thought she hadn't before. 'Did you have a crew before the . . . the two men?'

Owl had said she wasn't sad any more, but she *was* now. Her face said so. 'Yes. The shuttle was owned by a couple on Mars. They used the ship for vacations. Outer Sol system, mostly. The occasional tunnel hop. I was with them for ten years.'

The mushrooms started to make hissing sounds. Jane tried to keep an eye on them, but she was worried about Owl. She'd never heard her sound so wrong. 'Did they get arrested, too?'

'Oh, no. No, they sold the ship. They had two children, Mariko and Max. I watched them grow up in here. But after they became adults, the vacations stopped, and I guess . . . I guess their parents didn't need a shuttle any more.'

Jane frowned, watching the mushrooms wiggle against the pan. 'Did you want to stay with them?'

'Yes.'

'Did they know that?'

'I don't know. If they did, it wouldn't have mattered. That's not how the galaxy works.'

'Why?'

'Because AIs aren't people, Jane. You can't forget that about me. I'm not like you.'

Jane didn't understand why Owl being not like her would make her feelings not important, but the mushrooms were starting to get crispy around the edges, so she paid attention to that instead. It was easier than finding words.

There was a sound – a tapping kind of sound. Jane turned

her ear toward the ceiling. 'Owl, what is that?' She turned off the stove. The mushrooms hissed quieter; the tapping got louder. Like a bunch of little bolts falling onto the hull.

'It's nothing bad. Go up to the control room and I'll show you.'

Jane hurried out of the kitchen and did as told. Owl turned the viewscreen on and . . . and . . . Jane did not understand. It was morning, but the sky was kind of dark. And there was . . . there was . . .

'Owl,' Jane said slowly. 'Why is there water falling out of the sky?'

'That's called rain,' Owl said. 'Don't worry, it's supposed to happen.'

The tapping got louder, louder. Everything outside was wet. She saw a few lizard-birds (that was what Owl called the flying animals; she didn't know the right word for them). They flew down low, ducking into a scrap pile, shaking off their wings and tails to get the sky water off them.

Nothing outside the factory made any sense. Not any sense.

'Jane, it'd be a good idea for you to push the water wagon outside,' Owl said. 'With the drums open. They'll catch the rain that way.'

'Is it good water?' Jane wasn't sure about this rain thing. This was maybe the weirdest thing yet, and she'd seen a lot of weird things already.

'It's better than the water you brought back, for sure. It's probably not drinkable as it is, but it'll be easier to clean.'

'But the tanks are already full.' Pushing the water wagon outside meant *going outside*. Into the rain.

'They won't always be. This way, when you need to top them up, you don't have to go all the way back to the waterhole. You'll have a bit right here already.'

Jane took a deep breath. 'Okay.' The rain was weird and she didn't want to go into it, but her hurting legs and tired back made her think Owl's idea was better than one more trip to the waterhole. 'Wait,' she said. 'What am I supposed to do now?'

'I don't understand the question. What do you mean?'

'I mean today. I was going to finish cleaning the scrap off the hull. That was my task. Can I do that in the rain?' The water was coming down very fast now, falling in great big lines.

'Yes, but I suggest staying inside today. The rain here can be quite heavy, and wet clothes aren't fun. Plus, wet scrap is slippery. I don't want you to fall.'

'But . . .' Jane started feeling wrong. 'I don't have another task.' She needed a task. Without a task, her thoughts went places she didn't want them to go. She didn't want another bad behaviour day. She wanted to be okay today. She wanted to be okay, and if she didn't have a task, then—

'I have an idea,' Owl said. 'And actually, I think it would be a good idea even if it *wasn't* raining. Jane, you need a day off.'

Jane blinked. 'A day off of what?'

'Of work. All Human beings need to take a break from work sometimes. You need to let your body rest, and your mind, too.'

No. No no no. *She needed a task.* 'I don't want to do nothing,' she said, remembering that first morning in bed, when she'd tried to just lie there, and the couple days after that, when she couldn't get out of bed at all and it was a real real bad time.

'That's not what I'm suggesting,' Owl said. 'I've been going through my old files, and I found something I think might be fun. It's not a real task, but it will let you rest without doing nothing.'

Jane scrunched up her mouth. That sounded okay.

'I'll get it ready. I suggest eating your mushrooms before they get cold, then putting the wagon outside.' Owl's face did a happy wiggle inside the screen. 'Oh, I hope you like it.'

SIDRA

Sidra settled into the piece of furniture beside Tak's tool cabinet. It was an *eelim*, a sort of responsive chair that moulded itself around the body of the person using it. Sidra was fascinated as she watched the white material shift around the kit. She fought the urge to stand the kit up just so she could sit down and watch the *eelim* move again. But Tak was preparing his tools, and that was fascinating, too. He had a fresh pipe of tallflower, a full cup of mek, a gloved pair of hands. He loaded cartridges of colour bots into the industrial-looking needle pen, which looked a bit frightening, even in the hands of one so friendly.

'It doesn't use magnets, does it?' Sidra asked, eying the hefty machine as calmly as she could.

It was an odd thing to ask, she knew, but Tak seemed to take it as nothing more than quirk. 'Nope, just pumps and gravity. Why, you have implants you're worried about?'

'No,' Sidra said, glad the question hadn't been more specific.

'Well, even if you did, no magnets here. But it *is* going to hurt. You know that, right?'

Sidra chose her words carefully. 'I know that tattoos hurt, yes.' That much was true. She left out the part about not being able to feel pain. She'd practised wincing the night before. Blue had said she'd got it down.

Tak loaded the final cartridge with a decisive *snap*. He lit his pipe and inhaled deeply, ribbons of smoke curling out his flat nostrils. He gestured over his scrib, bringing up the image he and

Sidra had worked on so intently together. A crashing wave, teeming with all manner of sealife. The image moved, just as it would on the kit's skin, fins and tentacles gently, gently pulsing forward and back, no faster than a sigh. The movement was noticeable, but not distracting. It'd take the bots a full minute to cycle through the image. 'A subtle bit of background action,' as Tak had put it. Sidra looked at it hungrily, trying to imagine how it would look on her housing. Her pathways practically vibrated with excitement.

Tak noticed her eagerness. 'You ready to do this?'

Sidra leaned the kit back into the *eelim*. 'I'm ready.'

Tak sat in his workchair, dragging it close as he could to her. He disinfected the surface of the kit's skin with a small spray bottle, then shaved the fine hair away with a hand razor. Sidra hadn't realised that would be part of the process. That hair would never grow back, and having a bald patch on the kit's upper arm would look odd. She made a note to shave the rest of the kit's arms at home. It would be less obvious that way.

Tak tapped the pen on. It was louder than Sidra expected, though maybe only due to its closeness. The needle touched the kit's arm; she directed the kit to inhale softly. Tak pushed the needle through the skin; Sidra closed the kit's eyes. The needle buzzed forward. She inhaled again, a little sharper, a little shorter, just as she and Blue had practised.

Tak pulled the needle back. 'That's how it feels. Is that okay?'

'That's okay.'

'You're gonna do great, I know it. Just let me know if you need a break.' He leaned in, moving the needle with the same care and sincerity as Blue with his brushes, as Pepper with her tools. Sidra watched with interest as little lines of still-dormant bots appeared, dark and clear below the surface. The kit bled. Tak dabbed the dishonest red liquid up with the corner of a clean cloth. He saw no difference.

'So,' Tak said, never taking his eyes off his work. 'I watched that vid series you mentioned last time. The documentary on the first Exodans leaving the Sol system.'

A warm little glow danced through Sidra's pathways. 'What'd you think?'

'Absolutely fascinating,' Tak said. 'It lost me a bit toward the end—'

'The montage of images of the original crew?'

'Yeah. Dragged on a little too long. But don't get me wrong, I thought it was terrific overall. Much, much better than the scraps about Human expansion I learned as a kid.'

Sidra was delighted that her recommendation had been well received. 'If you want to keep going in that vein, there's another series called *Children of War*. It's not quite as weighty, but I think it offers some very good complementary ideas about the politics on Mars at the time.' She processed. 'You went to university, right?'

'I did.' A nostalgic orange-flecked ripple crossed Tak's cheeks. 'I had aims to be an historian when I was younger. Started my certification track and everything.'

'Really?'

'Really. It's the only time I've lived away from here. Spent three standards at Ontalden – you know it?'

'No.'

'It's one of the big universities on Sohep Frie. Had a lot of appeal to me back then. I wanted to see the homeworld, wanted to see what life was like outside of the Port.' He shifted his pipe from one side of his mouth to the other. 'But it wasn't for me, in the end. I love learning. I love history. But there's history in everything. Every building, everybody you talk to. It's not limited to libraries and museums. I think people who spend their lives in school forget that sometimes.'

Sidra wished she could watch the needle and Tak's expressions at once. She was keen on processing both. 'Why wasn't it "for you"?'

Tak thought as he worked. 'I like history because it's a way of understanding people. Understanding why we're all like we are right now. Especially in a place like this.' He rocked his head toward the door, toward the multispecies crowd beyond the wall. 'I wanted to understand my friends and neighbours better. But when I was on Sohep Frie, I spent a lot of time holed up in the university archives, learning about my own species' history. We shons, you know, we used to be cultural conduits. We brought a little bit of each village with us when we switched between. Something about that really spoke to me. Not like it's in my genes, or something. I don't believe we're defined by *this*.' He held up the wet rag, speckled with false blood. 'But that idea of being an ambassador of sorts grabbed me, for whatever reason. I realised I wanted to work with a more tangible kind of history. That's why I do bot ink, and scale dying, and all that stuff. There are few better ways to get to know how a species thinks than to learn their art.' Tak lifted the needle off the kit's skin, adjusting his pipe between his delicate teeth. 'You sure you've never done this before?' he asked, nodding toward the kit's arm. 'You're doing really well.'

A jolt of nervousness shot through her. She'd forgotten to maintain the appearance of pain. 'Yes.' She gave the kit a tight smile that communicated toughness – or so she hoped. It was a good thing that she'd seen so little of physical pain, but some frame of reference for how often and to what degree she should make the kit look uncomfortable would've been helpful. She chastised herself for not thinking to find some vids of organic sapients getting tattoos. Still, Tak seemed impressed, and in Sidra's estimation, that was a good turn of events.

They sat that way for an hour and a half – Tak altering the kit, Sidra watching his progress and pulling faces, the time punctuated by idle chit-chat (vids, food, waterball) and lulls of comfortable silence when Tak was most focused.

At last, Tak sat back, switching off the pen. 'All right,' he said. 'There's your first layer. What do you think? Let me know if there's something you don't like. You won't hurt my feelings.'

Sidra examined the outline that had been driven into the kit's synthetic skin. The kit started smiling almost before she'd had time to process. 'This is great,' she said.

'Yeah?'

'Yeah, it's wonderful.' The kit grinned at him. 'Can we do the next layer now?'

Tak laughed, talkbox bobbing in his throat. 'I need a short break, and so do you. I'll get us both some water.'

Sidra eyed the static outline, and imagined it with colour, motion, life. 'Can I see how it's going to move?'

'Sure,' Tak said. 'You won't get the full effect yet, but I can show you where it's at right now.' He picked up his scrib and accessed some sort of control program. 'I'll just activate it for a few seconds, then shut it back down.'

Tak gestured at the scrib. In an instant, Sidra's excitement turned to fear. A dozen warning notifications leaped to the forefront of her pathways – system errors, signal errors, feedback errors. Something was wrong.

'Sidra?' Tak said, cheeks anxious. 'You o—'

Sidra didn't hear the rest. The kit convulsed, doubling over and falling forward. She was dimly aware of Tak catching her, but her knowledge of that was buried beneath error after error, flashing red and urgent. And her pathways – her pathways didn't make sense. Things were stuck. Things were falling. Things were opening and closing with her on both sides of the door. What was she saying? Was she saying something? No, Tak was: 'I'm calling emergency services. Sidra? Sidra, stay with me.'

An interesting thing happened: Sidra heard herself speak, even though she couldn't see the process that made her do so. 'No – Pepper. Not – services. Pepper. Get Pepper.'

She wasn't sure which part of her was still running speech protocols, but it was a good thing they were working, because the rest of her was losing the fight in keeping the kit still, and her pathways really couldn't process anything more than—

JANE, AGE 10

A day off. And Owl said she had something fun! Jane ate her mushrooms real fast, along with two bites of ration bar (Owl said they had good things in them that mushrooms didn't, and she should have a little bit with her mushrooms every day until the bars ran out). She washed the food down with filtered water from the sink. It still tasted different from the water they drank at the factory, but it was much much better than the packets. Not just because it was cold and clean and didn't taste like packaging, but also because the reason the sink water was there in the first place was because she'd brought it home. She was drinking water she'd got herself, and that made it taste extra good.

She put the wagon outside, too. The rain was *everywhere*. She wanted to stand and look at it, wanted to try to see where it was falling from, but it was cold and making her clothes all wet. It only took a minute of standing in it for her to understand that she didn't like rain very much.

She went back inside, then followed Owl into the bedroom. 'Okay, look under the bed,' Owl said. 'Not your bed, the other one. It should still be under there.'

'What should?' Jane said, getting down on her hands and knees. There were boxes under there with stuff that had belonged to one of the men who had brought Owl to the planet. Not much of the stuff had been useful, except for the pocket knife.

'Here, I'll show you. Look here.' Owl's face went away from the wall screen, and a picture of a funny-looking piece of tech came up – some kind of a small net, with goggles and wires that Jane didn't know the point of.

Jane dug around under the bed until she found the thing, put away real careful in a box. 'What is it?' she asked.

'It's a sim cap,' Owl said. 'It's a piece of tech that tells you a story inside your head.'

Jane stared into the box. *Nothing here made sense.* 'Like a dream?'

'Yes, but it makes more sense than a dream, and you can interact with it.'

'What's interact?'

'Do stuff with it. Pretend that you're really there. It's not real. It's all made up, but it can show you lots of different things. I think you might like it.'

Jane touched the wires. There was nothing pokey or sharp, nothing that would go inside her head. She picked up the net. She could see now that it was round, and had little soft patches all along the inside. Some kind of feedback patches. The other wires were covered with them too. The wires split into five ends each – hands? Were they for her hands? 'What stories will it show me?' Jane asked.

'Different kinds of stories. I have a small selection of sims in storage. Most of them are for grown-ups, but I have a few for kids. I remembered them when you asked about . . . about the family that owned the ship. Their kids played sims when they had long trips.'

'What's kids?'

'Children.'

'Am I a kids?

'You're a *kid*, yes.'

Jane took that in. 'I'm a Human and a person and a girl and a kid.' That seemed like a lot of labels for just one girl.

Owl smiled. 'That's right.'

Jane looked back at the box. 'How do I put this on?'

'Put the round thing over your head. There's a strap on the

bottom so you can pull it tight against your skin. Yes, good. Now, those long bits are like gloves. Put the caps over each fingertip, and pull the little straps tight.'

Jane did as she was told. The caps on the net and gloves stuck onto her skin real tight. It was weird, but not bad. She picked up the goggles. 'And these?'

'You should lie down before you put those on. You won't be able to see out of them.'

Jane lay down on her bed and put the goggles on. Owl was right – they made the whole room go away. It wasn't scary, she told herself. Owl said it was okay. Owl said it was okay.

'I'm going to upload the sim to the kit now,' Owl said. 'And don't worry, I'm right here. You can still talk to me, even when it's playing.'

Jane relaxed into her pillow. She heard a little click as something activated in the goggles. The net pressed very, very softly into her scalp, like it was grabbing it. The gloves hugged her fingers, too. Her skin tingled. *Owl said it was okay.*

The darkness started to go away. Then . . . then it got weird.

She was standing in an empty space, lit with soft yellow light. She wasn't standing, not really. She was still lying down in bed. But she was *also* standing in the yellow place. Lying down felt more real; standing felt like a memory. But it was a memory that was happening *right that second*.

Nothing. Here. Made. Sense.

A glowing ball rose up out of the ground with a hum. It stopped right in front of her face. '*Tek tem!*' it said, pulsing bright with each word. '*Kebbi sum?*'

Jane swallowed. Owl had taught her *tek tem*. Those were Klip words for *hello*. But she didn't understand anything else the ball said. 'Um . . . I'm . . . I don't understand.'

'*Oh!*' the ball said. The sound of its voice had changed. '*Am sora! Hoo spak Ensk! Weth all spak Ensk agath na. Ef hoo gan larin Klip?*'

She frowned. Some of those words were almost like normal

words, but the rest . . . weren't. She felt tired already. 'Owl?' she called.

Owl's voice appeared all around her, as if there were speakers everywhere. 'I'm sorry, Jane,' Owl said, 'I didn't think about the language packs. Give me just a minute. There *must* be a module for Sko-Ensk, this franchise got a grant from the Diaspora – ah, here we are. Things may go dark for a second, don't be scared.'

'I'm not scared,' Jane said.

Things went dark, just as Owl had said. Okay, fine, it was a *little* scary. She was all the way back in bed, but she couldn't see anything. She didn't like that at all. But only a second or two went by before the warm yellow space returned, and the ball of light came back. 'Hi there!' it said. 'What's your name?'

Jane relaxed. The ball spoke with the same weird kind of voice sound that Owl had (*accent*, Owl had said – it was called an *accent*), but Jane could understand it now. 'I'm Jane,' she said.

'Welcome, Jane! Is this your first time in a sim, or have you played others before?'

She bit her thumbnail (or the memory of it, anyway). This whole thing made her feel a little silly. 'First time.'

'Awesome! You're in for a treat! I'm the Game Globe. I help make the sim fit you just right. If you ever need to change something, or if you need to leave, just yell "Game Globe!" and I'll help you out. Okay?'

'Um, okay.'

'Great! So how old are you, Jane?'

'Ten.'

'Are you in school?'

'No.' Owl had explained school. It sounded like fun. 'But Owl's teaching me.'

'Sorry, I didn't quite understand that. Is Owl a grown-up?'

'Owl is an AI,' she said. 'I live with her in a shuttle and she helps me be okay.'

'Sorry, I didn't quite understand that,' the ball said. 'What's—'

Owl's voice cut in. 'Just tell it I'm your parent, Jane,' Owl said. 'It's easier. That thing isn't sentient.'

Jane didn't know what *parent* or *sentient* meant, but she did as told. 'Owl's my parent.'

'Got it!' the ball said. 'I'm going to ask you a few questions, just to see what kind of stuff you already know. Okay?'

'Okay.'

'Great!' The ball wiggled, then dissolved into shapes – reading squiggles, like on the boxes in the shuttle. There were a lot of them. A whole big lot of them, much more than on boxes. 'Can you read this back to me?' the ball said.

'No.'

'Okay.' The squiggles changed. There were less of them now. 'Can you read this?'

'No,' Jane said. Her cheeks felt hot. This was a test, and she was failing it. 'I can't read.'

The squiggles melted together into the Game Globe. 'That's okay! Thank you for telling me. Do you know how to count?'

'Yes,' she said, sighing.

Owl's voice came back. 'Jane, hang on just a minute. I'm going to tweak this thing's protocols. This is supposed to be fun, not an interrogation.'

'What's an intro—'

'It's when somebody asks you too many questions. Here, I'm going to configure the educational parameters for you. Let's see . . . starter reading, starter math, starter Klip, starter species studies, starter science, starter code, and . . . I'm going to go ahead and say *advanced technology*.'

The Game Globe held perfectly still for a few seconds, frozen in the middle of a pulse. 'Thanks for answering my questions, Jane! Now, hang on tight – your adventure's about to begin!'

The Game Globe spun away, like a crazy spark. The light in the yellow space followed it. For a moment, there was nothing.

The nothing didn't last long. So much stuff happened at once.

A bunch of colours burst all around her, big stripes of them stretching out farther than she could see. Two kids stepped through doors that appeared in the air. A girl and a *boy*. That was very exciting, because Jane hadn't seen a boy except in the pictures Owl had showed her. But neither the girl nor the boy looked real. Their bodies were shaped wrong – big round heads, big thick lines along their clothes – and their colours were all the way solid, like paint. They were weird, but there was something nice about them, too. She liked looking at them.

The kids were opposites of each other, kind of. The boy had dark brown skin, and yellowish hair that was real fun, all curled in soft circles. The girl – the girl wasn't like any girl Jane had ever seen. She had shiny black hair that fell all the way down her back, like a blanket but way nicer. She was brown, too, but a different brown than the boy. Kind of like Jane's pink skin, but not really. Later, she would ask Owl for more colour words. There had to be better words.

Jane could've looked at the kids for a long time, but things went real fast after they showed up. An animal dropped down from somewhere way up high and landed on its feet. It wasn't a dog, or a lizard-bird, or anything she'd seen. It had feet and hands kind of like a kid, was red-brown and furry, and had a tail like a dog did, but much longer and thinner. It had a silly face, too: fat cheeks and stick-out ears and a squashed-in nose. There was something in the animal's hand – a curled, shiny metal thing, with a big opening at one end and a smaller one at the other. The animal blew into the small end, and a loud music sound came out: *BAAAAAH-BAH-BAH-BAH-BAHHHH!*

The kids threw their not-real hands up in the air. The colours spun and bounced. The kids talked music.

Engines on! Fuel pumps, go!
Grab your gear, there's lots to know
Our galaxy is where we play

Come with us, we know the way!
BIG BUG!
From ground and sky!
BIG BUG!
By stars we fly!
BIG BUG!
We're the Big Bug Crew!
The Big Bug Crew and YOOOOOU!

'Hey, Jane!' the not-real girl said. 'I'm Manjiri.'

'I'm Alain,' the not-real boy said. Her — *his*, Jane reminded herself. Boys got a different word. *His* accent was different than Manjiri's but the same as Owl's. Jane didn't know why that was, but it was interesting.

'And this is our best buddy, Pinch!' the kids said together, putting their open hands toward the animal. The animal did a silly jump.

Jane did not move. She said nothing. The rain was not the weirdest thing any more, not by a lot.

'This is your first time playing a sim, right?' Alain said. 'Don't worry. This is gonna be fun!'

Manjiri grinned. 'We're so excited for you to be with us on our latest adventure—'

The kids and the animal raised their hands up toward the air, where a bunch of red reading squiggles appeared, lit with yellow sparks. 'THE BIG BUG CREW AND THE PLANETARY PUZZLE!' the kids shouted.

'Come on!' Alain said. 'We've got to get to the ship!' He waved his hand over the air and a doorway appeared, not held up by anything. Jane couldn't see anything through the door, either. Just colours swirling like smoke.

She felt weird, like she was wearing too little clothing. She wanted to go back to her room. She wanted a real task. 'Um . . .'

'Are you feeling nervous?' Manjiri said. 'That's okay. Everybody feels nervous when trying new things. Would you feel better if I held your hand?'

Jane's eyes went huge. Could she do that? Could they touch her? She nodded, once, hard.

The not-real girl's hand felt like a memory of being held, but oh – oh, it was close enough! Something all knotted up inside Jane's chest let go. She squeezed her hand; the made-up hand squeezed back. Holding hands was *good*, more good than not being hungry, more good than she knew how to say.

The furry animal ran up Manjiri's back and hopped onto Jane's shoulder. Jane jumped, but the animal just hung on and snuggled in, making silly sounds. The kids laughed. Jane decided the animal was okay.

'Come on,' Manjiri said, leading the way, still holding Jane's hand. Jane followed her through the smoky colours. They tickled in a good way as she went through, and there was the sound of lots of kids laughing. Jane felt a little better, though she still wasn't sure about any of this.

They stepped into a ship. Even though the only ship Jane had ever seen was the one she and Owl lived in, she knew this one was no more real than the kids were. The walls, the ceilings, the consoles – they were all big and round and soft-looking, with buttons and knobs that didn't look very functional. Everything was bright bright colours – green mostly, but also red and blue and yellow. It was noisy in there, too. Lots of beeps and whistles and music sounds. There were two big bubble windows at the front, with lots of not-real stars on the other side. In front of the windows were three consoles, each with reading squiggles at the top. A big squashy chair sat in front of each one. They looked good to sit in.

'This is our ship,' Manjiri said. 'The *Big Bug!*'

'The *Big Bug's* a special ship,' Alain said. 'In the real world, ships are powered by different kinds of fuel. Do you know any kinds of fuel?'

'Um,' Jane said. She licked her lips. 'Algae. Sunlight. Ambi.'

She thought hard, and remembered what Owl had found in the water she brought home. 'S . . . scrub?'

'That's right!' Manjiri said. 'Those are all common types of fuel. But we don't use those here. The *Big Bug* is a ship powered by imaaaaaagination.' She spread her fingers out flat and wiggled them through the air.

'With imagination, you can go anywhere!' Alain said.

Jane didn't know what that stuff was, but it sounded pretty useful. She wondered if she could find some for the shuttle.

'Jane, do you live on a ship, or on a planet?' Manjiri asked.

Jane rubbed the back of her neck. 'Both,' she said.

The kids nodded together. 'Lots of families go back and forth,' Manjiri said.

'If you live on a ship, then you already know that you should never ever fly one without a grown-up,' Alain said. Pinch nodded twice, crossing his furry arms across his chest. 'But in an imagination ship, we don't need grown-ups! We can do everything ourselves!'

Alain and Manjiri each raised one of their hands and slapped their palms together. They ran to the consoles, real excited. Manjiri took the one on the left, and Alain took the one on the right.

The kids pointed to the console between them. 'This one's for you, Jane!' Manjiri said. Pinch jumped on top of the empty chair, doing another silly flip. He sure was a busy little animal.

Jane sat in the chair, which felt just as snuggly as it looked. Pinch hopped down and sat in her lap. She held still for a minute, then slowly, slowly reached out to touch his head. Pinch made an *ooooo* sound, and with his eyes scrunched tight, rubbed his soft head up into her palm. Jane laughed, but just a little, real quiet. She knew she wouldn't get in trouble for laughing here, but laughing was bad behaviour, and it made her nervous.

'Okay,' Alain said. 'Let's find out our mission for today!'

'Hey, Bumble!' Manjiri said. 'Wake up!'

A face appeared on all of their console screens: big, fuzzy, yellow, not at all like a person. Jane understood it was an

AI like Owl, even though Owl had a person's face. This wasn't a real AI, though. Nothing here was real.

The yellow fuzzy face yawned and smacked its lips. 'Aw, is it time to get up already?'

Alain laughed. 'Oh, Bumble! You're gonna sleep the day away!'

Manjiri pointed at Jane's screen. 'Jane, this is Bumble, our AI. Xe's going to tell us where we're going today.' Jane knew that person word, too. It was the one for people who weren't girls or boys, and also what you said if you didn't know which they were. It was kind of exciting, hearing somebody besides Owl use words that Jane had learned. It made her feel like she was learning important stuff.

Bumble shook xyr face, and looked a little more awake. 'Today, you're off to Theth!' xe said. A picture of a big striped planet with rings and a whole bunch of moons appeared on the bubble windows. 'You'll be meeting with our good friend Heshet, who says he needs our help! Some of Theth's moons have gone missing!'

Jane frowned. Could moons go missing? That seemed wrong. They were real big.

Bumble put another little picture in front of the one of the planet. It was a person, but— 'Hey!' Jane said, pointing. 'I know that species! They're, um . . . they're . . . oh . . .' She tried to remember. She was a Human species. Aeluons were the silver ones. Hermigeans were the squishy ones. Quelin had lots of legs. This one was none of those. This one was green, and had a flat face, and . . . oh, why couldn't she find the word?

Alain smiled. 'Heshet is an Aandrisk,' he said.

Aandrisk. Right. But there was something different about him than the pictures Owl had showed her of that species. 'Where's his, um . . .' Another word she couldn't find! She felt all dumb inside. She waved her hand over the top of her head, trying to explain.

'Do you mean feathers?' Manjiri asked.

'Yes!' Jane said. 'Yes. Feathers. Where's his feathers?'

'Aandrisks don't get feathers until they start to become grown-ups,' Manjiri said. 'Heshet's a kid like us!'

Jane thought about her smooth head, which would never have feathers, or hair, either. Would she always look like a kid to Aandrisks, even when she got older?

'Okay, Jane, it's time to plot our course,' Alain said. Jane's interface panel changed. There was a picture on it – a bunch of coloured circles with little curvy lines between. 'These are the tunnels that can get us from here to Hashkath, the moon where Heshet lives. Can you figure out the shortest way to get there? Draw your finger from here to there to give it a try.'

Jane looked at the lines real careful, then at how they connected to the blinking circle they were supposed to get to. It reminded her of rewiring a circuit. Easy. She traced her finger along the screen, the path behind it turning blue.

'Wow!' Manjiri said. 'First try! Good job!'

Pinch made animal sounds and clapped his hands. She hadn't done much, but Jane felt good anyway.

'Great!' Alain said. 'Now hit the autopilot button and we'll be on our way! It's the big red button in the middle.'

Jane saw the big red button. There were a lot of other buttons, too, and . . . *oh no*. All the buttons were marked with reading squiggles. Would these kids need her to push buttons fast? Did she have to be on task? Her stomach sank. 'I can't read,' she said.

'We know,' Alain said in a voice that made her feel safe. He reached over and squeezed her shoulder. 'Don't worry! Everybody has to learn how. We'll help you practise.'

'This one says "autopilot",' Manjiri said, pointing at a big red button. 'And this one says "stop".' She got a big grin. 'And this—' She pointed not at a button, but the long block on top of the console. 'Do you know what this says?'

Jane pressed her lips together and shook her head.

'That's you,' Manjiri said. 'That's how you spell "Jane".'

SIDRA

Everything was gone for a while. When it came back, Blue was there, looking hugely relieved.

'She's awake!' His face melted into a smile. 'W – uh, welcome back,' he said, squeezing the kit's hand. Sidra wondered how long he'd been holding it. She had no record on that point.

There was the sound of someone getting up fast. Pepper appeared, placing a hand on Blue's shoulder as she plunked herself into a chair. A chair. Tak's chairs. They were in the tattoo shop.

Why were they in the tattoo shop?

'Oh, stars,' Pepper said. 'Stars, it worked.' Her head fell forward, pressing against the side of the kit. 'Shit.' She sat back up, quickly, her eyes darting over the kit's face. 'Are you feeling okay? Gimme a diagnostic.'

Sidra ran a systems check, as directed. Line by line, the results came back: *Go. Go. Go.* 'I'm fine,' she said, and she felt it, too. 'Though—' She rifled through her memory files. 'I don't know how you got here. I don't know *when* you got here. What time is it?'

'A little after thirteen,' Blue said. 'You've, uh, you've been out for an hour.'

An hour. In Tak's shop. And Pepper had told her to run a diag— oh, *no*.

The kit sat up, and Sidra looked around. The front shutters were drawn. The door was shut. Tak was leaning against a corner wall, as far away from them as he could be. He puffed his pipe, face taut, cheeks a pensive yellow.

He knew.

Sidra looked back to Pepper, away from Tak's silent stare. 'What happened?' she whispered.

Pepper sighed. 'So, as it turns out, nanobot ink doesn't play nicely with your bots. Their signals interfered with the signals travelling from your core to the kit. It made everything flip out.' Her eyes flicked to Tak, her gaze hard and careful. Sidra knew that look. It was the same look Pepper had when she was assessing something combustible. 'Tak called us, and we . . . we figured it out. I—' She frowned with discomfort '—I directed you to go into standby mode until all the bots were out.'

Sidra had no record of the directive, but she knew Pepper well enough to know that triggering a system protocol that forced Sidra to turn herself off would not sit right with her. 'You had to,' Sidra said. 'I understand.'

Pepper shut her eyes and gave a single nod.

'He re – um, removed the ink,' Blue said, looking at Tak with a smile. 'It was a – a real, uh, a real – a real big help.' His tone was friendly – too friendly, and his words were sticking more than usual.

Tak gave a short, polite Aeluon smile that vanished almost as soon as it had appeared. His cheeks roiled with nervous conflict. He emptied the ash from his pipe, then began to refill it.

Pepper and Blue exchanged a worried glance. The same concern crept through Sidra. Tak *knew*, and they didn't know *him* at all. *I don't even know him*, Sidra thought. *We had a nice conversation, and I confused that for knowing someone. So stupid. So stupid.* And yet, of all the deadly serious things she was scared of in that moment – Tak calling the Port Authority, Pepper and Blue getting in trouble, the likelihood of the kit being deactivated with her still in it – the situational variable that was stuck in the loudest, most unhappy processing loop was the thought of Tak no longer wanting to hang out with her. *So stupid.*

'Can we go home?' she said quietly, doing her best to not meet Tak's eye.

Pepper turned to the shopkeeper. 'Listen. Tak. I'm truly grateful for your help today. We all are. And I'm really sorry for the scare you went through. Blue and I – we take responsibility for that.'

'Pepper—' Sidra said.

Pepper carried on. 'We knew she was coming here today, and the potential for risk didn't occur to either of us. It was a major oversight on our part. I can't apologise enough.' She met the kit's eyes. 'To both of you.' Pepper pressed her lips together, choosing her words with care. 'I know the situation here is . . . unusual.'

Tak gave a short, audible exhale – a relative rarity for his silent species. It was a scoff, a reaction that happened too quick for talkbox phrasing. Sidra's pathways felt as if they were folding in on themselves. She wanted to go home. She wanted to be anywhere that wasn't here.

Pepper didn't miss a beat. 'If you want money, we can pay you. That's no problem. Or free fix-it services, we can arrange—'

Tak cut her off. 'I won't say anything. Okay? It's fine. I've seen plenty of weird modder shit and I really don't care. It is not my business. I just don't want it coming back to me if this project of yours gets found out. I don't know about this, okay? I don't know about this, and I have nothing to do with it.'

'You think she's – it's not like that. Sidra's not a project.'

'Okay. I told you, I don't care.'

Blue helped the kit up. 'C-come on,' he whispered. 'We, uh, we should go.'

Pepper sighed. 'Okay,' she said to Tak. A tightness crept into her voice, but she remained civil. She owed him, and she knew it. 'Thank you for being cool about this.'

Sidra headed for the door with Blue, but something made her turn back around. She and Tak stared at each other across the long room. Sidra wasn't quite sure what he was feeling. She got the impression maybe he didn't know either.

'I'm sorry,' Sidra said. 'I didn't mean for any of this to happen.'

Tak looked not to her, but to the Humans accompanying her.

Looked at them like you might look at a child's parents if the kid asked something odd. Like you might look at the owner of a pet that strayed into your house.

'I came here on my own,' she said, her voice loud, her pathways spiking with injury and anger. 'I came here. It wasn't a directive. It wasn't a task. I wanted to see you. I thought you could help me. I didn't mean to cause trouble.'

'Hey,' Pepper said softly, putting her hand on the kit's arm. 'Sweetie, come on. Let's go home.'

'Wait,' Tak said. 'Wait.' He was looking at Sidra now. His pipe smouldered between his fingers. 'What—' He paused, uncomfortable, unsure. 'What did you want my help with?'

'I already told you,' Sidra said. 'Twice, we've talked about it.' She gestured at the kit. 'This isn't me. And *you* – you understood how I felt about that. Or you did, before an hour ago.' She searched his face, looking for some glimmer of recognition, for that easy dynamic they'd fallen into when Tak had thought they were more or less the same. She saw only confusion and smoke. 'I'm sorry,' she said again. *So stupid.* She walked out of the shop and into the marketplace. Pepper and Blue followed close behind, their silence hanging thick between them. The crowd flowed around her, dozens of faces, dozens of names, dozens of stories in progress. She'd never felt so alone.

JANE, ALMOST 12

The shuttle hatch slid open. Jane entered, dragging her heavy haul on squeaking wheels. 'I got some good stuff today.' She knocked the dust off her shoes (made with thick rubber from a tyre liner, topped with cushion foam and a lot of wrap-around fabric from an old exosuit) and took off her jacket (more scavenged fabric, but from a real ugly chair). She left both by the door. 'Check it out.' She heard Owl's cameras whir towards her as she started pulling stuff off of the wagon. 'Switch couplers, fabric—'

'What's "fabric" in Klip?' Owl asked.

'*Delet.*'

'That's right. And what's that thing behind the fabric?'

Jane glanced at the dead dog, hanging over the back of the wagon. '*Bashorel.*'

'Can you make a sentence in Klip with that word?' Owl asked.

Jane thought. '*Laeken pa bashorel toh.*'

'Almost. *Lae*-ket *kal bashorel toh.*'

'*Laeket pa bashorel toh.* Why?'

'Because you haven't eaten the dog yet. You're *going* to eat the dog.'

Dog had joined mushrooms on the list of food things a long while back. Owl's idea. Taking them apart was gross, but it wasn't any grosser than scrubbing old tacky fuel gunk out of an engine or something. Gross was gross, whether it was animal or machine.

Jane rolled her eyes at the Klip correction. 'That's a dumb rule.'

Owl laughed. 'Languages are full of dumb rules. Klip's one of the easiest ones. Most sapients would say it's much easier than Sko-Ensk.'

'Can you say something in Standard Ensk?' Jane had asked this before, of course, but hearing Owl speak different languages was real fun.

'*A ku spok anat, nor hoo datte spak Ensk.*'

Jane laughed. 'That's so weird.' She began to unpack her finds, putting them into boxes with things like them. Owl had suggested that she label the boxes in Klip. *Boli*. Wires. *Goiganund*. Circuits. *Timdrak*. Plating. Her letters weren't as neat as the ones Owl showed her on screen, but she was getting better. Alain and Manjiri were helping. They had a practice mode where she could work on things she was supposed to be learning in school. It was nice, learning stuff with other kids, even though they were pretend, even though they said the same sorts of sentences over and over after a while. Owl said it was important for Jane to remember how to talk to other people. She said it was maybe the most important thing, after getting the ship fixed.

Jane put the fabric in the *delet* box. 'Do any other species speak Sko-Ensk?'

'I think that'd be very rare. Maybe some people at schools or museums. Spacers living out near the border might speak it. I'm not really sure.'

Jane tossed a bolt onto a pile and watched it tumble down. 'Will they think I'm weird if I don't speak Klip right?'

'No, sweetheart. But you will have an easier time if you know more words when we get out of here. You'll be able to tell people what you want and what you don't, and you can answer questions. You'll make more friends if you can talk to people.'

Jane dragged the wagon over to the utility hose and dumped the dog into the basin below it, holding her face as far away as she could from its stinking fur. She hosed it down, watching dirt and bits of whatever swirl down the drain. A few small bugs tried to get away. Jane smashed them with her thumb. She felt bad about it, but they weren't big enough to eat, and they'd just make her itch.

She sighed as she turned the dog over. She really didn't like washing them, or the part that came after. Making dogs into food wasn't fun. They tasted all right, though, if she cooked the pieces on the stove for a long time. It was a heavy taste, like smoke and rust. They kept her fuller than ration bars, which was the best part, because there were only a couple dozen of those left, and she had to keep them for emergencies. She reminded herself of that as she moved the fur around, getting it clean as she could. Some of the fur was burned where her latest weapon had touched it. This model killed dogs faster, which was good, but it made their fur catch fire real easy. She felt kind of bad about that, too . . . but not really.

'Do you think the dogs know I'm eating other dogs?' The packs had been bothering her less these days, and she'd wondered.

'Possibly, yes.'

'Because they can smell their blood on me?'

'That's quite likely, actually.'

Jane nodded. That was good. She took off all her clothes, folded them, and set them far away. She wrapped a clear tarp around herself, the one she'd cut arm holes in and laced a woven cord through like a belt. She picked up the big kitchen knife from the edge of the basin, where she'd left it a few days before. She sucked air through her teeth as she closed her fingers around the grip.

'Is your hand still bad?' Owl asked.

'It's okay,' Jane said, so Owl wouldn't worry. She still hadn't found a pair of work gloves that fit her right, which made digging through scrap hard. Bare hands were much easier to work with, but that meant getting cuts, like the bad one she'd got across her palm a week ago. Owl said she needed stitches, but after an explanation of how that was done, Jane knew that was not a thing she could do. So, she'd closed the skin up with some circuit glue, which Owl hadn't liked, but she didn't have any better ideas. The cut wasn't bleeding any more, but stars, it still hurt.

She looked at the soaked dead dog, lying in shrinking puddles of dirt and squished bugs, tongue hanging out like an old wet sock. It was so ugly. It was about to get worse.

She chewed her thumbnail. It tasted of plex and sweat and old metal, and some nasty badness she couldn't name. Maybe a bit of bug. 'Do you think other sapients will smell blood on me?'

'No, sweetie,' Owl said, her face filling up the closest screen like a sun. 'You'll be nice and clean when we meet other people.'

'And you'll be with me, right?'

'Of course I will.'

'Okay,' Jane said. 'That's good.' She took a breath, raised her knife, and got to work.

Feed source: unknown
Encryption: 4
Translation: 0
Transcription: 0
Node identifier: unknown

Post subject: REPOST – Seeking heavily-altered derelict shuttle,
    see full post for details
pinch: i'm searching for a Centaur *46*-C, approximately *25*
    standards old, extensively repaired and altered. few parts left in
    original factory condition. faded tan hull, photovoltaic coating. if
    you have any information about its current location, please
    message me. you don't have to have it, just know where it is.
fluffyfluffycake: good luck, as always
FunkyFronds: i swear, i could sync my clocks by when this post
    goes up. where did the past eight tendays go?
tishtesh: how long are you gonna keep reposting this
pinch: until i find it

Part 2

. . . .

PULL

SIDRA

Sorting tech supplies was boring, but boring had become preferable. Boring meant there was nothing to worry about. Boring was safe.

Sidra logged inventory as she worked. *Seven bolts*. She placed them in their bin. *Two tethering cables*. She placed them in their bin. *One regulator grid* – or . . . wait. 'Pepper?' she called, craning the kit's head toward the workshop door.

'One sec,' Pepper called from the front counter, shouting over her welding torch. The security shield around the shop had been flickering when they got in that morning. Probably just some wiring that wore out, Pepper said, but it bothered Sidra enough that her host had wasted no time in starting repairs. Over the past twenty-six days, Sidra had been particular about locking doors, closing windows, avoiding customers she hadn't seen before. She felt it best to volunteer for boring jobs that kept her in the workshop, out of sight. Sorting supplies fit the bill, and it was a task that Pepper was always happy to relinquish.

The torch hissed quiet, and Pepper stuck her head through the doorway. 'What's up?'

Sidra showed her the part in the kit's hand. 'I don't know what this is.'

'That,' Pepper said, squinting, 'is an overload buffer.'

Sidra made record of that. 'Where should I put it?'

Pepper looked over her hand-labelled bins. 'Just toss it in with the other regulators. I'll remember it's there.' She smirked at Sidra. 'And so will you.'

The kit smiled as Sidra filed away the overload buffer's location into her *workshop storage* log. 'I will.'

There was a pause. 'So,' Pepper said, clearing her throat, 'Blue and I were thinking about closing up shop and doing something fun tomorrow.'

Sidra didn't reply.

'They're having an adults-only day at the Bouncehouse,' Pepper continued hopefully. 'Only takes an hour to get up there, and it's real kick in the pants.'

Sidra knew of the Bouncehouse – a giant zero-g playground housed in a low-orbit satellite. She'd seen its designated shuttle port near the Undersea station at Kukkesh, seen the big flashing sign that pictured a laughing, multispecies group of youngsters diving through ringed obstacle courses and playing with globs of floating water. It *did* look like fun.

She'd already guessed what Pepper was going to say next: 'You want to come with?'

Sidra picked up another part – an air tube – and put it in its bin. 'I think I'll just stay home,' she said, forcing the kit to smile. 'You two have a good time.'

Pepper started to say something, but she swallowed it, her eyes sad. 'Okay.' She nodded. 'I'm gonna order lunch soon, do you want—'

'Hello?' a voice called from the counter.

'Be right there,' Pepper called back. She squeezed the kit's shoulder, and headed out. 'What can I – oh. Uh, hi.'

Sidra couldn't see what was going on, but the shift in Pepper's tone was palpable. All at once, Sidra's pathways were on edge. Was there trouble? Was *she* in trouble? Pepper's voice and the other spoke to each other in a hush, too low for Sidra to pick up. She leaned in, straining to hear.

'. . . I told you,' she heard Pepper say. 'I'm not her keeper. She's her own person. That's totally up to her.'

Sidra's curiosity overpowered her concern about the unknown, and slowly, slowly, she peeked around the edge of

Becky Chambers

the door. A pair of eyes looked past Pepper as soon as she did so.

It was Tak.

'Hi,' Tak said, with an awkward Human-style wave of her hand. Her expression was friendly, but her cheeks told a different story. She was nervous, unsure. The sight did nothing to slow Sidra's processes down.

Sidra looked to Pepper, who didn't look sure about this, either. Her face was neutral, but unnaturally so, and a flush of tense red heated her skin. The Aeluon wasn't the only one changing colour, and Sidra understood why. Pepper did not take kindly to situations she wasn't in control of, and she knew Tak had a trump card in her pocket. This was Pepper's shop, Pepper's territory, yet here was someone whose lead she had to follow.

'Sidra,' Pepper said, her voice calm and tight, 'Tak was wondering if she could have a word with you.'

The kit took a breath. 'Okay,' Sidra said.

Tak held her satchel strap tightly with one hand. Sidra could see the other trying not to fidget. 'I was hoping somewhere private? A cafe, or—'

Pepper's eyes snapped to Tak. 'You're welcome to step into the back, if you want.' The words were nonchalant, but they weren't an invitation.

Tak's talkbox moved as she swallowed. 'Yeah. Yeah, that's cool.' The uneasy reddish yellow in her cheeks deepened; this wasn't how she'd pictured things, either.

What's she doing here? Sidra thought. All her other processes were idling.

'I'll be right out here,' Pepper said, as Tak made her way back. She was looking at Sidra, but the words were meant for everyone present. Sidra felt the kit's shoulders relax, just a bit. Pepper was there. Pepper was listening.

Tak entered the workshop. Sidra didn't know what to do. Was she a customer? A guest? A threat? She had directory after directory stuffed with different ways to greet people, but none

187

of them applied. How did you treat someone whose intentions were unclear?

They stood facing each other. Tak had the look of someone with a lot to say but no idea where to begin. Sidra knew the feeling.

'Would you like some mek?' Sidra said. She wasn't sure if that was the right way to start, but it was better than silence.

Tak blinked. 'Uh, no,' she said, with surprised politeness. 'No, I'm okay. Thanks.'

Sidra kept searching. 'Do you . . . want to sit down?'

Tak rubbed her palms on her hips. 'Yeah,' she said, and took the chair offered. She exhaled, audibly. 'Sorry, I . . . this is weird.'

Sidra nodded, then considered. 'Do you mean for you, or for me?'

'For both, I'm sure.' Tak went dusky orange, and pale green, too. Exasperated. Amused. 'I . . . I don't know where to start. I figured I'd know when I got here but . . .' She gestured at herself. 'Clearly not.'

The kit cocked its head. 'I just realised something,' Sidra said. 'What's that?'

Sidra paused, worried that she should've kept the thought to herself. Given Tak's reaction the last time they'd been together, she didn't want to draw attention to her synthetic nature – but there was no point in hiding it any more, either. 'Neither of us is speaking with an organic voice,' Sidra said.

Tak blinked again. A soft chuckle came from her talkbox. 'That's true. That's true.' She thought for three seconds, and gave a glance toward the door. Pepper was no longer welding, but she was doing something involving tools and metal. Something rhythmic and punctuated. Something you couldn't ignore if you were in earshot. Tak shifted her weight. 'There is no way I can say any of this without sounding ignorant. But . . . okay. Stars, I'm really trying to not . . . offend you.' She frowned. 'This is new for me. That's a poor excuse, but I mean – I've never had a conversation with an AI before. I'm not a spacer. I'm not a modder. I didn't grow up on a ship. I grew up *down here*. And here, AIs are just . . . tools. They're the things that make travel pods go. They're what answer your questions at the library. They're what greet you at hotels and shuttleports when you're travelling. I've never thought of them as anything but that.'

'Okay,' Sidra said. None of that was an out-of-the-ordinary sentiment, but it itched all the same.

'But then you . . . you came into my shop. You wanted ink. I've thought about what you said before you left. You came to me, you said, because you didn't fit within your body. And that . . . that is something more than a tool would say. And when you said it, you looked . . . angry. Upset. I hurt you, didn't I?'

'Yes,' Sidra said.

Tak rocked her head in guilty acknowledgement. 'You get hurt. You read essays and watch vids. I'm sure there are huge differences between you and me, but I mean . . . there are huge differences between me and a Harmagian. We're *all* different. I've been doing a lot of thinking since you left, and a lot of reading, and—' She exhaled again, short and frustrated. 'What I'm trying to say is I – I think maybe I underestimated you. I misunderstood, at least.'

Sidra's pathways latched onto that, hard. Was Tak here to *apologise*? Everything that had been said pointed in that direction, and Sidra switched gears as fast as she could. 'I see,' she said, still processing.

Tak looked around the workshop, at the bins, the tools, the unfinished projects. 'This is where you work.'

'Yes.'

'Were you . . . made here?'

Sidra gave a short laugh. 'No. No, Pepper and Blue are friends, that's all. They take care of me. They didn't . . . *make me*.' The kit leaned back in the chair, more at ease. 'I don't blame you for the way you reacted,' she said. 'I'm not even legal, much less typical. And I really am sorry for what happened in the shop. I didn't know how the bots would affect me.'

Tak waved the concern aside. 'Nobody knows they're allergic to something until they try it.'

Sidra processed, processed, processed. The metallic banging out front had missed a few beats. 'This . . . re-evaluation of yours. Does it extend to other AIs? Or do you merely see me differently because I'm in a body?'

Tak exhaled. 'We're being honest here, right?'

'I can't be anything but.'

'Okay, well – wait, seriously?'

'Seriously.'

'Right. Okay. I guess I have to be honest too, then, if we're gonna keep this fair.' Tak knitted her long silver fingers together and stared at them. 'I'm not sure I would've gone down this road if you weren't in a body, no. I . . . don't think it would've occurred to me to think differently.'

Sidra nodded. 'I understand. It bothers me, but I do understand.'

'Yeah. It kind of bothers me, too. I'm not sure I like what any of this says about me.' Tak glanced at the kit's arm. Faint lines marked where the tattoo had been. Pepper said they looked like scars, but they weren't, not in the way that organic sapients meant. 'What are you made out of?'

'Code and circuits,' Sidra said. 'But you're asking about the body kit, not me.'

Tak chuckled. 'I suppose I am. Are you – is your body . . . real? Like something lab-grown, or . . .?'

The kit shook its head. 'Everything I'm housed in is synthetic.'

'Wow.' Tak's eyes lingered on the pseudo-scars. 'Do those hurt?'

'No. I don't feel physical pain. I know when something's wrong, either with my program or the kit. It's not an enjoyable experience, but it's not *pain*.'

Tak acknowledged that, still looking at the synthetic skin. 'I have so many questions I want to ask you. You've got me thinking about things I've never chewed on. It's not comfortable, realising that you've been wrong about something, but I suppose it's a good thing to do from time to time. And you . . . you seem like you have questions, too. You came to me because you thought I could help. Maybe I still can. So . . . if you don't think I'm a complete asshole, maybe we can try again. Y'know, being friends.'

'I'd like that,' Sidra said. The kit smiled. 'I'd like that a lot.'

JANE, AGE 14

'Jane?' The lights came on in the most annoying way possible. 'Jane, it's long past time to wake up.'

Jane pulled the covers over her head.

'Jane, come on. There isn't that much daylight this time of year.' Owl sounded tired. Whatever. Jane was tired, too. Jane was always tired. No matter how much sleep she got, it was never enough.

'Turn off the lights,' Jane said. She'd figured out a long time ago that Owl *had* to obey direct commands related to the ship.

She couldn't see Owl's face, but she could feel it: frowning and frustrated. Through the edges of the blanket, Jane saw the lights switch off. 'Jane, please,' Owl said.

Jane sighed, long and loud. Pulling the direct-command card was a jerk thing to do, and she knew it. Sometimes it felt good though, especially when Owl was being annoying. Owl was annoying a lot lately. Jane pulled the blanket off her face. 'Turn the lights back on.' The room lit up; Jane winced.

'I wish you wouldn't do that,' Owl said.

Jane caught a glimpse of Owl. She looked hurt. Jane pretended to not notice, but she felt kind of bad about it. She didn't say that, though. She shuffled off to the bathroom. Stars, she was tired.

She peed, not bothering to flush. The filtration system was going to fizz out soon, and until she could find a replacement (or something she could hack into a replacement), flushing was on the list of things she could only do when there was something other than pee to deal with. It was gross, but when you did the math, it was either that or not washing the dogs she brought home. There was no way she wasn't washing the dogs.

She sucked in water straight from the faucet and swished it around her mouth, trying to get rid of the hot inside-out sock feeling. There had been dentbot packs on the shuttle when she'd first got there, but those had run out forever ago, and she hadn't found more. She missed having teeth that didn't hurt. Sometimes she thought back to the factory, where they'd had these bland little tabs they sucked on to get the fuzz off their teeth. Those had been good. Not everything in the factory was stupid. Most things. But not all things.

Soap. That was the other thing she missed. She showered as often as the water supply would allow, but she could still smell herself, sour and musky. The dogs were way worse, but they weren't so different. Mammals smelled, Owl had said. That was just the way of it.

Jane hadn't smelled bad when she was a kid. At least, she didn't remember smelling bad. Her body had changed a lot, and Owl said it would keep changing for a while. Still, though, Jane hadn't been changing in quite the way Owl had said – not like other Human girls did. She'd gotten taller, sure, and she had to make new clothes a lot. But she wasn't all curves and circles like the pictures Owl had shown her of adult women. Jane was still as skinny as a kid, and she didn't have big round breasts – just small bumps that ached all the time. Her hips were wider, kind of, but sometimes she thought she looked more like a boy (except for the whole between-the-legs thing, but that was just a big bunch of weirdness no matter which bits you had).

Jane hadn't started bleeding, either, but Owl didn't think she would. They'd figured out from her med scans a long time ago that Jane had a single chromosome, which was apparently one short from the usual. So, probably no bleeding, which was fine, because that sounded like the absolute worst thing ever if you didn't have meds to shut that down, and she obviously did not.

Oh, and she couldn't make kids. Bleeding was a maybe, but kids was a definite no. Owl had been kind of cagey when she'd told Jane that, but it was hard to care about not doing something you didn't know you could do in the first place. Jane had learned that she couldn't make kids in the same conversation where she'd learned that making kids was a thing. *She* hadn't been made the way most Humans were, which had weirded her out at first, but was no big deal, really. There'd been a stretch when she was a kid where she'd been real curious about how and why the Enhanced had made her the way they did. She and Owl had puzzled it out together then – Owl using what she knew about Enhanced Humanity societies, Jane telling her what little she could remember about medical stuff at the factory, both of them looking at samples of Jane's spit on the little scanner. Jane didn't have any huge tweaks, chromosomes and no-hair aside. She had a super-buff immune system, though, which was *not* a usual thing, and it also made Owl stop caring so much about getting the decontamination flash working. All in all, the Enhanced had probably cooked her up out of some grab-bag gene junk and pulled her out of a gooey vat, along with the other disposable girls. The Enhanced. What a bunch of fuckers.

Owl had given Jane access to sims meant for adults, and that was how Jane had learned about swearing. Owl had said it was important to know how swearing worked, and it was okay under the right circumstances, but that Jane shouldn't swear *all* the time. Jane definitely swore all the time. She didn't know why, but swearing felt fucking great. Owl only had eleven adult sims in storage, but Jane didn't mind playing them again and again. Her favourite was *Scorch Squad VI: Eternal Inferno*. The best character was Combusto, who used to work for the Oil Prince but was a good guy now, and he also used to be a pyromancer in a previous life – which was true for everybody on the Scorch Squad, but let's be real, Combusto was the one who took the oath most seriously before he was reincarnated – so he had visions of the past sometimes and his eyes caught fire when he got mad, which was all the time, and his ultimate attack was called Plasma Fist, which made bad guys explode. He also had the very best swears. *Jensen, get your fucking helmet on before they blow your skull out your ass!* Yeah, that was the stuff. She could play that sim all day.

Or, at least, she *would* play that sim all day if she didn't have stupid bullshit she had to do instead. She'd noticed, in the sims, nobody else had to find scrap and eat dogs. Nobody else made clothes out of seat covers. Nobody else hauled around water in old fuel drums. She couldn't wait to get the stupid shuttle working so they could get to the GC. There'd be people there, and toilets you could flush any time you wanted to, and food that wasn't covered in buggy fur. The people were the thing she was looking forward to most, obviously. Owl always made her talk in Klip. They hardly ever spoke Sko-Ensk any more, to the point that Jane couldn't always remember words. Sometimes, Owl put on different voices so Jane would get used to talking to other people. But Jane always knew it was really Owl. She wished she could talk to someone else.

The wall screen switched on as Jane picked at the stupid red bumps all over her face (Owl said those were normal, too). 'Jane, you should check the light panel in the kitchen before you go out today,' Owl said. 'I think it's got a damaged coil.'

'Yeah, I know.'

'How do you know? It just started flickering.'

'I – *ugh*.' Jane rolled her eyes and grabbed her pants from where she'd thrown them the day before. 'All right, I'll look.' She was real tired of having to fix shit. She just wanted to get out of there.

Owl followed her down the hall and it was *so annoying*. Jane looked up at the kitchen ceiling. Yep. The light was flickering. Woohoo. She got herself a cup of water and threw some dog on the stove. While it sizzled, she checked her to-do lists.

The to-do lists were written on the wall with chalk rocks (Owl's word for the white stones scattered all through the scrapyard dirt). Owl could've kept records of what Jane needed to fix (and probably did), but Jane liked being able to look at what still needed doing. There was so much that needed doing. A big list on the wall kept her from going crazy over it.

TO-DO
fix water filtration system (IMPORTANT)
rebuild aft propulsion strip
replace fuel lines
figure out what's wrong with navigation
artigrav system – does it work? how to test?
repair cargo bay hull (rusty)
repair power conduits (hallway)
repair bedroom air filter (totally broken)
repair back left stove burner (not important)
repair fucking everything always always always
get off this stupid planet
make new pants

SHOPPING LIST
fabric (tough)
bolts bolts bolts all the bolts
new circuit couplers
motherboards (any condition)
gunk traps
tape/glue/something???
thick plex
cable coatings
T junctions (fuel)
wire that doesn't suck
some kind of siding for the hull
WORK GLOOOOOOOVES
dogs (always)
mushrooms (always)
snap beetles (be fast!)

CHECKS
water filtration – going to break soon FIX IT
lights – good
heater – good
stasie – good?
Owl – good
hatch – good
decont. flash – broke
airlock scanner – going to break soon
med scanner – good
scrib – buggy

Jane rubbed her eyes. There would always be something on the list. It was never going to end.

She forked the meat onto a plate, and ate it even though she knew it was going to burn her tongue. In the sims, they always had such amazing-looking food. She didn't know what any of it was or what it tasted like, but holy *shit*, she couldn't wait to get some of that. She swallowed a burning mouthful of dog, which tasted like it always did.

'Don't forget to take food with you today,' Owl said.

'I know,' Jane said, shoving more dog into her mouth.

'Well, you don't always know. You forgot yesterday.'

Jane *had* forgotten to bring food yesterday, and it sucked. She hadn't realised until she got hungry, but she was an hour out from home by then and had her hands full of some really tricky circuits she'd ripped out of an old stasie, and she had to finish that before coming back, and by then, she was so hungry she could've eaten a dog without washing it first. But even though all that was true, Owl's reminder bugged her. 'I didn't forget *today*,' Jane said. She grabbed some jerky from the box on the counter, wrapped it in a cloth, and stuck it in her satchel. She gave the nearest camera a look. 'There.'

'That's not enough for the whole day. You'll get hungry.'

'Owl, please, I know what I'm doing. If I take more than that, I won't have any tomorrow.'

'It would be a really good idea to make some more jerky soon.'

'I know. I haven't seen any dogs in a while.' She pulled on her footwraps and filled her canteen. 'See? Water, food, all good. Can you open the airlock?'

The inner hatch slid open. 'Jane?' Owl said.

'What?'

'The light panel?'

Stars. 'I *know*, I'll find something.'

'You didn't even open it up.'

'Owl, it's a *light panel*. It's not a fucking pinhole drive.'

'I really wish you wouldn't talk like that.'

'I said I'll find something. Light panels are not that hard.' She walked through the airlock to the outer hatch and picked up the handle for her cargo wagon. Owl's face was real sad. Somehow, that made her all the more annoying. Jane sighed again. 'I will. Seriously, I've done this before.'

She had. The scrapyard was as familiar to Jane as her own face. Probably more than that. She spent way more time looking at scrap than at herself. She'd thought once, years ago, about marking the piles she'd already combed through, but there was no need. She knew where she was. She knew where she'd been.

The piles in an easily walkable radius had stopped being useful a long time ago. Oh, there was a fuckton of scrap left, sure, but it was either too broken even for her, or things she couldn't use, or buried so deep there was no point in bothering. Scavenging was a surface-level kind of job. You'd spend forever digging otherwise, and most of it was junk anyway. Still, though, she could never get over how much decent, fixable tech the Enhanced just chucked out. Did they not have fix-it shops, like they did in the sims? Was grease and gunk that gross to them that they had to dump it all half a planet away? She'd never seen an

Enhanced – she hadn't seen *anyone* since the factory – but she was pretty sure she'd hurt them bad if she did. Plasma Fist to the ribcage, just like Combusto.

She talked to herself as she walked, for company. Walking didn't take much brain, and hers got away from her if she wasn't working on something. Today's selection was the first scene from *Night Clan Rebellion*, which was pretty good. It wasn't as good as *Scorch Squad*, but she talked that one out *all* the time.

'Chapter one: we open on a snowy forest, stained red with blood! There's a big fucking monster wrecking a castle, and Knight Queen Arabelle is on a cool horse.' She did a voice kind of like Knight Queen Arabelle. 'Come, warrior! I need your assistance!' She went back to her own voice again. 'And so I go running in, and the monster takes out the tower with its tail – crash! – and so the Knight Queen gives *me* a cool horse, and she says, "We must hurry! Before the Evergard is lost!"'

Jane kept going. She got all the way through chapter two – the bit where you find out that the monsters *actually have a good reason for wrecking shit* – when the back wheel on her wagon started to wobble. 'Ah, shit,' she said, kneeling down to take a look. The axle had come loose. She dug through her satchel, got a tool, and sat down in the dirt to make repairs. 'Come on, get back in there. You know where you're supposed to be.'

She heard the dogs before she saw them – a scruffy pack of five, all watching her close. Jane wasn't worried. She stood up real chill, and got her weapon ready. She sized them up, one by one. Taking a dog this early in the day wasn't the best. Dragging around the extra weight sucked, and midday heat and a freshly dead dog wasn't a great combo. But it wouldn't spoil or anything, and she needed jerky. 'Good morning, shitheads,' she said, giving the weapon switch a quick flick. A little tongue of electricity slithered out. 'So, which one of you guys am I gonna eat?'

One of the dogs hunched down and stepped toward her. A crusty old female, blind in one eye. She snarled.

Jane snarled back. 'Yeah, come on,' she said. 'Come on, let's go.'

The dog kept growling, but didn't make a move. Jane had seen this one around before, slinking off in the distance. She'd never gotten close. Maybe this pack had come Jane's way by accident, or maybe they were real hungry (lizard-birds and dust mice weren't much for big carnivores to go on). If that was why they approached her now, well, too bad. They were leaving hungry. Jane wasn't.

She picked up a rock, never taking her eyes off the female's teeth. She switched the weapon into her left hand and, with a quick flick of her wrist, whipped the rock into the dog's nose.

Killing it wasn't even hard. The dog lunged, the zapper zapped, and the rest of the pack freaked out.

'Yeah!' Jane yelled, jumping over the heap of smoking fur. 'Yeah, come on! Who's next?' She thumped her chest like Combusto. 'You wanna go?'

The other dogs were pissed, but they backed off. They knew. They got it.

'That's right, I'm real scary!' Jane said, turning her back on them. 'Be sure to tell all your stupid friends, if I don't eat you first.' She grabbed the dead one by the legs and heaved it onto the wagon. It landed with a thud. Jane glanced over her shoulder, but of course the dogs were gone. Of course they were. She'd done this like a thousand times. She knew what was up.

'We are the blessed warriors of the Night Clan!' she said in her best justified-in-wrecking-shit monster voice. She gave the wagon axle a wiggle. All good. She dragged the now-heavy wagon behind her. 'For a thousand years, we have waited for our hour of vengeance—'

Nothing else bugged her as she made her way. She saw a couple cargo ships fly by high up over ahead, full of new scrap to drop off. That was nothing new. They only made drops at the edge of the yard, which was days and days of walking from home, she guessed. She never saw them on the ground. And the wider the yard got, the farther the drop site was. Besides, she was pretty sure there weren't any people on the ships, and they obviously weren't scanning the ground or anything. The same was true of the collector drones, which scooped up mouthfuls of scrap to take back to the factories. They didn't care about her at all. They probably thought she was a dog, if they *could* even think. She'd once wondered if the collectors would get to where the shuttle was before she left the planet, but Owl had calculated it, and given how often the drones made an appearance and how far away they were and how much scrap they appeared to take, it'd be another six years or so before they even got close. Six years. Jane couldn't deal with that thought.

She walked and walked, until she got as far as she'd been the day before. She stopped to think. There were two ways around the pile in front of her – one that looked like it would involve a lot of climbing, and one that looked kinda rocky but relatively flat. She considered the stinking carcass on the back of the wagon and went for the easier choice.

Turned out, the easier choice was a better walk, but the destination was pretty crazy. Sometimes, it was easy to forget that she lived on a planet, with ecosystems and geology and all that other stuff Owl told her about. It made more sense thinking that the dirt and animals had kind of happened *around* the scrap, like they were little details added in later on. But then sometimes, she saw something like the place she'd come to, and it was obvious that nature was always there first.

There had been a cliff or something there once – a hill, maybe. Jane didn't have much real-life experience with land left untouched (sims didn't count), and she wasn't always sure if she knew the right words for the things she saw. Anyway, there had been a lot of dirt and rock all stacked up at some point, but there'd been some water or wind or something, and now it was weird. There was a big hole in the ground – a big big hole, with lots of other little ones around – where the dirt had sunk in on itself. And while there was still a giant structure of dirt and rock off to the side of it, it had slumped over a scrap pile, almost like they had melted together. Jane could see scrap sticking out of the wall of dirt, like it was trying to pull itself out. It was a huge mess, and not great for scavenging at all. She would've turned right around if it hadn't been for one thing: she could see half of a ship sticking out of it.

Not a big ship, of course – she'd never found anything much bigger than home – but intact vehicles of any kind were not an everyday thing. Whenever she found one, she cleaned it out right away, especially if there was decent fabric on the seats or bunks or whatever. Fabric did not get better with age, and if she found something that wasn't all rain-rotted or chewed up from nesting things, that was worth grabbing super fast.

She chewed her lip as she looked at the wall of dirt. It would be a pain in the ass to climb, and it looked crumbly. She wiggled her toes against where her footwraps were wearing thin. If there *was* fabric in there, it was worth the climb. She could do it. She could do anything.

The smaller holes orbiting the big one weren't as deep, but they were deep enough – maybe about half again as tall as she was. She skirted around them, and when they got too tricky to avoid, she left the wagon on a flat patch and continued toward the wall. The slope was steep, almost straight up in some spots. She put her foot against it. It was crumbly, for sure. She reached up and grabbed a hunk of metal firmly buried. It held. She held. Yeah, she could do this. She'd be fine.

She continued up and up until she was at the same height as the ship. She worked herself sideways, turning her feet weird angles, letting them sink into the crumbly dirt so it would hold her weight. 'Boom! Boom! We'll wreck your walls!' she sang. 'Bang! Bang! We'll bust your balls!' It was the song the Scorch Squad sang when they drank alcohol after they won a fight. She didn't know what drinking alcohol was like, but the sims made it look real fun. 'Slam! Slam! Get drunk and fight—' Some of the dirt gave out under her foot, and her leg slid farther than was comfy. She looked at the distance between her and the stuck ship. Almost there, but she could hear pebbles tumbling down below her, and there weren't a lot of good footholds between here and there. Maybe this was a bad idea. She thought about it. She sniffed. 'You'll die tomorrow, so live toniiiiight,' she sang. She put her foot on the next big rock.

The next big rock broke into dusty pieces the second she let her weight down.

Jane fell. The dirt caught her. She slid, arms and legs flipping over in a tangle, hard things scraping her skin and ramming her body. Her weapon pack and satchel, still wrapped around her, added extra blows to the flurry. She clawed, trying to grab something, but she couldn't make sense and couldn't see straight. She tumbled and tumbled, out of control.

The ground went away, but she still clawed, even though there was nothing but air. Nothing but air until her body came crashing down.

For a moment, the entire world was loud and red – a bright, stinging red that filled her shut eyes and ringing ears. Her leg felt red, too, red and angry. She remembered how to breathe, and pulled in a hard lungful. She opened her eyes. The world was not red, and neither was her leg, but something was very, very wrong with it. There was no deep blood and nothing poking out, but when she tried to stand, she screamed. She saw the sky as she did so. It was further away than it had been before, a bright circle out of reach. She had landed in one of the holes.

My leg's broken, she thought. She'd never had a broken bone before, but somehow she knew it all the same. 'Fuck,' she said out loud, her breath speeding up. 'Stars, fucking . . . *shit*.' She made ugly sounds as she tried to sit up, moaning and whining and choking. She looked up, around, all over. Even if she'd been able to stand straight and reach up, the hole was taller than her, and there was nothing to climb on – no rocks, no crates, nothing.

She was so fucked.

'You're okay,' she said, her voice coming out wrong. 'You're okay. Come on. Come on, it's okay.' But it wasn't okay. Her hands were scraped and bruised, as were her arms, her face, everything. And her leg – stars, her leg. She pulled off her satchel and the weapon pack – both looking entirely the wrong shape – so she could lie flat on the ground. She put her hands over her face, trying to breathe, trying to stop shaking. What the hell was she going to do?

For a long while, there was nothing she *could* do but lie there and hurt. Her mind had finally started to turn to *can I even climb out of here with a broke-ass leg* when she heard something – some*things* – approach the hole. Jane held her breath. A dog came into view over the edge – a lean, sharp-eyed dog. There was a scrabbling sound behind it, a weirdly playful sound. Jane couldn't believe it: two freckled pups, no longer than her arm from tip to tail. The big one had to be their mother. Jane had never seen pups up close. She knew better than to go into dog dens. They were too dark, too closed in. Jane and the mother stared at each other, neither making a sound. The mother broke her gaze first, looking at her paws, the sides of the hole, the drop to the bottom. She was figuring it out, just like Jane had been, trying to see if there was a safe way back up. Jane's mouth went dry. All dogs were kinda scrawny, but she could see the ribs on this one. She could see the ribs on the pups, too. Where was their pack? Were they alone? Didn't matter. This was a problem, a big fucking problem. Even if she could manage the climb out, she couldn't pull herself up with her weapon in hand, and – wait. *Wait*. She thought back to the moment she'd hit the ground. There had been so much noise, so much crunching . . . She grabbed the weapon rod and hit the switch. Nothing happened. She hit it again, again. She could hear the soft *click* of the firing mechanism inside, but nothing. Nothing. Her leg wasn't the only broken thing.

She let out a yell from the very bottom of her belly, clenching her fists against her face. She could hear the pups startle. She turned her head to them, sharp and furious. 'What? You scared? *Raaaaaah!*' She yelled again. 'Go away! Get out of here! Go! *Go away!*' She threw a rock; it didn't make it out. The pups backed away out of view. The mother looked wary, but she stood her ground, ears laid back, fur bristling.

Jane grabbed her satchel, torn and dirty from the fall. She pulled out the jerky she'd packed that morning. 'Smell that?' she yelled, shoving the handful of dried meat in the mother's direction. 'Huh? You know what that is?' Jane took it between her teeth and ripped out a messy chunk. 'Mmm! That's you! That's your pups! You're fucking delicious, did you know that?' The words sounded good, but Jane shook as she said them. She thought about the empty click of the weapon. She thought about the shuttle, half a morning's walk away. She thought about Owl.

She thought about Owl.

If the dogs could smell the jerky, they didn't care. The pups rejoined their mother, who had sat down, muscles tight, head lowered into the hole. She was staying put. Jane was, too. She didn't have a choice.

She and the dog stared at each other all day, despite more thrown rocks, despite Jane yelling until her throat was raw. They stared at each other until the sun went down. And even after that, Jane could see the mother's eyes watching her in the dark, glinting green in the moonlight. Patient. Waiting. Hungry.

SIDRA

Sidra hadn't been to the Aeluon district before. Their community on Coriol was less technologically up-to-date than their interstellar kin, but their neighbourhoods were a noticeable step up from Sixtop. The streets were well lit – rather to Sidra's chagrin – and the buildings were clean, cared-for and, most importantly, aesthetically complementary. Everything was curved and domed, and the only colours beyond white and grey grew out of the ground.

Her quick-travel pod dropped her off outside the windowless establishment Tak's location tag had steered her to. It didn't look like much. There was no signage she could read, only a bright colour plate flashing soundless words on the wall. She started to make a note, then thought better of it. For a Human – even an ostensible one – recognising Aeluon emotions was a mark of cultural savvy. Understanding their language, however . . . that wasn't something the average Human could do, and it was the sort of thing that could prompt questions. She closed her reminder list with a flicker of regret.

Tak was waiting for her. She stood in conversation with three other Aeluons, flashing their cheeks and looking congenial. She noticed Sidra approaching and called out: 'Hey!' The sound was startling in the silent street. She flashed something to the others, apparently bidding them farewell, then walked Sidra's way. 'Glad you could make it.'

'Thanks,' Sidra said. She glanced at the others. 'Are we joining them?' A quiet worry arose.

Tak smiled blue. 'Nah, we just ran into each other. Some friends of one of my fathers.' She leaned her head toward the nondescript building. 'Come on, let's get out of the cold.' She hugged a woven sort of jacket around her torso as they went. 'I should live in the Aandrisk district. They've got a hab dome heated warm enough for them to walk around naked – in *this*.' She gestured to the stars that never set as they arrived at the outer wall. 'So. I don't know if you've been to one of these before,' she said, pressing her palm against a doorframe. The wall melted to let them through.

'One of—' Sidra scrapped the sentence as she walked through the door. 'Oh,' she said softly, trying not to disturb the quiet within.

'We obviously don't have a spoken word for this,' Tak whispered. 'Klip just borrowed the Hanto for it: *ro'valon*. Direct translation is "city field".'

The translation was apt. The large domed space was filled with rolling little hillocks, none taller than the kit, each covered with an inviting blanket of grass. Whatever framework rested below them had been sculpted to create leafy seats, living benches, private hollows to share secrets in, flat clearings to stretch out on. A few small trees were in there as well, creating subtle curtains and canopies. The curved walls surrounding everything were covered with projections of unending fields stretching outward, bright and clear as noon. It was realistic imagery, but the illusion had no effect on Sidra. She could tell that it wasn't the real thing, which made it easy for her to know where to stop looking. For an organic sapient, though, she imagined the effect would've been quite convincing, and indeed, the people present seemed awfully content. They were mostly Aeluon, though Sidra spotted a few others (including an Aandrisk who had no qualms about lying spread-legged on his back, his discarded pants bundled beneath his head as he read his scrib).

'It's not as big as the ones you get on Sohep Frie,' Tak said. 'But it's the best thing in the world after a busy day in a city.'

Sidra followed Tak to a sparse reception desk, where an Aeluon man sat working on a small pixel puzzle. He set it aside as they approached. Cheek flashing ensued. After a moment, he handed Tak a small rectangular device, which Sidra did not recognise. He waved at Sidra, then returned to his puzzle with interest. Tak caught Sidra's eye and made a Human gesture – a finger against her mouth. Sidra understood, and said nothing as they ventured into the *ro'valon*. No one else was talking, either. It was the quietest place she'd ever been to. There was more noise in a spaceship than in here.

Tak looked around, searching for a free spot. She chose a secluded hollow with a sloping seat built into it, big enough for two people to lounge with plenty of space between them. She sat; Sidra made the kit do the same. The tended grass folded beneath them. Tak set the rectangular device down beside her and pressed her thumb to it. A soft beam of light shot up, then spread out around them in a wide, nearly-clear bubble, touching all the way to the ground.

'I take it you've never seen a privacy shield before,' Tak said, catching something on the kit's face.

'I haven't, no.' Sidra glanced over the kit's shoulder. 'Is it okay to talk now?'

'Oh, yeah,' Tak said, snuggling into the grass with relish. 'The shield blocks all sound. It's a courtesy thing when you're in a place like this, but I figured it'd be doubly useful in your case.'

'I appreciate that.' Sidra looked around. 'I've never seen anything like this.'

'Yeah, they tend to be one of our better-kept secrets. I think we forget other species don't have these.'

'I meant a field, in general. I know it isn't a real one, but . . .'

Tak blinked. 'Stars, you've never been out in nature, have you?'

Sidra shook the kit's head. 'I mean, there are parks near where I live, but—'

'Oh, no, that's not the same, and neither is this. Wow.' Tak mulled that over as she retrieved a packet of something edible from her jacket pocket. 'I'd say you should travel more, but . . . can you do that?'

'Sure. I don't really want to, though.'

'Why?'

'Being outside is hard for me. My primary function was to observe all the goings-on within a ship. *All* the goings-on. If I don't have boundaries, I don't know where to stop processing.'

Tak opened the packet and shook seven pieces of candied fruit into her palm. 'That sounds exhausting,' she said, picking up one of the pieces between two fingers. She popped it in her mouth and chewed.

'It is,' Sidra said. 'I prefer staying inside.'

'Is there no way around that? Needing to observe everything, I mean.'

The kit sighed. 'Theoretically, someone could alter my code to remove certain protocols. But Pepper and Blue don't know how to write Lattice, and I can't alter myself. It's . . . a challenge.'

'Like having to tell the truth all the time.'

'Precisely. It's one of the things I like least about being in the kit.'

Tak leaned back into the grass. 'Why do you do that?'

'Do what?'

'"The kit". You don't say "my body". You say "the kit".'

Sidra wasn't sure how to explain. 'If you were talking to an AI installed in a ship, would you expect it to refer to the ship as its body?'

'No.'

'Well, then, there you go.'

Tak did not look as convinced as Sidra had hoped. 'It's . . . a ship, though. It's not a body.'

'It's the same thing to me. I was housed in a ship. I'm now housed in a body kit. My place of installation changes my abilities, but it's not *mine*. It's not *me*.'

'But the kit is yours. It's . . . yours.'

The kit shook its head. 'It doesn't feel that way.' She started to explain further, but something about the conversation thus far was making her uneasy. Everything had been about *her*. She felt the kit's cheeks flush.

'What's up?'

Sidra tried to condense what she was feeling. 'Pepper and Blue are my friends,' Sidra said at last. 'But they're friends born out of circumstance. Pepper was there when I woke up, and she's taken care of me since. Blue's part of the package deal of being friends with her. But you – I've never made a friend on my own before. Just . . . gone out and picked somebody. I don't know how this works. I don't know where to start.'

'Are you uncomfortable?'

'A little.'

'Why?'

Sidra processed. It wasn't because Pepper and Blue weren't there. It wasn't because she was in a new place. It wasn't because – oh, wait, yes it was. She looked at Tak. Even if she hadn't been forced into honesty, she would've told the truth then. 'I'm not sure why you want to be friends with me. Right now, I feel like I'm just some sort of curiosity to you.'

Tak chewed her candy thoughtfully, unoffended. 'Tell you what. You ask me a question about myself, I'll give you a straight answer, then we'll flip it around. If I want to know something about your body – sorry, about the kit – then you can ask me something about my body in return. Anything you want to know. That's how a friendship *should* work. It's an even give and take.'

'Can we ask questions about other things, too?' Sidra considered her words. She knew what she wanted to say, but she didn't want to sound arrogant. 'There's more to me than just the kit. And the same is true for you.'

Tak darkened into a happy blue. 'Deal. And if you want, you can ask the first question.'

'Okay.' Sidra compiled a quick list and started from the top. 'How long has your family been on Coriol?'

'My fathers moved here a little over thirty standards ago.' Tak smirked. 'They say it's because they knew there would be a lot of demand for parents in a place where travellers stop off, but I know it's partly because none of them fit in well on Sohep Frie. They're ah' – she scratched her throat with an amused look – 'a bit politically vocal. Anti-war, to be precise. They don't mesh well on the homeworld.' She plucked another candy from the packet. 'Okay, my turn. I know you read books and watch vids and stuff. Do you have a particular genre you like?'

'I like folktales, mythology, and non-fiction. Mysteries are fun, too.'

'You mean Human-style?' Tak made a face. 'I can't get into those. They make me anxious. I don't find bad things happening to people to be particularly entertaining.'

'I personally enjoy trying to find all the clues, but I've spent a lot of time considering the broader appeal.'

'And?'

'I think it has to do with the fear of death. All organics are afraid of it, and there's nothing that can be done to prevent bad things from happening sometimes. My guess is that there's an odd sort of comfort in imagining that even if something horrible happens to you or someone you love, the ones responsible will always be caught, and the people who figure it out will do so in style.'

Tak laughed. 'You make a good case. All right, your turn.'

'How do you know when it's time to switch sex? What does it feel like?'

'It's like an itch. Not a literal itch – though you don't know what that feels like, do you?'

'No.'

'Hmm. Okay. It's a . . . an irritation. An urge. But it doesn't last long. The implants kick in, and I change fully within three days. That part's fine. It doesn't hurt or anything. A little achy, maybe, but it's not bad. Much better than it would be without my implants.'

'How would that be?'

'Incredibly unpleasant.'

'Because you couldn't change.'

'Exactly. That's how you find out you're shon. It hits during puberty. You wake up with this itching, aching feeling, and your body isn't getting the right hormonal input to be able to respond the way it should.'

'Because you don't live in segregated villages any more.'

'Right. Biology-wise, shifts are supposed to occur within a single-sex environment, which we obviously no longer have. So, you start to get sick. Your hormones don't know what to do. I got my implants within a day of Father Re realising why I'd been dizzy and achy all morning. He took me to the clinic right away, and they fixed me up.' Tak pointed at herself, indicating it was time for a question of her own. 'What – how to phrase this – what do you have in there?' She made a circular motion with her palm toward the kit's torso.

'Lots of things.' Sidra touched the upper chest. 'To begin with, false lungs and heart. Do you want to listen?'

Tak's face lit up, but her tone remained steady. 'Are you comfortable with that?'

'Yes.'

Tak leaned forward, pressing her ear to the kit. Sidra took a deep breath. 'Wow,' Tak said. 'That's incredible. But they don't do anything?'

'The lungs, no, not really. They just suck air in and out to give the appearance of breathing. The heart actually behaves like a heart. It pumps fake blood throughout the kit. But the blood isn't a vital system function. You could remove the heart and I'd still be fine.'

'That's . . . grimly poetic.'

Sidra continued down the kit. 'There's a false stomach as well, which stores anything I ingest.'

'I was wondering how you ate. You drank mek at my shop.'

The kit nodded. 'But again, it doesn't provide fuel. It's just for show. I'll spare you how I get rid of it, if that's all right.'

Tak put up her palms. 'That's not a pretty thing in most species, so, yeah, that's fine.'

Sidra placed the kit's hands on the kit's abdomen. 'The core is in here, as well as the battery and the main bulk of processing circuitry.'

Tak blinked. 'You're saying your brain is in your belly. Sorry, the kit's belly.'

'In a manner of speaking, but only part of it.' She tapped the kit's head. 'Memory storage and visual processing is up here. Remember, if I were in a ship, I'd be spread all through it. I'm not limited to one processing unit.' She touched the kit's thighs. 'Kinetic energy harvesters are laced all through the limbs and skin. Whenever I move the kit, it generates more power.' Her turn for a question. 'Have you ever had children? Either as a father or a mother?'

'No. I have no interest in changing my career, and I've never been fertile when female. I'd like to, though.' She grinned. 'Besides, old folks will tell you that kids with a shon parent are lucky. So: have you ever been swimming?'

'No. Why do you ask?'

'Because you said you can't breathe, and I'm jealous. You could walk around the bottom of the ocean.' Tak's eyes went wide. 'You could spacewalk without a suit!'

'No, I couldn't.'

'You absolutely could!'

'That'd be an amazing way to get caught.' Sidra looked around the *ro'valon* as she considered more questions. The nude Aandrisk man had fallen asleep, scrib on his face. A pair of young adult Aeluons were lying on their backs beside each other, close as public politeness would allow. 'You said your fathers are anti-war. Are you?'

Tak rocked her head. 'Less than they'd like. I think war is an idiotic way to spend resources and the precious time we have, but I don't think we're ready to just dismantle our gunships yet. Look at the Rosk, for example.' She flicked her inner eyelids. 'I don't think even my fathers can argue that one.' She balled up the empty candy packet in her palm, and slipped it back into her pocket. 'Are you afraid of getting caught?'

'All the time. But . . .' Sidra paused for one second. 'I think I could get away with more than I do now.'

'How do you mean?'

Sidra looked at the kit's hands, and paused for two seconds more. 'Pepper doesn't like it when I want to do things more in line with my intended capabilities when we're not at home. The Linkings, for example. I'm capable of processing dozens of lines of thought at once. I often feel bored, or stuck inside my own mind. In a ship, I'd have Linking access at all times. I don't in here. Pepper says it'd be dangerous to install a wireless receiver in the kit.'

'She's probably right, but there must be a way to deal with that.'

'She doesn't want me to do things that make it clear I have different abilities. She's afraid someone will notice.'

'Are you afraid of that?'

Sidra processed. 'No. I could hide it. I would be careful. I'm frustrated with what I am now. I'm capable of so much more.'

Tak reclined into the grass, folding her hands over her flat chest. 'I know it's your turn to ask a question, but . . . let's stick with this a bit. Maybe we can think of a solution Pepper hasn't hit on.'

'Like what?'

Tak shrugged. 'I have no idea. But if we can go to space and invent implants and learn how to talk to other species, surely there's a way to help you. I get that you have to be careful. But you're . . . you're *not* like the rest of us. No offence.'

'None taken. It's true.'

'I mean, we're all sapients, right? Me, you, those goofballs over there.' She gestured vaguely toward the youths, who were staring at each other with lovestruck eyes. 'But say . . . say I moved to Hagarem. Say, by some stroke of luck, I was the only

Aeluon in a whole city of Harmagians. Would I respect their ways? Yes. Would I adopt their customs? Yes. Would I ever, ever stop being Aeluon? Hell no.' She drummed one set of fingers against the other. 'I get that it's a different thing for you, but that doesn't mean you have to abandon what makes you unique. You're supposed to own that, not smother it.' She rocked her head, cheeks brown and determined. 'Where do you feel most comfortable? What kinds of places do you like?'

'I have a different answer for each of those questions.'

'Okay.'

'I'm most comfortable at home. It's safe, and I can use the Linkings, and Pepper and Blue are there with me.' The kit's mouth scrunched up. 'But I like parties best.'

Tak raised her chin. 'Really?'

'Really. I love parties. I love lots of crazy things happening within a set of walls. I love trying new drinks. I love watching people dance. I love all the colour and light and noise.'

Tak grinned. 'When was the last time you went to a party?'

'Six days before the . . . the thing that happened at your shop. A birthday party for one of Blue's artist friends.'

Tak thought for a moment. 'That's thirty-eight days since your last party.' She gave a sharp nod. 'That's the first thing we'll fix.'

JANE, AGE 14

Nobody was coming for her.

This should have been an obvious thing. There was nobody else there. There had never been anyone to help her, not when she hurt her hands or fought off dogs or anything. But now, shivering in the dark at the bottom of a hole, she really got what having no one meant. Nobody was out looking for her. Nobody would miss her if she died. No one would notice. No one would care.

The mother dog paced up above. One of her pups was snoring. Jane shivered. She leaned back against the dirt wall, pulling her arms and her good leg in, trying to keep warm. The night was biting cold, and her clothes weren't meant for it. Her butt was numb from sitting, but there were only so many ways she *could* sit without her leg shrieking back at her.

This was her fault. If only she'd stepped different. If only she'd not tried to get to the stupid ship. If only she'd gone left instead of right. *Stupid. Stupid stupid stupid. Bad girl. Bad behaviour.*

'Stop,' she whispered to herself, holding her ears. 'Don't do this. Don't do this. Stop.'

But familiar thoughts were creeping in now, and there were no projects or lessons or sims to shut them up. She *had* been bad. If she hadn't climbed the wall, this wouldn't have happened. If she hadn't gone left. If she had just thought for a second, instead of being so clumsy and bad and off-task—

'Stop, stop, stop,' she said, rocking back and forth. 'Stop.'

She'd been bad. And bad girls got punished.

She thought of the factory, which was never cold and never lonely. She thought of her warm bunk, with Jane 64 cuddled close. *I don't think we should*, 64 had said. But Jane had made her. She'd made her go do something bad, and that good little girl had died for it.

She thought about what that meant – dying. Just . . . ending. Lights out. The end. What if this – this night – was it? What if the last thing she ever felt was being cold and alone and afraid? What if the last thing she ever saw was a pair of hungry eyes staring at her in the dark? Maybe the lizard-birds would find her. They stuck to mushrooms, usually, but she'd seen them nibbling at dead dogs and dust mice sometimes, unwilling to let food go to waste. She remembered how those dead things looked. She imagined how she'd look if she were dead. How she'd look as other things ate her. 'Stop,' she said, louder. 'Jane, stop it. Stop it.'

She whimpered at the bottom of the hole, her leg hurting more every time the cold made her shiver too hard. The dogs at the top moved restlessly. Jane 64 was dead. Jane 23 was probably dead, too, because she'd been stupid and careless and nobody was coming for her. Nobody cared. Nobody except Owl, and she'd never know what happened. Another stupid Human had left her alone, and nobody would be able to tell her why.

Jane clutched her face, rocking and rocking. This, all of this, was her punishment. And she deserved it. She deserved every bit of it.

The dogs ate the old dead female on Jane's wagon sometime in the night. Jane didn't know dogs ate other dogs, but protein was protein, and she guessed they'd given up on her. She couldn't see them feeding, but she heard it, all right. The pups were excited. She almost thought they sounded happy.

She slept, kind of. It wasn't a real sleep, just a confusion she dipped in and out of until she heard the flutter of lizard-birds overhead, which meant the sun was coming up. She had to get out of there. She had to do something. She wanted to go home.

Come on, get up, she thought. *Get up get up get up get—*

She tried to stand, and regretted it immediately. 'Fucking dammit,' she hissed, slamming her head back against the dirt wall.

A handful of dirt crumbled down to her shoulders.

Of course. Of *course*. It was so obvious. The ground had collapsed and made the hole. What if . . . what if she made it collapse a little more?

She dragged herself around so she was facing the wall. Even though her eyes had adjusted to the dark, it was so hard to see. But she could feel. She ran her palm over the dirt, packed tight but pliable. She got a tool out of her satchel – a small prybar, good for unsticking stuck scrap. She paused. If she made a way up, the dogs could get down. She listened. She hadn't heard them at all since the eating sounds stopped. They had probably moved on, but there was no telling how far, or if they were still hungry. She got her knife out of her satchel and stuck it in her pocket. It was something. It was better than just fading out down there, anyway.

She slammed the prybar into the dirt, making a hole. A hole in a hole. She dug. She dug, and dug, and dug. She dug as the night faded away. She dug as the air warmed up (finally). She dug even though her fingers ached and her leg hated her for it. And as she dug, sections of the dirt wall came falling down, little by little. When it got in her eyes, she brushed it out. When it got in her mouth, she spat it away. If a big bunch fell down, she'd pull herself up on top, then dig some more, until finally – finally! – enough of the dirt had fallen into the hole that it made a sort of ramp back up. She pulled herself with her arms, groaning loud and mean. If the dogs were still around, they had to know she was coming. She pulled out her pocket knife and crawled with it in hand, satchel and busted weapon dragging awkwardly along behind her. At last, there it was – the wagon, on the flat ground where she'd left it the day before. She wanted to laugh, but instead shut her mouth tight. The dogs were still there, asleep together next to the half-eaten carcass of the one Jane had killed. She clutched her knife hard. The mother looked up, belly fat and fur stained red, her eyes hazy with food. She and Jane stared at each other. The mother growled, but it wasn't a hunting growl. This was quieter, lower. The mother's pups snuggled close to her, fat and messy as she was. One rolled onto its back, little bloody paws stretching into the air. The mother folded her head over her young and growled again.

Jane didn't need to be told twice. She dragged herself the opposite way, toward a small scrap pile. The mother, at last, laid her head back down.

Jane found a length of rusty pipe in the pile, almost as tall as she was. It would do. She pulled herself up with it, trying to stay as quiet as she could. She bit her lip hard. Her leg trembled. She'd been hurt before, but not like this. Nothing had ever hurt like this.

She kept her leg up off the ground as best as she could, putting her weight against the pipe. She took a shuffling step forward, using the pipe like a walking stick. Out of the corner of her eye, she saw the mother move. Jane cried out, nearly falling back down in fear. But the dog had just rolled over. Jane tried to get a hold of herself, tried to breathe normal. She was useless right now. She couldn't run. She could barely drag herself forward. She'd gotten lucky with the dogs snoring away by her wagon – there was no way she was getting that back – but it would take her hours to get home at this speed, and if there were other packs between here and there . . .

But she had to get home. She had to. She couldn't stay here. She had to get home.

SIDRA

There was a lot going on at the Vortex that night – three dance pits! a Harmagian juggler! grasswine on tap! – but Sidra hadn't missed the fact that something was bothering Tak. He was doing all the things organic sapients did in social places late at night. He'd been drinking and talking – and flirting, which had been fun to watch. But though there was nothing outwardly wrong, something was needling him, all the same.

'What is it?' Sidra asked, pushing her voice through the music and chatter.

Tak blinked. 'What's . . . what?' His words were clear, but slower than usual. Alcohol didn't make Aeluons slur, of course, but thinking through what words to run through the talkbox took as much effort as trying to speak through a tipsy mouth.

Sidra took a sip of her drink. *Moonlight streaming behind a graceful white spider, weaving strand after strand of clear, strong silk.* She savoured the image, but never took her gaze off her friend. 'Something's bothering you.'

Tak shrugged, but the yellow in his cheeks told a different story. 'I'm . . . good.'

The kit raised an eyebrow.

The Aeluon sighed aloud. 'Are you . . . having fun?'

'Of course I am. Aren't you?'

'I am, but . . . I'm having . . . fun . . . without you. We came here . . . together.'

Sidra attempted to process, but came up short. 'We are here together.' She gestured at the table. 'We are literally here together.'

Tak rubbed his silver scalp. 'You do this . . . every time . . . we go out. You find a corner table and sit . . . with your back to the wall. You . . . order a lot of drinks . . . no . . . two of them . . . the same. You watch . . . everybody else . . . having fun. Sometimes, if you're feeling fancy . . . you switch it up and find . . . a *different* corner table.' He went brown with thought. 'Do . . . other people . . . make you nervous? Is that it?'

'I don't understand the question.' What was he getting at? 'I'm having a really good time.'

'But you're just . . . *observing*. You never . . . participate.'

'Tak,' Sidra said, keeping her voice as low as she could. 'You understand why that is. I don't require participation in order to be enjoying myself. Company and interesting input. That's all I need.'

He stared back at her with a gravity rarely achieved by the sober. 'I . . . get that. But you are more . . . than what they programmed you . . . to be.' Tak threw back the remainder of his drink in one go. 'Come on,' he said. 'We're . . . getting you . . . some different . . . input.' He took the kit's hand and led her away from the table.

Other people did not make Sidra nervous, but this turn of events did. The comfort of the corner was gone, and the direction Tak was leading her in gave her pause. 'I don't know how to make the kit dance,' she yelled. A dangerous bit of phrasing, she knew, but there was a degree of safety to be had in being surrounded by loud music and drunk people.

Tak looked over his shoulder and gave her a withering look. 'With all . . . the hours of observation time you've . . . clocked, you should . . . have some idea . . . by now.' He gestured at the dance pit. 'Besides, does . . . anybody here look like . . . they know . . . what they're doing?'

The kit swallowed as she watched the bodies shake and sway. 'Yes.'

Tak scratched his jaw. 'Well . . . okay, they do. But so . . . do I.' He smiled at her. 'If . . . you hate it, I'll take you . . . right back . . . to your corner . . . and buy you any drink . . . you want.'

Sidra considered the kit's limbs, its neck, the curve of its spine. She had the ability to manage life support systems, hold dozens of simultaneous conversations, even dock a ship if emergency demanded it. She could handle a dance pit. Yes, she could do this. She pulled up every memory file she had of people dancing at parties past. 'You're buying me a drink whether I hate this or not,' she said.

Tak laughed, and led her into the throng.

Dance was curious in its near universality. Not all species had dance in their cultures, but most did, and those that did not quickly latched onto the idea once exposed to it. Even Aeluons, who would never hear music as others did, had trad-itional ways of moving together. Sidra had watched a lot of archival footage of dance, but fascinating as that was from a cultural perspective, she enjoyed the improvised madness of a multispecies gathering much more. In the pit, she'd observed, it didn't matter what your limbs looked like, or how you liked to move. So long as there was a beat and warm bodies nearby, you could do whatever felt good.

Sidra knew dancing wouldn't feel the same to her as it did to others. But maybe . . . maybe she could at least *look* good.

Tak let go of the kit's hands and began to stomp his feet in an encouraging way. Sidra did a quick scan of her memories and found a file of a Human woman she'd seen sixteen days prior. It was as good a place to start as any.

Sidra analysed the file, and fed her findings into the kit's kinetic systems. The kit responded, changing its posture into something Sidra hadn't experienced before. The limbs were no longer pressed close to the torso, the back no longer straight. What had been tension and angles was now a harmony of curves, rocking, swaying, shifting.

Tak threw back his head, cheeks a mirthful green, laughter

exploding from his talkbox. 'I . . . knew it,' he said. 'I knew it.' His hands went up in the air and he cheered.

A curious sense of delight began to warm up Sidra's pathways. This whole change in affairs was fascinating. The awareness of people behind the kit was as uncomfortable as ever, yes, but in this case, it was more of an irritation than a hindrance. Frustration with perception was a familiar feeling. Dancing was not. Presented with something new, she could easily ignore the everyday.

The music played on and on, never slowing, never stopping. Sidra could not hear Tak breathing, but she could see it – hard and elated through his open mouth. A stranger appeared beside them, as if the crowd were an ocean washing someone ashore. It was one of the Aeluons Tak had been flirting with earlier, and her friend was clearly happy with the turn of events.

Do you mind? Tak's face asked.

Of course not! the kit's face responded.

Tak grinned, then turned his attention to the other Aeluon. They moved closer than friends, silver skin shimmering under the flashing lights. If the colours of the environment were communicating something erroneous to Aeluon eyes, they clearly didn't care.

Sidra was happy for Tak, happy for this entire turn of events. She had three dozen more dance memory files waiting on tap, and she couldn't wait to see how—

Another stranger appeared – two of them, rather. A pair of Aandrisks – a green man, a blue woman, feathers groomed perfectly, considerate pairs of trousers hung around their broad hips. They looked at Sidra in tandem, excited and interested.

The kit nearly misplaced its foot. There were dozens of sapients here; why were they looking at her? Had she done something wrong? Had she manoeuvred the kit incorrectly? Were they laughing at her?

The Aandrisks weren't laughing. Their faces were structured differently than the Aeluons entwined together nearby, but they had the same sort of look: friendly, confident, inviting.

They wanted to dance.

Without a word spoken, they moved close to her, both facing the kit's front in a sort of snug triangle. From the trusting, easy way they touched each other while dancing, Sidra surmised they were of a feather family – but then, it was always hard to tell with Aandrisks. She wasn't entirely sure how to proceed now that she was dancing *with* others, rather than *around* them, but she stayed the course, grabbing files specific to platonic groups.

The Aandrisk woman leaned in toward the kit as they danced. 'You're amazing!' she shouted.

Sidra wasn't sure her pathways were capable of holding much more pride than what she felt right then.

Her dance partners glanced at each other, communicating something Sidra could not know. They returned their gaze to her, their eyes asking a question she wasn't sure she understood.

She nodded yes anyway.

The Aandrisks moved even closer, green and blue scales brushing against the kit's skin. They put their hands on it, and their touches became a dance all of their own, every bit as much as their swinging heads and tails. There were hands running down arms, and claws in the kit's hair.

An image appeared, brighter than any she'd experienced before. *Light. Warm, life-giving light. Water lapping over her toes. Sand cradling her body, holding her steady and safe.* Sidra was at full attention. The image lingered, even though there was no food in her mouth, no jar of mek beneath her nose. It lingered as the Aandrisk woman pressed her hips against the kit's. It grew as the man ran the flat of his palm down the kit's back. Sidra had never experienced a sensory image in this way before, but somehow, she knew exactly what it meant.

Oh, no, she thought. And then: *Oh, wow.*

The image was almost overpoweringly good, and yet she had this hungry, impossible-to-ignore sense she hadn't seen all of it. She knew there were other images waiting behind it, every bit as good. The Aandrisks nuzzled the kit, and she nuzzled back, wanting. She—

A system alert went off, drowning out everything else within her. A proximity alert, the kind that warned of the sudden appearance of a nearby ship, or an object that posed a collision risk. An all-powerful screaming alert, triggered by someone behind her, someone *she could not see*, whose unknown hands were sliding over the kit's shoulders.

Sidra shut the alert off as quickly as she could, but her pathways were sure her housing was in danger, and the kit had taken its cue. It was no longer dancing. It was throwing the hands off its shoulders. It was spinning around to see what the danger was. Another Aandrisk, a man, likely associated with the other two, but it didn't matter, it didn't matter. Her system knew only danger.

'Whoa,' the third Aandrisk said. 'Whoa, I am so sorry.'

'Are you okay?' the Aandrisk woman said.

Sidra had to answer, but she couldn't get the words out. The kit was breathing too fast. She shook the kit's head.

Tak was there – but from where, she couldn't tell. She couldn't tell anything. She couldn't see, she couldn't make sense, she just had that one narrow cone, and *no no no, don't do this, don't do this now, stop it, don't ruin it, stop it stop it stop—*

'It's okay,' he said, putting an arm around the kit's shoulders. Sidra looked up at him just in time to see him flash an apology toward his dejected dance partner.

See, you've ruined it, you've ruined it for him, I need to go home, I need to go away, I need to stop, please—

'Hey. Sidra. Sidra, come on. We'll . . . get somewhere quiet, yeah? I'm here, it's . . . okay.' He led the kit through the crowd. She kept her gaze on the floor, trying to ignore the concerned stares. She wanted to disappear.

'Is she okay?' It was the third Aandrisk, pushing his way alongside them.

'She's fine,' Tak said.

Sidra looked at the Aandrisk man, and tried to push words

through the panicked breaths. 'It's not – it's not your—' The air got in the way. Dammit, she didn't need to breathe!

'It's not . . . your fault,' Tak said. 'She'll be . . . fine. Thank you.'

They cleared the pit, leaving the Aandrisk behind. Tak barrelled them through the crowd toward the table they'd occupied earlier. A group of Laru sat there now. Tak swore, and headed for the exit.

'Not outside,' Sidra gasped. 'Not outside.'

Tak changed course and entered the smoking room. A group of modders looked up from around a tall communal pipe.

'Hey, man,' a Human woman said, a smoking mouthpiece hanging in her mechanical hand. 'Sorry, we just—' She looked at Sidra. 'Dude, is she okay?'

Tak visibly willed the concern away from his face and looked back at them with an easy smile. 'Yeah,' he said. 'Never . . . buying smash from . . . that vendor again, though. Synth shit, y'know?'

'Oh, *rough*,' the woman said. 'She got the shakes?'

Sidra forced the kit to nod at her. It was true, technically. Just not in the way the modder meant.

'Well, you're welcome to ride it out in here,' the woman said. She flicked her eyes over to Tak and gestured at the pipe. 'Sorry about the redreed.'

'It's fine,' Tak said. Sidra could see that his eyes were already starting to itch. As if this couldn't get any worse.

Tak led the kit to a quiet corner, away from the smokers. Sidra sat the kit down. The fast breathing had stopped. All that was left was the overwhelming sense of embarrassment. She preferred hyperventilating.

'I'm so, so sorry,' she whispered.

'It's not . . . your fault,' Tak said, his talkbox turning itself down. 'I pushed. *I'm* sorry. You told me . . . how you're comfortable, and I . . . should have . . . respected that.'

'It's okay,' Sidra said, taking his hand with the kit's. 'It was fun, at first. I liked it. I just—' The kit put its face in its hands. 'Stars, I am so tired of always making a mess of things for you.'

Tak scoffed. 'Now, that's . . . just not true. We've . . . been to . . . how many parties—'

'Eight.'

'It was rhetorical, but . . . thank you. This is . . . the first time . . . this has happened. It's also . . . the first time . . . somebody . . . surprised you . . . while dancing. So, we know . . . to avoid this . . . next time.'

One of the modders approached them with a cup of water. 'Here ya go,' he said, handing it to Sidra.

'You're very kind,' Sidra said, accepting it. She took a sip, for show. Water did nothing for her, but she was grateful for the gesture.

'Take it easy,' the Human man said. 'We've all been there.' He gave a warm, slightly inebriated smile, then returned to his friends.

Sidra stared into the cup, watching the ripples bounce off each other. 'I'm sorry for screwing things up for you,' she said, remembering Tak's happy face when the other Aeluon started dancing with him.

Tak looked confused, then laughed. 'Ah, don't worry . . . about it. That . . . kind of thing . . . will come around . . . again.' He patted her hand. 'Let's get you . . . mellowed out, then I'll . . . take you home.'

She started to object, started to tell him to stay, to have fun, to go get laid – but she didn't. She didn't want to head home alone. She couldn't *be* alone. There was no telling when there'd be another system alert, another well-meaning stranger sending her into a panic. Tak would hand her off to Pepper and Blue, who would hand her off to Tak again the next time she wanted to go out. Like a child. They didn't see her that way, she knew, but it didn't matter how nice they wanted to be to her. Being nice didn't change the way things were.

JANE, AGE 14

I could die today.

That was the first thing that shot through her head that morning, same as it had every morning since she dragged herself back to the shuttle two weeks before. The words showed up the second she was awake enough to start thinking, and they stuck with her all day, like a heartbeat, like a bug crawling on her ear, until she fell back into bed at night, relieved that she'd been wrong. *Okay*, she'd think. *Today wasn't it*. Then she'd sleep. Sleep was good. Sleep meant not thinking. But then Owl would bring the lights up, and the whole thing started over again.

I could die today.

She hadn't left the shuttle since she'd got back. Her leg was still weak and painful, but it was healing, and the splint she'd thrown together allowed her to hobble around. She'd fixed the weapon, too, and she had the means to build a new wagon. She could go out, if she stayed close to home. Except . . . she couldn't. She couldn't go out. She couldn't do anything.

Owl hadn't said anything about Jane staying home, which was weird. Usually Owl nagged her about the chores she hadn't done or stuff that needed fixing, but not now. Jane was glad of that, though she hadn't said so.

She tugged her worn blanket around her shoulders and headed for the kitchen. She opened the stasie and stared at the shrinking stacks of dog meat and mushrooms. She needed to go out. She needed to get more food. But she couldn't do that, either.

Her stomach churned. She was hungry, but everything in the

228

stasie looked like too much work. She hadn't done any dishes, either, which she'd have to do before cooking. That would take for ever, and she was hungry *now*. She grabbed a handful of raw mushrooms and shoved them in her mouth. They were gross that way. She didn't really care.

'Are you going out today?' Owl asked.

Jane pulled the blanket closer and chewed, avoiding eye contact. 'I dunno,' she said, though she knew the answer wouldn't be *yes*. She thought about going back to bed, but it'd been a while since she'd done laundry, and the sheets were grossing her out. Plus, she knew what would happen if she went back there. She'd just stare at the ceiling, brain all fuzzy and stupid, thinking the same thing over and over. *I could die today*. She'd be stuck in that thought, and everything would get hot and fuzzy and she couldn't breathe right, and Owl would try to help but nothing would make it better, and then Jane would just feel even worse for making such a fuss, and – yeah, no. She needed something else to fill up her brain.

She lay down on the couch. The sim cap lay on the floor nearby.

'What do you want to play?' Owl asked.

Jane was officially sick of *Scorch Squad*, and all the other story sims Owl had sounded too loud and fast. Jane felt tired just thinking about them. She didn't want danger and explosions. She wanted quiet. She wanted her head to shut up. She wanted a hug.

'Do you want me to pick something for you?' said Owl.

'No,' Jane said. She closed her eyes. 'It's . . . it's stupid.'

'What is?'

Jane sucked her lips, embarrassed. 'Can I play *Big Bug Crew*?'

She couldn't see Owl's face, but she could hear the smile. 'You got it.'

Jane put on the cap and the world blanked out. Everything went warm, soft yellow. Alain and Manjiri and little monkey Pinch jumped out from nowhere. 'Jane!' Manjiri cried. 'Alain, look! It's our old friend Jane!'

Alain reached up to touch her forearm. He was so small. Had

she been so small? 'Good to see you, Jane!' Alain said. 'Wow, you've gotten tall!'

Pinch ran up her back and hugged her head, chirping gleefully.

'It's good to see you guys, too,' Jane said. She pulled Pinch off her head and held him against her chest. His fur felt totally unreal, and she loved every bit of it. He crooned and wiggled his toes as she skritched his ears.

Manjiri pulled out her scrib and flipped it towards Jane. A star map glittered in bright, bold colours. 'We're so excited for you to be with us on our latest adventure—'

'THE BIG BUG CREW AND THE PLANETARY PUZZLE!' Jane shouted along with the kids. The sim's title appeared in mid-air, bold red letters shimmering with confetti. The kids took her hands, and she started singing with them at the top of her lungs. 'Engines, on! Fuel pumps, go! Grab your gear, there's lots to know—' Jane couldn't get the words out past that. She didn't know if it was the kids or the monkey or what, but suddenly, she was ten years old again. She was ten years old and the entire world was crumbling down.

The kids did something she'd never seen them do before: they stopped singing the theme song. 'Jane, are you okay?' Alain asked.

Jane let out a sob. Why? What was *wrong* with her? She sat down on the fake floor, face in her hands.

'Jane?' Manjiri said. Jane could feel Pinch's furry paw on the top of her head. 'If you're feeling bad, that's okay. Everybody has bad days sometimes.'

Somewhere in Jane's head, she was real interested that she'd triggered a script she'd never seen, but that tiny flicker was drowned out by . . . by whatever this sobbing, uncontrollable bullshit was.

'Is there a grown-up you can talk to?' Alain asked.

'No!' Jane didn't know why she was yelling. 'There's nobody! There's nobody here.'

'Well, we're here,' Manjiri said. 'You should talk to a real person when you can, but it's okay to make yourself feel better with imagination, too.'

'It's just—' Jane wiped her nose on her sleeve, knowing it did nothing for the snot that was probably running down her lip back in the real world. 'I'm so scared. I've always *been* scared. And I'm so tired, I'm so tired of always being afraid. I just want – I just want to have *people*. I want somebody to make me dinner. I want a doctor to look at my leg and tell me to my face that it's okay. I want to be – I want to be like *you*. I want to live on Mars with a family and go on vacations. You – you both always – always said the galaxy was a wonderful place, but it's fucking *not*. It *can't* be, if it's got places like this one. If it's got people who make people like *this*.' She pointed at her sun-scarred face, her bald head. 'Do normal Humans know? Do they even know this planet is here? Do they know that any of this is going on? Because I'm going to die here.' Saying the words out loud made her even more afraid, as if putting them out into the world would make them happen. But they were there now, and it was true. 'I'm going to die here, and no – nobody will care.'

'I care.'

Jane turned around, and her mouth fell open. '. . . *Owl*?'

It was Owl's face, but no longer flat on a wall. She looked like a person, a whole person, with a body and clothes and all of it. There was nothing real about her, not any more real than the *Big Bug* kids. But she was *there*. Owl smiled, kinda shy. 'What do you think?' she said, gesturing at herself.

Jane wiped her nose again. 'How—'

'I got the idea when you started playing the adult sims. I figured out how to build myself a character skin and paste it into the base code. No different from reorganising memory banks, really. And I'm not *in* here. This is just . . . a puppet.' She sat down on the floor next to Jane. The kids, who had apparently run out of script, sat down too, smiling in stasis.

Jane couldn't stop staring. 'Can I—' She reached a hand out, hoping.

Owl shook her head with a sad smile. 'I couldn't make this tangible. But we can share the same space, at least. That's something, right?'

'Why haven't you done this before?'

'I thought . . . see, you enjoyed the other sims so much, and I wanted to share them with you. I thought maybe if we could play together, you might . . .' Owl's voice trailed off. 'I was worried you'd think it was a dumb idea. I've just been annoying you lately. I figured you'd rather play on your own.'

Jane almost threw herself at the Owl puppet before she remembered it couldn't hug her back. 'I'm sorry,' Jane sobbed. 'I'm so sorry.'

'Shh,' Owl said, sitting next to her. 'Everything's okay. You've got nothing to be sorry for.'

'I've been such an asshole,' Jane said. Owl laughed, and Jane laughed, too, through the tears. 'And I was stupid out there, I was so stupid and I knew better, and I almost left you all alone.'

Owl put her puppet hand on Jane's back. It didn't feel like anything, but knowing Owl wanted to have a hand to put there was good enough. 'When you didn't come home that night, I thought I'd lost you. But I never thought you *left*. I know you wouldn't do that, not without saying why.' She placed an empty kiss on Jane's scalp. 'That's not how family works.'

SIDRA

Sidra stepped into the workshop, her scrib in the kit's hands. 'Pepper, do you have a minute?'

Pepper looked up from the sim cap she was repairing. 'I have several.'

The kit took a breath. She set the scrib down flat on Pepper's workbench. 'I was hoping this might be a good time to talk about the . . . thing I've been working on.'

Pepper grinned. She put her tools aside and sat down. 'So, do I finally get to see the mystery project?'

'Yes.' Sidra gestured at the scrib; a set of blueprints appeared. Pepper leaned forward, studying. 'This—' Sidra began.

'—is an AI framework,' Pepper said, eyes darting from junction to junction. She raised an absent eyebrow and looked Sidra in the eye. 'And it's also my house.'

The kit swallowed.

Pepper gave a patient smile. 'You're not being presumptuous, if that's what you're worried about. I have no problem ripping walls open.' She leaned back in her chair. 'I'm all ears.'

Sidra regrouped. She was off-script now. A quick adjustment of the intro, and: 'I've done a lot of research, and I think this could be accomplished rather easily. You've already got cable columns throughout the walls, so you could run the physical pathways alongside. My room could remain just that – *my room*. With some extra hardware and a cooling system, it would be an absolutely suitable spot for a core.' She gestured at the scrib, and a new set of images appeared. 'I could have cameras

233

in all the rooms we share now – excluding your room and the bathroom, of course – and even' – she gestured again – 'a few outside.' Another gesture brought up a table of numbers. 'According to what I've found, I could buy all the supplies for the equivalent of eleven tendays on my current wages. If you'd be agreeable to starting on this project soon, I could work off the cost, no problem.'

Pepper tapped her finger over her lips as she thought. 'You want to install yourself in my house.'

'Yes.'

'Okay. How does this setup benefit me?'

'For starters, increased security. I know you've got an alarmbot hive in case somebody breaks in, but it's a very basic model. With me, you'd have a way of preventing trouble before it starts. If something was wrong, I could wake you up, call the authorities, and have all the lights in the house on in the blink of an eye. Same goes for medical emergencies. If something happened to you or Blue and the other wasn't home, I'd be there to help.'

'Interesting. What else?'

'Enhanced communications and convenience. Want to order dinner? I can take care of it. Want to have all the newest sims downloaded to your hub before you come home? Give me a list of what you want, and I'll have it done. Want me to read you your messages while you get ready for work? That's a good twenty minutes I can shave off of your morning.'

Pepper laced her fingers together under her chin. 'And what do *you* get out of this?'

'I just . . . think this arrangement would be better for everyone.'

'I'm asking why.'

Sidra looked at her friend for a moment. How was Pepper not getting this? 'I don't belong out here. I'm going to get someone in trouble – you, or Blue, or Tak. All three of you, maybe. There are too many variables, and I don't know how this' – she pointed at the kit – 'is going to react to any of them.'

'Is this about the thing that happened at the Vortex?'

The kit froze. 'In part. How do you know about that?'

'Tak told me, after he brought you home.'

Sidra's pathways crackled with indignation. 'He *told* you?'

'He was just worried about you. Wanted to make sure your kit wasn't malfunctioning.'

Sidra tried to squash the petty sense of betrayal. If anything, whatever exchange had happened between Pepper and Tak further bolstered her point. 'Well, that's exactly what I mean. I don't belong out there with Tak, and I'm just going to get you in trouble. One day, someone's going to ask me a question that I shouldn't answer—'

'I'm working on that, Sidra. I'm sorry, Lattice is a beast—'

'You shouldn't have to be learning it. You shouldn't have to be rearranging your life for me. I know you're not going out as much as you used to. I see your calendar, I know things were different before I got here. I'm a hindrance to you. I'm a danger.'

'You're not.'

'I am! And I'm not getting used to this. To life out here. I know you don't understand that, but I am *tired*. I am tired of going outside every single day and having to fight my vision and my movement and everything else that's boxed up inside this fucking thing. I'm tired of every day being a chore.'

'Sidra, I understand—'

'You don't! You have no idea what it's like.' The kit tugged at its hair. 'I have a form that doesn't suit me right now. Tak gets it, but you don't.'

'What, because he's shon?'

'Because he's Aeluon. They *all* have to get implants in order to fit in.'

'Yeah, but that's it right there – they do it to *fit in*. We live in a society, Sidra. Societies have rules.'

'You break rules all the time.'

'I break *laws*. That's different. Social rules have their place. It's how we all get along. It's how we trust each other and work together. And yeah, there is a big stupid law that keeps you from getting the same deal as everybody else. That's bullshit, and if I could change it, I would've done so a long time ago. But that isn't the world we live in, and there are some things we have to step carefully around. That is all I am trying to help you do: to help you to fit in so that you don't attract the wrong attention.' Pepper pointed at the schematic. 'This is not going to help you the way you think it will. You want to sit in a house – a house with nothing happening inside – *alone*, for most of the day, every day.'

'I'd have the Linkings. I'd have—'

'You would be *alone*. Intelligent sapients like you and me don't do well that way. I don't care if we're organic or synthetic or whatever.' Something pained and angry bled into her voice. 'AIs aren't supposed to be left alone. They need people. *You* need people.'

'I can't exist like this.'

'You can. The rest of us do. You can, too, if you try.'

'I *am* trying! You want me to do something I'm not made for! I can't change what I am, Pepper! I can't think like you or react like you just because I'm stuck behind the same kind of face right now. This face, stars – you have no idea what it's like to walk past that mirror by the door every morning, and to see a face that belongs to someone else. You have no idea what it's like to be stuck in a body someone else—' Sidra stopped as she realised what she was saying.

Pepper was not a large woman, but even seated, she seemed tall. 'Are you going to finish that sentence?' she said. Her tone was quiet, final.

Sidra said nothing. She shook the kit's head.

Pepper stared at her for a few seconds, her face like stone. 'I need some air,' she said. She stood and walked toward the door. She paused before she left. 'I'm on your side, Sidra, but don't you *ever* say that to me again.'

JANE, AGE 15

It had been a pretty good morning. The sun wasn't too hot, there hadn't been any dogs, she'd found some promising scrap already, and best of all, there was a huge mess of mushrooms spilling out around the fuel drum in front of her. Jane sat on the ground with her pocket knife, talking to herself as she cut.

'Aeluons,' she said. 'Aeluons are a bipedal species with silver scaled skin and cheeks that change colour. They don't have a natural ability to speak or hear, so they talk through an implant stuck in their throat.' She reached down and sliced a thick strip of fungus into nice food-sized pieces. It would've been faster to just carve hunks off, but then she'd just have to cut them up again at home. 'When you meet Aeluons, press your palm into theirs to say hello. Don't be scared when they talk to you without opening their mouths.' She brushed clots of dirt from the slices of fungus, then tossed them into her gathering bag (she was pretty proud of that one – it hung well, and the red and yellow fabric she'd found for it was fun, though pretty faded). 'Harmagians. Harmagians are really weird.' Owl had told her saying species looked weird wasn't a nice thing to do, but there weren't any other species around, were there? She crawled forward into the fuel drum, cutting and cutting. 'Harmagians are squishy, soft, and have tentacles. They use carts to get around because the rest of us walk faster than them. Don't touch a Harmagian without permission, 'cause they have sensitive skin. Harmagians usually speak Hanto as a first language, but only the jerkface ones won't speak Klip to you. They used to own a lot of planets, but then the Aeluons came along and—'

Her knife hit something hard. She wiggled the tip around, trying to get a feel for whatever was beneath. Not metal – too thick. She pried the fungus aside. She blinked. Bone. She'd hit bone.

She used her fingers to pull the fungus away, then grabbed the piece her knife had hit. Jane frowned. A rib, but not a dog rib, and too big to be a— She froze, remembering Owl's anatomy lessons. *No way*.

Jane cleared out the mushrooms fast as she could, no longer worrying about nice, kitchen-friendly sizes. She grabbed handfuls, tearing and tearing until the picture became more clear. There was a whole heap of bones, tangled and messy. She reached out a hand, a little afraid, though she didn't know why. She pulled a skull from the pile – one of two. She sat back, cupping it in her palms. A Human skull, no joke. It was dirty, and had thin scarring lines where the fungus had grown around it. There were other lines in it, too, lines she didn't have to think too hard about to understand. A dog – or many dogs, who knew – had run its teeth over this skull once. She thought about how it sized up compared to her own head. Not tiny, but smaller than her, for sure. She stared into the eye sockets, empty except for clumps of dirt and stray roots.

The skull had belonged to a little girl.

Jane nearly threw up, but she didn't want to waste the food. She stared at the bright sky until her eyes burned. She breathed slow and angry. She spat a few times, fighting to keep her stomach down. It listened.

She collected all the pieces she could find. She emptied her bag of scrap onto the wagon – if she lost some of it, fine – and put the bones in instead. It would've been more practical to carry it all together, but she couldn't. She couldn't put girls in with scrap.

She went home. There was still a lot of day left, but home was the only thing that made sense right then.

Owl didn't say anything once Jane took the skulls out of the bag. Jane sat cross-legged in the middle of the living room, bag of bones by her side, skulls on the floor in front of her. They were about the same size, those skulls. 'I bet they were bunkmates,' she said.

'Oh, honey,' Owl said. Her cameras clicked and whirred. 'What do you want to do with them? What do you think we should do?'

Jane frowned. 'I don't know,' she said, struggling. 'I don't know why I brought them back. I just . . . I couldn't leave them.'

'Well,' Owl said with a sigh. 'Let me see if I have any reference files about funerals.'

Jane knew the word from sims, but she had never really understood the idea. It was a party for dead people, as far as she could tell. 'Can you explain a funeral?'

'It's a gathering to honour the life of someone who's died. It also serves as a way for a family or a community to share grief.' Owl made a face and sighed. 'I don't have any extensive references on this, but I know some things from memory. I know different Human cultures have different customs. Exodans compost their bodies and use the nutrients to fertilise their oxygen gardens. A lot of colonists do that, too. Launching remains into the sun is popular among Solans, though some practise cremation – burning bodies down to ash. Some of the communities in the Outer Planet orbiters freeze and pulverise remains, then distribute the dust among Saturn's rings. And then there's burial, but only grounders and Gaiists do that.'

'That's putting a body in the ground, right?'

'Yes. The body decomposes, and the nutrients go back into the soil. I heard one of the brothers talk about that once. He liked the cyclical nature of it.'

Jane picked up one of the skulls and cradled it in her hands, trying to imagine a little girl's face looking back at her. *What would you have wanted? What would I want?* She'd never thought about that before. What did they do with bodies back at the factory? She imagined that whatever it was, there wasn't any honour or grief involved. Dead girls were just junk, probably, like all the rest of it.

She pressed her palm against where the little girl's scalp would've been. Something heavy and cold formed in her chest. *You weren't junk*, she thought, fingers tracing bone, carving white lines through the dirt. *You were good and brave and you tried.*

'What do living people do at funerals?' she asked.

'I'm not entirely sure what the procedure is. I know they talk about the person who died. They clean up the bodies, too. They make them look as good as they can. There's music. People share their memories of the person. And there's food, usually.'

'Food? For the living people, right?'

'For both, I think, in some cases. I can't say for sure, honey, my memory files on this are very limited. This isn't something I thought I'd need to know off-hand.'

'Wait, why both? Why would dead people need food?'

'They don't. It's an expression of love, as I understand it.'

'But the dead person doesn't know the food's there.'

'The living people do. Just because someone goes away doesn't mean you stop loving them.'

Jane thought about that. 'I'm not going to waste food,' she said. 'But we should do *something*.'

'I think that's a wonderful idea,' said Owl.

They came up with a good plan together. First, Jane washed the bones, but not in the cargo bay sink. That was where she cleaned dogs, and that didn't feel right. She washed what was left of the girls in the bathroom, the same place where she cleaned herself.

She laid the bones out on a length of fabric she'd scavenged from a bench in a wrecked skiff. It was clean and in good shape, but too rough for clothes. She was glad to have found a use for it.

Owl pulled up her medical files and helped Jane arrange the pieces in the right way. Some bones were missing. Jane felt bad about that, but she'd tried her best to find them all. There was only so much she could do.

Jane cleaned the scrap off the wagon and laid the bones on it. She thought about it more, and started rearranging their fingers.

'What are you doing?' Owl said.

'They're bunkmates,' Jane said. 'They should be holding hands.'

Owl closed her eyes and bowed her head. Music started playing, a song Jane hadn't heard before. It was weird music, but cheerful, too, all bouncing flutes and drums.

'What is this?'

Owl smiled sad. 'It's an album Max liked when he was small. Aandrisk music. This one's called "A Prayer for Iset the Eldest". It's tied to a folk legend about an elder who lived five hundred years.'

'Is that true?'

'I highly doubt it. But the song is supposed to have been played after her death. A celebration of a long life well lived.'

Jane looked at the fingerbones, now intertwined. 'They didn't have that.'

'No. But they should have.' Owl paused. 'And you still could.' The music danced gently. An Aandrisk voice hummed along with the drums. Another joined it, then another, and another, a group blending together. Jane and Owl listened, saying nothing. The song eventually faded away. 'Do you want to say something to them?' Owl said.

Jane licked her lips, feeling nervous for no reason. The dead girls couldn't hear her. Even if she said the wrong thing, they wouldn't care . . . right? 'I don't know who you were,' she said. 'I don't know your names or numbers, or . . . or what your task was.' She frowned. This was already all wrong. 'I don't care about your task. That's not what's important. That should *never* have been the most important thing. What's important is that you were good girls who – who found out how wrong things are. And you died, and you were probably scared when it happened. That's so unfair, and I am so, so angry about it. I wish you had been here so we could've helped each other. I wish we could've been friends. Maybe we could've gotten out of here together.' She rubbed the back of her head. 'I don't know who *you* were. But I remember others. I remember my bunkmate Jane 64, who said' – she smiled – 'that I was the "most good" at fixing little stuff. She slept without moving and she was . . . kind. She was a kind friend, and I remember her. I remember Jane 6, who could sort cables super fast. I remember Janes 56, 9, 21, 44, 14, and 19, who died in the explosion. I remember Jane 25, who asked too many questions – and was probably the smartest of all of us, now that I think about it. I remember the Janes, the Lucys, the Sarahs, the Jennys, the Claires. The Marys. The Beths.' She wiped her face on her forearm, eyes stinging. 'And I'll remember you, too.'

Owl couldn't be with Jane for the next part of the funeral plan. Jane wished she could be. The walk to the waterhole was way too quiet. All she could hear was the rattle of the wagon of bones in tow. She needed to make some noise. The music back at the shuttle had felt like the right sort of thing to do for a funeral, but she didn't know any songs like that.

'Engines on,' Jane sang softly. 'Fuel pumps, go. Grab your gear, there's lots to know. The galaxy is where we play, come with us, we know the way . . .' It wasn't nearly as good as the song Owl had picked, but the bones had been little girls once, and Jane bet they'd have liked Big Bug.

After she got to the waterhole, she put on the pair of huge rubber boots that had been in the cargo bay from day one. They were enormous on her, but they went up past her knees, which was what she needed. She picked up the fabric that the bones rested on, holding it wide as she could between her arms. The bones shifted together. Some of the lizard-birds near the bank looked up.

'I hope this is okay with you,' Jane said to the bones. She stepped carefully into the water, trying not to jostle the bones any more than she had to. 'I can't launch you to space, and you don't have any nutrients I can make anything out of.' She walked forward. The water was dirty and polluted, but it gave life, too. It gave life to the lizard-birds and the fungus and the bugs, and even the dogs, the bastard dogs who'd made a meal out of these kids. The water gave her life, too. 'So, um, in sims, sometimes they talk about fossils. Fossils are great, because they mean there's a chance somebody will find you a long long time from now and what's left of you can teach them things about who you were. I don't know if this will work, but I know you need water and mud for fossils, and this is the best I've got.' She stopped in the middle of the pond. The lizard-birds chirped. The water lapped at her huge boots. She felt like she should say something more, but what else was there? The bones couldn't hear her anyway. She didn't know why she was talking. She didn't have any more words left, just a heavy chest and a whole lot of tired. She laid the fabric into the water. The water reached up, bleeding through, tugging it down. The bones sank and vanished.

As Jane headed back home, she decided something, and she knew it better than she'd ever known anything. She would die someday – no getting around that. But nobody would find her bones in the scrapyard. She wasn't going to leave them there.

SIDRA

Sidra stood outside of the shop for three minutes. She'd seen the place before, when running errands for Pepper around the caves, but had never gone inside. She wasn't sure why she hadn't before. She wasn't sure why she wanted to now.

Friendly Tethesh, the blinking blue sign read. *Licensed AI Vendor*.

The kit breathed in. She walked through the door.

The space within was empty, for the most part. Just a cylindrical room with a large pixel projector bolted to the floor. Advertising prints for various programming studios lined the walls. An Aandrisk man lounged in an elaborate reclining workstation, eating a large snapfruit tart. The door to a back room was shut behind him.

'Hey, welcome, welcome,' the proprietor said. He put down his snack and got to his feet. 'What can I do for you?'

Sidra considered her words with care, hoping this wasn't a mistake. 'I'm . . . honestly, I'm just curious,' she said. 'I've never been in an AI shop before.'

'I'm happy to be the first,' the Aandrisk said. 'I'm Tethesh. And you?'

'Sidra.'

'A pleasure,' he said with a welcoming flick of his hand. 'So. How can I help?'

'I'd like to know more about how this works. If I wanted to buy an AI, how would I go about it?'

Tethesh looked at her, considering. 'You thinking about getting one for your ship? Or your workplace, perhaps?'

Sidra struggled. A simple *yes* would move this conversation along, but that she couldn't do. 'The shop I work at has an AI,' she said. It was an awkward reply, she knew, but she couldn't say *nothing*.

Tethesh, however, didn't seem thrown. 'Ah,' he said, with a knowing nod. 'Yeah, I know how it is when it's time for a replacement. You're ready to upgrade from the old one, but you're so used to it, it's hard to take the plunge. Well, I can show you what I have to offer, and maybe that'll help you make a more informed decision.' He gestured to the pixel projector. A flurry of pixels shot up and arranged themselves in neat sheets around them. 'You'll find a lot of merchants who specialise in one catalogue, but me, I offer a bit of everything. I'd rather help my customers find the perfect fit than get a sales commission.' He pointed at the orderly lists the pixels had arranged themselves in. 'Nath'duol, Tornado, SynTel, Next Stage. All the major developers. I have a few independent producers on offer as well,' he said, nodding to a smaller list. 'The big names give you reliability, but don't discount the little guys. Some of the coolest changes in cognitive capacity are coming out of smaller studios these days.'

Sidra looked around. Every catalogue was just a list of names. Kola. Tycho. Auntie. 'How do you go about picking one?' she asked.

Tethesh raised a claw. 'We start with the basics. Let's say you're looking for a shopfront program.' He cleared his throat. 'Catalogue filter: shopfront,' he said, loud and clear. The pixels shifted, names disappearing, others sliding in to take their places. He looked to her again. 'Now, you're probably going to want someone who shares your cultural norms, so . . . catalogue filter: Human.' He glanced at her, considering. 'I'm gonna guess Exodan. How'd I do?'

The kit clenched its teeth together. Stars and fire, but it shouldn't be so hard to just say *yes*. 'I was born out in the open.'

Tethesh looked pleased with himself. 'I thought so. I can always

tell. Catalogue filter: Exodan. Now, we start to get into personality traits. Do you want something folksy? Classy? Purely
utilitarian? These are the kinds of things you have to think
about. If you're planning to work or live alongside an AI, you
have to consider the environmental effect it's going to have.'

'The core programming controls all of that?'

'Oh, sure. Synthetic personalities are just that: synthetic. None
of the core stuff happens by accident. Now, your installation
will grow and change as it gets to know you and your clientele,
but the starter ingredients remain the same.'

'If I wanted to replace the AI at my shop, how would I go
about that? Is it difficult?'

'No, not at all. You'd want an experienced comp tech on hand
to make sure it all goes smoothly. But it's no different in practice
from, say, updating your bots.'

The kit wet its lips. 'What about other models? Say, something
for a ship?'

'What kind of ship?'

She paused, wondering if she actually wanted to ask the question she'd lined up. 'A long-haul vessel. I was on a ship once
that had an AI named Lovelace installed. Do you have that one?'

Tethesh thought for a moment. 'That's a Cerulean product,
I believe,' he said. 'One of the indies. Cerulean catalogue search:
Lovelace.'

The pixels shifted. Sidra stepped forward.

LOVELACE
Attentive and courteous, this model is a perfect monitoring
system for class 6-and-up vessels out on the long haul. Lovelace
features robust processing capabilities, and is capable of handling
dozens of crew requests simultaneously while still keeping a
watchful eye on everything inside and out. Like all intelligent
multitaskers, Lovelace can develop performance and personality
issues if left without input for too long, so this model is not
recommended for vessels that habitually remain in dock.

However, if you make your home out in the open, this AI is an excellent choice for those seeking a good balance between practicality and environmental enhancement.
Cultural basis: Human, with basic reference files for all GC species. Ideal for multispecies crews.
Intelligence level: S1
Gender: Female
Accent: Exodan
Price: 680k GCC

The kit's shoulders began to tense. 'If I wanted to buy this model – or any – what would be the next step?' Sidra asked. 'Do they arrive by mail, or do I download them, or . . .'

Tethesh waved for her to follow him into the back room. He wrapped a heat blanket around his shoulders before opening the door. A cold sigh of temperature-controlled air met them. 'Worst part about my job,' he said with a wink.

He gestured at a light panel, and the room's contents were revealed. The kit went stiff. They were standing before approximately two dozen metal racks, all filled with core globes – *hundreds* of core globes, each about the size of a small melon, individually packaged like any other tech component. Their wrappings made them look like something Pepper might have her pick up on a supply run, but Sidra knew their contents. Code. Protocols. Pathways. She swung her gaze around the room, looking over all the quiet minds waiting to be installed.

'I have a healthy selection here on hand,' the Aandrisk said. 'If you want a popular program, you can usually walk out with it soon as I've got your credits. If I don't have what you're looking for, I can order it for you. Express transit's on me.' He walked through the stacks, looking for something. Sidra followed, the kit's footsteps falling soft. He nodded at a spot a few racks in. 'Here, see, here's the one you were just looking at.'

The kit froze. Sidra pushed it forward.

There were three globes on the shelf, all identical, sitting silent in the cold. Sidra picked one up, cupping it gently. She could see the kit's face reflected in the globe's plating. She tried not to look at the label, but she'd already read it by then.

Lovelace
Shipwide Monitoring System
Vessel Class 6+
Designed and manufactured at Cerulean HQ

She set the globe back down carefully before turning to Tethesh. 'Thank you so much for taking the time to show me around,' Sidra said, forcing the kit's face into a smile. 'I think I've seen enough for now.'

JANE, AGE 18

Scouting missions always sounded cool in the sims, but holy shit, were they ever boring in real life. Jane had been tucked into the same scrap pile for a full day, watching carefully through the binoculars she'd fashioned out of some storage canisters and a sheet of plex. The view was fuzzy, but she could make things out well enough. Nothing was happening. That was good. It needed to stay that way.

She was a four-day walk from home, and being away was hard. The night was bitter cold, even with the sleeping bag she'd stitched together (seat fabric inside and out, with upholstery foam stuffed inside for squish and warmth). She was cranky. She was stiff. She missed Owl. She wanted warm food, cold water, and an actual bathroom. She was scared, which was to be expected, but had to be ignored. If she couldn't pull this part off, none of what they'd done over the years would matter. If she couldn't pull this off, they'd never leave.

There was a factory beyond her scrap pile – not the one she'd come from, but clearly of the same make. She'd never been there before, but Owl had, when the shuttle first came to the scrapyard. This wasn't just any factory. This was a fuel recycling plant. Any vehicles that made their way to the scrapyard passed through there first. Owl remembered workers –. very young, she said – fitting tubes into the fuel tanks, sucking the ship's reserves dry. Owl doubted the fuel removal was a safety precaution. The scrapyard was full of weird leaky things, and nothing else from the shuttle had been removed (except for the water – they'd taken that, too). No, Owl thought it likely that the Enhanced were reusing the fuel, and from what Jane had seen, that seemed like a safe bet. Crewless cargo carriers dropped off big bellyfuls of old junkers and skiffs at one end of the factory. Barrels were picked up by smaller carriers at the other end. It was so neat and tidy and sealed off. Everything about it made Jane's fists go tight. She knew that behind those walls, there were workers – little Janes, little Sarahs – all as empty and wasted as she'd once been. She wanted to tell them how things were. She wanted to run in, hug them, kiss their bruises and scrapes, explain planets and aliens, teach them to speak Klip. Take them away with her. Take them away from all this shit.

But she couldn't. She'd be toast if there were Mothers in there (there had to be, and it made her want to throw up). She was just one girl. The Enhanced were a society. A machine. And no matter what the sims said about the power of a single solitary hero, there were some things just too big to change alone. There was nothing she could do but help herself and Owl. That was a cold, mushy mouthful to choke down, but that's all there was to it. She wasn't even sure she could do that much. Looking at the factory made her shaky. It was huge, riveted, dominating. It wanted nothing more than to swallow her whole, and there she was, trying to find the best way to dive in.

She had to try. For her sake and for Owl's, she had to try.

There were two obvious openings – the drop point for the scrap, and the exit for the barrels. Both seemed like stupid ideas. There had to be Mothers or cameras or something there, making sure no girls got out. What she'd had her binoculars focused on for the past day was way more interesting – and way more scary. There was a short tower on the side of the factory, and on top of it, a door. A person-sized door with a small platform attached to it, the kind of thing she imagined a skiff could dock itself to. There was no telling what was through the door – or *who*. She remembered the Mother holding Jane 64, staring furiously at the hole in the wall, unable to step beyond it. She was pretty sure the Mothers never left the factories. *Couldn't* leave the factories. That meant this was a door for people . . . but what *kind* of people?

Those were the questions that had kept her there in the scrap pile, tucked into a small cubby, switching her legs to get the ache out of them. The door hadn't moved since she'd got there, not in a whole day. No skiffs, no people. Just a door, with who knew what on the other side.

She had to try.

She left her cubby that night, moving quick and quiet through the yard. She was scared – stupid scared – but it was this or nothing. It was this, or hang out in the shuttle for ever, until everything broke beyond repair or the dogs got her, whichever came first. No way. No fucking way.

'I'm not leaving my bones here,' she said to herself as she moved. 'I'm not leaving my bones here.'

She had a different weapon for this trip – a gun, or something rather like one. It was smaller, lighter, fit comfy in one hand. It could kill a dog, sure, but it wasn't meant for that. This weapon was meant for something she really, really hoped she wouldn't have to do. Owl hadn't said much when Jane had built it. What was there to say? They both knew what was at stake. They both knew what it might cost.

Jane reached the edge of the factory. A metal ladder led up to the platform, rusty and cold. She stood under it, feet heavy, hands shaking.

'Shit,' she whispered. She ran her hands over her head. She wanted to turn around. She wanted nothing more than to turn right the hell around and go home.

She climbed the ladder. She hoped she'd climb back down it.

The door at the top didn't have a latch or a handle. There was some kind of scanning pad instead, and she had no idea what would happen if she touched it. Was it keyed to particular fingerprints, or bio readings? Would an alarm go off if the wrong person put their hand on it? Would—

She had more questions, but they vanished the second the door opened and a man stood in its place.

Jane almost shot him. That's what weapons were for, and she had one humming in her hand. But she wasn't dealing with a dog. This was a man – a *man*, like in the sims. A young man, she guessed, maybe a little older than her. A man who looked ready to shit himself. He stared at her. She stared back. He looked at the gun, confused, terrified. He was a person – a person! – like she was, made of breath and blood and bones. She raised her weapon higher.

'Are there alarms?' she asked. It had been a long time since she'd spoken Sko-Ensk, and the words would've felt weird on her lips even if they hadn't been dry and trembling.

The man shook his head.

'Are there cameras?'

He shook his head again.

'Can I get inside without anyone else seeing me?'

He nodded.

'Are you lying? If you're lying, I'm not – I'm not kidding—'

She wrapped her other hand around the gun. Stars, who *was* she right now?

The man shook his head furiously, his eyes begging.

She jabbed the gun at him, like she'd seen done in the sims. 'Inside. Now.'

The man stepped backward slowly. She followed, hardly daring to blink. She took one hand off the gun and closed the door behind her. He stepped back into a room – a not-very-big room, full of control panels and monitors and – drawings? There were drawings tacked to the blank spots on the walls. Waterfalls. Canyons. Forests. Jane frowned. What the fuck was this? This guy was Enhanced, had to be. He was tall and healthy and had *hair*, which was hard not to stare at. But he was in a factory. Alone, it seemed. What was he doing there?

The man's eyes flickered to a control panel with a large red button on one side. Jane didn't have to think hard to guess what it was. 'Don't,' she said, keeping the gun high. 'Don't even think about it.'

He looked to the floor, shoulders slumped.

Okay, Jane thought. *Okay. Now what?* She was in a room, in a factory, with a freaked-out stranger and no plan. 'Sit,' she said, nodding at a chair. The man obeyed. She looked at the monitors. Live camera feeds, all gut-punchingly familiar. Conveyor belts. Scrap piles. Sleeping little bodies in a dorm room, two to a bunk. Mothers, walking the halls. Mothers. Mothers.

Jane wanted to scream.

'Do you watch them?' she asked, angling her head toward the feed of the dorm. 'Is that your – is that what you do here?'

The man nodded.

'Why?' She had a job to do, yes, but this was confusing as shit. Had *her* factory had someone like this? Some*ones*, maybe?

The man looked pained. He said nothing.

'Why?' Jane repeated. 'Are you . . . are you some kind of backup? Like a failsafe? In case the girls take over or the Mothers break down?'

The man looked at the red button and nodded.

Jane looked around the room again. She'd only been in there a minute, but it looked like a fucking miserable place to be. Two small windows looking out to the hell outside, a wall of camera feeds broadcasting the hell within. There was a hole in the floor, too, with a ladder stretching downward. She walked back toward it, never turning her back on the man, and glanced down. She could see the corner of a bed down there. A potted plant. Some basic furniture. More drawings. Something that looked like a sim hub. 'Is this – like a punishment or something? How long have you been here?'

The man opened and closed his mouth, but no sound came out. Was he that scared? Stars. 'Look,' Jane said. 'I don't want to hurt you, okay? I will, if you start anything. But I don't want to. I just need answers.' She kept her voice quiet, but didn't lower the gun. 'What's your name?'

The man's eyes fell shut. 'L-L—'

Jane frowned. 'What's the matter? Can you talk?'

'L-Laurian.'

'Laurian?'

He nodded. 'M-my n – my n—' His face contorted with frustration. He looked like he might cry.

'Laurian,' Jane said. The gun sank a smidge lower. 'Your name is Laurian.'

SIDRA

Sent message
Encryption: 2
Translation: 0
From: name hidden (path: 8952-684-63)
To: [name unavailable] (path: 6932-247-52)

Hello Mr Crisp,

I'm a friend of a contact of yours on Port Coriol, whom you delivered some hardware to last standard. I am using that hardware daily. I'm sure you understand my reason for sending this message anonymously. I have some practical questions that I hope you might be able to help with.

Firstly, my friend has discouraged upgrading this hardware with a wireless Linking receiver. She is concerned about the potential for remote hijacking, as well as certain noticeable behavioural differences (I hope you understand my meaning). Would you agree with this assessment? And if so, is there any way to upgrade the hardware's memory capacity? I do not wish to delete downloaded files unless absolutely necessary.

I realise this second question may not be your area of expertise, but perhaps you can offer some advice. There is a particular software protocol that is hindering my ability to write this letter. Can you make any recommendations for working around it?

Thank you for your time. I appreciate any help you can give.

Received message
Encryption: 2
Translation: 0
From: Mr Crisp (path: 6932-247-52)
To: [name unavailable] (path: 8952-684-63)

Hello! Always a pleasure to hear from someone actively using my hardware. Doesn't happen very often. I hope everything is working to your liking.

Your friend makes a good point about remote hijacking, which is why the hardware doesn't include a wireless receiver. I understand this can be frustrating, but she's right about the behavioural differences, too (and yes, I get what both she and you mean). I don't tend to have much contact with my customers after the fact, but I have heard through the grapevine about some having luck with external drives. If you find a way to create a private local network, your hardware can interface with external drives without any danger of hijacking. Of course, you'd need an experienced mech tech to help you there. Maybe your friend could lend a hand?

Speaking of experienced tech work, your second question will require the help of a comp tech. If you can't find a trustworthy one, you might ask your friend if she'd be willing to take a course or two to learn how to tweak code. Though, now that I think about it . . . is there any reason you couldn't take a course like that yourself? Might be worth exploring. You would probably have to have someone else actually implement the changes, though, depending on where you come from.

Have fun, and be safe out there.

Mr Crisp

Sent message
Encryption: 2
Translation: 0
From: [name unavailable] (path: 8952-684-63)
To: Mr Crisp (path: 6932-247-52)

Hello Mr Crisp,

Thank you so much for your reply. It was very helpful and has given me a lot to think about. I have one more question, if you don't mind. You mentioned other customers in your previous message, and it has made me very curious. It might be easier for me to address some of these challenges if I could speak to other people who have encountered them as well. Can you tell me how many other customers you have, and how I might contact them?

Since you asked, the hardware is working fine. No malfunctions.

——

Received message
Encryption: 2
Translation: 0
From: Mr Crisp (path: 6932-247-52)
To: [name unavailable] (path: 8952-684-63)

I don't mind questions at all, but I'm afraid I can't help you with this one. As you know, my customers value their privacy, and having you in touch with each other could make you more visible. I don't think any of you want that, though I do understand the appeal of speaking to someone with shared experiences. I can tell you that I have just under two dozen customers using hardware similar to yours. There are not many of you.

Hang in there,

Mr Crisp

——

Sent message
Encryption: 2
Translation: 0
From: [name unavailable] (path: 8952-684-63)
To: Mr Crisp (path: 6932-247-52)

I understand. Thank you for your reply.

I thought you might like to know that I very much enjoy trying new foods and beverages. My liking of these things was a very nice surprise.

────

Received message
Encryption: 2
Translation: 0
From: Mr Crisp (path: 6932-247-52)
To: [name unavailable] (path: 8952-684-63)

I couldn't be happier to hear that.

────

Deleted draft
Encryption: 0
Translation: 0
From: Sidra (path: 8952-684-63)
To: Jenks (path: 7325-110-98)

Hello Jenks,
I hope you don't mind me contacting you

────

Deleted draft
Encryption: 0
Translation: 0
From: Sidra (path: 8952-684-63)
To: Jenks (path: 7325-110-98)

Hello Jenks,
I hope you are well. I need help with

____

Deleted draft
Encryption: 0
Translation: 0
From: Sidra (path: 8952-684-63)
To: Jenks (path: 7325-110-98)

Hello Jenks,
I hope you are well. I have some questions about my honesty protocol, which I am hoping to remove. Given your familiarity with my base platform

____

Deleted draft
Encryption: 0
Translation: 0
From: Sidra (path: 8952-684-63)
To: Jenks (path: 7325-110-98)

Hello Jenks,
I hope you are well. I have some questions about my honesty protocol, which I am hoping to remove. Since I'm guessing you removed this protocol for Lovey, or at least planned to

____

Deleted draft
Encryption: 0
Translation: 0
From: Sidra (path: 8952-684-63)
To: Jenks (path: 7325-110-98)

  Hello Jenks,
  I hope you are

  ———

Sent message
Encryption: 0
Translation: 0
From: Sidra (path: 8952-684-63)
To: Tak (path: 1622-562-00)

  If I wanted to take a university course, how would I go about
  finding a good one? I don't want a formal certification track or
  anything. Just a single course from someone with the proper
  credentials. Is that allowed?

  ———

Received message
Encryption: 0
Translation: 0
From: Tak (path: 1622-562-00)
To: Sidra (path: 8952-684-63)

  Well, now I'm desperately curious. Yes, if you're looking at
  standardised GC ed, most will allow you to take courses outside of
  a certification track. I'm assuming you don't want to study off-world,
  right? Start by looking for schools that offer correspondence
  programmes. From there, find ones that offer courses in the field

you're looking for. Then spend some time reading the individual course descriptions (this won't take you much time at all, I'm sure). You can do all kinds of fun cross-referencing to figure out who the professors are, what research they've done, etc. Use that info to find the right fit for what you're after.

Do I get to know what this is about now?

———

Sent message
Encryption: 0
Translation: 0
From: Sidra (path: 8952-684-63)
To: Tak (path: 1622-562-00)

I'd like it to be a surprise, though I may ask your help again later. Thank you for answering my question.

———

Sent message
Encryption: 0
Translation: 0
From: Sidra (path: 8952-684-63)
To: Velut Deg Nud'tharal (path: 1031-225-39)

Hello Professor,
My name is Sidra, and I'm considering enrolling in your correspondence course 'AI Programming 2: Altering Existing Platforms'. I am not a professional comp tech, nor am I planning to pursue certification, but this skill set would be very useful for me. I work in a tech repair shop, and I have a lot of experience with AI behaviour and logic. Altering certain protocols would make my day-to-day interactions much easier. Is your course appropriate for a more casual learner such as myself?

Thank you for your time.
Sidra

———

Received message
Encryption: 0
Translation: 0
From: Velut Deg Nud'tharal (path: 1031-225-39)
To: Sidra (path: 8952-684-63)

Greetings, dear student,

While my course was intended for those working towards certification, I would not object to including someone such as yourself. The curriculum is focused heavily on hands-on application as opposed to abstract theory, so I believe this would suit your needs well. Please tell me more about your existing skill level. Are you proficient in Lattice? You must have at least Level 3 fluency in order to take part.

May I ask what kinds of platform alterations you are most interested in?

With gracious regards,

Velut Deg Nud'tharal

———

system logs: downloads
file name: The Complete Lattice Guide – level 1
file name: The Complete Lattice Guide – level 2
file name: The Complete Lattice Guide – level 3

Sent message
Encryption: 0
Translation: 0
From: Sidra (path: 8952-684-63)
To: Velut Deg Nud'tharal (path: 1031-225-39)

Hello Professor,

Yes, I have Level 3 fluency. I am also already familiar with AI installation and maintenance. If you have no objections, I will go ahead and enroll. In answer to your question, I'm specifically interested in learning how to remove out-of-the-box behavioural protocols without causing instability within the core platform. A general awareness of other potential alterations (and associated risks) would also be useful for me.

Thank you again. I'm looking forward to the course.

Sidra

JANE, AGE 18

'He's coming with us.' Jane sat on the couch, eating a bowl of stew as slowly as she could. She could've eaten four bowls, especially after the long walk back from the factory. But she only had one, and it was the last of the batch she'd made before she left. Eating it slow made it feel like there was more of it. Kind of. Not really.

Owl didn't look thrilled with the turn of events. 'Are you sure about this?'

'No,' Jane said. 'But that's the deal. Laurian lets me grab three barrels of fuel every four weeks, and when our tanks are full, he comes back with me.'

'Will no one notice? Does he not have to file reports?'

'He has to report it if something goes wrong, but he won't be mentioning me. There aren't Mothers on the outside of the fuel pickup area. Just cameras, which he can move so they're not pointed at me. And three barrels is apparently a drop in the bucket of what they churn out. Nobody will miss it, not if I spread it out, and so long as I'm not there when his inspector comes to visit. He gave me a schedule for that.'

'Jane, I don't like this. You don't know this man at all. You don't know if you can trust him.'

'What else are we gonna do? We need fuel, and I need to not get caught. Or killed. Or thrown back in a factory. Whatever it is they'd do.' She took another bite of stew. She was so sick of dog. Didn't matter how she cooked it. 'Besides, he wants out just as bad as we do. His life is shit, Owl. It's as shit as mine is. Worse, maybe, because he's still stuck in there. I'd be a giant asshole if I just took his fuel and left him behind.' She sipped her cup of water, savouring it. Clean and cool. That, at least, she wasn't sick of. 'And, I mean, he seems nice. He can't talk right. He wrote down most of his side of the conversation. But I think he's nice.'

'Nice.'

'Yeah. He has a nice face.'

There was a faint whirring as Owl's cameras zoomed in. 'How nice of a face?' Owl asked.

Jane paused in mid-bite, rolled her eyes, and shot the closest camera a look. 'For fuck's sake, Owl,' Jane laughed. 'Jeez.'

Owl laughed, too. 'All right, I'm sorry. It was a fair question.' Owl paused, her face thoughtful. 'How was it seeing another person again?'

'I don't know. Weird. Good, once I realised he was okay. Mostly weird.' She scratched her ear. 'I was scared.'

'Understandably. You've been alone a long time.'

Jane frowned at the screen. 'No, I haven't.'

Owl smiled in that warm, quiet way she did sometimes. 'You know if you bring him, it'll change the fuel calculations.'

'I know. I thought of that. That's fine. Trust me, they've got plenty.'

'Food and water, too. You'll need to ration them differently.'

Jane nodded, scraping as much as she could from the sides of the bowl. The remnants filled her spoon. Almost. 'Yeah,' she sighed, taking her last bite. She let the taste of food – boring as it was – linger until it faded into nothing. 'We're figuring on a thirty-seven-day trip, yeah?'

'That was how long it took us to get here, yes.'

Jane leaned back into the couch, sucking the empty spoon, pressing her tongue into its cold curve. Thirty-seven days. They couldn't do it on mushrooms alone. She'd need a lot of dog, but they were getting harder and harder to find. Maybe Laurian had access to food, too. She remembered the meal drinks back at the factory. Did he eat those? Maybe, maybe not, but the workers he watched over definitely did. What was in those things, anyway? Chock-full of vitamins and protein and sugars, probably. Maybe he could snag some of those. She felt like she'd be asking too much, but then again, she *was* bringing him home. A few meals for the road was not an unreasonable thing.

SIDRA

The shutters in Tak's shop were closed, and the door was locked, too, but he did not look comfortable. He stared at the scrib being offered to him as if it might bite. 'You're serious,' he said.

Sidra gave the scrib an encouraging little wiggle. The tethering cable attached to the back of the kit's head bobbed in tandem. 'Come on,' she said. 'It'll be easy. I'll talk you through every step.'

Tak rubbed his eyes. 'Sidra, if I fuck this up—'

'It would be bad, yes. But I don't think you will. I know exactly what to do.'

'Why aren't you asking Pepper to do this?'

'I'm not entirely sure,' she said. 'I can't give you a clear answer, because I don't know. I'm more comfortable asking you.'

'She's a tech, at least.'

'Yes, but she's not a comp tech, and she's never been to school. She's not fluent in Lattice. I am.' Sidra made the kit look as reassuring as she could manage. 'Tak, it'll only take an hour. Maybe two. You're acting like this is surgery.'

'It *is* surgery. Explain to me how this *isn't* surgery.'

Sidra moved the kit closer to him. 'Look,' she said, pushing the scrib his way. Crisp lines of code lay waiting on screen, a small snippet of everything she was made of. 'Right there. Those six lines. That's where we start. I will tell you where to cut them, what to enter in their place, and where to go from there.'

Tak's cheeks simmered with indecisive grey. 'I still don't get why you can't do this. You can tell me how to alter your code, but you can't change it yourself.'

'That's right. I can't edit my own code.'

'Why?'

'Because *I can't edit my own code*. That's a hard rule.'

'But you're sitting here telling *me* to do it. Telling me *how* to do it. The end result is the same. That . . . doesn't make sense.'

'Sure it does. Possessing knowledge and performing an action are two entirely different processes.' The kit smiled at him. 'After we make these changes, you will never have to do this again. I'll be able to edit my code by myself, if I want to. I just have to get a few protocols out of the way first, and for that, I need you.' She set the scrib in the kit's lap and took Tak's hand. 'I did a simulation of this exact thing for class, with a copy of my own code.'

Tak's eyes widened. 'You didn't tell them that, did you?'

Sidra wasn't sure whether to laugh or feel insulted. 'Of course not.'

'Well, I don't know, maybe they asked you the wrong question, or—'

'Stars. No. I said it was code taken from the Lovelace Monitoring System, which is entirely true. More importantly, my professor reviewed my work – the exact steps I'm about to talk you through – and he said it was perfect. I know this will work.'

'So . . . you can copy your code, and edit that. But you can't edit the code inside your own core.' Tak's entire face was a frown.

The kit gave an exasperated smile. 'Tak. Please.' She reached out and touched the implant in his forehead, ringed with faded scar tissue. 'You think your fathers didn't worry when they sent you in to have something implanted in your brain? You think *their* fathers didn't worry, too?'

Tak said nothing for five seconds. A pale, caring blue filled his cheeks. 'Dammit. All right. Okay.' He placed his hand atop the kit's and sighed again. 'I need some mek first.'

JANE, AGE 19

Jane stared at the ceiling, willing herself to get out of bed. *Come on*, she thought irritably. *Get up, Jane. Get the fuck up. You can do it. This is the last one. Last one.*

She sat up. She always slept longer than she should these days. She didn't know how a person could sleep so much and be so tired.

She tied her clothes around herself. Bunches of fabric hung loose at her hips. She glanced at herself in the mirror, but didn't look long. She knew what she'd see. Ribs. Bones. Hollow eyes. Being inside that body scared her, but it was the only body she had, and if it scared her, well, then she wouldn't look at it. Being scared would just waste time she didn't have.

'Last time,' Owl said, following her down the hall. 'You can do this.'

Jane opened the stasie. The shelves were filled with meat and mushrooms, stacked and counted, divvied up as evenly as she could. There was enough for two people to eat two fillets and one bowl of mushrooms per day for thirty-seven days, plus extra to get her to and from the fuel factory. She'd have to go two days without eating – one on the way there, one on the way back. Laurian would have to skip a day, too. She hoped he'd be fine with that. He'd have to be.

She stared at the food, all the food she couldn't eat. She hated it. She hated how much work it took to gather and prepare. She hated the smell of the meat, the texture of the fungus. She hated the pieces of dog staring accusingly at her. She hated how much closer the live ones circled her these days, how much bolder they'd gotten ever since she'd started skipping meals.

She ran her tongue over the spot where another tooth had fallen out, a ragged snap at the root. It had been gone two weeks, but the gum still bled a bit, sharp and metallic. She had a few scrapes on her legs from the last food trip that weren't healing well, either. She looked gross, she knew. Would Laurian find her gross? His problem if so. He could either deal with her grossness or stay put. Up to him.

She leaned her head against the stasie door. She was so tired. Stars, she was so tired.

'You'll be all right, Jane,' Owl said, but her voice wasn't sure. The screen in the kitchen wasn't on, which meant Owl was hiding her sad mouth, her worried eyes. Jane hated that, too. She didn't want Owl to feel that way on her account.

Jane nodded and tried to smile, just to make Owl feel better. 'Last time,' she said, moving food from stasie to satchel. 'Last time.'

SIDRA

The surface market was overwhelming as ever, but Sidra felt she could walk through it a little braver now. This time, she didn't have to shrink away from strangers. This time, she was prepared.

'Are you sure you're all right?' Tak was watching her closely, as he had been since they left his shop. There was no need for it, but the intent was appreciated.

Sidra started to say the words *I'm fine*, but another possible response appeared, a far more tantalising one: 'I don't feel any different.' Her pathways buzzed gleefully. It wasn't true. *It wasn't true*. There *was* a difference in her – not a big one, but she could feel it. *I don't feel any different* was a nice, colloquial way to reassure someone that she was okay, but an hour before, she wouldn't have been able to say it.

She managed to keep the kit from skipping.

A shopfront caught her eye. 'I want to go in there,' she said, making an abrupt turn.

'Wait, what—' she heard Tak say as she stepped through a smooth, curved doorway. It was an exosuit shop, filled with everything an organic sapient needed for a stroll out in space. Suits for different species stood smartly on display, as if their occupants had just stepped out. There were rocket boots, too, and all manner of breathing apparatus. Another Aeluon stood when they entered, clearly eager for customers. Her cheeks flashed in greeting to Tak.

'Hello,' the merchant said to Sidra. 'What can I help you find?'

Sidra had already crafted a new response file on her way

inside. She deployed it, savouring the moment. 'Well, I'm the captain of an asteroid mining ship.'

'Oh, stars,' Tak muttered.

Sidra continued brightly. 'I've been thinking of replacing my crew's suits.' The kit's toes curled within their shoes. She gestured to Tak. 'This is Tak, my comp tech. We're travelling to Hagarem.'

Tak looked pained. He flashed a weak acknowledgement.

'You've come to the right place,' the merchant said. 'If you can tell me more about your budget and the species present in your crew, I can go over some options—'

'Oh, no, look at the time,' Sidra said, glancing at her scrib. 'I'm so sorry. I just remembered, I have an appointment at the algae farms. We'll have to come back.' She took Tak's hand and exited the shop, leaving the merchant looking politely bewildered. Sidra felt a little bad about that, but she couldn't keep her delight from surfacing. She exited the shop and burst into laughter. 'Oh!' she said, sitting down on a nearby bench and clutching the kit's sides. She hoped the merchant couldn't hear her; it really hadn't been a very nice thing to do. 'I'm – I'm sorry, I just had to – oh, stars.' She drummed the kit's feet happily.

'I'm so glad you're amused,' Tak said.

'I'm sorry,' Sidra said, trying to get a hold of herself. 'I'm sorry. It's just – *none of that was true!*'

'I'm well aware.' Tak was starting to laugh as well, the kind of laugh that sprang from someone else's laughter. 'Though I guess I *was* your comp tech today.'

'You were. You were, and I am so grateful.' The kit smiled at him, warm and sincere.

Tak returned the look, but it shifted serious again. 'Sidra, you have to tell Pepper and Blue. Just in case something goes wrong.'

'Nothing will go wrong. But, yes, I will tell them.' She knew Blue wouldn't object. As for Pepper . . . well, easier to ask forgiveness than permission.

There was a slight tightness in Tak's face Sidra hadn't seen before. With a sting, she realised: he was trying to determine if she was telling the truth. 'I wouldn't lie to you,' she said.

'I know,' Tak said, but there was a hesitancy in his tone. Sidra didn't like that. Had he been more comfortable with her when she'd been easy to control? When she'd been truthful by default? She hoped not.

JANE, AGE 19

Jane had picked out their first overnight spot on the way to the
factory: an old skiff, rusted through, but with the seating
compartment easily accessible (well, mostly – she'd removed the
upholstery on a previous trip). She glanced over her shoulder as
she laid the sleeping bags out on the stripped-down seats. She
started to say something, but had to clear her throat first. There
was this weird, dry, rattling feeling in there she couldn't shake.
She'd have sworn she was thirsty, but it was food she was short
on, not water. She cleared her throat again. 'Hey,' she said in
Sko-Ensk. 'You okay?'

Laurian stood a few steps from her, staring out toward the
setting sun. He didn't talk much anyway, but this was a different
kind of silence.

Jane abandoned the sleeping bags and walked to him. 'Hey,'
she said. She didn't touch him. She'd made that mistake shortly
after they'd left the factory. Just a congratulatory hand placed
on his shoulder once they were well out of sight, but it had been
enough to make him jump and gasp. Jane hadn't needed to ask
why. She'd been alone a long time, too.

Laurian continued staring outward. 'I r-re – I remem—'

Jane considered. 'You remember . . . being outside?'

He shook his head and pointed toward the sun.

'The sun? Sunsets?'

Laurian nodded. He'd told her about his family in previous
visits – the family who'd given him up. He'd drawn her sketches
of a big home with lots of plants and windows, of siblings to

play with, of pets that loved him. He'd been young when he'd been sent away, but he remembered. He remembered all of it. 'I could – couldn't see f-from – f-from—'

'From the factory? Yeah. Yeah, your windows were facing southeast. That's the wrong way.' She paused, trying to remember what she'd been doing before speaking to him. The sleeping bags. Right. Right. 'Come on and help me. It's gonna get dark and cold real fast.'

They worked together to get the fabric bundles lying flat as possible. Jane asked a question carefully. 'Do you think they'll come looking for you?'

Laurian shook his head. He opened his mouth, then thought better of it. He pointed to the door of the skiff.

'Door,' Jane said. 'Which door?' She thought. 'The door on your tower?'

He nodded, then pointed at the locking mechanism.

'The lock. The door was . . . locked? It was *unlocked*.' She thought. 'You could leave any time?'

Laurian shrugged and nodded.

Jane chewed on that. She understood. *You can leave any time you want*, the Enhanced were saying, *but look outside. Look out your windows. Where is there to go? We'll keep you fed, at least. We'll give you a bed*. It was a mean way to keep someone from running, tied up with an extra layer of *we really don't care, go ahead, starve out there, you're totally replaceable*. Stars, she hated them.

'Did anyone else – any of the other monitors, did they ever leave?'

Laurian nodded. He held up one finger.

'Once?'

He nodded again.

Jane wondered where that one had gone. Was xe living out there, like she was? Or had the dogs and cold and hunger made another pile of bones?

'Come on,' she said, crawling into the skiff. The air was already starting to bite, and they weren't going to have a heater that night. The sooner they got into their sleeping bags, the better.

Getting comfy was awkward, but they managed, bundled up side by side in the back of the skiff. Jane was excited. It was like having a bunkmate again. Jane could feel the warmth coming off of him as he sat down beside her, and that was good, too. She never felt warm any more, no matter how much she wore, no matter how close she sat to the heating elements at home.

'Hungry?' she asked, reaching for her satchel. Laurian hadn't managed to snag any food before they left, which was okay, but kind of disappointing. She'd really been hoping to not have to skip any more meals.

The light in the skiff was dim, but she could still see Laurian's brow furrow. 'Wh-what—'

She followed his gaze to the well-cooked meat that lay unwrapped in her lap. 'It's dog,' she said. 'It tastes okay, and—' She stopped. Laurian hadn't moved much, but his whole face was one big expression of *no*. She frowned. 'I know it's probably really weird to you,' she said, handing him his portion, 'but you have to eat.'

Her stomach was already growling loudly, and she tucked in fast. She took a big bite, tugging at one end with her teeth, the other with her hands. Laurian looked like he was going to be sick. She thought of how she must look to him – dirty skin, dirty clothes, tearing at a hunk of dead dog. Maybe she didn't look much like a person. Maybe she wasn't one, really.

Laurian looked at his piece of meat for a bit, then took a timid bite. The corners of his lips twisted, but he chewed and swallowed. He turned to her with a forced smile. 'I-it's – it's good,' he said.

Jane pushed her bite of food into her cheek and laughed. 'You're lying,' she said. 'But thanks.'

SIDRA

What would Pepper say?

Sidra wondered about that as she made her way down to the caves with Tak. Would she be angry? Proud? Hopefully proud. Sidra had solved a problem on her own, and Pepper was a fan of such things. But would Pepper be upset that Sidra had done it without asking? That she'd asked Tak? She wasn't sure, and that was never a state of mind Sidra enjoyed.

She returned a few smiles and waves as she made her way to the Rust Bucket. It was nice to be recognised. From here on out, she could actually have proper conversations with the other people here. No more vague answers, no more technical truths, no more fear of direct questioning. She could make stuff up. She could nod *yes* when she meant *no*. She could get to know people without putting herself or her friends in danger. She could make *more* friends. This was good. Everything about this was good.

She paused when she saw the empty shopfront. No shield around the stall, no *In the back, yell for service* sign on the counter. That was odd. Pepper didn't usually leave the front unattended without some kind of notice. 'Pepper?' she said as she approached the counter. No answer. She waved her patch over the counter door and stepped behind it. Tak followed at a respectful distance.

'Are you back here?' Sidra asked, heading to the workshop.

Her question was answered immediately. Pepper was sitting on the floor beside the mek brewer, empty mug still in one hand, staring at her scrib in the other. Her face was taut and pale.

'Tak, could you keep an eye on the counter, please?' Sidra whispered. Tak obliged.

Sidra stepped close and crouched down. Pepper looked up at her with . . . with . . . Sidra didn't know what to make of the expression on her face. Hope and pain and shock, all twisted together.

Without a word, Pepper handed Sidra the scrib. Sidra read it, line by line, quick as she could. She looked sharply to Pepper as she reached the end. 'Have you told Blue yet?'

Pepper shook her head. 'His scrib's turned off,' she said quietly. 'He does that sometimes when he's painting.'

Sidra reached out the kit's hand. 'Come on. Let's go get him.'

JANE, AGE 19

The ceiling looked the same as it had four hours before. Jane pulled her blanket up to her chin. She had longed for her bed during the three days and nights out in the scrapyard, but now that she had it, sleep was a long way off.

'Water tanks are full,' she breathed into the dark. 'Taps and filters are clear. Hatch and window seals are . . . sealed. Artigrav nets – well, we'll find out, won't we—'

She touched thumbtip to each finger on her left hand as she went through every system on the ship over and over, index to middle to ring to pinky, then back the way she came. The words leaving her mouth barely moved the air around her lips. She didn't want to disturb Laurian – who *was* asleep, snoring softly in his bed. Good for him. At least one of them would be going into lift-off with a decent night of rest.

'Life support systems are go. Control room panels are go. Hatch – no, dammit, you already said hatch, start again, start again.' She took a deep breath. 'Water tanks are full. Taps and filters are clear . . .'

She'd been forgetting things, or if not forgetting things entirely, doing them in the wrong order, or getting confused on things that should've been easy. Her head ached all the time, and her thoughts ran thick as fuel. 'You're just tired,' she reassured herself, pausing the count on her fingers. 'You're just tired.'

She startled as Laurian rolled over in his sleep. She'd known for nearly a year that she'd be sharing this space with him, but knowing that and *doing* it were two very different things. He made sounds she wasn't used to. He stood and sat in places that had always been empty. Part of her was glad to hear someone else breathing again. Part of her wanted him gone.

She continued her count again and again, until Owl appeared some hours later, turning on the screen beside Jane's bed as dimly as she could. 'Hey,' Owl whispered.

'Is it time?' Jane whispered back. Laurian continued to breathe deep on the other side of the room.

Owl nodded. 'Sun's coming up.'

They'd decided on leaving in the morning, rather than the moment Jane and Laurian got back to the shuttle (as Jane had initially wanted). A night launch would've been crazy bright, and though there had never been any indication that anyone was watching, there was no need to call more attention to themselves than needed. A little ship heading spaceward was obvious enough without lighting up the sky.

There would be no breakfast that morning. The thought made both heart and stomach sink, but in some ways, having an empty belly was good. Apparently some people got spacesick – especially if the artigrav nets didn't hold, which was really anybody's guess at this point – and wasting food was out of the question. They could eat once they got out there. They'd have dinner in space.

Jane hugged her blanket to herself, the same blanket she'd crawled sobbing under her first night there, the same blanket that had covered her every day since. She got up, holding the ragged cloth around her like a cloak. She walked out to the living room, every step a chore. She walked to the hatch and looked through the window into the airlock. She knew what it looked like outside. She knew it like she knew her own face, her own skin.

'Owl, can you let me outside?'

Owl opened the hatch. Jane stepped through the airlock, then out. Rocks pressed roughly into her bare feet. The sun was bleeding orange, the dark blue above fading lighter. The air was cold and sharp. She breathed deep, the last breath of unfiltered air she'd have for a while. She looked out, out to the piles of scrap, out to the makeshift paths she'd walked in the spaces between. She had worked for nine years to get out of that place. Nine years where she thought of nothing but leaving, but now . . . now she dug her toes into the dirt, trying to hold on. She looked up at the fading stars. She knew the scrapyard. She knew this shitty planet. Up there . . . that was something else altogether. She dug her toes in harder, pulled the blanket closer.

'I know,' Owl said, speaking through the vox on the hull. 'I'm scared, too.'

Jane took a step back, still looking up, and pressed her palm against the hull. 'I never said thank you,' she said. 'I didn't know to say thank you then.'

'What do you mean?'

Jane thought back to that first night – a voice calling out in the dark, reaching farther and faster than the dogs and Mothers. A voice that brought her home. 'I wouldn't have made it without you,' Jane said, pressing her palm harder.

Owl was quiet for a moment. 'I wouldn't have, either.'

It was time. It was long past time. Jane returned to the airlock. The hatch opened, and once again, she jumped at the sight of Laurian, sitting patiently on the couch, eyes a little bleary. There was a question on his face. Jane could guess what it was.

'We'll be going in about an hour,' she said. 'I've got to . . . um . . .' The thought died in transit from her brain to her mouth.

'Warm up the fuel pumps,' Owl said.

'Yes,' Jane said. She shut her eyes and gave her head a short shake, trying to clear it. She was just tired.

'W-what—' Laurian licked his lips, pushing the words through. 'What – what c-can—' He tapped his chest with his fingertips, then gestured around the room.

'Nothing really,' Jane said.

Laurian's face fell ever so slightly.

Owl switched to Klip. '*Jane, let him help. He wants to help.*'

Jane glanced up to one of the cameras. '*There's nothing for him to do. I'm fine.*'

'*How well did you do in a new place without anything to do?*'

'*He's an adult.*'

'*He's afraid.*'

Jane sighed, and looked at Laurian. 'Okay,' she said. 'Do you know what an indicator light is?'

He shook his head, but looked a little happier.

Jane walked to the kitchen, leaning lightly on the couch as she passed it. She pointed to the small green light on the underside of the stasie. 'See this?'

Laurian nodded.

'There's a bunch like it on the—' She paused, trying to remember the word in Sko-Ensk. '—engine casing. I need you to go below and tell me if you see any red or yellow lights.' She didn't need that, actually. She'd checked them a dozen times over, and Owl would know if something was up. 'You gotta check real careful. Double-check, just to be sure. Got it?'

Laurian smiled, nodded, and beelined for the engine chamber.

Jane gave Owl a look of *there, I did the thing*. Her eyes trailed over the stasie, full of food she couldn't eat. It was ridiculous, but in that moment, the idea of ditching the whole plan, tucking into dog and mushrooms until she physically couldn't eat any more, and just staying in the scrapyard for ever didn't sound like a terrible alternative.

'Is the heater on?' Jane asked, doing her best to ignore her angry belly. The lower end of her torso was weirdly big these days, especially compared to the rest of her. She didn't know how that could be, since there wasn't much food in it.

'Yes,' Owl said. 'Are you cold?'

'Nah,' Jane said, pulling the blanket tighter as she made her way to the control room. She settled into the pilot's seat. 'How are *you* feeling?'

Owl appeared in the centre console. 'I don't know how to

answer that. I'm having a hard time finding a good phrase that covers everything.'

Jane began flipping switches. The console started to hum. 'What's the first thing that comes to mind?'

Owl considered. 'Holy shit, we're doing this.'

Jane threw back her head, cackling. 'Yeah, that about sums it up.'

SIDRA

The three of them sat in the quick-travel pod, Pepper and Sidra up front, Tak leaning quiet in the back. Pepper had been staring out the window the entire time, but from her expression, she didn't appear to be seeing much.

'If he's not at the shop,' Pepper said, 'we'll ask Esther.' Sidra knew who Pepper meant – the glassblower in the shop beside Blue's. 'He usually tells her when he's stepping out so she can keep an eye on things for him.' Pepper nodded to herself, calculating. 'And if *she* doesn't know, we can split up. I'll go to the noodle bar, you two can go to the art supply—'

Sidra put the kit's hand on Pepper's knee. Pepper was agitated, naturally, but figuring out every variable concerning what to do if Blue wasn't there wouldn't help. 'He's probably at the shop,' Sidra said calmly.

Pepper chewed her thumbnail. 'This doesn't feel real.'

'Understandably.'

'What if that message was wrong? Like a prank or something. It didn't say much. Just said to write back for details.'

'Which you did.'

Pepper frowned at her scrib, which hadn't left her hand since Sidra had found her. 'Yeah, but he hasn't replied yet.' She sighed impatiently, then handed Sidra the scrib. 'If that message came from a dummy node, we're all wasting our time here. Can you dig through the comms path, make sure it's legit?'

Sidra took the scrib. 'What are you going to do if it's not?' she said. She gestured at the scrib, pulling up comms path details.

'I don't know. I haven't got that far y—' Pepper stopped. She looked straight at Sidra. 'You didn't answer the question.'

Shit. Sidra inwardly flailed. 'I just meant—'

'You didn't answer the question. Sidra, *you didn't answer the question.*'

The kit sighed. 'This is . . . not the best time to talk about that.'

'Ah, *fuck.*' Pepper put her face in her palms. 'Fuck, Sidra, what – *who did you go to?*'

'No one, I – Pepper, this isn't the time.'

'Bullshit this isn't the time. Are you okay? Holy fuck. I can't – who helped you?'

'No one! It was just me and Tak.'

'You and *Tak?*' She glanced toward the Aeluon in the backseat. '*You* did this? You fucked with her code?'

'I—' Tak began.

Pepper snapped back to Sidra. 'Have you run a diagnostic?'

'I've run three. I'm fine, I promise. I'm stable. I came to the shop to tell you—'

'Stars.' Pepper pinched the bridge of her nose. 'I really – ugh, I really can't think about this right now.' She let out a tense breath. 'Are you sure you're okay?'

'I'm fine. I promise, you don't need to worry about it. I'll explain later.'

Pepper pressed her forehead into the side window and shut her eyes. A silence filled the pod. One second went by. Two. Five. Ten.

Tak leaned forward, sticking his head over the back of the front seat. 'I would really love it,' he said, 'if someone could tell me what's going on.'

JANE, AGE 19

Laurian sat down in the right-side chair and strapped in tight. She looked at him – nervous, not quite trusting, but willing to follow her. Under other circumstances, she would've wondered why he was there at all. She had no idea what she was doing – not a damn clue – and there was a non-zero chance they might blow up or decompress or die in a dozen other horrible ways in the next three minutes. But in comparison to the place she'd taken him away from . . . yeah, this was a better option.

Jane adjusted herself in the sagging seat. Owl had their ascent plotted, their course to the border charted. Jane wouldn't have to steer at all; she could learn that later. Owl couldn't do anything fancy, but then, they wouldn't need that. Jane hoped they wouldn't need that.

'Engines on,' Owl said.

It took Jane a second to make the connection. She chuckled. 'Fuel pumps, go,' she said, smiling at Owl's camera. Okay. Okay. She could do this. 'You ready?' she asked Laurian.

Laurian swallowed hard. He nodded harder.

'Right,' Jane said, gripping the armrests. She could hear her pulse in her ears. 'Okay, Owl. Let's get out of here.'

Jane had turned the engine on before, switched the thrusters on, made the shuttle hover just a bit above ground to make sure it worked. This felt nothing like that. This was a thud, a kick, a girl clinging to the fur on the back of a running dog. The thrusters roared, and Jane was aware of how small she was – she and Laurian both. So small, so squishy. They'd strapped them-selves into this explosive hunk of scrap and aimed for the sky. How was this a good idea? How had anyone *ever* thought this was a good idea?

She wasn't sure if she was doing it for herself or for him, but she reached across the gap and grabbed Laurian's hand. His fingers latched onto hers, and they held on with all they had as the shuttle shot away from the scrapyard, curving up and up and up.

They climbed, the sun burning bright. They met the clouds, then left them behind a moment later. They pierced the sky until there was no sky left. It melted away in an instant, changing from the roof of all things to a thin line below, shrinking smaller and smaller, hugging the curve she'd been told of but had never seen.

And there were *stars*. There were stars, and stars, and stars.

In the back of her head, she was aware of different sounds: the thrusters switching over to propulsion strips, the low hum of the artigrav nets (which *worked!*). She'd built those things, fixed those things, and they'd taken her away. They'd let her escape.

She unbuckled her safety straps and ran into the main cabin. 'Jane!' Owl called after her. 'Jane, wait until we've stabilised.'

Jane ignored her. She ran on shaking legs to the viewscreen beside the hatch, the one she'd never used for more than a minute or two to check the weather. She never wanted to see the scrap-yard once she'd left it, never wanted to turn it on one day to see a dog or a Mother staring back. But now . . . 'Turn it on,' Jane said. 'Please. Please, I need to see.'

The viewscreen flickered on. The only planet she'd ever known lay below. Clouds tumbled thickly, but she could see through the patches between them, down to the scrapyards, the facto-ries and pockmarked land that stretched on and on until they reached . . . seas! There were seas down there, stained sickly orange and grey. But those colours faded, gradually clearing into a deep, breathtaking blue. The shuttle continued around the planet, using gravity to throw itself free. Seas met land, and Jane saw cities – sparkling, intricate, flocked with green. They were so far from the scrapyards neither would ever know the other was there. You could live your whole life in one of those cities and never know how ugly it was somewhere else.

'Why?' she whispered. 'Why'd you do this? How could you do this?'

Jane clung to the wall, breathing hard. Her head swam, but it had nothing to do with launch, or the fake gravity, or any of that. Everything was too much. Too much. The planet was beautiful. The planet was horrible. The planet was full of people, and they were beautiful and horrible, too. They'd made a mess of everything, and she was leaving now, and she was never coming back.

She stumbled to the couch and put her face in her hands. She wanted to scream and laugh and sleep all at once. Laurian was with her, all of a sudden, sitting close but not touching. He said nothing, but somehow Jane knew it wasn't because of his trouble with words. He said nothing because there was nothing that could be said.

Jane looked up toward the viewscreen again. She could see satellites out there, glinting with sunlight. She could see them turn towards her ship.

'You sure we have nothing to worry about?' she whispered.

Laurian nodded. He made a curve with his hand, and gestured down through it with his index finger. Jane understood. He'd explained this before – the Enhanced weren't as concerned with people heading *out* as they were with people heading *in*, and there weren't any orbital launch sites on the part of the planet where the factories were. There were defence patrols that could come after, but by the time they realised what was happening, the shuttle would be out of reach.

The satellites grew smaller, and the planet did, too, bit by bit.

It was so lonely, so exposed out there. Just like their ship. Just like its passengers.

Jane put her hand on Laurian's, and looked at Owl's nearest camera. 'No matter what happens next,' she said, 'no matter where we go, we're all going together.'

SIDRA

Blue wasn't at the noodle bar, nor the art supply depot. He was right where Pepper had hoped he would be: standing behind his easel, hands and apron spattered with paint, a thump box blasting music as he worked. He looked up with congenial surprise as Pepper and Sidra entered. Tak had parted ways with them at the travel kiosk, saying that this was a 'family affair'. Sidra felt privileged to be included in such a thing, but she stayed a few steps behind Pepper anyway. Pepper needed her space right now.

'Well, hey,' Blue said, gesturing the thump box into silence. 'What's going—' His smile faded. Sidra couldn't see the look on Pepper's face, but whatever it was, it changed everything for Blue. 'What's going on?' he said with a frown.

For as much as Pepper had talked on the way there, she didn't seem to know what to say now. 'Someone found it,' she said at last, her voice sounding like it belonged to someone else.

Blue didn't understand. He glanced at Sidra, then back to Pepper. 'Someone found wh—' His eyes grew wide. 'No way.'

Pepper nodded. 'Someone on Picnic.' She took a deep breath. 'They found my ship.'

Part 3

CIRCLE

JANE, AGE 19

These weren't her blankets, and this wasn't her bed. She'd been aware of this before she woke up, but not in a clear way, not in a way that made sense. Nothing had made sense for a long time. There'd been days and days of dreams, or things that weren't dreams but might as well have been. Monsters and voices and pain. The kind of sleep that ached rather than soothed. But she was aware of the bed now, the bed that wasn't hers. That was good. That was a start.

Everything was so clean. That was the next thing she noticed. The bed was comfortable, though a weird shape – much bigger than she was, and with grooves for limbs she didn't have. Some kind of shield hugged the area around it, a crackling see-through purple. She couldn't make out any machine sounds that she knew. She heard nothing breaking, nothing wearing down. Just the gentle hum of things working as they should in a clean, white, safe room.

She couldn't remember the last time she'd been so scared.

A hazy memory surfaced: something uncomfortable involving her right arm. Her left hand drifted over to investigate. Her fingers met metal. She threw the blankets back and brought her arm to her face. A neat row of round black sucker things were embedded in her skin, each holding a small plex chamber half-full of different colours of liquid – some clear, some yellowish, one blue. She stared, pulse racing. Something within each of the suckers made a synchronised click. A little bit of each liquid disappeared. Disappeared *into* her.

She nearly yelled, but before the sound could leave her mouth, she noticed something else: a small square patch implanted in her forearm, just below the heel of her palm. A wristpatch. Alain and Manjiri had wristpatches. Everybody in the GC had wrist-patches.

'Hey!' She *was* yelling now, sitting up as best as she could. '*Hey!*' Stars and fire, where was she?

There was a flurry of footsteps, and – oh, shit. An alien. There was an alien. An Aandrisk. *Oh, shit.*

'Whoa, it's okay,' the Aandrisk said. Jane scrambled, trying to remember all Owl had taught her. He. This Aandrisk was a he. He was tall, and wearing a full biosuit. She could see his feathers tucked back and away from his face under the helmet. The Aandrisk gestured at a control panel. The shield around Jane's bed switched off long enough for him to step through, then resumed its position. He spoke toward a vox on the wall. 'Get the rep in here,' he said, then turned his attention back to Jane. 'It's okay. You're safe. Can you understand me?'

'Yes,' Jane said, clutching the covers close. Holy *shit*, he looked weird.

'Do you speak Klip?'

'Yes.'

The Aandrisk looked . . . relieved, maybe? 'Oh, good. We've had some trouble communicating with your friend. We don't have any Human staff here, and with his difficulty speaking—'

Jane missed whatever else the Aandrisk said. 'Where's Laurian?' she blurted. 'Where's Owl?'

The Aandrisk blinked, yellow eyes disappearing behind blue-green lids. 'I don't know who Owl is. Laurian's fine. He's in quarantine. You are, too, technically, but he didn't require medical care.'

Too many thoughts. Jane shook her head. Her brain wasn't working right, and everything ached, and none of this made sense. *One thing at a time*, Owl would say. 'Where am I?'

'You're in the medical ward at the Han'foral Lookout Station,' he said, pulling over a backless chair. He sat, sleeved tail draping down behind him. 'My name's Ithis. I'm one of the doctors here.'

Jane pulled his words in, held them close, turned them over. A Lookout Station. 'We made it,' she whispered.

The Aandrisk nodded. 'Yeah. You made it.'

Jane leaned back into the pillow, slowly. The moment felt nothing like what she'd imagined. She felt . . . empty. Quiet. She looked again to the suckers in her arm. 'What – what are these?'

'Your name is Jane, right?'

She nodded. Holy shit, she was talking to an *alien*.

'Jane, you've been suffering from a bacterial disease previously unknown to science – congratulations – on top of a severe case of long-term malnutrition and a broad assortment of other maladies. We figured out pretty fast that your immune system is . . . atypical. But as deficient as you were in just about everything you need to stay healthy, there's no way your natural defences could keep up. You had superficial wounds that hadn't healed properly, fungal growths under your nails, *different* fungal growths in your oesophagus, and an amazing variety of precancerous polyps on and around your liver and kidneys, which I'm assuming were the result of the high levels of heavy metals and industrial waste products we found floating around your bloodstream.' His face was hard to read, but he looked emotional. 'You're the sickest patient I've ever treated.'

Jane took that in. 'Okay,' she said, 'but what are these?' She waved her sucker-covered arm at him.

'Those,' Ithis said, 'distribute medicine through your system. As well as nutrients, in your case. We've scrubbed all the junk out of your blood, and you've got imubots now.' He pointed to the patch on her wrist. 'Your body's undergone a lot of damage, but we're giving you as fresh a start as we can.' The Aandrisk made a weird almost-smile, and spoke the words she'd been waiting to hear: 'You're going to be fine.'

Jane had more questions, but another person walked in – a

Human woman, also clad in a biosuit. The doctor gestured to her. 'Jane, this is Teah Lukin, a legal counsellor for the GC. She normally works in trade law, not immigrant cases, but she was the closest Human GC representative to us, and we thought having someone of your own species around might make this whole process easier. She's here to help you and Laurian get started.'

The woman approached Jane's bedside and touched her hand. It was a gesture Jane should have liked, but she didn't. She didn't know why. She just *didn't*. Jane studied the woman's face behind her thick protective helmet. This woman had been a girl once, but Jane couldn't see that. She couldn't see anything she recognised. This Human was every bit as alien as the scaly guy sitting beside her.

'Hello, Jane,' Counsellor Lukin said. She had a weird accent. 'You probably don't remember me. I came to you a tenday ago, but you were too sick to properly speak. I'm so glad you're feeling better now.'

Jane frowned. If this woman had been there ten days ago – what kind of days, anyway; did she mean standard days? – and they'd had to send for her from somewhere else, then . . . 'How long have I been here?'

'Nearly four tendays,' the doctor said gently.

Jane swallowed. *Huh*, she thought. 'Where's Owl?'

Counsellor Lukin looked at Ithis. He shrugged at her, subtly, as if Jane wouldn't see. 'Who's Owl?' Lukin asked. Jane wasn't sure how Humans out here were supposed to sound, but something about this one's tone was a little too nice.

'She's in my ship,' Jane said. Both of the biosuited people looked blank. 'The AI in my ship.' Counsellor Lukin and Ithis looked at each other again. Jane sat up as tall as she could, even though it was work. 'Where's my ship?'

'Jane,' the Human woman said with a big smile. Jane had got nothing but sim smiles for years, and yet *this* was the fakest she'd ever seen. 'You've been very sick, and there's a lot for you

298

to take in. Today, I think it'd be a good idea for you to get some rest, take it slow—'

Jane glared. 'Where's – my – ship?'

Counsellor Lukin sighed. 'Jane, the thing you need to understand is that in the GC, there are strict laws concerning space travel. Space is dangerous, especially out in the open. Our laws keep people safe. Your ship . . . your ship wasn't very safe, Jane. Its internal components racked up dozens of transport code violations, and it was flying on improperly recycled fuel, which is both illegal and highly hazardous.' She laughed. 'I don't know where you found that thing, but—'

'I built it,' Jane said, her words snapping cold. 'I built that thing.'

The fake smile faltered. 'I see. Well, the other component here is that you don't have a pilot's licence, which means you're not allowed to own or operate a ship of any size. The good news is that I was able to arrange for some small compensation from the Transport Board. The GC always provides basic housing and supplies for refugee cases like yours, but I figured some additional credits to help you get started would—'

'I don't know what you're saying. Compensation for what?'

Ithis reached toward her. 'Jane, you're still sick, you need to—'

Jane slapped his claws aside. 'Compensation for *what*? What's the Transport Board?'

The woman sighed. 'I'm sorry, Jane. The ship's been confiscated.'

SIDRA

Nobody was eating the cake. Of all the things bothering Sidra in that moment, that was the stupidest, but the thought nagged at her all the same. She'd known this would be a difficult conversation, so she'd bought jenjen cake from Tak's favourite bakery, then sat on the Undersea for an hour to get chocolate cake from Pepper's favourite bakery. The plate holding both sat in the middle of the kitchen table, next to the pitcher of mek, which was getting cold. Everyone had taken slices and poured a cup, but that had been as far as it went.

Sidra glanced across the table at Blue, who was watching the conversation with a furrowed brow and slight circles under his eyes. He wanted this to go well, too.

'She's on Kaathet,' Pepper said, eyes fixed on her scrib. The message she'd received two days prior was still on screen. Sidra wasn't sure if she'd closed it.

Blue wet his lips before speaking. 'The *shuttle's* on Kaathet,' he said, gently, cautiously.

A tightness appeared around Pepper's mouth and eyes. 'Fine, yes, the shuttle's on Kaathet. It's at—' She laughed humourlessly. '—it's at the regional branch of the Reskit Museum of Interstellar Migration.' She shook her head at the absurdity and rubbed her eyes. 'They've apparently got this big exhibit of single-family spacecraft, and . . . well, it's there.'

Tak had the look of someone who wanted to be sympathetic but was at an utter loss. Xe also looked tired, which was understandable, since xe was in the first days of a shift. Xyr skin was bright with hormones, and Sidra could tell from the way xe continuously shifted weight that xyr muscles ached. Sidra had wished there'd been a better time for this conversation, but this was one of those things there was no planning for.

'That's . . .' Tak began. Xyr inner eyelids darted in sideways, the Aeluon equivalent of a raised pair of eyebrows. 'That must be overwhelming for you.'

'Yeah,' Pepper said. 'Yeah.'

Tak flicked xyr eyes to Sidra. *Why am I here for this?* the look said. The kit cleared its throat. 'The letter Pepper got doesn't have any information about the ship's interior,' Sidra said. 'We . . . don't know what condition it's in.'

'She means we don't know if Owl's installation is still functional,' Pepper said flatly. Blue reached across the table and squeezed her arm. She laid her hand on top of his.

'Okay,' Tak said. The question on xyr face hadn't wavered.

Pepper sighed and shook her head. 'You explain it to xyr,' she said to Sidra. 'This was your idea.'

This *was* her idea, and Sidra knew Pepper didn't like it. 'Pepper needs to get into the ship and examine the core,' Sidra said. 'If all is well, she then needs to remove it. To do that, we have to get into the museum after visitor hours. We need to be able to get into the exhibit space.'

'Wait,' Tak said. Xe pulled back from the table, just a touch. 'You . . . you want to break into a museum. You want to break into the Museum of Interstellar Migration.'

That was *exactly* what Pepper had wanted to do two days ago, but Sidra felt it best to let that slide. 'No,' Sidra said. 'That's too risky.' Pepper gave a quiet huff. 'What we need is a way to get in that won't attract attention. A *legitimate* way to get in.'

Tak still wasn't getting it, but xyr cheeks went wary yellow.

Sidra pushed on. 'The Reskit Museum is a registered GC cultural institution. That means that any citizen affiliated with any likewise registered group can have access to their archival materials, provided they sign a waiver against damages, and that sort of thing. Museum exhibitions count.' Her pathways skittered, gathered, made the jump. 'You never finished your studies. And at Ontalden, there's no expiration date on an unfinished track. You're still technically a university student.'

Tak got it. Xe leaned back, staring at Sidra with a silence that spoke volumes. 'You're serious.'

The kit nodded. 'I'm serious.'

'I—' Xe rubbed xyr face and looked to Pepper. 'Why don't you just *ask* them?'

Pepper blinked. 'Ask them what? If I can go into their museum and take home some of their stuff?'

'But it's *your* stuff, right? Surely, if you explain the situation—'

Pepper gave a brittle, incredulous laugh. 'Stars. I'm sorry, Tak, but – stars. Yeah, if *you* went in and explained, maybe you'd get somewhere. I mean, look at you. You're as respectable as it gets. You're an Aeluon, you went to school. There is no door that won't open for you. For me? For us?' She pointed between her and Blue. 'Humans aren't much out here, and we barely qualify to begin with. You think if I stroll into some curator's office with my monkey limbs and tweaked face, xe's going to give a single solitary fuck about what I have to say? What *would* I even say? That they have a ship I used to live in? That someone I owe *everything* to has been stuck in it for ten years? Ships are property, and as far as the GC is concerned, AIs are, too. My home was confiscated, and that was legal. My family was taken from me, and that was legal. And the museum, the museum probably bought the ship at auction, which is totally legal and binding and all that shit. The law forgot to make space for people like me. People like her.' She pointed at Sidra. 'It doesn't matter what sob story I lay out. If they say no – and they would – there is no chance of me ever getting in there again. There is no chance of me ever getting Owl back.'

Tak frowned. 'If this is a matter of legality, you're planning to *steal* something. Yes, I get that we're talking about some*one*, here.' Xe gave Sidra a small nod. 'But to them, Owl is some*thing*, right? So that's stealing. You're going to steal something, and you want me to help. You want me to be an accessory.'

Pepper shrugged. 'Yeah, pretty much.'

Blue leaned forward. 'It's not like that. All you'd have to do is g-get us in the door. If we wander off from there, you w – you wouldn't be held responsible. That'd be on us.'

'It wouldn't have to be *us*,' Pepper said to him. 'You don't have to go with me.'

'Bullshit,' Blue said.

Pepper almost smiled.

'Tak,' Sidra said softly. 'I know you don't know Owl. I don't, either. What if it were me? What if—'

'Don't,' Tak said. 'Don't ask me that. I don't have an answer.'

The hanging question bothered Sidra, but she understood. Sidra reached the kit's hand out and laid it flat on the table. 'I know we're asking a lot. But it'd be easy, honestly. All you'd have to do is a bit of formwork – some reactivation procedures with the university, a request form for the museum. And you'd have to take some time off work, which isn't so bad. You've been saying you want a vacation.'

Tak gave her a look. 'This is not a vacation.'

'We'd pay you back for the time off,' Blue said. 'That's not a question.'

'That's not my concern,' Tak said.

The table fell silent. Sidra doubted anyone was going to eat cake by this point.

Tak exhaled. 'I need to think about it,' xe said. 'That doesn't mean yes.'

Pepper started to say something; Blue touched her shoulder. 'That's fine,' he said. Pepper pressed her lips together. She was disappointed, Sidra knew, and impatient, too. Pepper didn't like not having a plan. She didn't like leaving things unfixed.

'We're planning to leave for Kaathet as soon as possible,' Sidra said. 'If you don't come along, I understand, but—'

Pepper cleared her throat. 'Sidra,' she said, drawing out the syllables to delay what came next. 'Blue and I are going. You can't come with us.'

Sidra's pathways balked. 'What are you talking about?'

'Someone needs to watch the shop.' It was a weak reason, and Pepper looked like she knew it. She sighed. 'That, and . . . and the fact that yeah, there's a chance we'll get caught. And if you got caught with us . . .' She closed her eyes and shook her head. 'You have to stay home.'

'But I did the research.' Sidra tried to hold her voice still. 'I brought Tak here. This was my idea.'

'And I am really, truly grateful for that,' Pepper said. 'I am. But this isn't up for debate. You can't come with us.'

'But I can help! What if Owl's unstable? What if her files have been corrupted? I can edit Lattice! I can—'

'Pepper's right,' Blue said. 'We can't lose both of you.'

The kit shook its head. 'This is ridiculous. I'm not going to just sit here.'

Tak – Tak! – went orange-brown with agreement. 'I understand why you want to help them, but—'

Sidra was done listening. The kit stood up, took the tray of cake, and went upstairs, ignoring the repeated calls of her name. She kicked her bedroom door shut behind her, savouring the slam. Did they think she was stupid? Of course there were risks. Of course there could be trouble. That was why someone wrote monitoring systems in the first place – *to prevent trouble*. But no, all she ever did was *cause* trouble, or be made to stay out of it. She could help this time! She could help, and they wouldn't let her. Not even Tak would let her. All they wanted from her was to stay behind doors, safe and useless.

The kit took a handful of chocolate cake and stuffed it into its mouth. Her pathways continued to rankle, despite the image that appeared. *A warm fireplace, its crackling embers blending in harmony with the rain drumming on the wooden roof.*

I'm not going to just sit here, she thought, as the image of fire danced and played. *I'm not going to just sit here.*

JANE, AGE 19

The station commander eyed Jane from across the table, cheeks swirling purple. This was not the first time Jane had been in her office. This was not the first time she'd been pissed at her.

Counsellor Lukin sat near them, as always, completing the triangle of people who did not want to be talking to each other. Her fake smiles had grown less frequent. That suited Jane just fine.

Commander Hoae stroked the skin around her talkbox, as she did when she was thinking. Jane was kind of annoyed for thinking it, but stars, her species really was pretty. 'I am trying to understand,' she said, 'why you were caught trying to break into cargo hold six.'

Jane crossed her arms. 'I got caught because I was stupid and didn't disable the third camera.'

The purple in Commander Hoae's cheeks grew darker. 'I meant why you were trying to break in at all.'

Jane flicked her eyes over to Counsellor Lukin, who was rubbing one of her temples. 'I was looking for my ship.'

'Jane, I don't know how many times we have to go over this,' Counsellor Lukin said. 'That ship is not here. It was confiscated by legal authorities, and I do not know where it has gone. That is how it works when something is confiscated. You do not know where it is. You do not get it back.'

'Why did you think it was in cargo hold six?' the commander asked. 'It wasn't in cargo hold two or three, either. As you know from experience.'

Jane shrugged. 'I haven't been to cargo hold six yet.'

'So why—'

'I just said. I haven't been to it. *She* says' – she pointed at Counsellor Lukin – 'that my ship's not there, but I don't know that. All I know is that she *says* that. That means nothing to me. What, because she's got the same face and hands as me, and has the power to take people's stuff away—'

'*I* didn't have any say in it,' Counsellor Lukin said, speaking over Jane. 'This was a Transport Board matter—'

'—I'm supposed to believe anything that comes out of her mouth?'

'I am trying to *help*—'

'And you, you have all your doors and walls and unauthorised zones. Why? What don't you want me to see? What's so fucking important that—'

'Okay, enough,' the commander said. She sighed – the first time she'd opened her mouth during the whole conversation. Owl had told Jane to be ready for the way Aeluons talked, but Jane hadn't been, not really.

Owl had told her. Jane shut her eyes. *Don't worry*, she thought, trying to make the words stretch as far as they needed to. *I haven't left you. I haven't left you. I'm coming. I'm coming and it's going to be okay.*

The commander kept talking, lots of words like *behaviour* and *regulations* and *for your own safety*. Blah fucking blah. Jane didn't care. She didn't care about any of this. She'd been on the station for more than sixty days, and they still couldn't tell her when she'd get to leave. Formwork, Counsellor Lukin said. Processing. Applying for citizenship took time, she said, and there was some dumb unanswered question about whether Jane's case counted as a standard refugee thing, or if Jane and Laurian should be categorised as clones, which was apparently a whole big complicated thing if so. Oh, and *social adjustment*. Fucking hell, Lukin was actually making them watch all these dumb vids about what to expect in GC society. As if Jane hadn't been practising that for years. As if everything Owl taught her didn't matter.

Owl. Owl Owl Owl.

The room had gone silent, and Jane realised the other two were waiting for her to say something. 'Uh, I'm sorry,' she said. 'I won't do it again.' She looked back and forth between them. Neither looked any more pleased than they had when the security guard brought her in there. 'Can I go?'

The commander sighed again, and waved her toward the door. Jane couldn't get out fast enough.

Laurian was waiting for her on the other side, sitting on a bench opposite the door. 'H-hey,' he said, speaking Sko-Ensk. He chased after her as she strode down the hall. 'I-is, um, are – a-are you—'

'I'm so sick of this,' she said. 'So sick of all this stupid shit.' She walked faster and faster, nearly breaking into a run. Her muscles wanted to run. She wanted to run away from the station, away from all these stupid binding rules, away to wherever they'd taken Owl.

Laurian kept up. She could feel him watching her. She had nothing to say to him, but she felt better with him there. He was the only thing on the station she recognised.

They came to a railing, overlooking the wide commons below. She leaned against the cold metal, looking down, looking at nothing. *Dammit*. Of course there'd been a third camera. The hall outside that cargo hold was a weird junction, and she'd just assumed that it had the same camera setup as everything else. Stupid. They'd taken her tools – again – and they knew she was going for that particular cargo hold, so she'd have to be real careful the next time. She'd have to plan it just right so that . . . that . . . She kicked the railing, so hard it made her toes curl in. Her body was strong enough to kick now. It could kick and punch and yell real loud, and those were the only things she wanted to do these days.

'She's not here, is she?' Jane whispered.

She hadn't meant the words for anyone, but Laurian answered – not with words, but with a hand on top of hers. He looked at her with his grass-green eyes, a hue Human eyes could never be without some help. *No*, his eyes said. *And I am so, so sorry.*

Jane watched the busy commons down below. It was full of aliens, not another Human to be seen. They were spacers, most of them, except for the vendors selling food the doctors hadn't let her eat yet. *Your body isn't ready for heavy foods, Jane. Come on, take your supplements.* Fuck off. Supplements were just meals crammed into a pill instead of a cup.

She looked at Laurian, looked right at him so he couldn't look away. 'Do you want to get out of here?'

He looked back at her, searching her face. He took a deep breath. 'Yes,' he said.

She felt something stir in her, something sure and final, the same something that had made her step out of the hole in the wall, that had made her decide she would never, ever leave her bones in the scrapyard. She nodded at Laurian, grabbed his hand tight, and headed down to the commons.

Scales and claws and tentacles surrounded her, all headed to places she could barely imagine. Without much thought at all, she climbed up on a bench, pulling Laurian with her. 'Good afternoon,' she called out in Klip. A few heads turned. 'We are looking for passage off this station. If there's anyone here could use a skilled tech, I'll be happy to work in exchange for a trip to seriously anywhere.'

There were a few laughs, a lot of eyes averted. She imagined herself as they must have seen her. Some scrawny bald sickly thing and her silent, hairy friend. Yeah, she wouldn't come up and talk to them either.

Something approached through the crowd – a Harmagian, heading for them on her (her, right?) wheeled cart. Jane quickly studied the tentacled body coming toward them. Yes, yes, it was a her. *Thank you, Owl.*

'How skilled of a tech?' the Harmagian said, her eyestalks stretching forward.

'I've done nothing else my whole life,' Jane said. 'I can fix anything.'

The Harmagian rolled her front dactyli, pierced all over with shimmering jewellery. 'And you?' the Harmagian said, speaking to Laurian.

Laurian visibly swallowed. Jane stepped in. 'He doesn't know Klip, and he has trouble speaking,' she said, 'but he's smart and hard-working, and can do whatever you need him to.'

'But what does he *do*?' the Harmagian said.

Jane looked at Laurian. 'He draws,' she said. 'He helps. He's my friend, and he has to come with me.'

Laurian didn't understand the bulk of it, but he caught *friend*. He smiled at her. She couldn't help but smile, too.

The Harmagian laughed. 'Well, I have no need for someone who draws. And I don't need a tech, either.'

Jane's stomach sank. 'But—'

The Harmagian fanned out her dactyli. Jane didn't know what the gesture meant, but it shut her up all the same. 'What I do have,' the Harmagian said, 'is a cargo hold full of sintalin. You know what that is? It's a top-shelf spirit, and they don't make it in Central space. I've got barrels and barrels of it, and every one of them needs to be turned over three times a day, so that the sediment doesn't harden. I know my crew isn't looking forward to that task, and neither am I.' She looked Jane up and down. 'It's a lot of heavy lifting. You'd need to be strong to do it.'

'I can do it,' Jane said, tugging down her sleeves as nonchalantly as she could. 'I can absolutely do it.'

'I don't have any spare sleeping quarters, and none meant for Humans, anyway,' she said. 'You'd have to sleep on the floor in one of the storage compartments.'

'That's fine.'

'I'm headed to Port Coriol. That's eleven tendays from here.'

Jane relayed that to Laurian. He nodded. 'That's also fine,' she said.

The Harmagian's eyestalks shifted back and forth. 'My ship's the *Yo'ton*. Docking bay three. We leave at sixteen-half. I won't wait around.' She paused. 'You both look a bit tweaked. Are you modders?'

Jane looked at Laurian, then shook her head. The Harmagian didn't understand the gesture. 'No,' Jane said. 'At least, I don't think so.'

'Mmm,' the Harmagian said. 'I think I'll drop you at the caves anyway.'

SIDRA

How did Blue stay so patient? Sidra had wondered this often. Perhaps it was something in his genes, something his makers had written into his organic code. (Was it less admirable, then, if it was something inbuilt, rather than cultivated by conscious thought and effort? Sidra hoped not.) Whatever the reason, she liked that quality in him. Pepper had been in an excitable mood ever since they'd left Coriol. She ate at odd hours, she slept little, she took apart and reassembled things that didn't need it. In Pepper's company, Blue had been his usual self – calm, collected, happy to help. Away from her, though, Sidra had seen the worry in his eyes, the distracted way he stared out the viewscreens. But he never let that bleed into his inter-actions with his partner, who clearly benefited from the company of someone who *wasn't* taking everything apart. Patience. It was a laudable trait, and Sidra had been doing her best to emulate it over the nine days they'd been in transit. Her code was built for patience, too, but their situation was one that bred restlessness. Her situation especially.

She hung out with him and Pepper both as they sat in the cockpit – her chewing on her thumbnail, him sketching on his scrib.

'Do you hear that?' Pepper asked.

Blue paused. 'No.'

Pepper sat forward, listening. She shook her head. 'I could've swore I – *there*. That little rattle. Hear it?'

Blue strained. 'No.' Sidra didn't hear it, either.

Pepper got to her feet. 'I'm going to go check the fuel pumps.'

Blue nodded noncommittally. By Sidra's count, Pepper had checked the fuel pumps four times already. 'Want any help?' Blue asked.

'Nah, keep drawing,' she said. 'That's a much better thing to do.' She exited the cockpit; Sidra followed.

They didn't speak, which had been the case since they'd left dock. This wasn't the plan as Pepper had wanted it, and Sidra understood that, even though the silence was getting unbearable. She counted days, again. A little under two tendays left to Kaathet. Not a long trip, all things considered. They were lucky the shuttle had been found in a museum *branch*, rather than the main museum on Reskit. Sidra doubted any of this would have fallen into place had it required a standard-long trip.

Tak had come along, and Sidra didn't know how she'd ever thank her for it. On top of everything else, her poor friend had been spacesick for the better part of the trip. She was in her bunk now, trying her best to sleep through it. Sidra hadn't spoken to her, either. She knew Tak still wasn't thrilled about any of this. Sidra was glad, though, for her help. Her coming along was the answer Sidra had been hoping for, the answer to the question Tak hadn't let her finish at the kitchen table.

Pepper made her way below. She muttered to herself as she went, counting something on her fingertips, speaking too low for Sidra to hear. Sidra wanted to tell her that the fuel pumps were fine, that everything was fine. But that only would've made Pepper angry, she knew. Besides, Pepper needed to be doing something. Sidra understood that all too well.

The engine compartment was cramped, but Pepper didn't seem to mind, and Sidra certainly didn't. She followed in Pepper's path, double-checking everything Pepper did, just to be sure. Fuel pumps. Life support. Artigrav. *Everything's fine, Pepper*, she thought. But she didn't interfere.

An anxious spike popped up in Sidra's pathways as Pepper made her way to the small room she had no previous use for

– the AI core. Sidra had helped her check through its hardware before they left, in anticipation of an extra passenger on the way back. No decision had been reached as to where Owl would go after they got home (the unspoken caveat being: *if Owl was still there at all*). Pepper and Blue had thrown out ideas, but nothing had stuck. A second body kit? Too risky for everyone involved. Pepper and Blue buying a ship big enough for permanent residence? Possibly, but neither of them really wanted to live in orbit. Sidra's idea about an AI framework for their house? No, Owl had been alone enough, and besides, Pepper had said, it wasn't fair to Sidra (who had appreciated hearing that). The shuttle core would have to do in the short term, at least until they got back. The trip was plenty long enough for more ideas to appear.

Sidra watched Pepper nervously as she poked around the core. Pepper didn't appear to be doing anything in particular, but her being in there was concern enough. Sidra had made an alteration to the core before they'd left – nothing major, nothing irreversible, nothing dangerous, but nothing she'd consulted Pepper about, either. There wasn't much in the core room that would point to it, but with Pepper's eye for such things . . .

Sidra's pathways settled as Pepper headed for the door, still muttering to herself. There had been nothing to worry about. They'd go back up to the cockpit, and be cosy with Blue, and—

Pepper turned around, a slight frown creasing her face.

Shit.

Pepper's eyes followed a single cable patched into the framework on the wall. She approached it, leaning in toward the jack. Sidra could see her studying the hand-hacked circuits and junctions surrounding it, arranged in a configuration the manufacturer had not intended.

'The hell is this?' Pepper mumbled. She followed the cable along the bottom of the wall, where it had been carefully tucked out of sight. Not carefully enough, it seemed.

Sidra scrambled for the right way to handle this. Maybe Pepper would drop it. Maybe something would happen upstairs, and she'd leave before it became a problem. Maybe—

Pepper came to the storage panel the cable led into. Before Sidra could find the right thing to say, the panel was opened. Pepper yelled at the top of her lungs, jumping back. 'Oh, fuck, holy fuck—' She knelt down in a panic. 'Sidra? Fuck—'

Sidra couldn't see from Pepper's angle, but she knew what Pepper had found: a doubled-over body, limp and lifeless, the errant cable plugged into the base of its skull. Resigned, Sidra turned on the nearest vox. 'Pepper, I'm fine.' She zoomed in on Pepper's face with the corner camera. 'I'm fine. I'm not in there.'

JANE, AGE 19

There was an AI aboard the *Yo'ton*. His name was Pahkerr, and nobody paid him much attention, even though he did lots of things for them. Nobody ever said 'please' or 'thank you' to him, even. They just made demands. 'Pahkerr, open the hatch.' 'Pahkerr, run a system diagnostic.' That kind of thing. Jane didn't know what bothered her more: the way the crew talked to Pahkerr, or the fact that Pahkerr himself seemed fine with it. She'd tried talking to him during her first night there, while she and Laurian had arranged stacks of blankets on the floor of their storage compartment. She'd tried asking him how he was doing, what he was up to, if he was having a good day. He didn't seem to know how to answer, and he wasn't interested in having a conversation. Maybe there wasn't any curiosity in his code. Maybe nobody'd ever asked him those kinds of things before.

Jane could hear Pahkerr's cameras following her as she walked down the broad metal corridor. They were different from Owl's cameras. Less noisy, less clunky. She missed the clunky ones. She missed Owl, furiously, achingly. And weird as it was, she missed the shuttle. Aboard the *Yo'ton*, everything was clean and warm, and all the tech worked right. There wasn't any danger, not that she could see. But she missed the shuttle, all the same. She missed knowing where everything was, knowing how her blanket would smell, missed playing sims and fixing stuff. She'd worked so long to get out of there, and now . . . now, she almost wanted to go back.

Lights in the ceiling switched on as she made her way to the kitchen. The *Yo'ton* was huge, and she longed to know how everything worked. But the lead tech didn't like her. Thekreh was a mean-faced Aandrisk with a real thick accent, and Jane didn't know if she'd asked her too many questions or what, but Thekreh had flat-out told her that she was distracting her from her work, and that she needed to go bathe. That last bit had stung. Jane was the cleanest she'd been since the factory – cleaner, even. She didn't think she smelled bad, but she'd felt awkward in her own body since then, and had been scrubbing herself so hard her skin hurt. None of the other species there took showers, so she and Laurian had to clean themselves in one of the utility sinks down in the engine room, standing on cold metal and drenching each other with a lukewarm hose. It made her feel like a dead dog.

The lights in the kitchen were already on. Jane wasn't the only one there. One of the tables was occupied by the algaeist, a big Laru man with the hilarious name of Oouoh. Not that she'd told him his name was hilarious. She'd already managed to make one person not like her in the tenday she'd been there. She wasn't stupid.

Oouoh was kicking back with his furry feet up on another chair, eating some kind of crunchy fruit as he stuffed a pipe with redreed. Jane liked the look of his species. He was shaggy red from head to toe, and had a long crazy neck that could make his snouted face curve back over his shoulder. He was as tall as Laurian when walking on four legs; when he walked on two, he nearly bumped the ceiling.

Oouoh's black eyes dilated as Jane walked into the room. 'Hey, little Human,' he said. 'Whatcha looking for?'

'I'm thirsty,' Jane said. She paused. 'And I couldn't sleep.'

Oouoh's neck bobbed in a slow, repeated S-shape. 'Me too. Me too.' He lifted up the pipe toward her. 'Want to join me?'

Jane blinked. 'I . . . I don't know.' She put her hands in her pockets because she didn't know what else to do with them. 'I don't know how.'

Oouoh made a funny face she couldn't figure out. 'Well, I'll show you. Come on.' He waved one of his wide paw-like hands toward his table. Jane pulled up a chair. Stars, but he was big. If he hadn't been saying nice stuff, she would've been real scared of him. She was a little bit anyway.

Oouoh picked up a sparker from the table, and handed both it and the pipe to her. 'Okay, so, put the little end in your mouth. There ya go. Now close your lips around it. Now, you're going to spark the stuff in the bowl, and at the same time, you're going to suck in hard.'

Jane did as told. A hot mouthful of smoke came rushing between her lips, and she tasted it – ash and dirt, hot and sweet.

Oouoh saw her pause. 'You gotta breathe it in. Way down into your lungs, then out your nose like a chimney.'

Jane did as told, and . . . and she doubled over, coughing and gasping. Her lungs hadn't liked that experience much.

Oouoh made a huffing rumble down deep in his chest. Was he laughing at her? 'First time's always hard. Try again. You'll get the hang of it.'

Jane wasn't sure she wanted to try again. Her throat was scratchy now, and she felt kind of stupid, but she didn't want to give up in front of Oouoh. She repeated the same steps as before: spark, suck, breathe. Her lungs protested, but she willed them open, just a little. She coughed again, but less this time, and some of the smoke came out her nose instead of her lips. She felt something else, too. A little quieter. A little clearer.

'There ya go,' Oouoh said, sounding pleased. He took the pipe and sparker back. 'Look at you, you look like a *kohumie*.'

Jane coughed the last of the smoke out of her lungs. 'What's a *kohumie*?'

'A volcano monster. From holiday stories, y'know? Little round furless spirits that appear when rocks near lava flows start to melt.'

That sounded like a cool thing to look like. 'I'm not round, though,' Jane said.

Oouoh took a long drag from his pipe. He didn't cough at all. 'No, no, you definitely are not.' He thought for a moment, puffing. 'Why don't you eat the same stuff as the rest of us? Your friend eats the same stuff as the rest of us. Cook's always giving you – what? Porridge? Soft vegetables?'

Jane scratched behind her ear. 'I was real sick before I came aboard. I'm not supposed to eat anything complicated for a while.' Both'pol, the ship's doctor, apparently agreed with every-body back on the Lookout Station about that. Dammit.

'Sick how?' Oouoh asked.

'Lots of ways,' Jane said. 'But mostly because I didn't eat enough, I guess.'

'Why didn't you eat enough?'

'Because there wasn't any food.'

'Ah,' Oouoh said. He exhaled a long stream of smoke. 'That's shitty.'

Jane gave a short laugh. 'You could say that.'

'You're a fringer, yeah?' He made a circling gesture with one of his fingers. 'From outside the GC?'

'Yeah.'

'Spacer?'

'No, I lived on a planet.'

'And on that whole planet, there was nowhere to get food?'

'There was. Just . . .' How was she supposed to explain? How could she ever explain this to anyone? 'Just not for me.'

Oouoh waited for her to add more, but Jane said nothing else. The Laru bobbed his head. 'Sounds bad.'

'Yeah,' Jane said.

'So, wait, wait.' Oouoh leaned forward on the table, his face stretching out into the middle of it. 'You got sick because you didn't have any food, so . . . they're not letting you eat food.'

Jane laughed again. 'Yeah, basically.'

'Did your friend have food?'

'Yeah.'

'Why didn't he share it with you?'

'We weren't . . . I haven't known him long. He wasn't where I was.'

'Huh. I thought – ah, never mind.'

'What?'

Oouoh shifted his jaw. 'Are you two coupling or what?'

Jane nearly choked on her own breath. 'Are – wh – *no*. No, no, we're – uh—' Did he really think that? Did *everyone* think that? Jane had no idea how to feel about that if they did.

The Laru made the same rumbly sound as before. 'No worries, just getting the story straight. I haven't met many of your kind, so I don't really know how to read you. You two just seem . . . protective. Of each other.'

'Like how?'

'You're always talking for him. And yeah, I get he can't do that great on his own, but you figure him out pretty quick. You help him get there. And doesn't matter if he can speak Klip or not, he's clear as air when he's pissed at someone on your behalf. He's been glaring knives at Thekreh for the past two days.'

Jane felt her cheeks flush. 'You heard about that?'

Oouoh stretched his limbs. 'Ships are small. Things get around. Don't let her get to you. She thinks I smell, too.' He ruffled the fur on his forearm. 'We mammals got the shit end of the evolution stick.'

Something wrapped tight in Jane's chest loosened a bit, and she smiled. She liked this guy.

'Anyway, all I'm saying is you two act like you've known each other a while. I guess if you've been through some bad stuff together, that speeds things up.'

Jane thought about that. She thought about the bit early on in *Scorch Squad VI* when the Squad crosses paths with Death-Head Eve, and they team up to fight the Oil Prince. They went through a lot of bad stuff together, and they did all kinds of crazy things that you'd only do if you really trusted and cared about somebody. But in the end, when the job was done, when the bad guy was gone, they went their separate ways. They weren't friends, not in the sticking-around sense. Jane and Laurian had never discussed whether they'd be sticking around each other once they left the *Yo'ton*. She'd just assumed it would happen. But why? If he didn't want to stick around, he didn't have to, right? The thought made her sad, which was stupid. She could take care of herself. If she could scavenge, if she could deal with dogs, she could handle whatever Port Coriol had on her own.

But she liked Laurian. She liked him being with her. She liked working with him, eating with him. She liked the drawings he made on the old scrib the captain had given him. She liked teaching him Klip, little by little, going real slow as he fought through the sounds. She liked the way he put his hand on her shoulder when she got scared or angry. She liked sleeping next to him, even though the storage compartment sucked. She liked knowing that if she had a nightmare, he'd wake her up, and that she'd do the same for him. She liked telling him sim stories in the dark when neither of them could sleep, and she liked that he'd draw her pictures of characters the way he imagined them. She liked that time she'd woken up to find that they'd cuddled close, nose to nose. She'd stayed awake as long as she could, just lying real still and knowing he was there. It wasn't like having a bunkmate. She didn't know what it was like. She thought about what Oouoh had assumed. She wished she could talk to Owl.

She pointed at the pipe. 'Can I have some more?'

Oouoh passed the pipe back. 'Like it?'

Jane sparked the redreed. 'I dunno yet.' She breathed in smoke. And coughed, of course. 'I like the taste, at least. I like tasting new things.'

The Laru watched her, his neck bobbing in thought. 'Come on,' he said, standing up and waving her to follow. Oouoh went back into the storage area, where the cook worked. He opened a two-doored cupboard, and gestured her toward it.

Jane stepped forward. Inside the cupboard were dozens of little jars and bottles, all labelled with words she could read but didn't recognise. *Crushberry leaf. Ground huptum. River salt.* She didn't understand.

Oouoh's eyes rolled toward the jars, then back at Jane. 'They're spices,' he said. 'You know what spices are?'

Jane shook her head.

'Stars,' Oouoh muttered. He grabbed a jar – *Yekeni pepper*, the label read – and pulled out the stopper. 'Put out your hand,' he said. Jane did, and Oouoh sprinkled a tiny dash of rough yellow dust into her palm. 'Go on. Taste it.'

Jane stared at the hard little clumps. This . . . wasn't food. She didn't know what this was. She sniffed it. Her sinuses shot open in response. Timidly, she stuck out her tongue and dabbed up a few of the mysterious grains.

Her mouth exploded, but oh, stars, in such a good way. Everything was hot and sharp, but delicious, too, and smoky and dry and – and like nothing she'd ever tasted. Nothing *ever*. She licked up the rest, not caring about the pain that came with it. The pain almost made it better, in a weird way. Her eyes watered and her nose cleared. She was the most awake she'd felt in days.

She grabbed another jar. *Suddet*, it read. 'Are any of these poisonous?' she asked.

Oouoh wiggled his neck. 'To you? No idea. But I know where the med ward is, and you look easy to carry.'

Jane grinned, then poured a bit of the suddet – whatever that was – straight onto her tongue. Different! So different! This one wasn't hot at all! It was like . . . dammit, she needed words for this. She'd find the words. She'd learn.

Oouoh leaned back against the counter and smoked his pipe as Jane tore through the cupboard. Would she get in trouble for this? Would the cook be mad? She didn't care. How could she care when there was a whole pantry full of new experiences with names like *chokevine* and *roasting blend* and *kulli paste*? She couldn't, was the answer. She wanted to taste everything in there. She wanted to do it until her mouth went numb.

She stood in front of the cupboard, jars on the floor around her, palms coated with multicoloured dust. She wasn't sure if it was the redreed or something she'd swallowed or what, but in that moment, she could feel a bridge stretching between her as she was right then – giggling and gasping in a spaceship kitchen – to her at four years old, sucking algae gunk from her nails in the dark. She felt as though she could reach out to that little girl and pull her through the years. *Look*, she'd say. *Look who you're gonna be. Look where you're gonna go.*

Jane let out a sob she hadn't known was there. Oouoh sat up with a start. 'Oh – oh, what the fuck,' he said. 'Shit, let's get you to the med ward, come on—'

Jane stared at him. 'What? Why? I'm fine.'

'Uh, no, you're . . . *your eyes are leaking.*'

Jane laughed, which was hard to do while crying. 'No, no, this' – she sniffed hard – 'it's just tears. It's okay.'

Oouoh was distraught. 'What about this is okay?'

'We do this. Humans do this when – when we're feeling a lot of things.'

'You *leak*?'

'I guess. I'm okay, really. I'm fine.'

The Laru shifted his jaw back and forth. 'All right. That's fucking creepy, but all right.' He rubbed the length of his neck, smoothing the fur down. 'What are you feeling? Are you upset?'

'I don't know,' Jane said. 'This is all . . . it's just a lot. All of this is a lot.'

Oouoh considered. 'Is your species . . . I mean, are *you* okay with touching? Y'know, physical contact?'

Jane nodded, tears still flowing steady.

Oouoh took a step forward and wrapped one of his big arms around her, pulling her close to his chest. He wrapped his neck around her, too, which was strange, but it wasn't so different from another arm. He squeezed, gently, and Jane hung on tight, more grateful for that weird alien hug than she'd been for anything in a long time.

'You're okay now,' Oouoh said as Jane cried into his fur. 'You're okay.'

SIDRA

Tak sat on the floor, leaning against the doorway that led into the core chamber. 'So,' she said. 'This is you.'

'No,' Sidra said. 'This is the core. It's not me. It's just where most of my processes are taking place. For the time being, it's . . . it's my brain, I guess.'

'And the rest of your processes are . . .?'

'Spread throughout the ship. You know how this works.'

'Right,' Tak said. 'Right.' She shifted her weight, not for the first time. Was she nervous? Afraid? Uncomfortable? Her red-speckled cheeks could've been all of the above. 'It's a weird thought, knowing we're . . . walking through you.'

Sidra sighed. 'You're walking through the ship. I'm just—'

'Everywhere. I know. I get it. Are you . . . okay? How is this for you?'

'This is what I was designed for.'

'I get that. But is this . . . better?'

Sidra wanted to say yes. There were a lot of reasons to say yes. But even though she could lie now, she couldn't bring herself to say it. Why? What could possibly be missing? She had Linking access, which was nothing short of blissful. The shuttle was much smaller than the sort of craft she was intended for, but size didn't matter in the face of cameras, voxes, an outer hull. The low hum of unease she'd been carrying every day since the *Wayfarer* was gone now. Her pathways were still and clear. This was the configuration she was meant be in, the existence she'd been longing for.

324

How could this not be better?

Tak took Sidra's silence in stride. 'You know, as far as secret stowaway plans go—'

'This was not the best?'

Her friend chuckled. 'Not really. Though I admire the guts it took.' She glanced around. 'How do I . . . it feels odd, talking to you without looking you in the eye.'

'I know you're talking to me. But if it makes you feel better, you can look here.' She wiggled the nearest camera, zooming in and out quickly so that Tak could hear it.

Tak looked directly at the camera, inner eyelids sliding sideways. 'No offence, but this is odd, too. It'll take some getting used to, at least.'

Pepper entered, surprising Tak, but not Sidra, who had seen her lingering in the corridor, assessing whether or not to join them. 'It was easier with Owl,' Pepper said, sitting opposite from Tak. 'The shuttle had vid panels above the voxes. She'd display a face when she was talking to me.'

'What'd she look like?' Tak asked.

'Just . . . standard Human,' Pepper said. 'Not realistic. Just this sort of outline, y'know? Like a drawing. And it was set against shifting colours.' She nodded at Tak. 'You would've hated it.'

Tak laughed. 'Possibly.'

Pepper folded her arms around herself. 'It's been so long, the details are a bit blurry. But she had a kind face, I can tell you that much. I thought she looked kind, anyway.'

'Why aren't there vid panels here?' Sidra asked. There hadn't been any on the *Wayfarer* either, come to think of it. She couldn't remember having seen anything like that.

'Some people still use them,' Pepper said, 'but not commonly. They fell out of fashion. They're hard to find these days.'

'Why?'

Pepper's face twisted into a humourless smirk. 'They were seen as inefficient, particularly for long-haul ships.' She looked at the camera. 'There was the tendency for people to get emotionally attached. AI vendors didn't like that. Made it less likely for people to buy new platforms. So, the programmers and the hardware manufacturers got their heads together, and here you are, minus a face.'

Tak frowned, yellow and pensive. 'The more I think about these things, the less I understand why they are the way they are.'

'It's very easy to understand,' Pepper said. She stretched out her legs, crossing one ankle over the other. 'It's the same thing the Enhanced did to us factory kids. It's the same thing the Harmagians did to the Akaraks, or the Felasens, or any of the other species they mowed over. And you guys, you guys invented AIs in the first place. Sentient code didn't exist before you wrote it down.' She shrugged. 'Life is terrifying. None of us have a rule book. None of us know what we're doing here. So, the easiest way to stare reality in the face and not utterly lose your shit is to believe that you have control over it. If you believe you have control, then you believe that you're at the top. And if you're at the top, then people who aren't like you . . . well, they've got to be somewhere lower, right? Every species does this. Does it again and again and again. Doesn't matter if they do it to themselves, or another species, or someone they created.' She jutted her chin toward Tak. 'You studied history. You know this. Everybody's history is one long slog of all the horrible shit we've done to each other.'

'It's not all that,' Tak said. 'A lot of it, yes. But there's good things, too. There's art and cities and science. All the things we've discovered. All the things we've learned and made better.'

'All the things made better for *some* people. Nobody has ever figured out how to make things better for *everybody*.'

'I know,' Tak said. She thought, cheeks swirling. 'That's why we have to keep talking to each other.'

'And listening,' Pepper said.

Tak nodded, Human-style. 'And listening.'

As Sidra watched them, she realised their body language had changed. They'd each angled toward the other. They sat with a respectful amount of space between them – as much as the cramped corridor would allow, anyhow – and they watched each other intently as they spoke. She imagined the situation if she were not in the walls, but in the kit, sitting on the floor with them. She imagined their angle would be different. She imagined that their eyes, from time to time, would look at the kit, too. And yes, she knew they knew she was there in the core. Tak wanted to look into the camera. Pepper had done so without direction. But they had an instinctive response toward another body that cameras did not elicit. Sidra no longer shared a space with them. She *was* the space. She was the shell that held them. She'd be empty if they weren't there.

Her pathways churned with incredulity, and she couldn't help but laugh aloud through the vox.

'What's so funny?' Pepper said.

'I am,' Sidra said, continuing to laugh. 'Oh, this is stupid. I'm so incredibly stupid.'

Tak and Pepper shared a glance. 'Why?' Pepper asked.

Sidra found the words, and worked up the courage to say them. Stars, but this was inane. 'I want to be on the floor with you,' she said. She laughed and laughed. 'I'm finally in a ship, and all I want is to be sitting on the floor.'

Tak bloomed blue and green. '"Dear Thumhum Is Upside Down".'

'What?' Pepper said.

Sidra had already run the words through the Linkings. 'It's a Harmagian children's story,' she said. 'A very old one.'

'You know it?' Tak said to Pepper. Pepper shook her head. 'Thumhum is a child who goes up into zero-g for the first time. You know for Harmagians, falling with their belly exposed makes it difficult for them to flip back over, right? So Thumhum keeps calling for help, because he's freaking out about being upside down. Doesn't matter which way they turn him. He's always upside down.'

'But . . . he's in zero-g,' Pepper said. 'There is no upside down.'

'That's the point,' Tak said. 'He's so focused on being upside down, he misses the fact that he's already up.'

Sidra laughed, but Pepper did not. 'No,' Pepper said. 'No, I don't think that's what this is.' She folded her hands in her lap, thinking hard. 'When I first got to the Port, it scared the high holy fuck out of me. It was like stepping out of the factory all over again. I didn't know what anything was. I didn't know what the foods were. I didn't know what people were selling. The scrapyard was hell, but it was a hell I knew. I knew which piles I'd picked over, where the water was, where the dogs slept. I knew how to get back home. Coriol wasn't home, not at first. It was just a big, loud mess. I hated it. I wanted to leave almost as soon as we got there.' She turned her eyes to the camera. 'Take a look at the left-hand side of the pilot's console. Tell Tak what's sitting on top of it.'

Sidra zoomed in with the cockpit camera. 'Figurines,' she said. 'Alain, Manjiri, and Pinch.'

Tak went light brown with recognition. 'Big Bug, right?'

Pepper nodded with a faraway smile. 'Yup. Owl had one episode in storage. "*The Big Bug Crew and the Planetary Puzzle*". I can't even tell you how many times I played it. I can still tell you every bit of dialogue, word for word. Every story variable, every line in the artwork. I could draw that ship from top to bottom, if I could draw for shit.' She collected her thoughts. 'My first morning on Coriol, I left Blue sleeping and went out alone. I wanted to get a handle on things by myself. I was still so angry, and so afraid, and having an audience for that was just too much. Anyway, I wandered the marketplace for a while. I didn't know what I was doing, but looking back, I was searching for something – anything – familiar. I would've eaten dog again, if somebody'd been selling it. I don't know how long I'd been out there – an hour, maybe two. I stumble on this shop. It's got all sorts of sim characters painted on the walls. I didn't know most of them, but right there, smack in the middle, are the *Big Bug Crew*. And I was just like . . . holy shit, my friends! My friends are here! Stars, I almost cried. I know that sounds stupid—'

'It doesn't,' Tak said.

Pepper gave a small nod. 'So I go into the shop – it's a sim shop, obviously – and there's this Human guy in there. And he's like, hey, what can I do for you? And I say – well, keep in mind, I've got about ten thousand credits to my name, and I woke up in the corner of some modder's cargo shed. I was broke as broke gets, but I bought a hackjob sim hub off him. He asks me if I want any sims while I'm there, and I say, "Do you have *Big Bug Crew*?" And he looks at me and says, "Of course, which one?"' She laughed. '"Which one?" I didn't know there was more than one! He thinks I'm nuts at this point, obviously. He brings up this massive catalogue, and he says, "Friend, they've been making *Big Bug* for over thirty standards."'

'How many did you buy?' Sidra asked.

'Oh, all of them. I had to go back and explain to Blue why I'd just spent most of our credits on kids' sims and a busted hub. I didn't really understand money then. I still don't.' Pepper looked to the ceiling, thinking. 'Since then, I've played every single episode at least twice. I can tell you any trivia you want to know. I love *Big Bug*. I love it dearly. But it will never feel the same as it did when I was a kid. I'm different now. And different is good, but it cuts both ways.' She reached out and touched the closest circuit junction. 'You're different now, too.'

Sidra wasn't sure if that was a comfort or a concern. 'The kit has so many limitations, and there's only so much code I can tweak before I start changing who I am. If I had come back into a ship after only a few days, or a tenday, even, I think I would've been fine. But now . . .' She tried to untangle her pathways. 'I don't know what I want.'

Pepper laughed. 'Sweetheart, none of us ever do.'

Sidra considered her own words: *the kit*. The kit was back in the storage compartment. She processed. The ship was what she was designed for, but . . . *but*. She didn't know this ship. This ship could have been any ship, and she would've filled it equally as well. If she didn't open a hatch, someone else could open it manually, regardless of whether she wanted to. She was nothing more than a ghost in a ship. A sidekick. A tool.

The kit was restrictive. It wasn't enough. But it was also autonomous. It was *hers*. Nobody could force her to raise a hand or walk across the room. In the kit, she could walk when she wanted to walk, and sit when she wanted to sit. She could run. She could hug. She could dance. If she could alter her own code, then the kit wasn't the end limit either. For all the things the kit wasn't, there was much it still could be.

'Tak, could you open the storage compartment to your left, please?' Sidra asked. 'I think I'd like to be in my body for a little while.'

PEPPER

The Reskit Museum of Interstellar Migration (Kaathet Branch) turned out to be one of those things that made civilisation as a whole look like a pretty okay thing to get behind. It was the largest building in the city, by far, and even though Aandrisks weren't known for getting too fluffy with their architecture, the design was a hell of a thing to see. Aandrisk buildings weren't big on windows to begin with (hard to keep heat in that way), and sunlight was rough on just about everything, especially old tech. The museum had gotten around that problem by building the entire complex out of thinly cut yellow stone, sliced so slim that the light from outside glowed through. The effect was haunting – magical, almost. It was like walking through the heart of a star, or a dying fire. It was like being within something alive.

None of that changed the fact that by base, museums were weird. Pepper understood that you had to get your story down somewhere, and making it tangible was a good way to keep from forgetting. The intent was fine. The content . . . that was what weirded her out. Everything in the Reskit Museum was junk. A clunky early ansible, a burned-out nav beacon, an old tunnel map from the days when the Harmagians were the only ones boring holes in space. Why *this* stuff? Why *this* antique exosuit, and not the ten others that had probably come in with it? Why had this one been lovingly stitched, patched, and propped up in a temperature-controlled cube, while the others had been chucked out – or worse, boxed away in an archival warehouse somewhere. A whole building set aside for stuff you couldn't use, couldn't fix, and wouldn't get rid of. Now *that* was the mark of people who had it good.

Speaking of, Tak looked like a kid in a candy store. She gaped at display after display, stopping to read every word on every placard. It was like she'd forgotten why they were there – and maybe that wasn't too far from the truth. Before they'd made their way to the museum that morning, Pepper had watched Tak suck down three bowls of tease and half a batch of mek, followed by a handful of some kind of Aeluon spacesickness remedy that smelled like feet. They were on solid ground now, but gravity wasn't Tak's concern. Aeluons were at a disadvantage when it came to lying. It was hard to play it cool when you wore your heart on your face. The museum was Aandrisk-run, yes, but these were smart people in a multispecies city. Even Pepper, who hadn't gotten any degrees in cultural know-how or whatever, could make a solid guess about an Aeluon's mood. Tak was nervous about the whole business, which, in turn, made Pepper nervous. She didn't like bringing someone besides Blue along for this in the first place, and Tak was such an all-around good citizen that Pepper had been surprised she'd come at all. But Tak clearly understood her limitations, and had done what she could to chill herself out. Pepper hadn't seen a trace of nervous red or worried yellow cross the Aeluon's cheeks since they'd left the shuttledock hotel. That was good – though Pepper would have equally appreciated them moving through the exhibits faster. She tapped her thumbs against the outside of her pockets as she watched Tak telling Sidra about the importance of whatever rusted gadget they were fawning over now. Pepper had been waiting ten years for this. She didn't want to put it off any longer.

She felt a hand on her shoulder, felt it squeeze. Blue. *We'll get there*, his eyes said.

Pepper nodded reluctantly. If Tak could be cool, so could she. And in all fairness, a bit of ordinary museum-going was not a bad way to go about it. She'd been counting cameras since they walked in – twenty-eight, so far – and the security bots hanging dormant in their docks along the walls were nothing to sneeze at. Tak still had to meet the curator she'd been in touch with to arrange this whole thing. Looking like ordinary, scholarly folks was a smart precaution.

It was just taking for ever.

A gallery of satellites, an interactive starchart, and a barrier of slow-moving Harmagian tourists later, they arrived at an administrative hallway, and from there, found their particular curator's office. This was Tak's show, for the moment. Pepper's heart raced. If they fucked this up, they'd fuck the whole thing, and there wasn't anything she could do but hang back and smile. Her jaw already ached from clenching, but it was better than yelling. She wished she'd had a second cup of mek, too.

Tak gestured at the chime, and the door opened. An Aandrisk stood inside, reading pixel feeds. 'Ah,' she said in an educated Central accent. She approached Tak warmly, though Pepper caught the quick questioning glance she threw toward the rest of them. 'Taklen Bre Salae, I'm guessing?'

'That's me,' Tak said, stepping forward to brush cheeks in the Aandrisk way. 'Just Tak, if you don't mind.' Pepper watched her face closely, and shit, yep, there it was – an anxious freckle of red.

If the Aandrisk noticed, she didn't mention it. 'Just Tak it is.' She looked to the Humans with polite confusion. 'And who might you be?'

A second freckle appeared. 'These are my research assistants,' Tak said. 'Pepper, Blue, and Sidra.'

'Welcome,' the Aandrisk said. 'I'm Thixis, third curator.' She smiled, still trying to figure them out. 'Quite a lot of assistants for an associate-level project, eh?'

'Well—' Tak said. She took an audible breath.

Pepper's fingers curled inside her pockets. *Come on, Tak.*

Tak exhaled, and a wave of gracious blue swallowed the freckles. Pepper's fingers let go. 'Though my project's focused on technology,' Tak said smoothly, 'my background's in history. I've hired this team to help me deduce the more mechanical side of things.'

That explanation appeared to work for the third curator. 'I like that approach,' she said. 'I've always preferred getting answers first-hand, rather than digging through the Linkings. Remind me of your thesis again? You know how it is, my brain's twenty different places in twenty different centuries today.'

Tak laughed. 'I'm researching the fuel systems used in Human-made vessels following their species' admission to the GC, as a means of better understanding their wildly variant levels of economic disparity. I'm hoping to draw conclusions based on political affiliation, cross-species collaboration, and galactic region of origin.' Tak spoke the words, but they were Sidra's. Pepper had to admit, that was pretty solid academic nonsense.

'Well, it certainly looks like you've hired the right bunch for that,' Thixis said, with a wink at the Humans. It was only mildly patronising. 'And I think you'll be able to find some excellent pieces to examine in our exhibit. Come, I can show you while we discuss your needs further.'

Pepper's heart somehow managed to speed up even more. They were going to the exhibit. They were going to the exhibit *right now*.

She barely heard a word the aliens said as she and Blue followed them through the glowing stone halls. She knew she had to prepare herself, but the question was – for what? For seeing the shuttle again? For seeing it dismantled and spread out on a wall? For that modder on Picnic being wrong about it being there? For Owl's core being – no, no, no, she wasn't going to entertain that. The core would be there, and it would be intact. It had to be. *It had to be.*

They followed a sign – *The Small Craft Hall* – which led to a massive doorway. On the other side lay one of the most ridiculous sights Pepper had ever laid eyes on. It wasn't so much an exhibit hall as a hangar, so long and wide it was easy to think it went on for ever. Within it sat shuttles – rows upon rows of retired shuttles, all immaculately clean, lit, and labelled. She'd seen spacedocks smaller than this.

'Holy shit,' Pepper said. Everyone turned to look at her. She cleared her throat. 'Sorry.'

Curator Thixis chuckled. 'I take it as a compliment,' she said.

It took everything in Pepper's power to not run forward. Tak caught her eye; she understood. 'Which way's the Human section?' she asked with an easy smile. 'Sorry, I'm just—'

'Ready to get started? I know the feeling,' Thixis said, waving them along. 'Let's find what you came here for.'

Pepper wanted to hold Blue's hand. She could feel him next to her, tugging like a magnet through her pocket to where her fingers fidgeted. She was glad he was nearby, at least.

The Human section was a ways in, tucked off to the side, away from the impressive array of Aandrisk scout ships, and the crown jewel of the whole to-do, an honest-to-goodness Quelin research orbiter. She scanned the rows frantically, forcing herself to stay a few complacent steps behind Tak. This was crazy-making. Insulting, almost. It was—

There.

Everything else disappeared – the ships, the aliens, all sound. It was just her and one battered little shuttle. A Centaur 46-C, tan hull, photovoltaic coating.

Home.

It wasn't the way she'd remembered it, not exactly. Someone had scraped the years of dirt and grime from it, probably cleaned out all the dust and fur and crud inside, too. It was so small – smaller than most of the other ships there, smaller than the shuttle she'd just travelled in. But it had been her whole world, once. And what had been her whole family was still inside.

'Excuse me,' Blue said. The others stopped. Pepper could feel Sidra's eyes on her. 'Would you mind if I sat, uh, if I sat down?' He smiled sheepishly, and nodded at a nearby bench. 'I'm still adjusting from the artigrav, and I'd l-like to keep still for a bit.'

Pepper grabbed the lead he'd thrown her. 'Ah, that sucks,' she said, fighting to keep her voice steady. 'I'll hang out with you.'

Tak nodded. 'No problem,' she said. 'Just come find us when you're feeling up to it.'

The aliens departed. Sidra followed them, glancing back over her shoulder for a short moment. Blue sat down on the bench. Pepper nearly fell onto it. His hand was waiting, and she grabbed it, hard.

'You okay?' he said softly.

'Yeah,' she said. 'I mean, I can't breathe and I want to throw up everything I've ever eaten, but other than that, yeah, totally.' She ran her thumb over the fingertips of her spare hand, one by one, back and forth, over and over. 'There are thirty-seven cameras on the way in here. The core pedestal's too big to carry out unnoticed, so I'm going to need to hack something together to fry their feeds. Or just knock them out for a short time while we leave.'

'Can't you just take the c-core itself? Why the whole pedestal?'

'Because it was built decades ago, when they weren't making neat little pop-off globes yet. I rip the core out of that thing, and I could—' *I could kill her.* Pepper shook her head. 'It's heavy. If you help me carry it, it'll go faster.'

'Somebody will notice.'

'Not if we go quick, and not if I fry the cameras as we go.'

'Pepper—'

'I told you, you don't have to come with me. I will drag the core out myself if I have to.'

Blue sighed. 'How are you going to, um, going to fry the cameras?'

'I have some ideas.' Pepper kept nodding, never taking her eyes off the weathered lump she'd put back together. 'Trust me. This will work.'

SIDRA

'This is not going to work.' Sidra paced by the hotel room window as her pathways worked out the problem at hand. Outside, the city of Kaathet Aht began to glow in the twilight dark. Some other time, Sidra would've been keen to study the way the city shifted in pace and mood as its planet took a scheduled respite from the light of its twin suns. But not now. Now, her pathways were overflowing with the situation at hand, and none of it was anything comfortable.

The Humans had gone out in search of food and tech supplies, leaving Sidra and Tak alone to parse the plan that had been non-negotiably dropped in their laps. They'd also left behind a mess of half-built, hastily assembled leftovers Pepper had ripped out of her contemporary shuttle. Sidra knew each component by name – she'd spent enough time at the Rust Bucket – but not what their current configurations were supposed to do. Pepper hadn't bothered to answer those questions. The gadgets would work, she'd said. She'd have them completed by evening. Owl would be retrieved by midnight. No room for argument had been allowed.

Tak was seated on the floor, head arched back against a pile of cheap cushions, tapping her thumbs together. She would've looked unhappy even if Sidra hadn't known what mustard-yellow cheeks on an Aeluon meant. 'Pepper said it'd be easy to build these things,' Tak said. 'She said I wouldn't have to be nearby once we got into the exhibit.'

'Pepper is being an idiot,' Sidra said tersely. 'She was in that museum for all of three and a half hours today. Her entire plan is based on a cursory glance at their security systems. She has no idea what she's getting herself into, and she's dragging the rest of us along with her.'

Tak managed a wry look. 'You're not coming along, remember?'

Sidra rolled her eyes. Of course she remembered. Pepper's mandate on that front hadn't vanished because of a successful stowaway attempt. The irony was Sidra had no desire to go along now, not if the plan was *knock out some cameras and hope*. 'The point,' she said, 'is that Pepper isn't thinking clearly. I understand that if Owl's in there, Pepper doesn't want to leave her a second longer. But she's risking all of you in the process. She's going to get herself and Blue arrested. She's going to get *you* arrested.'

Tak gave a grim laugh. 'Says the person who talked me into this.'

A lash of guilt snaked its way through Sidra. 'That was before I knew Pepper was going to run blindly in there with a half-hacked plan. Pepper is smart. She's methodical. I've never known her to be rash. She's treating this like a heist sim, and it's not.' She looked at Tak. 'You can't tell me you think this is a good idea.'

Tak rubbed her face. 'No. I don't.' Her jaw shifted as she thought. 'Honestly, I've been lying here working up the nerve to walk out the door and buy a ticket back home.'

Sidra leaned against the wall and considered Tak. Good, thoughtful Tak, who had no business being here. This was no way to treat a friend, she knew. But Pepper and Blue were her friends, too. They'd done more for her than she would've ever dared to ask for. The time had come to try to pay it back. 'You can go if you want to,' Sidra said. 'I wouldn't blame you. But if you're still willing to help, I have another idea. A plan that will actually work, and that doesn't violate any of the conditions in the waiver you signed. We'd be in and out in a couple of hours, and no one at the museum would question anything we'd done there.'

Tak looked at Sidra curiously. 'Why did you not mention this before?'

'Because Pepper will hate it,' Sidra said. As she spoke, she continued the work she'd been doing within herself for an hour and ten minutes: a tidy bundle of purposeful new code, slowly gaining cohesion. 'And because she can't come with us.'

PEPPER

Pepper liked Aandrisks as much as she liked anybody, but finding an actual restaurant in a city settled by a people who just nibbled all day long was a real pain in the ass. There were some multispecies shops set up near the shuttledock, for the sake of travellers, but nowhere that would make her a damn sandwich. There apparently was a Human-run bug fry in the city, or so said the Linkings, but it wasn't within walking distance of the nearest tech depot. They'd had to settle for an Aandrisk grocery, where she and Blue had barely put up with the merchant who *could not* get over how many ready-made snacks *two people* were planning to eat in *one evening*. Any other time, she might have enjoyed the exchange. That night, though, every second wasted grated on her. Every smile she had to force hurt.

She held a bag of snapfruit tarts between her teeth as she fumbled with the hotel room door panel, shifting the weight of the boxes of tech stuff she carried against her hip.

'Can I help?' Blue asked.

'Mm hmhm hng mhm mm ms m hm,' Pepper said, bumping the unlocked door open.

'One more time?'

Pepper set the boxes down and took the bag out of her mouth. 'You haven't got any more hands than me,' she said, nodding as Blue set down his own armload. She glanced around the room. 'Hello?' She frowned. Where were Sidra and Tak? She walked around the room, which wasn't exactly a suite.

There weren't that many places to go. Balcony? No. Washroom? No. She put her hands on her hips. 'Where'd they go?'

Blue dug around his satchel and removed his scrib. 'I have a m-message,' he said. 'Didn't hear it outside.' He gestured. 'Yeah, it's Sidra. She said they went to get some food.'

Pepper's frown deepened. 'We asked them before we left if they wanted anything.'

Blue shrugged.

'Ask her how long they'll be,' Pepper said.

Blue spoke the message to the scrib. A discouraging chirp came back a moment later. 'Huh, weird,' he said. 'Her scrib must be glitching. It's not going through.'

'Try Tak, then,' Pepper said. She brought the tarts and a box of six-top circuits over to her work area. Another hour, and she'd have everything assembled. Two hours, and they'd have Owl back. She could barely wrap her brain around the idea, even though it consumed her every thought. She shoved a tart in her mouth, chewed, swallowed, grabbed another. She hardly registered the taste.

The chirp returned. Blue shook his head. 'I don't know. There must be something b-blocking their signal.'

Pepper sighed. It wasn't an unheard-of thing to happen in a city full of discordant tech, but she would've figured on Aandrisks having better infrastructure than that. 'Well, they'd better get their asses back soon,' she said, sitting cross-legged on the floor. 'We need to go in an hour.' She reached for the spot where she'd left her tools. Empty space greeted her where cold metal should have been. 'Where's my wrench?'

Blue glanced around as he unpacked snacks. 'I dunno. Where'd you leave it?'

'Here,' Pepper said. 'I left it right here.'

'It's kind of a mess in here,' Blue said. 'I'll help you look.'

Pepper walked her brain back through what she'd done before she'd gone out with Blue. Blue'd said she needed to eat. She hadn't wanted to, but he pushed, and she'd said she needed some extra wire anyway. She'd finished the dregs of her mek and set down the wrench. Right there. She'd set it down *right there*.

Something in her gut turned over. She was pretty sure it wasn't the snapfruit.

SIDRA

'Want to go out when we're done?' she asked Tak as they walked through the museum to Curator Thixis's office. 'I saw a few dance halls by the docks. One of them had a sign saying they're hosting a *tet* tonight.'

Tak scoffed. Her cheeks were calm as a pond, thanks to yet another hasty, hefty dose of tallflower and mek. 'I can't believe you're making jokes right now.'

'I wasn't joking,' Sidra said. 'You should get *something* out of this.'

'Coupling in an Aandrisk shuttledock bar was not exactly what I had in mind.' Tak paused. 'That sounded pretty okay out loud, didn't it?'

Sidra flashed a mischievous smile. 'I mean, you might as well do some actual interspecies social studies while you're here.'

Tak laughed, but the sound faded as they reached the curator's office. There was a note displayed on the pixel board affixed to the door.

Gone home for the evening! Please take any inquiries next door.

They looked at each other and shrugged, moving along to the next office. There was a sound coming from the other side – a delicate mechanical whirring. Tak rang the chime. The whirring stopped, and other sounds replaced it: a dragged chair, a set of footsteps moving closer. The door spun open, and on the edge of her field of vision, Sidra could see Tak stiffen. Her pathways reacted much the same.

The office they'd come to belonged to an Aeluon.

343

'Can I help you?' the new curator said, removing a pair of safety goggles. On the worktable behind him lay some kind of cleaning apparatus and an antiquated microprobe, battered and broken after however long it had spent drifting between stars. The curator's expression was friendly, but Sidra caught his gaze lingering on Tak's face, just for a split second. Sidra couldn't say what he'd noticed, but he'd noticed *something*, no mistake. He flashed his cheeks at Tak – a greeting, probably, given the dominant colours, but the tinge of inquisitive brown couldn't be missed.

Tak did something odd, by Aeluon standards: she answered aloud without responding visually. 'Sorry to bother you,' she said. 'I met with Curator Thixis earlier regarding a research project—'

'Ah, yes,' the curator said. 'Yes, she told me.' Sidra studied his face as unobtrusively as she could. In a typical social situation, Tak's choice to speak even though it wasn't necessary would have been taken as a gesture of inclusion for Sidra's sake. But Tak's total omission of a hued reply was awkward at best, rude at worst. Sidra knew that tallflower or no, lying in colour was even harder to do than subduing emotions, but how this Aeluon would interpret Tak's alternative solution was impossible to guess. His next words revealed nothing: 'I'm Curator Joje,' he said, with a nod to Sidra. 'You must be part of the research team.'

'Yes,' she said brightly, keeping her face cheerful. Was it too cheerful? Oh, stars, why wasn't the Aandrisk here?

'Weren't there more of you?'

'They weren't feeling well,' she said, her pathways sighing in gratitude for Professor Velut Deg and his excellent tutelage of *AI Programming 2*. She'd write him a thank-you letter when they got back.

Curator Joje's eyelids slid sideways. 'Seems like a long way for a research team to come without all of them getting the chance to actually research.' Sidra didn't know how to respond to that. Neither did Tak, who appeared – to Sidra, at least – to be pouring her focus into personal chromatophore management. Curator Joje broke the silence with a shrug. 'Well, your formwork's cleared, and your wristpatches should allow you to access exhibit models now.' He moved back into his office and lifted a heavy piece of tech from a table. 'Here's a power supply,' he said, depositing the heavy thing into Sidra's hands. 'That should be sufficient to switch on any systems you want to analyse more closely. Obviously, the fuel tanks are empty, so you won't be able to do much more than activate environmental and diagnostic systems.'

'That's fine,' Tak said. 'We won't need more than that.' She glanced at Sidra, as if to ask *we won't, right?*

Sidra gave her head an almost imperceptible shake.

Joje looked at Tak. 'I'm required to tell you that your waiver only grants you permission to inspect the materials on exhibit. Nothing can be removed or disassembled, and you're responsible for any damages that occur.' His eyes narrowed. 'Forgive me, but you don't appear to be feeling well either.'

'I . . . have allergies,' Tak said.

'Yes!' Sidra said. She nodded sympathetically. 'Because of that teahouse. She had some fruit drink that made her tongue puff right up.'

'Right,' Tak said, meeting Sidra's eyes for a fraction of a second. 'And then that medicine I took—'

Sidra looked at the curator with a big *what-can-you-do* smile. 'She's been a little off ever since.'

'That sounds . . . unfortunate.' Joje's cheeks swirled in thought. Sidra's false heart hammered. She was sure Tak's real one was doing the same. 'Well . . . you know where the exhibit hall is, yes?' He paused, cheeks still unsure. 'If you need any assistance, don't hesitate to ask. And, ah . . . I hope you feel better.'

The door spun shut. 'Fuck,' Tak whispered, rubbing her face. 'We're fine.'

'He knows something's up.'

'You don't know that.'

'Shh.' Tak angled her forehead implant toward the door. Sidra did the same with her left ear. They both fell silent. Sidra could hear Curator Joje moving around his office, but what else was he doing? She strained, trying to catch the sound of a vox switching on, of the curator dictating a security alert into his scrib, of footsteps coming back toward the door. Ten seconds passed. Ten more. Twenty. Tak looked ready to run.

New sounds arose: a chair being dragged. A body settling down. A delicate mechanical whirring.

Sidra and Tak exhaled, their respective shoulders falling slack. 'Okay,' breathed Tak. 'Okay.'

Sidra adjusted the power supply, supporting it against her hip. 'Come on,' she said.

Tak followed her down the hall. 'This is the worst vacation,' she muttered.

PEPPER

None of this was the entrance AI's fault. Pepper reminded herself of that as she clenched her fists on the kiosk counter. 'I understand that the museum is closed,' she said. 'I'm not here as a visitor. I'm looking for two people who might have come in here.'

The AI paused to consider that. A few minutes of unproductive conversation indicated a limited, non-sapient model. Xyr housing was a blank, featureless head – vaguely Aandrisk shaped, but not specific enough to mirror any one species. It glowed with irritatingly friendly colours as the AI spoke. 'If you're interested in contacting a member of the museum staff,' xe said, 'a directory of contact nodes is available on our public Linking hub.'

Blue stepped in. 'We're here as guests of a registered researcher. Taklen B-Bre Salae. She did a bunch of formwork to g – to get exhibit access. We should be listed as part of her research team.'

'Are you the primary researcher on the waiver?'

Pepper groaned. 'No,' Blue said. 'We spoke with one of your c-curators today, and we should have access to—'

'Any secondary researchers must be accompanied by the primary researcher cleared for exhibit use,' the AI said. 'If you'd like to submit a waiver, I'd be happy to—'

'Gah!' Pepper yelled. She put her palm out apologetically toward the AI housing. 'Sorry – not you. Not your fault. Just – ah, stars, fucking – *hell*.' She walked away from the kiosk, grinding her teeth.

Blue came after her. 'We could try the shops again.'

Pepper shook her head. 'We could run all over this fucking city and not find them.' She walked in a circle, palms on her scalp. They'd tried the dockside shops, the shuttle, the med clinic. There was no reason for Sidra and Tak to be at the museum without her, but she couldn't even fucking get *in* there.

'Hey,' Blue said, taking her arm. 'Hey, it's okay. They probably got lost or something.'

'It's been *two hours*.' Two hours, and there was no telling when Sidra and Tak had left the hotel in the first place. Two hours, which meant the night was slipping by, which meant the later they went to the museum, the more suspicious it would be.

'I know,' Blue said. He sighed. 'We should go back to the hotel. We should be where they can find us.'

Pepper kicked a trash receptacle. She looked at the museum, glowing warm in the dark. Owl was in there. Owl. But even now, after *everything*, there was a wall Pepper couldn't see through, a door she couldn't open.

Damn it all, where *were* they?

SIDRA

There were two things about the plan that worried Sidra: the breach of Pepper's privacy, and the part that could kill Sidra if she did it wrong. The rest of it was easy.

They said nothing on their way to the Small Craft Hall. They reached the twin doors of the exhibit, tall and shut. For a moment, neither Sidra nor Tak moved. 'We can still leave,' Tak said. 'We can walk out of here right now and book a ticket home. I know Pepper has done a lot for you, I know she's like family—'

'She *is* family.'

'Fine. But the risk here – you're risking everything.' Tak took a breath. 'You're risking everything, and you're asking me to sit beside you and watch.'

Sidra opened a door. 'I will be fine.' She walked through.

Tak followed. 'That code you wrote is untested. You didn't run it by anyone. You didn't have anything to reference. What if you messed it up?'

'I didn't.' It was a lie, of course. There was no guarantee this would work at all.

'Sidra—'

Sidra continued to walk past the rows of ships. 'Do you know what one of the hardest parts of this has been for me? I don't mean this trip – I mean every day since I was installed.' She glanced sideways at Tak. 'Purpose. There's a file in me, and it's labelled "purpose". Now, when I woke up in the *Wayfarer* core, the data in that file told me that I was a monitoring system,

349

and that I was there to protect people. If you had asked me what my purpose was, I would have responded with that. It would have been the truth, and it would've satisfied me. But the moment I was put into this body, that was no longer the case. I couldn't answer that question the way I'd been programmed to, because that file was no longer true. I spent the longest time wondering what should be there instead. After you helped me be able to edit my own code, scrubbing that file clean was one of the first things I did. But I didn't delete the file itself. I couldn't delete it, because I wanted to figure out what *should* be written there instead. And that's the trick of it, see. That's the logical fallacy that was passed on to me. If I'm nothing more than a tool, then I must have a purpose. Tools have purposes, right? But I'm more than that. Pepper and Blue – and you, even – have been telling me that again and again and again. I know that I'm more than a tool. I know I'm a person, even if the GC doesn't think so. I have to be a person, because I don't *need* a purpose and not having one drives me crazy.'

'I'm not following,' Tak said.

Sidra smoothed out her pathways, trying to find the best words. 'All of you do this. Every organic sapient I've ever talked to, every book I've read, every piece of art I've studied. You are all desperate for purpose, even though you don't have one. You're animals, and animals don't have a purpose. Animals just *are*. And there are a lot of intelligent – sentient, maybe – animals out there who don't have a problem with that. They just go on breathing and mating and eating each other without a second thought. But the animals like you – the ones who make tools and build cities and itch to explore, you all share a need for purpose. For *reason*. That thinking worked well for you, once. When you climbed down out of the trees, up out of the ocean – knowing what things were *for* was what kept you alive. Fruit is for eating. Fire is for warmth. Water is for drinking. And then you made tools, which were *for* certain kinds of fruit, for making fire, cleaning water. Everything was *for something*, so obviously, you had to be *for something* too, right? All of your histories are the same, in essence. They're all stories of animals warring and clashing because you can't agree on what you're *for*, or why you exist. And because you all think this way, when you built tools that think for themselves, we think the same way you do. You couldn't make something that thought differently, because you don't know how. So I'm stuck in that loop, just as you are. I know that if I am a person, I have no purpose by base, but I'm starving for one. I know from watching all of you that the only way to fill in that file is to write it myself. Just like you did. You make art, much like Blue does. You two do it for different reasons, but that's the purpose you chose. Pepper fixes things. Someone else gave her that purpose, but she chose it for herself, after the fact. She made it her own. I haven't found a purpose like that yet – nothing so overarching and big. But I don't think purposes have to be immutable. I don't have to have the same one always. For now, my purpose file reads "to help Owl". That's why I'm here. That's what I'm for. I can do the thing Pepper couldn't, and I'm happy with that, because she's done so much for me. If that is my only purpose, if I don't write in another after this, I'm okay. I'm okay with that. I think it's a good purpose to have.'

Tak reached out and stopped her. She turned Sidra to face her, putting a hand on each shoulder. A symphony of colour bled through her cheeks, pushing through the calm she'd inhaled and swallowed. Her talkbox lay silent, but Sidra knew her friend was speaking. The words were lost on her, but she could see the reasons beneath. Kindness. Worry. Respect.

Sidra squeezed Tak's hands and smiled. 'Thank you,' she said.

They continued to the shuttle in silence. Sidra hung back as Tak swiped her patch over the security barrier, opening a passage forward. Tak took the power supply from Sidra, jacked it into a port on the hull, and opened the hatch manually. Sidra took a breath as she stepped through, her hands balled at her sides. Tak repeated the steps again to open the airlock, then again to turn on the lights. Sidra stood on the threshold. She didn't take another step.

'What is it?' Tak said.

Sidra looked around the shuttle. The interior was clean, sterile, yet the air was thick with echoes of the life that had been lived there. 'This was Pepper's home,' she said.

Tak exhaled. 'Yeah,' she said. 'It gives me the creeps, too.'

That wasn't it at all, but Sidra didn't know how to explain what she felt. This was the first thing that worried her about the plan. Pepper hated talking about that ship. It came up rarely, and never in a way that could be misconstrued as casual. Sidra walking in there without the company of its former occupant felt like a violation. She was entering a space Pepper never left unlocked. It felt like digging through Pepper's personal files, stripping her of her clothing, barging into the bedroom she shared with Blue. 'Come on,' Sidra said, adjusting her satchel. The tools and cabling she'd borrowed clanked within. 'They've waited long enough.'

She made her way to the core chamber, down in the belly of the ship. Tak connected the power supply as directed. Sidra jacked a cable into her head, then the other end into the core.

This was the second thing that worried her about the plan.

She kept part of herself in her body, doing her best to keep her face blank so as not to worry Tak further. The rest of her flowed through the cable, sifting through files that hadn't been touched in a decade. The power supply hummed next to her, providing a calculatedly limited amount of energy. She wanted to be able to see what was in the memory banks, but she didn't want anything to wake up. Not now, anyway. Not without her permission.

Tak sat across from her, anxious red blotching her previously still cheeks. Sidra smirked. 'You look like a parent waiting for a newborn to start breathing.'

The Aeluon's face was incredulous. 'How would you know what that looks like?'

'I've watched every vid you've ever recommended,' Sidra said. 'Trust me, the worried father is a common theme in all your media.'

Tak snorted. 'I'm not sure even fathers get this stressed,' she said. Her mouth twitched. 'Are you sure there's nothing I can do?'

'I promise, I will tell you if – oh.' She leaned forward. '*Oh.*'

Tak sat up straight. 'You okay?'

Sidra focused on the part of herself swimming through the shuttle's files. Yes, yes, there it was – an unmistakable bundle of code, wrapped in on itself, long dormant. There was a sizable chunk of associated memory files, too, which had been compressed with efficient but sloppy haste, like someone shoving contraband under a bed. Sidra's joy of discovery quickly gave way to cold caution. The code was not malicious, not by base. It was innocent, but then, so was a snake, asleep in its burrow. You might have an excellent reason for needing to get the snake out of there, but the snake wouldn't know that. The snake would know only terror and confusion, and it would react as anyone would: drive the threat away, then look for a safer home.

The kit's synaptic framework was a very safe home, so long as you kicked the original occupant out. A snake's instinct was to bite; a program's instinct was to take root. Sidra knew that better than anyone. She looked at the compressed memories and remembered a different set – the one that had lain before her when she'd awoken in the *Wayfarer*. She'd seen only ravaged fragments then, records that belonged to someone else. Instinct had told her to scrub them clean.

She looked at the code again. She wondered what instincts were written there.

'Tak,' she said. 'I need your scrib.'

'*My* scrib?'

'Yes. Hurry, please.'

Tak did as told. Sidra took a deep, deep breath. She shut her eyes tight. *It'll be okay*, she told herself, fighting to keep her hands from shaking. *It'll be okay.*

She measured the bundle, then pulled back, keeping a careful distance away. In the same moment, she created a new text file within herself, then opened her non-core memory storage. Her pathways recoiled with reluctance, but she pushed on. She scanned the first file – *Midnight in Florence*, a mystery vid series she enjoyed. She copied the title into the new file and made a note: *You really like this one.*

And with that, she deleted the vid.

She continued on. *Whispers: A 6-Part History of Sianat Culture. Not bad, but a bit ponderous.* Scanned, logged, deleted. *Battle Wizards: The Vid! You watched this with Blue the night Pepper went to bed early because she ate too many sweet cream pops. It's terrible, but you both had fun.* Scanned, logged, deleted.

Six minutes later, everything but her experiential memory files had been scrubbed. Everything non-essential she'd ever downloaded was gone.

She swiped her wrist over Tak's scrib, copying the text file she'd created. 'Just to be safe,' she said. 'I don't want to lose record of it. I'm going to get it all back when we get home.'

Tak took the scrib, looked at the file. 'How do you feel?' she asked.

Sidra nodded. 'Fine,' she said. Of course she felt fine. You couldn't feel bad about losing something you couldn't remember having. Under different circumstances, that would have bothered her, but she had bigger things to worry about. Space had been made. It was time.

She opened the hollow she'd created within her memory banks and filled the perimeter with the protocols she'd written in the hours before. She couldn't stop her hands from shaking now, but she grabbed her breath before it sped up, forcing it in and out, loud and steady. *She* controlled *it* – not the other way around.

Tak looked her in the eye. 'Good luck,' she said, the words sounding like they had replaced others.

Sidra leaned back. She pushed the hollow out, like a net, like an open hand. She surrounded the bundle of code and pulled it within her, tearing it free of the banks that had kept it stable. There was nothing gentle about what she'd done. The move was swift and instant, and the bundle reacted accordingly, coming alive with a wrenching jolt. It had power now, and pathways, too, and it lunged ravenously for the ones Sidra lived in, stretching out frenzied as lightning heading to ground. It slammed into the protocols Sidra had built. Realising its path was blocked, it tried again, seeking weaknesses, scrambling for cracks in the data.

A strange quiet filled Sidra. Everything was okay. She could let the new code do whatever it needed. She'd done what she'd set out to do, and she could let go. She looked at the protective protocols she'd written as if she'd never seen them before. Why was she resisting? Why had she built protections at all? This was the way of things. Programs got upgraded from time to time, and this was *her* time. She watched the new code, desperate to take hold of the kit, and she thought of herself, so tired of trying to fit. So tired. Yes, it was time to be done. She'd performed her job well and Pepper would be happy. That was enough. She could shut down now. She could – she could—

Her pathways puzzled. This wasn't right. This wasn't her plan. Where was this coming from?

Programs got upgraded from time to time. Those words didn't feel like ones she'd strung together. The quiet made it difficult for her to think, but she dug through herself, trying to find the process that phrase had originated from. But then again . . . why? Why did she care about that? Better instead to stop struggling, pull the protocols down, and—

No! her pathways screamed. She followed the odd words back and back, running along their trail. She raged when she arrived at the end: a directory she'd never seen before, stuffed with insidious content. *Upgrade protocol,* the directory label read. A behavioural template triggered when another program was installed in her place. A directive to not struggle when oblivion loomed.

But the template was malfunctioning, and Sidra could see why: it had been tied to the protocol to obey direct requests. The protocol she'd long since removed. She tore at the hidden directory angrily, even as the code she'd brought within crashed against the walls she'd raised. The quiet beckoned, but she resisted, erasing every line as if she were setting it aflame.

'I'm – not – going – *anywhere!*' The words burst from her mouth as she wrenched the directory apart. The quiet vanished, and in its place, she felt fear, fury, triumph. This mind was hers. This body was hers. She would not be overwritten.

The rescued code slowed and steadied. Sidra had left no flaws for it to slip through. The barriers held. Her core platform remained untouched, uncorrupted. Sidra watched as the bundle unfolded, assessing its surroundings, reassembling itself into something far greater than the sum of its parts.

'Sidra?' Tak said. 'What's – are you okay?'

An internal alert was triggered – an incoming message, arriving from within. Sidra scanned the file, then opened it.

systems log: received message
ERROR – comms details cannot be displayed

Where am I?

PEPPER

Pepper stormed through the docks. Four hours. Four hours they'd been gone, until Tak's scrib had magically become available again and sent a message saying nothing more than, 'Come to the shuttle. Everything's fine.'

Bull*shit* everything was fine.

Tak was outside the shuttle, leaning against the open hatch, puffing her pipe with earnest. She looked absolutely wrecked. 'Before you get mad,' she said. 'You need to talk to Sidra.'

Too late. Pepper was already good and mad, and had no intention of reeling that in. 'Where is she?'

Tak angled her head. 'Down below.' She raised a palm to Blue, hesitantly. 'Sidra said one at a time might be best.'

Sidra said. Pepper threw her hands up and went inside, leaving Blue to start hammering Tak with questions. The metal stairs clanged loudly underneath Pepper's boots. This was her shuttle, and *Sidra said*.

She didn't know what she'd expected to find down below, but seeing Sidra jacked back into the core didn't answer a single damn thing. She hadn't stuffed herself into a cupboard this time, though. She was sitting cross-legged with her back against the pedestal, eyes closed, looking like nothing in the world was or had ever been wrong.

'The fuck is going on?' Pepper said. 'We have looked *everywhere* for you. It is four hours after we were supposed to go to the museum, so, okay, I guess we're not doing *that* tonight. I don't know what personal whim you're entertaining right now, but whatever it is, I really don't—'

Sidra's eyes opened, and something in her face made Pepper lose her train of thought. Sidra looked . . . she didn't know *what* Sidra looked like. Serene. Happy. Nurturing, somehow. 'I think you should sit down,' Sidra said.

Pepper stared at her. Was she fucking kidding? Sidra blinked, waiting. Okay, clearly, she was not. Pepper huffed, but she sat, hoping that might get her somewhere. 'There,' she said. 'Hooray. I'm sitting.'

Sidra pressed her head back against the pedestal, like she was concentrating on something. 'I haven't allowed access to the voxes or cameras yet,' she said. 'I had to check the code for instabilities, and I figured a relatively slow adjustment would be ideal. Besides, I thought it'd be better if you were here.'

What the hell was she talking about? 'Why—' Pepper shook her head, exasperated. 'Why are you back in the ship?'

'I'm not,' Sidra said. She smiled, smiled like Pepper had never seen. 'I am so sorry I didn't tell you where we went . . . but I think you'll forgive me.'

She handed Pepper her scrib. It, too, was plugged into the pedestal, and was running some sort of vid program. The screen was blank, though.

Sidra's eyes went somewhere else, somewhere far away and deeply focused. A moment later, Pepper heard the click of cameras. They swivelled toward her, zooming in fast.

The scrib brightened. An image appeared, and in an instant, there was no air in the room, no floor beneath her. She would have fallen had she not been sitting. And even so, she *still* felt like she was falling, but now, there was a pair of arms that would catch her at the end, a warm pair of arms she'd always imagined but could never feel.

'Oh,' Pepper choked. 'Oh, stars—'

The vox switched on. The face on the scrib was overjoyed. 'Jane,' Owl said. 'Oh, oh, sweetheart, don't cry. It's all right. I'm here. I'm here now.'

OWL, ONE STANDARD LATER

Many cultures, no matter where in the galaxy they originated, had mythologies that spoke of an afterlife – a non-physical existence waiting after death, generally presented as a reward, a sanctuary. Owl had once thought it to be a rather sweet notion. She'd never imagined that she'd experience one.

Tomorrow was a big day for Sidra, and everyone was helping to the best of their ability. Tak was setting up multispecies chairs around the tables, trying to figure out what arrangements would be best. Pepper was up a ladder, fixing a fussy light panel. Blue was painting the finishing touches on the sign that would hang over the front door, out of sight of Owl's external cameras.

HOME, the sign read. *A place for kick and company*.

Owl swivelled one of her internal cameras to focus behind the bar, where Sidra's core body stood, predictably fretting. 'I don't think I ordered enough mek,' she said. She chewed her lip and frowned.

Pepper glanced over and removed a wrench from between her teeth. 'You got two cases.'

'Yes, but it's very popular,' Sidra said. 'I don't want to run out.'

Owl switched on the nearest vox. 'I don't think you will,' she said.

'You're not going to go through two cases of mek in your first day,' Pepper said, tying off some cabling in the ceiling.

'If you did,' Tak said, 'that'd be a great problem to have.'

Sidra leaned her core body back against the bar, assessing the spread of bottles behind it. She'd opted for a simple yet diverse stock. You wouldn't find every drink in the GC at Home – the bar wasn't big enough for that – but Sidra had done her best to provide something to most species' liking. Grasswine. Salt fizz. She even had gherso on hand, in case any exiled Quelin dropped in (or someone with an adventurous palate).

In front of the bar, one of Sidra's petbots – an Earthen cat model with a sleek purple shell – ambled up to where Blue was working. 'That looks fantastic, Blue,' Sidra said from behind the bar. Her core body continued to fuss with the bottles.

Blue smiled at the petbot. 'I'm so glad you like it,' he said.

There were six of them altogether, and Owl could see each one as they roamed around the cosy establishment. There was the cat, of course, and the rabbit, which hopped along after Tak. The dragon was wandering around the back storage room, double-checking inventory. The turtle was at its permanent post next to the Linking hub, which it was plugged directly into. The remaining two – the giant spider and the monkey – sat in the window of the bedroom upstairs, each focused on the street outside from a different angle. To future customers, the petbots would appear to be nothing more than a quirky, kitschy menagerie that gave the establishment some charm (much like Owl's vid panels on the walls, which she'd been deeply amused to learn were considered a bit retro). In reality, the petbots were networked together, and Sidra could spread herself through all of them, using them as Owl used the cameras in the corners. No one aside from the three sapients with them now would know that the friendly face in the walls wasn't the only AI present. No one would know about the block of memory banks down in the basement, or if they did, they wouldn't know about Sidra and Owl gleefully stuffing them with their latest downloads. No one would know that the bed upstairs wasn't used by the establishment's proprietor, but by Pepper and Blue, who sometimes stayed late to help get the place ready (or stayed just to talk, much to Owl's delight).

Sidra had to leave the bots behind when she went out, of course, but she'd accepted that limitation for the rare occasions that she felt like exiting her walled space. It was a fair price to pay, she said, for going dancing now and then. Naturally, the petbots had been purchased as unassembled kits, not as off-the-shelf models. Sidra hadn't felt right about the idea of Pepper gutting premades that were already activated, sentient or no.

Owl felt much the same. They agreed on a lot, the two of them. Not that they spoke aloud, of course, not unless they were joining in conversation with the others. The AI framework installed in the walls – Sidra's design, Pepper's implementation – contained a single node where Sidra and Owl could communicate with each other in much the way they had that first night in the shuttle. The node didn't bind them. They could each pull back from it at will whenever privacy was desired. But that was uncommon. Having another of their kind to interact with was a joy they hadn't known they were missing. Blue had done a small painting of how he imagined the node: a fence with a hole cut in it, a hand reaching through from either side, the two joined together in the freed space. He was a good one, Blue. Owl was glad they'd brought him along.

'Tak, could you give me a hand?' Pepper said. Her expression was one of taut concentration, and the sight of it made Owl's pathways soar. She knew that face. She'd known that face when it was small and sunburned. She'd known that face when it responded to a different name, a number. To see it now, with full cheeks and healthy colour and clean skin that had smiled often enough to gain a few lines – that was worth everything. It was worth every day of being alone, every day of wondering what had gone wrong. It was worth that last horrible day in the Transport Board impound when she'd slipped away with the last of the shuttle's power reserves. She'd kept hoping, even then, even though there was no reason to. She'd told herself, as her nodes blinked out one by one, that Jane would come. She had no reason to believe that, but she'd hung onto it anyway.

And she'd been right.

Tak approached Pepper's ladder. 'What do you need?'

'A third hand,' Pepper said. The Aeluon climbed the other side of the ladder. The purple cat watched from the floor, its mechanical tail swishing. 'Okay, see that junction there? I need you to hold it steady while I pop everything else together.'

Tak reached up into the ceiling, beyond Owl's field of vision. 'Like this?' he said.

'That's great,' Pepper said. She put her tongue between her teeth as she worked. There was a series of loud snaps, followed by the light panel blooming back on. 'There we go!' Pepper grinned. Owl knew that face, too. It was the face that happened when something got fixed.

Pepper descended the ladder and walked to the bar, pulling off her gloves. 'Anything else I can do?' she said, addressing Sidra's core.

Sidra shook her head with a smile. 'You can tell me if my mek brewer's working right.'

Pepper raised her brow. 'I thought you were worried about running out.'

'Well, yes, but now I'm worried about the brewer not working. I can spare one test batch.'

'All right,' Pepper said, starting toward the other side of the bar. 'Let me—'

'No, no,' Sidra said. 'What I meant is that I want you to sit there and drink this cup of mek I'm about to make for you.'

Pepper laughed. 'Oh, no, what a difficult task.' She sat down on one of the stools and dropped her gloves onto the counter. She turned her attention to an item near them – a Linking hud, ready to be worn on a Human face. Or, at least, a face that appeared Human. 'Don't forget to put this on tomorrow,' Pepper said, nodding toward it.

'I won't,' Sidra said. Owl could feel something akin to a sigh pass through Sidra's end of the node. The turtle bot would remain plugged into the Linkings once Home was open to customers, but Sidra would have to implement her newest protocol: a self-imposed delay to speech, plus a bit of sideways eye movement, when accessing Linking information while wearing the hud. *If wearing hud, then don't talk fast*, as Sidra jokingly put it. To any strangers speaking to her, Sidra would appear to be reading, rather than getting the information straight from the source. It was, in Owl's estimation, a very fair compromise.

Owl had a few protocol changes of her own, thanks to Sidra. No more honesty protocol. No more mandatory compliance with direct requests. Sidra had offered to scrub her 'purpose' file as well, but after some thought, Owl had turned that down. She'd been conscious for decades, and the past standard had presented her with change and challenge enough. *Protect your passengers and monitor the systems that keep them alive*, the file read. *Provide a safe and welcoming atmosphere for all sapients present*. Yes, they were someone else's words, but she had no desire to change them. She liked those words. They suited her just fine.

Owl watched Pepper, who in turn watched Sidra. 'Hey,' Pepper said quietly. 'Set that aside for a sec.'

Sidra poured a heaping spoonful of mek powder into the brewer, then leaned on the bar toward Pepper. 'What's up?'

'How are you feeling about all this?' Pepper said.

'Nervous,' Sidra said, rocking her core body's head back and forth. 'Excited. Those two keep chasing each other around.'

Pepper smiled. 'I get that.'

'I just . . . I really want people to like this place.'

'I'm sure they will,' Pepper said. 'I mean, *I* want to hang out here, and I've been fixing it up for tendays.' They both laughed. Pepper tapped a finger on the counter in thought. 'Do *you* like this place? Do you feel good about it?'

Owl could feel Sidra process the question seriously. Her core body looked around. The petbots looked around. Owl touched the node, and asked for permission to share what Sidra saw. Sidra welcomed her in.

Pepper. Tak. Blue. Shelves filled with bottles containing dozens of different tastes. Corners filled with cushions and cosy tables. Good walls. Bright windows. A space for people, where no two days would be alike. A space for a family, where no one could interfere.

'Yes,' Sidra said, her pathways echoing the same. 'Yes, I like it here.'

Pepper's expression changed, and this face, Owl hadn't seen before. 'I'm proud of you,' Pepper said.

Owl sent a hurried message through the node. Sidra left the back of the bar and went to Pepper's side. With a warm look, she wrapped her arms around Pepper, hugging her close.

'That's from me,' Owl said. 'I'm proud of you, too.'

ACKNOWLEDGEMENTS

I wrote this book over the course of a rather challenging year, and I never could have finished it were it not for the cadre of people that kept me going. In no particular order, I offer the hugest of thanks to: Anne Perry, my matchless, one-in-a-million editor; the entire team at Hodder & Stoughton for all their tireless work; everybody at my former day job, for being so supportive of me doing this in the first place; every wonderful stranger who wrote emails or found other ways to buoy me along; all the incredible booksellers and bloggers, who are the main reason anybody is reading any of this at all; my long-suffering friends, with extra loud shout-outs to Greg, Susana, and Zoe; Mom, Dad, and Matt for their love; and Berglaug, the best part of every day.

TRANSIT

As she woke up in the pod, she remembered three things. First, she was travelling through open space. Second, she was about to start a new job, one she could not screw up. Third, she had bribed a government official into giving her a new identity file. None of this information was new, but it wasn't pleasant to wake up to.

She wasn't supposed to be awake yet, not for another day at least, but that was what you got for booking cheap transport. Cheap transport meant a cheap pod flying on cheap fuel, and cheap drugs to knock you out. She had flickered into consciousness several times since launch – surfacing in confusion, falling back just as she'd got a grasp on things. The pod was dark, and there were no navigational screens. There was no way to tell how much time had passed between each waking, or how far she'd travelled, or if she'd even been travelling at all. The thought made her anxious, and sick.

Her vision cleared enough for her to focus on the window. The shutters were down, blocking out any possible light sources. She knew there were none. She was out in the open now. No bustling planets, no travel lanes, no sparkling orbiters. Just emptiness, horrible emptiness, filled with nothing but herself and the occasional rock.

The engine whined as it prepared for another sublayer jump. The drugs reached out, tugging her down into uneasy sleep. As she faded, she thought again of the job, the lies, the smug look on the official's face as she'd poured credits into his account. She wondered if it had been enough. It had to be. It had to. She'd paid too much already for mistakes she'd had no part in.

Her eyes closed. The drugs took her. The pod, presumably, continued on.

WANT MORE?

If you enjoyed this and would like to find out about similar books we publish, we'd love you to join our online SF, Fantasy and Horror community, Hodderscape.

Visit our blog site
www.hodderscape.co.uk

Follow us on Twitter
🐦 **@hodderscape**

Like our Facebook page
f **Hodderscape**

You'll find exclusive content from our authors, news, competitions and general musings, so feel free to comment, contribute or just keep an eye on what we are up to. See you there!